PEOPLE IN THE PARK

By the same author

The Diary of an American Au Pair

People in the Park

Marjorie Leet Ford

Chatto & Windus

LONDON

Published by Chatto & Windus 2003

2 4 6 8 10 9 7 5 3 1

First published in Great Britain in 2003 by
Chatto & Windus
Random House, 20 Vauxhall Bridge Road,
London SW1V 2SA

Random House Australia (Pty) Limited
20 Alfred Street, Milsons Point, Sydney,
New South Wales 2061, Australia

Random House New Zealand Limited
18 Poland Road, Glenfield,
Auckland 10, New Zealand

Random House (Pty) Limited
Endulini, 5A Jubilee Road, Parktown 2193, South Africa

The Random House Group Limited Reg. No. 954009
www.randomhouse.co.uk

A CIP catalogue record for this book is available from the British Library

ISBN 0 7011 7403 X

Papers used by Random House are natural, recyclable products made from wood
grown in sustainable forests; the manufacturing processes conform to the
environmental regulations of the country of origin

Typeset in Horley Old Style MT by SX Composing DTP, Rayleigh, Essex
Printed and bound in Great Britain by
Mackays of Chatham Plc

For Phillip – always

Love Song

Sweep the house clean,
hang fresh curtains
in the windows
put on a new dress
and come with me!

The elm is scattering
its little leaves
of sweet smells
from a white sky!

Who shall hear of us
In the time to come?
Let him say there was
a burst of fragrance
from black branches.

William Carlos Williams

YOU TURNED UP a brick street and into a miniature forest. It was a garden, part wild, part civilized, a few acres of trees set in the most citified part of the city. The red brick street was bordered by a long lawn, with steps to the tennis courts. Perched at the tip of Russian Hill and looking over treetops to the Bay, these might be the prettiest courts in the world. They made you yearn to play tennis. The sound effects were nice too. Sometimes, along with the boings of the balls, you could hear sea lions barking. The Bay was close, and the sea lions were loud. You could hear the bells of the cable cars and a chorus of screams when the car shot over the crest of the hill, pitching to the water. The cable car sounded like a traveling playground.

When you walked by the lawn and the tennis courts, the brick became stairs through woods. On one side of the stairs there was, between patches of wildwood, a serene slant of lawn sprinkled with yellow dandelions. At the first landing, you entered what some people called the promenade. It was a long, shaded rectangle of formal dirt, sifted and red, like something they might have in Europe. They say that in times past, old Italian men played bacci ball here.

On two sides of the promenade stood lines of plane trees, poised like an honor guard. The trees were pruned for winter, so there were no leaves, just branches like stumpy arms. Early in February, pinpoints of green appeared on the amputated joints, and the pinpoints grew into tassels. These were the kind of trees that by April or May would have big broad leaves.

1

From the far end of the promenade a monument presided like an altar, dedicated to a poet most people these days had never heard of. The monument was framed by a triptych of tall-backed benches painted in old Italian tiles: blues, greens, creams, saffron, and a sienna red like the formal dirt, but brighter. Most people appreciated the agedness of these tiles, and the surprise they gave to this cool, green glen.

Down here, the woods baffled out the rattles and clangs of the cable cars, the musical tennis balls, and the barking sea lions. You heard doves cooing, the gardener's shears trimming the hedges, and sometimes a dog galloping up a path and springing, hoping to pluck a bird from the sky.

Friday

"ALL OUR DOGS here are purebred something-or-others," Frankie said to the stranger with the chocolate whippet. "All pedigrees. Except mine." She tilted her beer can to the scrub brush mutt who was trying to hump Napoleon, Pierre's fancy little poodle. Napoleon didn't even honor Buster with a snarl. He just raised his nose. That's where the word snooty comes from.

Frankie looked across at the people, standing in twos or threes around the borders of the rectangle. Over on the tile bench sat a girl so skinny she was ugly, busy listening to the psychiatrist with hair like a girl. Those two didn't even notice when the fat guy practicing T'ai chi almost fell in their laps. The woman who owned the flower store and the scottie talked to the couple who owned the video store and the dalmatian. Pierre, with the two toy poodles, brought his coffee mug every morning and a martini every night. Frankie got a kick out of Pierre. A burly guy like that, with a Jersey accent and a fru-fru name. A beret. When he talked he used his Gauloise like an exclamation point. He always looked like he needed a shave, but his two little poodles – jet-black Napoleon and snow-white Josephine – went to the beauty parlor once a week, to maintain their expensive hairstyles. She could hear the rasp in his Jersey accent as he told some story to the Englishman, whose dog was also a poodle, but tall. Dr. Hawthorne and his rottweiler ambled over just in time for the punchline.

When Frankie first got here with Buster, the promenade was

groomed with fine stripes, drawn through the dirt by the gardener's rake. Pretty soon a jumble of dalmatian dots, poodle pompoms, borzoi stilts and scottie fringes had chased and tackled and rolled with their paws around each other and scuffed away the stripes.

When the woman with the chocolate whippet sat down, all Frankie noticed was she was new. She'd never seen the dog, either. The only chocolate whippets she'd seen were in books. "You new?" She didn't intrude on the woman by looking at her.

Turned out this one was temporary. A professional dogsitter. "I have a two-week gig with those people who live in the penthouse."

Frankie followed the woman's finger, pointing through branches to the tall old building across the street with beautiful arched windows and bunches of trees at the top. They looked like bonsais from here, but up close, naturally, they would be full-sized. "I've never seen this dog," she said.

"The people have a roof garden. So they never take him out."

"Must be nice. Walking Buster's a pain."

"The dogs up here are beautiful!" the woman said.

"Where do you live?"

"I live in the 'hood. O'Farrell and Hyde. The dogs there are not beautiful."

"Oh, I know! I used to live down there. The dogs looked like they were made out of broom straw and twine. Different colors and textures of string and straw, and cashmere and angora too, all on the same dog. Heads the wrong size for the bodies. I used to manage an apartment house down there. Before I moved up in the world."

The dogsitter had an interesting hairdo. It was a two-colored crewcut – the roots brown, the tips canary yellow – like a neon halo. Frankie wondered how that would be done. "The building I managed down in the Tenderloin," she continued, "was half straight, half gay, and half black. Loud. Stereo wars. Judy Garland vs. John Lee Hooker."

The woman laughed at that. Probably what she did was, she cut her

4

hair to almost a shave and bleached it, maybe put some metallic dye on, then waited for it to grow into that science fiction type of outline.

"Up here, my job is easy," Frankie told her. "I don't even know my tenants exist except the first of the month, when the checks arrive in my box." To get some beer out now, she had to tip her face up. "You get a much better class of dog up here."

The woman let her whippet off the leash, but the dog didn't enjoy himself. He pressed his bones as close into the bench as he could and shook silently. Frankie studied the animal with the focus she'd need to draw it. The spine had a beautiful swoop, and every vertebra stuck out like a stud. The fur had the sheen of Swiss chocolate, but it vibrated – a sheath of jerks speeding over petrified bones like fast water rippling on rocks. She didn't know if she could draw well enough.

FRANKIE WAS AN artist, though she didn't call herself that. She loved to draw. When she drew she forgot to eat. Sometimes she forgot to open a fresh beer for three or four hours at a time. She forgot to smoke. She could have drawn all night, and often she did. Sometimes she drew all day and got irritated as hell when Buster started nagging her to go to the park. He had his ways. He jabbed his cold nose into her arm, made her pencil slip. At least her cat had more tact.

If she'd come along at a time when women were encouraged to have careers, she would have been a fulltime artist. She wouldn't have been Picasso, but she probably would have been able to get a job at Macy's, illustrating brassieres and Lay-Z-Boys and espresso machines. She'd enjoy that, although she preferred the human form. So maybe she was lucky. The way things were she could draw what she wanted.

As for her actual job, she did a man's work. Painting the apartments when they came vacant. Dealing with the electrician when the elevator broke. Relighting the boiler. Getting the plumber, or, more often, being the plumber. She did the bookkeeping. Kept the tenants in line. And whenever there was a vacancy, she was on call day and night. Her boss, Bill, he knew he had a good thing in her.

And if there was one thing you learned from managing apartments, it was how to keep people at a distance. You had to. Otherwise, life would be hell.

This chocolate whippet obviously felt the way she would if people ran up to her in the park and sniffed her privates and jumped to hug her and drag her to the ground. She could see this whippet was glad the other dogs didn't know it was alive. And then what? That little bichonne frisée hopped up the stairs through the woods and bounced past the other dogs straight to the whippet and stuck her nose right in his ear. Never mind if the ear was pressed back flat, giving a message. The puffball dog was just like its owner, Leone. Old Mrs. Leone was always welcoming every new person whether they wanted to be welcome or not. The petrified dog's tail dropped between his legs like a piece of wrought iron filigree on a hinge. But that didn't stop the puffball from sniffing there. That's where the word nosy comes from.

Now the Englishman was talking to Mrs. Leone. Except for her shoes, Frankie liked her. She was too old for high heels. Too old and too fat. Actually, she wasn't that fat. No fatter than Frankie, except in the bust. Stout-chested, she was. The whole engineering feat was held up on skinny little spikes. But even with those ridiculous shoes, old Leone set a high standard of dress for the neighborhood. She was rich enough to be a rich snob, but she wasn't a snob. The exact opposite of me, Frankie thought.

OVER BY THE monument, the fattish fellow with the pimples and the drawstring balloon pants kept lunging forward and upwards, left elbow and wrist angled so the fingers pointed ahead, right arm crooked the opposite way. One knee bent, the other leg straight out, he held his position as long as he could before stumbling to the other foot, trying to make it seem like he was graceful and intending to change feet. He'd never move from one pose to another until it was just past necessary. That was his problem. His dog was the borzoi. Maybe he got that dog because he'd heard people tend to look like their dogs. Too bad. Getting a borzoi didn't make him taller and thinner. But the dog appeared to have a balance problem that made it seem, in spite of the body build, to resemble its owner.

"You get a higher class of person up here in the high rent area," Frankie told the dogsitter. And from out of the bushes the psychiatrist's corgi flew low on four feet, no legs. Right after him sped the so-called golden retriever. "A higher class *in general*." Without being obvious, she tilted her can toward that dog's pathetic, emaciated owner. "That one over there? She's the exception. She doesn't belong."

"Who?"

"The owner of the speed freak chasing the corgi." She gazed in another direction and gave a description. "The one who looks like a seven-foot dragonfly in a sweatshirt. She's talking to the guy with the hairy legs. He's a psychiatrist."

"Wow. He doesn't look like a psychiatrist."

Frankie'd never thought of that.

"He's *much* too good-looking to be a psychiatrist."

Maybe Philo Righi was a phony too. Nobody called him Dr. Righi, the way they called Dr. Hawthorne Dr. Hawthorne. But in the morning, Philo Righi looked like a psychiatrist. All tweed, and the girly hair. He probably was a psychiatrist. She, though, the spider-legs, was no TV camerawoman. "Her name's Hillary Birdwood. Says she's a TV camerawoman. Can you imagine a station hiring that weak thing to man one of those great big cameras?"

"She does look about to break. Poor thing. Her neck's like a string. See? It's so thin it can't take the weight of her head."

"That's nothing. You should see how her neck bends when she has her glasses on. They weigh more than she does. You know the Hubble telescope? You can't even see her eyes, through them. She took 'em off to flirt with the psychiatrist. She forgets that a psychiatrist understands human nature."

"He seems to like her pretty well," the dogsitter observed, watching his long arms fly in gestures, making the skeleton laugh. "He really is great-looking, with that beautiful hair and that jaw. And look at his hands."

"Oh, believe me," Frankie said, "his hands are the most interesting thing about him. He doesn't need a dictionary. His whole vocabulary's in his hands. And his seat. See how it hops off the bench when he gets excited? And see how cunning she is? She's glued to everything he's saying, and she laughs. But, she hasn't actually said a word since we got here. That's because she knows a psychiatrist's job is to listen. He's off work now. She's doing his job."

She lit another cigarette and blew out. "Want one?" The dogsitter didn't. Frankie laughed. "That's why I smoke this kind. Nobody else does. They say sure, they'd like a cig, then they see the bent pack, hairy twigs of tobacco falling out both ends, and they decide they don't want a smoke after all."

Getting back to the insect: "It's all my fault she's here. She's my tenant. I screwed up. I called the station, and the right person wasn't in, so I just took some flunky's word for it. He said yes, Hillary Birdwood works here. He didn't know her salary, and for once I didn't insist on having the boss call me back. I just – got sloppy. I've had three vacancies already since the first of the year, and I must've panicked. That's no excuse, but it's all I can think of. It's my fault she can't pay the rent."

"Oh dear." This dogsitter was all sympathy. "But if she can't pay the rent, you—"

"That's what I told my boss, Bill, when her first rent check bounced."

"Oh dear."

"Bounced a check on my friends Ray and Pete, too. They own the corner drugstore, where I buy my beer."

"I didn't know that drugstore sold beer. They have no refrigerators . . ."

"They keep it way in the back corner, underneath the toilet paper. I think they keep it just for me. Me and Ray and Pete go way back. The store does too. Their grandfather started it just after the 1906 earthquake. Something like that. Ray and Pete cash my paychecks, so I never have to go to the bank. As a special favor to me, they cash my tenants' checks too.

8

When this deadbeat came along, using my reputation to recommend her, I was afraid they'd eighty-six me."

"But – maybe it was a mistake."

"Huh. My boss Bill, the owner of the building, he's just like you. Soft heart, soft head. He said 'Aw, Frankie. Let's give her another chance.' So. She blamed the bank. You've heard that one? She apologized like crazy and wrote a new check. That one bounced too. The third one was the charm. So. Count my blessings? She only bounced *one* on Ray and Pete. And of course they got a big apology. Apologizing is one thing she's good at."

"How sad!" the dogsitter said. "Because there really is something sweet about her. Look how tender she is with her puppy."

"She has nothing else to love. Nobody and no thing. She has no furniture. Sleeps on the floor. No clothes. Just that sweatshirt, and two dresses hanging in the closet."

"How do you know?"

"Looked!" She laughed so it sounded like the beer was getting to her, but beer never got to her. "I have keys." She caught disapproval in the dogsitter's eye. "I know, I know, you think it's like breaking and entering. I've heard that, from my tenants. But bouncing checks is illegal too."

She held her beer can upside-down and gave it a shake. No drops. "Buster! We've got to get going."

Heading out, she said, "Claims her dog's a golden retriever."

"Maybe I'll see you tomorrow?" the dogsitter called after her.

No need to answer.

DOWN IN THE basement she unlocked her apartment and relocked all the locks. For some air she opened the window looking out on the gravel roof of the garage. She went to the fridge for a fresh tall of Miller's and the leftover half can of Alpo. Spooning the meat into Buster's dish and mixing in kibble, she was careful to get the blending right so each mouthful would be tasty. She set the bowl on the floor and reached to the shelf for cat food. The saucer was empty, on the counter. When she set it

9

back, full, four light paws turned the corner of the kitchen door. "*Waa-waa*" came the cry. Frankie picked up her cat and set him by the dish. How long had it been, she tried to remember, since he could spring to the counter himself? Last year? She couldn't be sure. She stroked the silky old fur, getting thinner, as he leaned over his bowl. "At least you can still eat." She popped open her Miller's and watched the two animals enjoy themselves. When they'd finished, first the dog went over to his pillow and plopped down, then the cat went over and nuzzled a place for himself against the dog's belly. Frankie stayed for a minute while the two of them adjusted their bodies into comfort, the cat's back moving till it fit just right under Buster's chin. Buster moved his paw so gently to tuck the cat's old head in. When the purring and the snoring started, she took her beer upstairs, to size up what she'd have to do before she could show her top floor vacancy.

Through the window she watched the cable car, all lit up now, slipping along the tracks, its gonging and the noise of its riders a contrast to the smoothness of its sliding. Against the night she made out four silhouettes – a tall dog and a short dog and two humans. The long-legged dog pulled ahead on a taut leash, and the short dog's feet sped to keep up, like fast-motion in a Charlie Chaplin movie. The man's arms and legs swang, loose-limbed and sure-footed. The woman seemed contracted, folded into herself, with steps minced and uneven and – incomplete! When she took a step she never straightened her knee. She kept both knees bent, holding her seat about four inches closer to the ground than it ought to be. It looked like she was in training for Cossack dancing.

Frankie didn't need any help from the streetlight to see it was the Birdwood woman and the psychiatrist. He was still talking with his arms. She was looking *up*, into his face. Typical. Obviously, she thought if she kept her knees bent she could fool the guy's ego into thinking he was taller than she was. Frankie stood in her vacancy and muttered at the window, "Either sit down or stand up."

Friday: Temporary Inconvenience

FIRST THING IN the morning, about ten-thirty, Hillary Birdwood put on Tess's favorite CD, Mozart's flute concertos, and tiptoed toward the shower. As the flutes flew up and glided in formation, the winter sun warmed the wood floor, and Tess sat in the center of it, head tilted, one ear flopped and one lifted to the music. Untying the waist, Hillary let her pajama bottoms drop to the tiles and tossed the top off. Naked as a giraffe, except for her glasses, she stretched her neck around the bathroom doorway for another look at Tess, who sat alert as a music critic.

Amazed at the sight of Tess so quiet, Hillary set her glasses next to the sink, taking care not to make a clunk. When the rush of the shower misted out the Mozart, she continued the song in her head. It calmed her as she took on the dangerous job of drawing the razor over the row of bones lined up along each shin. She knew the Mozart so well that when she turned off the shower the music on the record was on the same note as the music in her mind. Stepping out, she scowled at the shower curtain. Army green. It was the only ugly thing in the apartment. Of course, it was just about the only thing in the apartment at all. She'd get used to it. Wrapping her head in the towel, wiping the steam from her glasses, and fastening the bra she didn't need, she felt grateful for the steam that clouded the mirror, so she didn't have to see the sharp blades and planes trying to poke through her skin, or the arms and legs that stretched on and on like telephone wires. She stepped into her jeans, belting the denim into pleats, and slipped on her sweatshirt, which flapped around her hips. Clothes never fit. With jeans, it was a choice between the right length or the right width. With sweatshirts, it was neither. Her arms outreached the sleeves by four inches, so she pushed the cuffs to the elbows. Of course, having so little flesh on her arms, the sleeves fell down, so she was always having to slide them back up. So they could slide back down.

It was tricky squeezing toothpaste when the tube had been punctured in a dozen spots, but she'd had a lot of practice. In the months she'd had Tess, she'd learned to put the toothpaste back in the drawer and to be sure the drawer was closed all the way, but she hadn't learned it perfectly. She might do fine for six mornings and nights in a row, but sooner or later she would slip up. It was lucky she had no furniture, except for the mattress on the floor, so the dog had only one place to bury her "bone." It was almost always under the pillow or under the sheets and blankets. Once in a while it was under the bottom sheet, which was a bother.

Praying that Tess would stay enthralled by the Mozart for just another two minutes, she tiptoed to the closet and got down her shoes and put them on – just a couple of seconds too late. She yanked her foot away from the puppy. "Tess! I just tied that shoelace. Why do you love to untie shoelaces?" While she re-tied this one, the puppy untied the other. This could go on all morning. This afternoon she didn't have to be at work by four o'clock – this was her night off. Tomorrow too. But she ought to hurry. Tess hadn't had an accident since they moved to San Francisco, but it would be unfair to challenge her too much. So for the moment she shut the dog in the bathroom, trying not to hear the frantic scratching on the door. She dreaded the day she would have to move out and let Frankie inspect the apartment for damages. Double-knotting her laces and letting Tess out of the bathroom, she took a look in the mirror. If any of her credit cards had had any credit left on them, she'd buy herself some clothes.

'Tess?" The puppy's face riveted to hers. "Tess? Want to go for a wah-alk?" The tail whipped and the body wagged. Tess was still a baby, really. She didn't understand English, but Hillary was trying to teach her key words and phrases. She'd mastered wah-alk. Now something harder. "Bring me your lea-eash." The dog stopped wiggling to concentrate. (What was that again?) "Bring me your leee-eash."

This excited Tess, who ran in darts wall to wall, making a racket on the wood with her toenails. When Hillary felt sure she didn't know what her leash was yet, she walked with deliberation to the closet door and lifted off the leash. "This is your lee-eash."

HILLARY HAD BEEN pretty good at not letting her money problems get her down. Temporary inconvenience, temporary inconvenience, she said over and over, a chant – aloud if she was alone with Tess, silently if she was on the bus or something. It was actually a handy chant, good for all sorts of things, like the tooth-holes in the toothpaste tube, the shoelaces, and even the glares from Frankie. Conversations with Frankie were temporary because they didn't last long.

As for the money thing, she'd get on her feet. She'd had three bi-weekly paychecks now, which (after a few tries) had paid the rent and groceries and the minimum balances on her credit cards. Finally this week she'd be able to pay a little over the minimum on one card, to shave away a little of the overage. You see, every time she was late in paying she got a penalty, and the penalty always put her over the limit, which earned another penalty and brought on another overage, and those overages on overages piled up and up and up. On each and every credit card, hundreds of dollars a month. Her plan was to get below the limit on just one card, so she'd be able to use it in an emergency. Then, little by little, she'd cut away the overages on each of the other cards. She'd get slowly, slowly on her way to paying down some balances. But it was like the time she went skiing in waist-deep powder and toppled. Her head and upper body lodged themselves in four feet of snow, her knees kicked in the air, but the skis were so heavy it was impossible to manipulate her feet. She

13

wore herself out trying to work her legs above the snow and to unearth her buried arms. She could breathe, but she wasn't sure how long she'd be able to keep it up. At that point in her life, she hadn't thought of the temporary inconvenience phrase. Anyway, it might not have been a temporary inconvenience if two people hadn't come along and hoisted her out.

This time, the job had toppled her. Meaning the no-job. The people who'd bought the station in Portland had laid off almost everyone. And there weren't a lot of TV jobs in Oregon. Of course there weren't a lot of television camera jobs anywhere, but there weren't a lot of jobs period in Portland. Even Hillary's parents were – not in trouble, but closer to it than they were used to being. They had a big house in the prettiest neighborhood, mortgage paid long ago. Their Volvos were both paid for. Everything was paid for. (They didn't believe in debt.) But her dad's insurance company lost money two years in a row and they talked about whether they actually needed to keep their membership in the tennis club. And then there they were stuck with a no-job daughter. They hadn't paid for her education to have her move back in with them. It took four months to find any job anywhere, four months of e-mailing everyone, running up long-distance bills, plane fares to interviews that didn't work out, a nightmare like the time skiing. Thank heavens for Visa and MasterCard, she often said, charging everything and getting out cash advances.

She'd allowed herself one splurge: Tess. She felt so depressed, she needed a puppy. She wanted a purebred, because she wanted to have some idea how the dog would turn out. She liked golden retrievers. And Tess was a special type, a rare silver-white. The other puppies in the litter were rust-colored and fluffy, like ordinary golden retrievers, but one was pale, with sleek fur. When the breeder gloated about having a silver-white, which he said was known to be the sweetest of all the golden retriever family, Hillary didn't admit she'd never heard of a silver-white. He assumed she knew, because everyone knew, and she should have known, but actually, she didn't know that much about dogs. At that time

14

she still had some credit left on one card, which she wiped out to pay the breeder, including fifty dollars extra for the extra-sweet silver-white. What luck, too! Every day she thanked heaven that in spite of the cost, she'd made the right decision. Tess actually turned out to be the sweetest dog that ever there was.

But the job problem ended up going on even longer than she'd imagined in her wildest dreads. She got Tess in the nick of time, just before she went totally broke. Or, face it. Broker than broke.

At least the money pressure was less intense here than when she lived in Portland, where her mother answered the phone. Her mom soon began to recognize that "Miss Green," at an 800 number, was trouble. And so was "Mr. Brand," and so were "Mrs. Evans" and "Miss Young."

"You have *four* credit cards?" Luckily she didn't find out that Hillary had five. As far as the credit cards were concerned, her mother said, "Sink or swim." As far as a deposit on an apartment in San Francisco, so Hillary could take the one job in the world that would have her, her father intervened. He wrote her a big check, although he said it slayed him to believe an apartment could be that much. The cost of housing in San Francisco was in the news all the time, but he just couldn't believe it was *that* high. "It is, Dad." But actually, it wasn't. It was true that there weren't any cheap apartments, but there were cheaper apartments than the one she got. It was just that she wanted a good safe neighborhood. For one thing, she'd have to walk Tess up and down the sidewalk after midnight, when she got home from her job, which was at night. Portland was a town. This was a city. The safer the better was all she could think. Anyway, pretty soon – like, in a few years – she'd be able to start paying her dad back. Eventually this money problem would be a thing of the past. Temporary inconvenience.

Then her first paycheck didn't come through the computer into her bank account the way it was supposed to. Bang-bang-bang, check after check. Big fines on every one, so she was getting more overdrawn by the minute. People say, It happened before I knew it. Well in this case, it did. When she got the computer problem straightened out, she wrote new checks to replace the bounced ones. It wasn't till the next day that she found out how deep the penalty problem was. Luckily, the bank didn't bounce all the little replacement checks she'd written, piling on even more penalties. They just bounced the big one. The most hideously embarrassing one. The rent.

She still cringed. She sometimes walked up the street and got an involuntary shudder, out of the blue. That whole period, when she couldn't answer the phone. She just sat alone in the empty apartment, the rings echoing, so loud, bouncing off the bare walls and bare floors. She counted, and counted the rings. On and on. Sixteen, once. No way would she answer. It couldn't possibly be anyone but Miss Green, Mr. Brand, Mrs. Evans, or Miss Young. Oh. It could have been the one her mother hadn't met, Mr. Kelly.

Luckily, she couldn't afford an answering machine.

AT THE HEAD of the leash, Tess pulled Hillary's arm up the sidewalk. A man waiting for a cable car said, "Who's walking who?" She smiled brightly, as if she'd never heard that one before. On the other side of Hyde, a man with three afghans on three colors of leashes had the same problem she had, but three times as bad. The biggest afghan barked nonstop, and the man kept yelling, "Shut up."

Where the brick street stopped and became stairs through the woods, Hillary always let Tess off the leash, just in time to keep her arm from being yanked from its socket. Here, the songs of the tennis balls and the sea lions gave way to the sound of Tobin's shears, shaping, and Tess's paws, galloping.

"No jumping!" Hillary yelled, as Tobin stumbled for his balance. Tess hadn't learned that phrase yet. Staggering at each attack of the dog's paws upon his chest and solar plexus, he ran his hand along the loose, silky, puppy fur.

Tobin had a great Father William beard and silver hair tumbling to his shoulders. He was a normal height, which meant he came up to about Hillary's chin, and he always stretched the same navy blue sweater over his round belly. "Like this sweater?" he asked. "Found it in the dumpster. Pretty good deal. Forty, fifty dollar sweater. Almost just like my other one." Tess jumped again to give the cheek above his beard another lick. Her tail thumped when she got more stroking. "Dog's growing fast. What is it, six months old?"

"Yes. When I got her, last September, I held her in my hand and I thought, how odd. She doesn't weigh anything. The next day, she seemed to weigh something. Now she weighs fifty-five pounds."

"Fifty-five." Tobin ran a hand down his beard. "Fifty-five."

Maybe fifty-five was his age.

"Exactly a third of my weight, if I lost ten pounds," he said. "I'd like to lose ten pounds."

Hillary wished she could gain ten. She'd even tried drinking cream. Her doctor in Portland had a chart for women that went up to six-two, almost her height. He, a great empathetic hero of a man, looked up into her eyes and told her not to worry about being underweight, she was healthy. He probably felt just awful for her, knowing she'd never find a man tall enough.

"Not much interested in travel," Tobin said.

"Hmmm?" She was watching his shears go over and over the same spot on the hedge, until that patch was flat as a wall, and then he went over it again. She was wondering how he knew when to stop.

"Been most of the places people want to go," he said. "The Alps, Scotland, Paris, Bavaria. Shaved once for a bike race in Italy." The little round leaves that dropped to the ground made a long stripe of shiny round dots in front of the hedge. "Didn't seem to make much difference. Could be if you were a swimmer . . ."

Tess shot up the cliff after a dove, who, after a fluttery takeoff, sailed to the crest of the hill and idled in the air beside the chain-link fence. Using the full leverage of her long legs, Tess launched her body like a rocket, her bark furious when the dove used magical means to elude her. When she could see the bird wasn't coming back, she took off down the hill and mapped out a track for herself – a huge oval pitching from the

17

top of the cliff to the lower terrace – and circled like an electric train. She wasted no energy on up and down, she just lowered her body so it practically scraped the ground and used her legs as propellers, leaning into the turns. Her ears pressed back, she followed the point of her nose and went like a Ferrari. The only break in her aerodynamic flight forward came once every minute or so, when she twisted her head to make sure Hillary was still there.

She always did that. She always checked up on Hillary, never let her out of her sight for more than a minute. The thing about Tess that hit Hillary in the heart was the way this big powerful puppy knew she was dependent. Tess was the first person who'd ever loved her this much.

"Ever had a dog?" she asked the gardener. This was when she noticed that he wasn't there.

"Hey Tess!" They might as well leave. "Tess! C'mere." This was the one command Tess ever obeyed. She knew better than to be left. But as they reached the promenade, Tess took off again. There was that older woman with the bichonne frisée, over by the monument. "No jumping! Tess, no jumping!" Oh no. Tess sped fast as a greyhound to that poor, sixty-plus woman on those heels. Hillary didn't know how she could stand up in those shoes in the first place. "*No jumping!*"

And look at that. Tess leapt   and landed on the ground in front of the lady. She sprang again. And she landed in the same spot! Up and down, up and down she boinged. Like a marionette being jerked. But only vertically. She never touched a paw to the woman. A miracle. She must have known she could knock her right off her little stilts.

Running toward her, Hillary called out, "Sorry! I hope she didn't scare you."

The woman was now clutching the back of a bench. Just in case. "She's a darling puppy," she said. "But she did scare me. You see . . ." She lifted an ankle to show the stiletto. "It's amazing. Do you think she could see that I'm vulnerable?"

Hillary couldn't believe it, but it seemed to be so.

The bichonne frisée and Tess had started playing dog tag, so Hillary

18

and the lady sat down on the bench, to be the spectators. The woman looked at her watch. "Posy needed a little walk, so here we are, but I only have five minutes. I have a luncheon meeting so important that I can't afford to be a minute late. Oh dear. Now we only have four and a half minutes."

Meeting? Important? Hillary wouldn't have thought this woman would do any kind of work. Could it be a meeting with her stockbroker? It would be rude to ask. But what would she talk about instead?

The woman had questions to ask Hillary. After they'd barely gotten started, their four and a half minutes were up. "See you later?"

Tobin seemed to be nowhere. And no one else was in the park either. Hillary and Tess went home to the four walls.

"WE'RE BACK!" SHE called out. It was almost four o'clock.

Tobin didn't bother to look up from his rake until Tess knocked it out of his hands and, bounding on to his chest, took his breath away. He stroked the dog and picked up his rake at the same time. "Ever see this place on a Friday afternoon?"

It was a Friday afternoon. Hillary walked to the monument and looked around.

"Friday afternoons I really do a job on this place." He picked up his rake. "I rake the dirt, get rid of all the footprints, make stripes. Friday afternoons, this place looks like a million bucks."

Tess was chasing one of those infuriating birds who could escape into the sky. Suddenly the bird didn't matter to her. She stopped barking, skidded to a stop, and crouched in her poised-to-pounce position. She beat a rhythm in the dirt with her tail. This meant another dog was coming. And, from around the corner of the hedge – the corgi. Which meant the psychiatrist, Philo Righi! Hillary shot to one of the green benches, hitting the seat and tucking her glasses into her sleeve just as Tess ran at the corgi, and her owner rounded the hedge.

"Philo." She kept her voice serene, like she'd been relaxing on that bench for hours, just looking out at the Bay.

19

Philo Righi was tall. But not as tall as Hillary. She preferred to sit when she talked to him. He ambled over in running shorts, his legs long and strong with lots of nice hair. She also liked the hair on his head. Maybe that cut would be called a bob. It was the color of polished teak, falling into waves he was always having to push back behind his ears. It was kind of a nice nervous habit that made his conversation even more interesting. She'd love to have a hairstyle like his. So would any woman, probably. But he had such a strong face and body the hair made him look even more like a man.

The corgi dodged Tess to scuttle over to Hillary. This dog wore short white socks, apparently attached to her long, fat stomach, which actually did scrape the ground. On the raked dirt, you could see the stomach print between the pawprints. As Philo Righi lowered himself onto the bench next to Hillary, the corgi stretched her neck up and placed her chin on Hillary's knee, to have her head stroked. This dog reminded Hillary of the Queen Mother; too bad she'd died. "I think your dog needs a hat," Hillary said. Tess jumped onto the bench to lean down and lick Philo Righi's ear, rapping her tail on the bench's back. Instead of pushing her off, the way most people would, Philo Righi grabbed her head and held it to his chest, caressing, "Hi, honey," he said to Tess, his voice as thick as the endearment.

Friday: Through Opera Glasses

ANNA LEONE'S APARTMENT idled above the city like a helicopter with lace curtains. A clock-face painted with angels and columbines smiled at fat babies holding up lampshades. Oil portraits looked out at a brindle cow, a series of still lifes, and a ship in the sky-blue sea. Pudgy upholstery of wine-red velvets and amber brocades invited you to sink in and adjust the fringed silk cushions; and on the mantle, a jumble of framed snapshots and formal photographers' portraits fought for space. A pair of stuffed vireos perched on a mossy branch in a rounded glass case, and a cracked porcelain cat slept on the hearth. In the dining-room the chandelier tossed rainbow darts against the walls, and the Bay outside was repeated in a dozen shapes of polished sterling and in a gilt-framed mirror so antique the glass seemed almost golden. Although the top floor Anna lived on was only six stories off the ground, the hill behind it dropped so sheerly that no tree or building got in the way of her panorama. The front of her apartment, where french doors opened to a balcony, faced the glade where everyone went to walk their dogs along paths beneath the pines. Anna saw shade on shade of green, shape on shape of leaf and needle, and here and there a bulging acacia tree blooming hot as mustard. Amidst it all, one blossoming crabapple stood out, light as a puff for dusting powder.

Once, when a cluster of dogwalkers stood by the tiled benches, Frankie had walked over with her newspaper folded open and said to Anna, "What do you put on your income tax form for occupation?

21

Socialite?" Along with a slight spray of beer, Frankie let burst a hoot of laughter. It was uncomfortable, because everyone stayed deadpan, pretending they hadn't heard. When Anna smiled, everyone burst forth laughing. Frankie then read a quote from the *Chronicle*'s society column, about the Giants' Opening Day: "Socialite Anna Leone was seen in the Mayor's box, eating Its-Its with her grandchildren." Back in her apartment, Anna went to the dictionary. "Socially prominent person" was the only definition Webster's gave. So she looked up "social" and waded through five and a half inches of fine print to find a definition that appealed to her: "Forming or having a tendency to form cooperative and interdependent relationships with one's fellows." This probably wasn't what the *Chronicle* had meant. They had probably meant "5a: of, relating to, or based on rank or status in a particular society or community" or, even worse, "5b: of, belonging to, or characteristic of the upper classes."

Fffft. She settled on "tendency to form cooperative relationships with one's fellows." That was what she was good at. It was also what made this apartment the most perfect place she could imagine for herself. After Joe died, when they were both fifty-three, the children begged her not to sell the house in Seacliff. That was thirteen years ago. Angela had gone East to college, and Joey lived in a fraternity house at Cal. They both needed a place to come home to, but they didn't live there any more. When she found this place, with its high ceilings and views and two bedrooms plus a library that could work as another guest room, Angela protested: "It's not a real home. It doesn't have a garden."

"But it does have a garden."

"What! That balcony?"

"No. The pretty little forest across the street."

"That *public park*?"

Anna had raised a snob. She'd first seen it coming when Angela was eight and corrected her great-uncle's grammar. "You mean you don't want *any* zucchini, Uncle Carlo." Carlo's face showed confusion and shame, and it didn't make him feel better when the child explained, "What you *said* is a double negative." It got worse in seventh grade, when Anna and Joe made the mistake of switching her to a private school. It was on a street you couldn't drive down at three in the afternoon, because the mothers, all used to having their own way, parked their foreign cars three deep in the street. Angela's fellow students had attitudes she picked up like lint. On her thirteenth birthday Angela opened a present her Great-Aunt Rosa had mailed from Bologna and said, "Eeeyew!" It was a satiny pink polyester blouse that Rosa had probably thought was just the thing in America. "I know you, Princess," Joe said to Angela. "You're *perfectly* happy with – *the best of everything*."

He admitted he'd stolen the line from Oscar Wilde. Years later, the way Angela pronounced "*public park*" reminded Anna of that "Eeeyew," and Joe's response to his little snob daughter. Anna said to Angela just, "I know you, Princess."

The two of them smiled. Their smiles became laughs. Together, they laughed more, until tears ran down their cheeks.

It wasn't the joke. It was Joe. Gone.

AS IT TURNED out, Anna enjoyed her new garden ten times as much as her old one. It flourished with fauna – human and canine. The park was for her what soap operas were for some of her friends. Stories unfolded there.

Love stories were what she liked best, and there weren't enough of them in real life. She was well past the age for love herself, but she sharpened all her senses to pick up what the younger people might be feeling. To both the men who'd wanted to marry her after Joe died, the answer had been automatic. Because her marriage really had been a romance. She still has his jokes to replay in her head. While so many people's sense of humor had to do with belittling someone, Joe's had been the opposite. Just yesterday, at a red light by the St. Francis, Anna heard herself laugh. She was remembering the time she'd worn a new dress to meet him at the usual spot, under the clock in the St. Francis. Joe stepped back to look her over. "Madame, you sure do make that gown look gorgeous."

23

That one, he told her, he'd stolen from Duke Ellington – who'd said it to Queen Elizabeth! But that didn't make the comment any less funny, or, to tell the truth, any less what he actually felt.

Through sixth grade, their daughter Angela had been proud that her father was famous, his name on plumbing trucks all over town. And then she went to Miss Burke's School.

"Tell them he's a businessman," Anna consoled.

"Entrepreneur!" said Joe.

He was a plumber who had a big payroll. Lots of trucks. A few buildings. He read books and gave money to the opera. On opening night he looked great in a tux.

THIS MORNING HAD started, as usual, in her red bathrobe, on her balcony, with her roll and her coffee and her opera glasses. Posy sat at her feet, nose twitching to pick up the news. The first person Anna saw on the promenade with the gardener was the Englishman, apparently discussing the graffiti that had appeared on the monument during the night. From the gestures the Englishman made, she saw he was angry. Of course the whole neighborhood was angry. Graffiti was certainly a problem. But when Anna got emotional, she got emotional about other things. She watched the Englishman wave his arm, she watched the gardener shrug, exaggerating how resigned he was. Her opera glasses were powerful enough to pick up the pinstripes in the Englishman's suit, a peek of light from his wingtips, the crease in his trousers. She saw how the Englishman resisted when the poodle tried to lead him, by the green leash with rhinestones, into the dewy ivy. The dog excreted on the path, and Anna watched the Englishman dip his hand into his pocket to pull out a sandwich bag, which he turned inside out. Bending at the knees and the waist, he cupped his plastic-mitted palm over the dog mound, used his other hand to whip the bag right side out and twirl it shut, stepping to the trashcan. Tobin raised his right arm in the Heil Hitler salute.

Seeing that, the Englishman's back rose even straighter than it had

24

been, tensed with shock. He pivoted and marched up the stairs. Naturally.

Anna must find a way to tell Tobin to be discriminating with this salute. Most people would misconstrue.

SHE WENT TO the kitchen to rinse out her coffee cup and heard a knock at the front door, and a second later heard the door opening. "*Buenas dias.*"

Seeing Anna at the sink, Morella rushed to grab the sponge, protesting, "You do-een my yob!"

When Morella laughed, hot pink shot to her cheeks. She had terracotta coloring and was round as a peasant painted by Botero. On the days Morella came, Anna made it a point to find an hour to sit down and talk – because it was fun, and because Morella needed the practice. Two years ago the conversation was so slow it almost hurt, because Morella knew hardly any words. "You should learn Spanish!" Angela advised. But that wasn't the point. When Morella brought her little boys and sat them down in the library with the TV tuned to Spanish stations, Anna had to fight the urge to intrude. They should watch American cartoons. If they didn't speak like natural-born citizens (which they were!) they'd be doomed to cleaning bussing tables for the rest of their lives. Anna kept her mouth shut about the Spanish TV shows, but she worked on a goal. By now, she and Morella could have a great time, gossiping in English. Such horrid stories Morella could tell. One woman made her work ten hours but only paid her for eight. She demanded that Morella lift huge things like desks and crates of books. Morella couldn't find the words to tell her she had a bad back. She did find the words to complain about the pay, but the woman just told her she wasn't worth her wages. And Morella understood this awful woman's English when she said, "All Latins are lazy and stupid."

Anna paid Morella for sixteen hours when she worked eight. But this didn't make up for what she had to go through with other clients.

25

"Anna?" Morella's voice came from the bedroom. She walked in with a stack of things from the lingerie drawer. "Anna, you gonna have to get new. See? These torn. These getting gray. This not pretty."

DRESSED IN A soft tweed of charcoal mohair, a fabulous red scarf, and tomato-red heels four inches high, Anna started with Posy across the street. At the lawn by the landing Tobin, in his black rubber boots, turned on the sprinkler. He saw her and called down, "I'll turn it off for you, Mrs. Leone." He did and stuck his arm straight out from the shoulder, palm and fingers parallel to the ground. Pumping up his small voice he chanted, "Extra, extra, read all about it / Raised right arm of Hitler / Found in a garbage can / In Yugoslavia."

She chuckled with him, hoping he wouldn't go through all the stanzas, about the goose-stepping knees and click-clicking heels and sundry severed body parts found in trash receptacles on all the world's great continents.

"Kind of dated, that poem," he said. "But 'the-former-Yugoslavia' doesn't scan. Never will. Lucky I keep writing. I've got a new one for you today, Mrs. Leone." He turned away to hide his pride. "I know you like my stuff."

"Oh no, Tobin, not this morning. I was just going to give Posy a little spin and then I have to speed along. The museum lunch is at eleven-thirty, but I have to be there by nine, since I'm chairman," and she was about to recite her list when she noticed he wasn't there. She saw the back of him taking two steps at a time to his shed. Oh dear. She looked at her watch, then suddenly sighed: "Romeo!"

"Well well *well!*" came a rich male voice. It was Dr. Hawthorne, turning the hedge after his rottweiler Romeo, who had already darted over to Posy. Dr. Hawthorne approached, thick silver hair six feet two inches above the ground, thumping his spade on his palm. She always looked forward to his outfits. Today he was wearing a red and green plaid flannel shirt under his tweed jacket with the two layers of elbow patches, and he'd tucked an ascot of fuchsia pink and tangerine under

26

the plaid shirt collar. She loved his dash. At the same time she wondered if he might be colorblind.

As they exchanged good mornings across the lawn, she was aware that her voice always picked up a sweeter tone whenever it was him she was speaking to. When he raised his spade and boomed to her, "I trust you carry one of these with you, at all times, in your pocketbook," she could hear that her laugh sounded like a wind chime. The odd effect the doctor had on her voice embarrassed her. Oh well.

"Imperative!" the doctor pronounced, waving the spade and striding to a far corner of the lawn, where he did a deep kneebend, spine straight as a gymnast, and slid the spade under a pile of dog do.

Men of forty weren't as fit as he was!

"Cannot tolerate these people who leave their dog's dirt around." He stepped to the trash bin and emptied the spade.

"So generous!" she said. "I clean up after my own dog, but I can't bring myself to clean up after other people's."

"You wouldn't mind if you carried one of these," he boomed, stentorian. (That was the word she imagined he'd use. He chose his words the way he chose his ascots.)

"I got it for you, Mrs. Leone." Tobin trotted down the stairs holding a sheaf of typing. "Kind of an epic." His voice was so soft it took hard listening to pick up the words. He paused to shuffle through the pages and enjoy a line or two before handing her the manuscript. When she protested that tomorrow would be a better day, he took the manuscript back.

"Tobin!" said the doctor. "I've been wanting to talk to you about these dandelions."

"Well," Tobin said, his voice barely making it out of his throat, "with the type of grass they've planted here, the dandelions just kind of grow."

"I'm sure you're aware," pronounced Dr. Hawthorne, "that there is a type of selective poison that kills the dandelions but spares the lawn."

"Wouldn't be surprised." Tobin looked uneasy. "I kind of like to go easy on poison."

"I'm with you one hundred percent, Tobin. But I know for a fact there are people who inhabit this park who are not in favor of dandelions."

"I kind of like 'em," Tobin said, just above a whisper.

"Exactly! To my mind, we need whatever we can get to give this place a countrified look. What this part of the city needs, with its urbanity of architecture and abundance of concrete, is a heath. A small relief of wilderness." He took a card from his breast pocket and selected a fine-pointed blue pen from his pocket protector. Anna noticed the pens in the plastic packet were arranged by color, black–blue–green–red–yellow, with two each of the red, blue and black – probably a narrow point then a broad tip. He wrote a phone number on the card. "Now you have my numbers at home and at my office. I want you to call me any time, if anyone gives you any trouble about the dandelions." He took the time to find exactly the right spot to re-file his pen. Anna looked on as Tobin took the card. She saw that Dr. Hawthorne had begun to frown at the ground. "It's not that I imagine I have absolute power to protect dandelions," he said, some uncomfortable gravel in his throat. "But I have used my influence to good effect on even more challenging matters in the past."

"Did you tell him about the tulips, Tobin?"

"Oh. Yuh." Tobin spoke to the ground. "Had to rip out the tulips. Some guy didn't like tulips. Said he was a C.E.O."

"A what?"

"Yuh. That's what he said. 'I. Am. A Ceeee. Eeee. Oh.'"

It was a relief when Tobin changed the subject by offering his poem. The doctor laughed his no-thanks: "I have twenty-four patients to see today. Romeo?" At the foot of the steps he turned to wave farewell with his spade.

Evenings in the park were like cocktail parties without the dresses. Now that it stayed faintly light until after six o'clock, there was always a little group – and usually a few drinks. Frankie always had her beer, Pierre his martini, and tonight a couple had spread a picnic on a bench, with pâté and cheese and plastic champagne glasses.

28

Tonight the Englishman had changed into jeans – crisp, clean, and ironed. He hadn't changed his topic. Graffiti. He was new in the neighborhood, she'd barely met him, and she was afraid he'd sense her boredom if the conversation stayed on graffiti too long. "Your accent is English so you must be . . .?" "Ah, yes. Indeed I am." He told her he'd commuted to London from a village called Snugwood. "Thatched cottages, the whole idyll. A bit of a bore for my wife. Chantal grew up in Paris." (His wife was named Chantal!) "Chantal wanted a city, so I gave her San Francisco."

THE BREAKABLE-LOOKING WOMAN was there, with her enormous puppy. The puppy ran up to Anna like an old friend. Don't jump, Anna silently prayed. And, of course, the puppy jumped. But not on her. The puppy seemed to dance for joy, high and higher, but never touching a paw to Anna. She petted the puppy and waved at her mistress, who was too absorbed in conversation to notice. Who could blame her? That young psychiatrist, Philo Righi, had a fascinating energy.

JOSH LEAPT UP the stairs, his skateboard under his arm. Anna had seen Josh transported by all kinds of vehicles: The baby buggy, the stroller, the trike, the two-wheeler, and now the skateboard. "Next thing I know, Josh, you'll be driving a car."

"Only a year and a half to go, Mrs. Leone," he said. "I turn fourteen in twelve days." He seemed to like her amazement. "Not soon enough, Mrs. Leone. I wish I was fifteen and a half right now. I've already got my dad talked into a car for me as soon as I get my license." His cider-colored eyes had a spot of fire. "It's not worth it, riding the buses. Know what I mean? I mean, I compare this year with last year, and this year is a whole lot worse. Like last summer was great for me, personally, and Christmas too, but the way things are in the city is worse. Much worse, man. If things keep going the way they're going I don't know what's going to happen." She gave him a questioning look and he answered. "Like, at least two people I know have pieces."

"What?"

"Yeah. This one guy has a rifle, and the other one has an Uzi. Oh. And this guy that beat the shit out of me, he's got a forty-five now." Josh checked her reaction and seemed pleased. But it wasn't his language that shocked her. "So I don't want to get near the guy. I mean, he's wired, wired on crack, and when you get that way you don't care. You waste people and it doesn't bother you. I'd rather not see him. I try to avoid him. Because he might have it out for me. Because he tried to beat the shit out of me that time on the bus but I ended up beating the shit out of him."

"Who are these boys?"

"They're writers."

"Riders?" she asked.

"Yeah, writers."

"You mean they just ride the buses back and forth?"

"Yeah, they ride the buses, but they write!"

"Write?"

"Yeah," he said. "Like South."

"South?"

"Yeah, South. That's what I used to write. Before I cleaned up my act. I mean, writers have tags."

"Tags?"

"Yeah. Like my last name's North, so I wrote South. My buddy Spike, that was easy. His was Pokey. 'Cause that's what spikes do. My buddy Chef, his tag was Cap'n Cooke."

"You mean you had codes?"

"That's it. Kind of."

"And you knew each other?"

"That's the whole point, man."

Anna was amazed, really flattered, at how he took her into his confidence. They had always had a rapport, she and Josh, since the tricycle days. "But you don't do this any more?"

"Naw." His skateboard was tucked tight into his underarm, so his

30

hands were free to stick in his pockets, giving him a manly stance. "Trouble is, people get it out for you if you crowd their territory, or especially if you write over them. I got in a lot of trouble that way."

"You mean, someone writes his tag and you write South on top of it so no one can read his tag?"

"You've got the picture." He was talking down to her now. "It's dangerous, man," he said, animated again, getting back to the point.

"So you'd write on the inside of buses?"

"Yeah!"

"Was it fun?"

"Oh yeah. It was kind of a thrill, really. It really was. Because you're standing up on the bus seat, writing, and there are people all around, and the bus driver, and you'd better not get caught. And you do it and you don't get caught – it's kind of a hit, it really is."

"But you stopped?"

"Yeah. Oh, we had one last fling, recently. But the wrap-up is I just decided it wasn't worth the hassle. The chance of getting caught and slapped with a big fine. It was great, though, you've got to admit." He rubbed his cheek, as if feeling a day's growth of beard. Anna looked closely, and she saw just baby skin.

BY THE TIME Josh said "Gotta rocket" and rocketed, all the people and dogs had left except young Philo Righi and the waif in the sweatshirt. Most of the light had gone too. Even the hyperactive puppy lay sleeping, a long heap on the ground, near the corgi, whose head lay on Philo Righi's running shoe. Philo and the girl didn't notice her when she walked past their bench to check the lights on the Golden Gate Bridge, just one long rope over the water. Turning back, Anna saw the couple like figures in a shadow box. And a shock came! Philo's long wrist shot up and his large hand slapped the girl's cheek! The girl's chin jutted out in surprise.

"Mosquito." It was amazing how clearly the sound of Philo's voice carried.

31

"Oh, thanks." Hers was harder to hear, but it sounded like thanks.

"It's dark," he said. "We'd better get going. I'm supposed to go to a black-tie party tonight."

"Oh!" The girl sounded cheerful and enthusiastic. Anna's heart sank, probably along with the girl's, until the next thought came to Anna: Next time maybe *you'll* be the one going to a black-tie party with him.

"You go that way, don't you?" Philo pointed up the hill to Hyde Street. "I go this way." He nodded down to Larkin. "But I don't think you should be going around by yourself at this hour. I'll walk you to your door."

FROM DOWN IN the woods, looking west, the Bay was smooth as that Midnight Blue perfume bottle Joe had given her for high school graduation. On this side of the bridge individual dots of yellow shone from windows, perfectly arranged lines of lights climbing the hills. Across the Bay the lights of Marin were just tossed, like glitter. Posy ran to Anna like a bouncing cloud, and the two walked up past the tennis courts to get an east-facing look. Coit Tower came into view, a gold pillar against a sky of deep lavender. Strings of incandescent beads draped the Bay Bridge from point to point to point, with round red lights at the peaks, like blinking cherries on sundaes. The cable car passed, a riot on rollers. Walking down Hyde Street, the tall reed of a woman seemed shorter. She walked unnaturally. Scrunched. Anna tried to calculate how tall she would be, next to Philo Righi, if she stood up.

Monday

MOST PEOPLE DIDN'T like Monday mornings. Said they didn't. Tobin didn't either, when he first realized. Before he opened his eyes.

He could've used another day off. Or, to tell you the truth, a day off. He was bone tired from writing all weekend. Back-breaking labor, writing. He was doing something different now. Stories. Like poems, but prose style. Plots, paragraphs. Hard for a poet to write stories. A poet didn't like to waste words. Chose every one for color and shape, to mean something. Harder to hold things together in a story. Could be it was possible. He'd see. Took concentration.

He didn't care what anyone said. He'd been a ditch digger. Summers, in grad school. So he knew, writing made you more tired than digging. It was the thinking.

"Maybe I'll retire and take it easy. Write a novel." People said that. Hmm. Could be a novel was easier than a poem. He hadn't tried novels. Why write them? He didn't read them. But stories were work.

So. It wasn't hard to understand why on Monday Tobin could've used a day off. But he got about an hour on the bus, transfers and everything, to wake up. When it came right down to it, Monday mornings were probably the best time of the week. He felt a lot of energy by the time the Union Street bus let him off at the corner of Hyde, by the ice-cream store. No temptation. Still closed. Sometimes the moon was still out, but not this day. Fog. He knew he'd made good time, because the electricity under the cable-car tracks hadn't started to hum. They switched it on at six.

His arms swung, as he walked up the block. There was a little slippage in his boots. Rubber. Worked out best for gardening. You were always walking through sprinklers, things like that. They looked like a toy soldier's boots, maybe. High to the knees. Yellow toes and yellow stripes around the tops. A lot of people found rubber boots uncomfortable, but that was because they got the wrong size. They thought they should fit right. A mistake. The rubber boots didn't give, like leather, so what seemed like a good fit ended up tight. Get a bigger size, wear a little thicker sock. Of course your feet slip around, but you get used to it. Before he got to the brick street he'd already gotten his keys out, ready to open the shed.

You might have thought he'd have girly calendars all over the walls. Typical male gardener. But he wasn't so much interested in that. Oh, he had one token nudie, but mostly he had photographs of the Alps, old windjammers, bicycle racers, that type of thing. He'd got them from calendars where the year had run out. Kind of brightened the place up. No windows.

He had his equipment in there, a phone, and a little work table. Kind of rickety. He had hooks for his tools, and shelves for his manuscripts and correspondence. A few reference books. Of course the phone books. He put his *Chronicle* down on the work table. He'd probably read it later. Maybe go down to La Petite Treat to have a glass of grapefruit juice. Usually did. Around ten o'clock. Nine, ten o'clock. Nice place. First thing he did any morning, before he set off one sprinkler, was check out all the cliffs at the edges of the park, with the low-growing cover and branches and leaves. He had to make sure the boys were up and had their acts together. All their gear stuffed into their backpacks. No cans lying around. No needles. If it got out that people slept here, Tobin was in deep water.

I'm not a policeman, he said to himself every morning, a spring of courage in his black rubber boots. Flashlight in one hand, his arms

34

swung maybe a little too much as he walked down the steps. I'm paid to be a gardener. It's not my job to know whether people spend the night or not. I've just got to see they don't sleep here in the day. On the way down the stairs he rehearsed. Okay, time to go home.

Couldn't say that. It'd make 'em feel bad.

Tobin shone his flashlight and pulled up a long, low branch. If he stayed on his knees there was just enough headroom to crawl around. He pointed his spot into all the places above the north wall that he knew were good for sleeping. All clear. Then he walked up past the tennis courts and went through the good spots along the east slope. Nobody home.

Relief. In a way he hated these guys. Some of them. But then he hated to bug them, too. Most of them made it a point to be gone by daylight, but they didn't have alarm clocks. One guy in particular, kind of a nice guy, had at tendency to sleep in. He wasn't a regular, of course. Showed up every couple of months. Tobin couldn't risk anybody sleeping in. He also didn't like repeaters. People got the idea this was their house.

He didn't like confrontations. That was not the job of a gardener. So, nobody home meant this was a good day. Might be a good week.

Up at the shed he got a handful of sprinkler heads, the long brass ones that rotated and sent out a big shoot. There was plenty of light from buildings and from the streetlights so he could see to attach the brass sticks to the different outlets on the different lawns, on his way down to the promenade. Good thing he'd been through Monday mornings before, so he didn't get a shock when he saw the place, even in the dark. Trashed. Beer cans, vodka bottles, Styrofoam. That Styrofoam stuff would last longer than the cockroaches.

And graffiti. On the benches, the monument, even the stairs.

Tobin had a system. He went into a squat-walk and used his free arm to sweep bottles, cans, and Styrofoam into big plastic garbage bags.

What did they call it? Instant gratification? Maybe this was what he liked about Monday mornings. He could get the garbage out of the way

35

in fifteen minutes. If it hadn't been for him, this stuff would have piled up so nobody could walk through any more.

The old Chinese gentleman was out on the promenade in his quilted silk vest. Faced the Bay. Did T'ai chi. They always did that. Put themselves in the most beautiful locations. It was supposed to rub off on their spirits.

The dog Tess ran out of the bushes and sprang on the Chinese fellow's bent knee, shot up to give him a lick on the mouth. He smiled and petted the dog. Graceful, how he got his balance back. Beautiful spirit, that Chinese guy.

"Tess! Tess!" yelled the Birdwood woman from somewhere in the park. Some of the neighbors around here didn't like people yelling before six a.m., but Tobin didn't know if it was his job to say it. He was not a policeman.

Strange, kind of. What was she doing here at this hour? She was a diller-a-dollarer.

"Tess!" Seemed pretty happy to see her dog. "Tess."

"A diller-a-doller-a-Hillary-hollers," Tobin said. Poet Laureate of the Park. "What makes you come so soon?" How'd that go? "You used to come at ten o'clock, and now you come at noon?"

"Rrrgh," she groaned. "I have to go to Sacramento this morning. Some dumb thing at the Capitol. The regular cameraman couldn't make it. The van's picking me up in ten minutes. I had to work last night, I always work Sundays, and I'd barely got to sleep when the phone rang. It was the middle of the night." She winced. "It's still the middle of the night. Tess! Come. Tess!"

Interesting to watch her run. A shame, to tell you the truth. Tall women are usually graceful.

Two bags full, Tobin hoisted one over each shoulder and walked them up to the corner for the city pick-up. Almost daylight. In the shed he got his bucket of stuff and his brushes. Time to work on the graffiti. Kind of a cold day for getting his hands wet.

Carrying his bucket down to the benches, he stooped to pet the

36

psychiatrist's corgi. Corgi'd scooted over to his boots. Must like yellow, that corgi. "Where's your boss?"

Looking over the top of the hedge, Tobin saw the psychiatrist guy down on the lower terrace. Camelhair blazer, gray slacks, lady by his side. Japanese, looked like.

The guy got around. Last time Tobin saw him, he had the TV camerawoman eating out of his hand. Now this little geisha in an executive outfit. Psychiatrist guy and pretty woman looked out at the Bay. Must be nice, Tobin thought.

Or, maybe not. He used to be a stud. To tell you the truth. Back in his bachelor days. His bike-racing days. It was okay. Something you went through. Moved on to something different.

Some guys didn't, of course. Even if they got married, they kept on proving their manhood. To themselves.

Sex? That was Tobin's favorite sport. His wife seemed to enjoy it.

TURNED OUT TO be a good day. The kids who wrote the graffiti had playschool magic markers. Washed right off.

The air was thick. Thick. The only color along Larkin was Mrs. Leone's bathrobe. Red. She stood out on her balcony like a cardinal in the mist. Tobin couldn't make out the details on the buildings. Tested his memory. Did that one have gargoyles? Monsters and medusas? Or flowers? Crests and laurels? The tallest one had delicate, fluted windows scaling the tower. He remembered that. The little Victorian tucked between had a lacy trim, white on white. When you could see it. Like a wedding cake except more the size of a *petit four*. Opera singer lived there. With her lover. People said that. He liked to think so. Wish she'd sing.

High noon. Sun up. Sky blue. Cable car. Tobin raised his right arm in greeting. People smiled. Most of them. Cameras clicked. Tape rolled. Tobin de Brettville, world-famous gardener. Half Fwench, half Scot. Photographed by the Sviss, the Aus-try-leans, and the Chah-pa-neese. Across Hyde, the Englishman's poodle. Venerable dog. Led a woman on a leash.

37

Guess that's glamor. He took in the glove-leather jacket, the long legs, the nice hips. Glossy hair, swinging. Chestnut, he thought they called it. Funny, because the hair didn't look like a chestnut. Maybe it looked like a chestnut horse. Gleam and movement.

Glamor was headed for Tobin. "'Ello, 'ello," she said. "You are Tobeen?"

"You know me?" Kind of embarrassing. "Tobin de Brettville!" he said. "World-famous gardener." Sometimes he didn't like the way his chuckle was so heavy on the inhale. Sounded like a goon. Snoring.

"Oh, Tobin!" she said in her accent.

Must be French, Tobin decided.

Said her name was Chantal. Said she'd heard about him.

"Oh," he said, frog in his throat. "Oh." Checked out his boots.

"You do such a beautiful job with this park!"

"Oh. Well. Uh. Looks like you've got the Englishman's dog there." Kind of a stupid thing to say.

"Yes. *Our* dog. Nigel is my husband."

Kind of sweet, the way she said that word. Uzz-band. Made it sound nice. "Guess you're French."

"Yes. Yes!" She looked at him, used her free hand to move aside the shine of hair that had fallen across one eye, bisecting the nose. Nice nose. She was blushing. Must be shy. He was shy.

"I love the way you make these bushes round. Like so many green beachballs."

"Oh. That's nice of you. I appreciate it." When he added "Yuh," the sound didn't come out.

"We love it. You keep our view so nice." Still blushing. "This is what we see when we look out the window. All the trees, and the round bushes, and the – geraniums." Zher-ah-niums. "We think it's a much better view than the Golden Gate Bridge or the lights of the city. We think those are kind of clichés, you know? We have our own little cable car coming by, and this big green garden."

"Oh. Glad you like it." He went back to sculpting his bushes. Kind of a long conversation.

Seemed like a pretty nice woman. He took another look. She followed her poodle up the brick street past the tennis courts. Nice walk.

THREE SMALL CHINESE boys, all the same height, carried peach ice-cream cones.

This was the kind of visual Tobin liked to start a poem with. The boys approached, pitching up Hyde Street. One slapped another on the back, he laughed and tipped forward, but the ice-cream cone stayed just where it had been, in front of him. All the boys laughed. The cones were lined up, tips pointed exactly down. Can you have tips at the bottom? Tips are tops. Interesting semantic question. Not that interesting. A quill tip? Tips aren't always tops. The peach scoops were round as juggling balls, and they stayed in symmetry as the boys squiggled and kicked up the sidewalk.

Something to see. Tobin liked to start a poem with seeing. Finding just the right words to show you. Then sometimes you figured out what it meant. Sometimes it meant something. Maybe not. You figured it out.

Clipping leaves and standing back to check the effect, he put ice-cream words together. Chinese boy words. And what came next?

When this bush was finished he'd lock his shears in the shed and take his yellow legal notepad down to La Petite Treat. Another glass of grapefruit juice. Squeezed fresh right on the spot. Best grapefruit juice in the city. Probably.

To tell the truth he'd like a sandwich. But he wanted to lose a few pounds. Stomach was getting out of hand. He went back to ice-cream words.

Hearts and Flowers

WHERE WAS TOBIN? Tess cantered ahead with springs in her big paws, through the bushes and hedges, and Hillary combed the foliage with her eyes. The two wound along paths padded with pine-needles to the north wall where the trail dead-ended and the cyclone fence cut up the hill. The hill was almost steep as a wall, so that even Tess had a hard time. She planted a paw and slipped back. At the top, she had to stand still and pant. Hillary hooked her long fingers through the links of the fence and pulled herself up with her arms.

There were no people, no balls, no sounds on the tennis courts. The dirt trail around the courts was only a foot wide, walled by chain-link on one side and tall shrubs pressing in from the other. Hillary had to keep moving branches back to clear a way for her body. At an open perch she stopped to take in the aerial view: the pattern of box hedges, steps, trees, and lawns; bushes, terraces, benches, and paths. It was a Mondrian design, without the Mondrian colors. Only the yellow acacia and the Italian tiles were bright, with the rest just muted greens and browns. Beyond the boundaries of the park, splendid old buildings lined Larkin, under a Kodachrome sky. The brilliance of the Great Meadow, the dome of the Palace of Fine Arts, and the sailboats crowding the yacht harbor were too far away to seem important. Within the monotone Mondrian, no Tobin.

IN A WAY, she wasn't sure she was happy she'd moved to San Francisco.

Everybody thought this must be the best place to live. Every tourist said so.

The scenery was pretty. People smiled. At work, people were pleasant. But then if you asked them if they wanted to go to a movie, they were doing something else. They didn't ask you over to dinner, they didn't offer to introduce you to some man they knew. In fact most of the people in this city didn't particularly care if you were alive. They might wish you weren't. It was crowded enough without you. You might get to the video store first and rent the movie they wanted to see. You might take the parking spot they wanted. How were they to know she didn't even have a television or a car? At least one good thing about being grotesquely skinny was that no one could accuse you of taking up too much space.

If it were Valentine's Day in this city, no one would give you a valentine. If it were your birthday, no one, except your mom and dad in Portland, would send you a card. No one would give you a party or a present or even go out with you for pizza.

It was Valentine's Day. And it was Hillary Birdwood's birthday. It always used to be the best day of the year, better than Christmas and the Fourth of July and the last day of school rolled into one. Hillary had always felt so lucky, to be the birthday girl on the day of love. All through grade school her mother had brought a heart-shaped sheet cake to her classroom on Valentine's Day, and a punchbowl and cups and punch with pieces of fruit floating in it. All the children loved it, and she got valentines from everyone.

The mail hadn't come yet, but she was sure she'd get a card from her parents. Probably the usual check – a dollar for each year. This year's check would amount to something. Twenty-seven. She might get a card from Jerry, her friend who'd moved to Minneapolis. And maybe she'd get one from Jan, in Portland.

Tonight she'd be working, so at least she wouldn't have to do something maudlin like treating herself to a movie, alone. Or going out to a nice restaurant alone. What a thought.

This was the kind of town where you met a nice man, a really good one, a doctor. And you talked for hours, and he liked you, and he was chivalrous and walked you home because he thought you shouldn't go around alone after dark. And he went to a black-tie party and you never saw him again.

Of course you were too tall. You'd be too tall anywhere.

Once she had read, in the *Oregonian* Sunday magazine, about a Swedish woman, six feet two, who had had two inches surgically removed from each thigh. That had left her at six feet. Big difference. Hillary wanted to be a maximum of five-eight, preferably five-six. The operation had probably ruined this Swedish woman's proportions. Hillary would never do that. But it really was a problem, finding a man tall enough.

FROM THE PATH around the courts, she could see just about everything, and it looked like Tobin hadn't come today. Maybe he had a cold. He might have taken the day off. Maybe his mother's illness had taken a turn for the worse. Hillary just hoped he wouldn't slough off like this very often.

Oh! There was a sprinkler going. Was it automatic? It could have turned itself on. But it was a black sprinkler hose, perforated, laid along the lawn. Someone must have slung it there. The spray it sent up went the whole length of it, gentle as mist.

Hillary and Tess spilled down the hillside, sending pine-cones skittering. Tess spotted the place in the hose where there was a leak and grabbed the spurt in her mouth, hurling and whipping the hose all over the lawn. "Tess! No! No! Tess!"

Bad dog.

Hillary didn't say those words. The dreaded words, bad dog. She never said them, except in the most dire circumstances. Tess's feelings were hurt so easily. Her ears pressed back, she got a look of pain in her eyes much worse than if she'd been hit. Hillary couldn't bear that look.

This was an easy situation. Hillary sprang into a skip, headed back toward the monument. "Tess! Tess," she called. "C'mon, Tess!" The puppy could be counted on to follow if she thought Hillary was leaving. She ran after Hillary, who caught her and clipped on the leash.

WHERE COULD HE be? Oh, of course. It was ten-thirty. He was probably down at La Petite Treat drinking his grapefruit juice. Writing his poetry.

It was so disappointing to come up here and have no one to talk to.

Here came a couple of people with cameras, speaking – some language. "Hello," Hillary said.

"Hello," they said, one word they knew, pleased to have a chance to use it.

Away from the sprinkler, it was safe to let Tess off the leash again.

"Tobin!" Hillary yelled. He swang his arms and his rubber boots up the brick road. Tess shot to him like a jack rabbit. "No jumping! No jumping!" Tobin looked down and caressed the dog, whose nose sniffed through his beard and hair, finding his ear for licking. Hillary walked up, leash wound round and round her wrist.

He gave her the raised right arm of Hitler.

She laughed. A big laugh of relief. "I thought you might not be here today. I thought you might be sick. Or something."

"Why?"

"Well, I looked around for you . . ."

"I haven't missed a day of work in eleven and a half years," he said in his soft, frog-throated voice.

"Oh." She and Tess followed him around, while he moved the sprinkler hose to a lower spot on the lawn. They followed him into the woods, where he walked with purpose, looking for something – pulling aside low branches and sticking his head under one shrub and another.

"Hey," he said, looking over at Tess sniffing through ivy. "Dog seems to be on to something." He started down the hill in her direction. "Could be thirsty."

Hillary followed. In the bed of ivy, Tess did seem to be licking or drinking.

"Some people look for gold," Tobin said. "I look for water. Found twelve outlets already, here in the woods. See? I had these pipes attached. Got 'em painted green. Nice, kind of."

That was a question. "Yes," Hillary answered. She had never noticed all the green pipes sticking up under the trees.

"Kind of goes with the vegetation." He clumped over ivy to Tess. "Oh, only a beer," he said, bending to pick up a brown bottle. Tess continued licking the lip as Tobin held it. "Dog likes beer, looks like." He tipped the bottle so the last drops fell out on her tongue. "Thought it might have been an outlet. Makes it easier, having sprinklers in the woods. Saves hauling hose."

"Hmm," Hillary said.

"I've really improved this park since I've been here." He resumed his search for water. Hillary followed until boredom overwhelmed her.

DOWN ON THE promenade, a girl sat on a bench. She wore jeans, and her blonde hair was thick and long, full of electricity. Where the streak of sun cut through the shade, golden sparks shot off. The girl held a book, and her head was bent forward so that the crackling bright hair hid her face and most of her upper body. Tess hurled herself at the girl, nudging aside the hair to lick her cheek, her ear, her eyelid. The girl gave a series of squeals. She pulled back a handful of hair to look around. The dog still kissed her. She looked about eighteen.

"Hi," said Hillary.

The girl squinted up and smiled and said hello, with an accent.

"Sorry about my dog. She's big but really she's only a puppy, a little over-enthusiastic, most people think. A little over-friendly. Hope you don't mind." The dog was still on the bench, tail thumping against the wooden back, nose exploring the girl's face. The girl had shut her book, keeping her place with a finger.

"I know I should discipline her," Hillary said, "but she's just impossible, and besides, it's sort of sweet really, I actually hate to squelch her."

44

"Sorry," the girl said, with a rueful smile. "I don't speak English."

Hillary looked down at the book. Albert Camus – *La Peste*. "Oh." She tried to think of something else to say, that the girl would understand. "*Bonjour!*"

The girl really smiled. "*Bonjour!*"

Unfortunately, Hillary could only think of two other words she knew in French. One was *escargot*. She smiled, searching her brain, and finally said the other one: "*Au revoir.*"

BEAUTIFUL DAY. *BEAUTIFUL* day. Ike's fifty-second Valentine's Day was going to be a beaut. He and the kids got a jump on the daylight. Without turning on the light he lifted Smoke, the twenty-five-pound ginger cat, off his chest and onto Meg's feet, next to Maude, the tortoiseshell kitten. Pulling on jeans and a T-shirt, he tiptoed the length of the railroad flat to the kids' room. Cracking the door, he gave a stage whisper: "Hey gang!" The three afghans sprang up and presented themselves to get leashed, and padded ahead of him to the front porch – Molly the goofy black puppy at the head of the line, followed by Goldie the dumb blonde, then Moe, the old cuss. He zipped up his jacket – black satin jacket with San Francisco Giants in orange script – and felt in his pocket for the cap. The air had a bite.

The street they had to walk up first was the steepest street in the world. They said so the other night on *Evening Magazine*. It got your heart started. After that it was a breeze – a gentle climb to the top of Russian Hill Place, in time to watch the sun smear its colors across the sky like a finger painting. Just like a finger painting! The lights on the bridge had a few more minutes to go before they'd call it a night. Everything was calm up here. With leashes slack, the four of them strode down Russian and up Nob, with the flags lined up in front of the Fairmont and the perfect flower beds around the lawn of the Pacific Union Club. All the people in all the hotels were still sound asleep. In front of the Huntington, Ike pointed through the glass doors of The Big Four. "See that, guys? See that piano? That's where Daddy played

Thursday night. You impressed?" Down in the Tenderloin, which was more his kind of place, a few of the prostitutes had already dolled themselves up for work. Or maybe they just hadn't finished up yet, like the lights on the bridge. To a teenager with hardly anything on except makeup he said, "Aren't you afraid you'll catch cold?" He fished a couple of bucks from his jeans and handed them to her. "Buy yourself some coffee and get some sleep."

This was their Valentine Marathon. Opera House, the projects, Pacific Heights, the Marina – at the beach he unleashed the afghans and let them fly, long fur floating after them. Ecstasy. They cut a six-mile circle through the city and got home to the park after all the dogwalkers had gone to work. Nobody was around except a girl with long hair, reading. By now the whole family looked a little beat, except maybe the baby. On the long rectangle leading to the monument, Molly darted forward. Backward. Left right left. She was chasing a big bright butterfly. She looked like a cartoon of a black mop gone nuts. The red leash wound around Ike's knee, then around his other knee, tangling with Moe's blue leash and Goldie's green one. Ike tried to extricate a leg. It was tricky, because the butterfly was enjoying this dance, keeping a distance but not too much. Now Ike had to hop around, like the dog, trying to keep his balance on one foot as he twirled the other in the air, hoping the red leash would disengage. The girl on the bench had stopped reading.

"Hello," he said. She had hair like Lady Godiva. He rotated his raised foot and shook his leg from the knee, but the red leash clung. It wound tighter. He tugged, but it was clumsy because of so many leashes. The girl seemed to be enjoying this. "How're you?" he asked, hopping.

The kid's smile took on an apologetic look. "Sorry. I don't speak English."

"Oh. Too bad." He stood with both feet planted, the butterfly gone and the puppy suddenly a sleeping heap of fringe on the ground. The red leash was now wound around only one ankle. "What do you speak?"

She looked at him quizzically and shrugged. "I don't speak English."

Ike leaned closer to see the book. "*La Peste! The Plague*. Great book.

46

Great book." He dragged out the word great to show how much he meant it, and said it again. "Great book." Seeing her smile of incomprehension, he said, "Aw." Taking off his baseball cap and running his fingers through his hair he said, "It's been a long time since I read that book. A long time. Read it in translation, of course." He transferred the red leash to his left hand, with the others, and extended his right arm for a handshake. "Ike Bartholomew."

"Martine Noisetier." She put her hand forward to his.

A lovely voice. A nice girl, really. A very nice girl. "Well! Too bad you don't speak English." He lifted his foot and gave it a wag, to slide the leash from his ankle. From over by the stairs he turned to give the kid his farewell salute, a very solid motion from the elbow, using his palm like a spatula to smear a flat arc on the air. "So long."

He and the dogs walked down the brick street, headed for mommy and the cats. She'd be up and dressed and working in her studio, and the coffee would be burnt.

He had a valentine for her. This could be the best song he's written so far. Love song. No words, just a very haunting little tune. He knew it was good, because he tried it out Saturday night at his yacht club gig. He got a hand from four or five tables, which almost never happens, plus a twenty buck tip from one guy. Tonight he was playing at Moose's, and he'd talked Meg into coming. He even had a speech prepared to introduce the song. He was going to say, "Here's lookin' at you kid." But that didn't say what he felt. Maybe, "This is dedicated to my love." Or, "To the one I love." No. "To the love of my life." That said it. To the love of my life.

VALENTINES. WHAT A waste. Frankie's buzzer never stopped bugging her. First a long gold box for Cherie La Rue on the second floor. How original. Each rose probably cost enough to feed a third world kid for a year. Buzz! A five-pound box of See's chocolate for Mrs. Bettencourt – the last thing she needed. Buzz again. The ugliest flower arrangement ever concocted, for Mrs. Haas. That one took the Lifetime Achievement

47

Award for bad taste. By the end of the day Cherie La Popular had received deliveries from five different florists, and every tenant but the alleged TV camerawoman had received at least one or two deliveries.

Usually Frankie was the only one in the building who didn't get any valentines. The only thing better about this year was that she had company. All day she had the comfort of knowing that no way would anyone send flowers to the Birdwood woman. Then at seven, after Buster had had his walk and Frankie had finally got settled down to draw, another buzz blasted her concentration. Opening the door she snapped, "Working late, aren't you?" "I'm sorry, Madame, we've had a misery of work today." His accent sounded Russian, and his face looked exhausted. He held out a bonsai pine and read from the card, "Hillary Birdwood and Tess." A toy fire hydrant had been stuck under the little tree in the planter. When she was subtly fingering the envelope to feel if it had been tucked shut or sealed, the man stooped to pick up a huge arrangement, standing by his foot. He stumbled under its weight and read, "Frances Clark."

"Me?" Branches of apple blossoms, long-stemmed peach-colored roses, and sprigs of mimosa. The envelope said her name. While the man was still holding up the vase she opened the card. It said, "Happy Valentine's, Frankie. Hang in there – Bill."

What did she want with flowers? They'd only wilt, and drop petals and pollen, and make a mess, and she'd have to dispose of the carcass. And nothing was more boring than washing a vase.

"Goodbye," she said to the delivery man. No wonder he had to work till seven o'clock. He probably had to stick around to snoop on everyone he delivered to. Frankie set both arrangements on the floor and opened the envelope that said Hillary Birdwood. "Love, Mom and Dad."

She'd been right all along. No one would send flowers to Birdwood.

VALENTINES USED TO be the biggest disappointment of the year, with the kind of guys Frankie used to go with. But it didn't get to her any more.

And she wasn't completely neglected. Bill, her boss, had asked her again this year to have dinner with him and his wife. "No thanks," she told him. "I'll have a business dinner with you sometime, but I'm not going out with you and your wife. Nothing against your wife."

DEADLINES WERE TOUGH for Tobin. He wasn't a sprinter, he was a long-distance guy. He'd thought he'd have his poem done and typed by the weekend, so all he'd have to do today was roll it in a scroll and tie it up in a big red bow. But here it was the due date, and he still hadn't wrapped it up.

Started with three ice-cream cones. Peach. Everything moving around them, the round scoops moving too, but with balance and symmetry. A mysterious alignment of rounds. He was creating a symploce, a figure starting with the word "peach" repeated again and again at the beginning, ending with repetition of the word "scoop." Maybe too ambitious. Wasn't working. Last minute, he went through two glasses of grapefruit juice at La Petite Treat. Pen failed him on the yellow pad. The poem was about love, and the world in flux. Him and her.

Rats.

Maybe she'd rather have a scarf. He'd have time to get off the bus at Walgreen's, pick up something. Something for his mom, too. Then on the bus he could write his mom some quickie about motherhood. She liked rhymers. Unfortunately, his wife had taste. He couldn't just knock off a couplet for her.

Maybe something would come to him while he was mowing the lawn.

A scarf would be the thing. The poem would come in its time. He'd get a scarf for his mom too. Miranda probably wouldn't mind if his mom got a scarf and a couplet and herself only a scarf.

IT BEING THE final hours of the Day of St. Valentine, Dr. Hawthorne had gone to his garden and snipped a twig of azalea that was a brilliant shade of cerise – a tad heavy for a boutonnière, but the general effect was festive. He tied a red handkerchief around Romeo's neck and set off up the hill to the park, where, strolling a path, he wondered if he could afford to indulge in memories of things past. He was weighing the risk factors – the degree of pleasure as opposed to the possibility of overwhelming ache, sadness of the quoth-the-raven-nevermore variety – when the little bichonne frisée bounced out from the woods. "Well, well, well!" his baritone rang. With a nice rhythm he thumped his spade against his thigh, waiting. But instead of Mrs. Leone, four children pitched up to the top of the stairway and ran after the dog. "Posy, come! Posy, *come!*" Two girls and two boys, very smartly dressed, were having trouble catching the dog's attention. He made his voice a stern growl: "Whose dog is this?"

It was their grandma's. The taller girl, about nine, said, "It can't do any tricks."

"But this is a very intelligent dog," the doctor stated. "You can teach it to shake hands right now. Watch." Concealing that he had the advantage of prior knowledge that the dog had, in fact, succeeded in mastering this accomplishment on occasion, he reached into his breast pocket to pull out a rolled newspaper. "Always carry one of these in your pocket at all times," he advised the girl. "Any intelligent dog understands this." He snapped the paper against his arm, making quite a bang. The children gave a start and the dog stopped in its tracks, an expression in the eyes that was a mix of terror and curiosity. "Now! We have her attention. Sit!" The dog dropped to a sitting position. "Stay." When he paced about to survey her profile he noticed that the stub of tail under her frilly white rump twitched. Getting close to the dog and facing her, he did a kneebend and reached a hand to Posy's paw, commanding "Shake." The dog's paw popped up and Dr. Hawthorne shook it. "Good dog, brilliant dog, what an intelligent beast you are!" To the children he explained, "It is an excellent idea to lavish praise upon the dog when it does what you say." They were impressed and fell upon Posy with congratulatory hugs and kisses. "You're exhibiting exactly the correct response to a job well done," Dr. Hawthorne told them. "Praise is what the animal loves, and it will encourage the animal to do whatever you ask. Here. You try it." He handed the newspaper to the oldest. It took a while, but she succeeded with the cracking of the newspaper and the startling of the dog. "Posy, sit!" The dog did not sit. "May I make a suggestion? It may work better if you deliver the command without preceding it with the name. Instead of Posy, sit, try Sit." And the girl had success. And so did each of the children, in turn, except the smallest, a boy. "You can practice with Romeo," the doctor suggested. Romeo was immaculately trained, giving the boy a joyful sense of accomplishment.

"You see?" Dr. Hawthorne said with solemnity. "Two intelligent dogs. Just remember always to carry a newspaper with you, and to keep it rolled in advance. And now. You are all obviously intelligent children." They seemed to agree. He took the azalea from his lapel and presented it to the boy with the bow tie. "And any intelligent child can memorize a message, and when the time comes, present it. You must present this flower to your grandmother, with a bow, and say – repeat after me – Happy Valentine's." They repeated it – and even bowed – and ran. They were intelligent children.

COLOR DWINDLED AROUND the park bench Chantal and Nigel had chosen. They had watched the pines go from green to charcoal-gray, the acacias from mustard to nothing but silhouette. The Bay's silver had deepened to pewter, with that rope of lights stretched across it. Only Roger, who had always been a shade of charcoal, stayed the same. Nigel was about to present Chantal with her valentine. It wasn't a thing but a thought. An idea. He had gotten it several weeks ago, and it had taken self-discipline to save it until the last hours of Valentine's night. Whispering, he unwrapped his gift.

GATHERING THE STACK of handmade valentines into her left hand, Anna used her right to carry the bud vase with the azalea to the bedside table. She hadn't had an anonymous valentine since she was twelve. She did some arithmetic. Fifty-four years ago today. Heavens. Taking a cup of herb tea to the balcony, she thought about the "tall old man who likes big words."

The moon floated high above the pine trees. The streetlight and the moonlight made it possible for her to see, near the top of the stairs, a man with a tall backpack entering the park. She had seen that same backpack climb the steps a few nights ago. Again she was glad it wasn't raining.

The hot tea hit the spot.

For some reason – well, for many reasons – the moon always reminded her of Joe.

HE HEADED FOR his hutch, on the north wall of the park. Long time ago, he used to think you shouldn't own more than you could carry over one arm. Over the years he'd picked up enough for two arms, so he'd had to get this backpack. It cost ten dollars, "as is." At the top of his pack he had three hamburgers in a bag, rummaged from the bin in back of the McDonald's across from the Opera House. The law only allowed them to keep food in the warmer for so long, and then they had to throw it out. The man competed with others most days, but tonight he got lucky and scored four. He'd eaten one in the parking lot, an appetizer before walking the two uphill miles to this park, still starving.

The woods were hushed. No traffic. It was so quiet you could hear the hum of electricity in the cable-car tracks. By the bench on the lower terrace, he stopped to look back at the city, the gold lights arranged on the flatland leading to the black Bay. Miniature headlights moved like a river across the Golden Gate.

Hunger rushing him, he started up to the hideout he'd found the other night. Up in the thickets the pine boughs blocked the moonlight, but there was some light deflected from the street below. He didn't have to take out his flashlight. Hand over hand, he climbed the cyclone fence to the path around the tennis courts. Battling the shrubs that crowded the path, he made it to the two trees that marked the spot. He pulled a branch aside to crawl in, and a shrill male voice screamed, "Fuck you! Fuck you!"

His heart jumped. Expletives, like shrapnel, exploded in his head, but he had trained himself to keep still. He simply growled and turned away muttering, "Wrecked my evening."

He had to find a place. Continuing along the high path, he considered checking out a couple of possibilities that looked like there'd be room under the overgrowth, but he didn't want to face a repeat of that last encounter. He came to the shed, a low cement building. No windows. Door locked. He faced Hyde Street – a row of tall buildings, stacks of windows, all dark. He took off the backpack. God, the shoulders. Getting old wasn't going to be fun.

At the top of the pack were the three hamburgers. Still standing he tore into the first one. Finished. Next. Finished. He could have had more. It was his first food in two days, and there were dozens of burgers in the bin. But he didn't like to be a pig. You never knew how many people would eventually come looking – maybe more famished than he was.

There was a comfortable spot just next to the shed, padded with pine-needles, like a mattress. The trouble was, it was exposed. If he could only count on himself to wake up before daybreak, it could be a good night. He'd be able to see the stars. It wasn't really like being in the mountains. The stars were muddled here. But they were stars.

What the hell. He yanked the sleeping bag from his pack and laid it out. He didn't take his shoes off before he climbed in. He never did. He couldn't afford that kind of vulnerability. But it felt great to untie the laces. He never took off his jacket, either, with the switchblade in the pocket. It was sharp. He'd never used it, except to shave. Not lately.

He'd brought the final hamburger into the bag. Before he took a bite he unbuckled his belt and unzipped his fly. This was comfort. He'd just better remember to wake up before sunrise.

That fourth hamburger satisfied him. He crossed his arms behind his neck and lay there, looking up at a cloud passing underneath the moon.

FOOTSTEPS. HE TENSED. Where was he? He was in church. But that was a dream. It was a big church, like a cathedral. He was in the balcony. But he wasn't. He was in his bag, his stomach on hard earth. The footsteps stopped. Right by his head. He made an eyehole in the bag's hood. A dim yellow dot moved along the ground in front of his eyehole. He pulled up his head, hooded by the bag. Against the blackness, there was something blacker. Black boots. Snapping his jeans, zipping his fly, he made out eyes, nose and cheeks in a mass of hair.

Was this still the dream? It looked like God.

"Ever hear of Glide Church?" the countenance said, voice hoarse, hard to hear.

The flashlight blinded him. Just yesterday he'd looked in the mirror in a public toilet. Not pretty. His skin was mottled and hard, and so were his eyes, like battered marbles. But those eyes weren't tough enough to take this spot without a flinch.

"Glide Church."

"What?"

"People tell me that's a pretty good place to sleep," said the voice. "Beds there, things like that. Pretty good people. Don't hassle you."

In the bag, he rubbed his eyes. On top of all the basic hardships, he'd worked up an allergy to whatever the bag was made out of.

"Downtown, by Union Square. Nice walk. Downhill. Here. I've got something for you. List of places you can stay. How long, whether it costs a dollar a night or what. I typed it up. Friend of mine drew a map. The guys at the drugstore let me xerox fifty copies, free." The voice kept talking, "Pretty nice guys, at that drugstore." The boots walked to the shed.

The sound of rattling. Keys? The camper stuffed his bag into his backpack and scooted his shoes through the woods. He'd tie them later. By the time the shed door opened, he was on the brick street, running. Way down the cable-car tracks, he looked back to see a light coming from the shed door, showing the man holding something (a piece of paper?) and a flashlight moving to the bushes.

54

Roses

"THIS PARK ISN'T the best place to sleep, to tell you the truth." He was folding the sheet that told all the shelters and places for free food. The guy was gone.

At least he hadn't had to make a decision about whether he'd give him the cash for a glass of grapefruit juice. He'd been thinking about it. Philosophically he was against it. Encouraged them to come back. And basically he hated these guys. But sometimes he imagined himself in this kind of situation and felt tempted to help out. He hadn't ironed out his thinking. Depended on how he felt.

It was true, what he told the guy. Before he noticed the guy wasn't there. This wasn't the safest place in the world. Once he found a suitcase full of women's underwear. Some days there was glass up the brick street, from broken windshields. One morning he found blood on the sidewalk.

He went back in the shed to thumb off a couple more sheets from his stack, in case there were more guys out there. Winking at the nudie, he promised to fix that door squeak for her. Kind of cute, that nudie. He'd like her even if she had clothes on. He folded the sheets, getting ready for his rounds. Lots of rabbit hutches in this park. So far no rabbits.

Over by the cyclone fence he found one. The guy with the scab-colored jacket and the foul mouth. He was wrapped up in a plaid blanket. To tell you the truth Tobin didn't like this guy. He used his boot to tap him on the shoulder. The guy bolted awake and screamed, "Fuck you! Fuck you! Fuh-uh-uck you!"

Ugly. "Go fuck yourself." Tobin's voice was soft, but his heartbeat was up. He tossed a sheet of information over to the guy, who screamed again.

"You're going to have to leave," Tobin told him, "or I'll have to get the police." He walked away. He didn't like to involve the police. He'd give the guy half an hour.

Kind of a lousy way to start the day. Tobin tried to be charitable, but some guys pushed him too far. Up at the shed he got an armload of brass sprinkler heads to attach to the outlets. The sun was coming up behind Coit Tower. Lots of pink this morning.

Here came the Englishman with the poodle, and his wife, the Frenchwoman. Pretty nice woman. Funny though. It was kind of early for her. Seemed like she ought to be asleep still.

"Hello, Tobin," both of them said, his accent English, hers French.

"Kind of weird guy down there," Tobin answered. "Very messed up."

"Not the one who shouts obscenities," said the Englishman.

"Yeah that guy. Wish he'd find some other park."

"Tobin!" said the Frenchwoman. Chantal. Pretty name. "Tobin, Nigel gave me an idea for Valentine's Day."

Kind of neat phrase. He could have used that for his poem.

"We need your advice."

"Oh. Oh. Well, maybe I can help you. Maybe not."

"We want to make a rose garden. For everyone. Over there." She pointed to the corner by the building they lived in, where the sidewalk became a stairway, and Greenwich stopped being a street and became nothing but steps zigzagging down to Leavenworth.

"See that patch that's planted with agapanthus?" asked the Englishman. It was a piece of land big enough to park a couple of big trucks, if the blue flowers weren't there. Probably a lot of people would rather have parking places.

"Agapanthus are freeway flowers," Chantal said. "Common." She wrinkled her nose. Nice nose.

"Don't mind Chantal. She's a snob. Our idea is, we think we could plant roses there. Chantal is going to pop the question to our landlord. If he'll terrace the land and put in irrigation, we'll furnish the roses and the labor. We'll buy them, plant them, look after them, and so forth. I reckon there's enough room for fifty bushes."

"We want mostly hybrid teas," Chantal said.

"We're long-time rosarians," Nigel said.

Rosarians. A religion. Wasn't it?

"Chantal's won a total of three ribbons at the Chelsea Flower Show. In Snugwood we bought a crumbling old yeoman's house with acres of weeds. At the moment it's let to a rock star. But we've kept on a gardener. We spent years making our garden, with roses you wouldn't believe. They're Chantal's children."

"Nigel misses them," said Chantal.

He took a handful of her hair and gave it a yank. "We'll get official labels from the Royal Horticultural Society and stick them in the ground. So all the people in the neighborhood, and the tourists, can know them by name."

"*Tout le monde* can learn something about the roses!"

"Chantal's a regular evangelist, aren't you, darling? – But you know, that's what rosarians are. When you're initiated into the International Society of Rosarians, you take a pledge that you will help as many people as you can to grow good healthy roses."

So it was a religion. Kind of.

"Every blossom has a personality," Chantal said. "And it changes in its lifetime, just like a person. It's one way when it's a baby, and another way as it gets more age, until it blooms itself out and the petals fall off."

"Tobin knows that, darling. He's a gardener. And that's why we need your advice, Tobin."

"About irrigation," Chantal said.

"Oh. Oh. I could probably help you out. I know quite a bit about that.

57

Not too many people know that about me. Irrigation, sprinkler systems, I know quite a bit about that."

"Excellent!" said Nigel. "Because we don't. In England it rains so much we don't need sprinklers."

DOWN AT LA Petite Treat Tobin and Chantal needed a table for four, to spread out their things. It was a window table just off the sidewalk, with plenty of light. She had a toasted bagel and cream cheese and cup after cup of coffee. He had grapefruit juice, a cheese omelet, a side order of ham, home fries, wheat toast and raspberry jam. He usually had just grapefruit juice. But when he had breakfast he had breakfast.

She had a notebook, and he was drawing in it. He drew different kinds of pipes, some that sweated water into the ground, some that dripped water onto the top, some that shot out a spray. He explained the advantages and disadvantages of each type of system. At the table, as sketches and words went onto the pages, Tobin's head and Chantal's stayed lowered in concentration. At one point Chantal looked out the window, and her expression stopped dead. Tobin followed her gaze. There was that guy in the jacket the color of dried blood, standing on the sidewalk, looking in. Both of them turned away. Both of them imagined he was screwing up his pinched little face and pushing it right to the window. Both imagined him taking his right hand out of his pocket and giving them the finger. But neither of them looked.

Laundromat

IT WAS A nice day, and she had all twenty-four hours of it off. Plus tomorrow. Plus Sunday until five p.m. She sat by the telephone trying to lift the receiver. There was a woman at work she liked, although she was in Sales. Leslie. About her own age, really friendly. Maybe Leslie would like to go to a movie or something tonight. Leslie didn't have a boyfriend either. She did seem to have a lot of friends though. She would probably be busy. Hillary didn't want to push it.

What was the worst thing that could happen? Leslie could say no. Well, the very worst thing would be that Leslie would not be doing anything but would say no anyway. But then she'd never say that to Hillary, so Hillary wouldn't know. But she might suspect. And Leslie would know. She'd feel sorry for Hillary.

Oh for heaven sakes. "*Come on!*" she said. Tess jumped for her leash. "No, I didn't mean you, Tess." Tess sank back to her lie-down position on the mattress, disappointment written all over her body. You're being mental, Hillary said to herself. (Mental was a term of her mother's. Mentally Hillary took back the word, but she had to admit she was nuts.) She told herself, Leslie would probably like to do something with you. One of us has to ask first. She lifted the receiver and dialed the station's number.

"KRMX," said the machine, and started through its "voice tree," telling which number to press to get where – leading you to more choices of numbers to press when you got there.

Hillary hung up.

She'd better rehearse this. Maybe she shouldn't say she was completely free, for tonight or anytime in the day tomorrow or tomorrow night or during the day Sunday. She should pick a specific time and stick to that. Well, tomorrow night was less short notice than tonight. But the lines were long at the movies on Saturday nights. Long on Fridays too, though. Either way, Leslie wouldn't want to stand in line. Of course they could go to an early show tomorrow. There was nothing wrong with being completely flexible for one day or night of the weekend. So she'd say she was busy tonight but would really like to get together tomorrow. So what was she doing tonight? Well, she'd met this guy, he was a doctor . . . But then tomorrow Leslie would want to know how it had gone. Maybe Hillary should think of Tobin and his wife as her engagement for tonight. These friends of hers she'd met in the park. Or, maybe she didn't have to come right out and say she was busy tonight, just let that be the assumption. In high school her mother had heard Hillary making up elaborate lies to the boys she didn't want to go out with (the only ones who asked her) and had advised her, "Keep it simple. Just say sorry, I can't. The more involved you get in your excuse the more it sounds like a lie." Hillary added in for herself, *the more it will hurt his feelings*. She followed her mother's advice, with the boys. Though it hurt. Her motive for keeping her excuse simple with Leslie had only to do with her own feelings. Good reason!

She picked up the receiver again. Punched the station's number. Waited through the entire list of choices and punched five, for Sales. Leslie was out to lunch. (At two-thirty p.m.) Hillary didn't leave a message.

She might as well get started on her laundry. She walked over to the mattress and said, "Tess. Off!"

Tess looked up and wagged her tail.

"Off! Off!" Hillary pulled the dog off and started yanking the sheets. This was one of Tess's favorite games, getting a corner of the sheet between her teeth and tugging against Hillary. The only defense was to let the sheet go limp until she could distract Tess long enough to gather up more of the sheet, bit by bit. She found the tennis ball and threw it, and when Tess ran for it Hillary collected part of the sheet in a small heap until she had to interrupt herself again and throw the ball. And again. It was a long process, changing the sheets. Putting the clean set on would take even more time, because as she spread the fresh sheet, Tess would leap under it, jumping and twisting until she was a squirming bundle of white. Hillary would get into the game. "Where's Tess? Where's Te-ess?" She'd pretend to look all around, making her feet loud as she checked all the corners of the room, making her voice worried. "Te-ess?" Tess always fell for this. She got agitated and tried to fight her way out of her swaddling. When the whimpering and struggling got too bad, Hillary always had to unwrap Tess and say, "Oh! There's Te-ess!" Tess loved the sheet game.

She slipped into other jeans, out of her sweatshirt and into one of the chewed sweaters she couldn't wear anywhere but the laundromat. With Tess's "help," she stuffed everything into a pillowcase and checked her wallet for quarters. She found her keys.

And then she went back to the phone to try Leslie once more.

Still not back. Of course not. Those people in Sales spent all day at lunch. Lunch and getting their nails done. Oh. They also went to the gym. She'd try again around three-fifteen. Maybe four. It was lucky she had decided on Saturday instead of Friday. It really might seem weird to be just making your plans for the evening at four o'clock that afternoon.

THE LAUNDROMAT WAS called The Missing Sock. It had a tiled floor, and here and there, a tile just the same color as the other tiles had a picture of a sock on it. These socks looked so real that Hillary always found herself swooping down to pick one up. The door said No Pets, but there was nobody in there but an old Chinese woman who probably didn't read English, so Hillary led Tess inside. When the water in her machine started swooshing she stepped outside to get a paper. The place to get papers, if you were broke, was a few doors

61

down at La Petite Treat. There were always abandoned *Chronicles* on the tables.

That homeless guy with the maroon jacket and the horrible hair was on the sidewalk between the laundromat and La Petite Treat, so Hillary hoped he wouldn't notice that she suddenly pulled Tess into the street to cross, just missing being hit by a cable car. She turned the corner and stood there watching from behind the wall of the ice-cream store until the guy had walked down past Green Street.

IT WAS LESS embarrassing to steal a paper when she could pick one up from a sidewalk table, but today there weren't any outside. Usually nobody noticed if she stepped into the restaurant and slipped out again with a paper. She always had a polite smile and a nod prepared if anyone should be looking. She tied Tess to a No Parking sign and prepared her entrance. Today there were three tables where people had left papers. She casually moved toward the one closest to the door and had all four sections between her thumb and fingers when she noticed Philo Righi at the far side of the room. He was with a small blonde woman, very cute. They were both in running shorts, so Hillary could see what lovely, normal legs she had, not overly long, just nicely in proportion with the rest of her enviably small little body. The knees were a pinky white, not freckled like Hillary's. And this woman's knees had a little plumpness. Even though she was sitting down, it was obvious they weren't knobs.

Hillary thought she might be able to back out, unseen. It would've been great if she could have just walked out forward, but that hole Tess had chewed in the back of her sweater was a raggedy gap the size of Greenland on the map. It was right at the shoulder blade, showing lots of skin and bra strap, not to mention that the shoulder blade was sharp enough to cut you. So, she was just stepping backwards through the door when Philo saw her and popped up off his chair and shot up his long arm. She started a little wave and a polite smile. She still hoped to find a way out, but actually she was afraid she was stuck. With Philo's black

62

eyes locked into hers, she couldn't just evaporate. "Hi," she said, all happy, walking toward Philo instead of away.

Tess was still tied to the No Parking sign, and the whimper from outside had become a howl. She noticed a couple of people lowering their newspapers to look toward the street, unpleasant expressions on their faces. She pretended not to notice.

The closer you got, the prettier she looked, the little blonde. She was kind of Marilyn pale, but fresher. Her hair was tied back by a handkerchief scarf.

"This is Hillary," Philo said. "One of the wonderful neighborhood characters I was telling you about. Hillary, meet my colleague, Dr. Marijka Chernikev."

"Doctor!" Hillary said, impressed, smiling.

"No no no!" said the blonde.

"She hasn't got her R.D. yet. June."

Hillary was embarrassed to let anyone know she didn't know what an R.D. was. Registered dietician? But that wasn't a doctor. She smiled more. Her face was beginning to hurt.

"An R.D.," the blonde woman said, "is Philoese for Real Doc."

"Oh," said Hillary. What was she going to say next? It was so hard to think of things, at certain moments.

Tess's yelping had reached an almost steady high that was like the sound of torture. A male voice from somewhere barked, "Is somebody going to do something about that dog?"

"Oh!" Hillary said, backing away on her stilt-legs. It was perfectly clear to her that backing was the best thing to do right now. "Sorry, Tess is really getting to be a problem." At the door she waved, smiled, nodded.

BACK IN THE laundromat, the washer still ground, not yet to the final stage, where the vibrations get violent. Hillary stepped over a sock on the floor (was it a real one? – no) and sat down with her newspaper. "Sit!" she said to Tess. Tess sat. "Good girl. Good girl." As she found the movie

63

section, the machine chugged to a standstill. "Stay!" She dug more quarters out of her jeans for the dryer. Of course Tess walked over too. Clothes and quarters in the dryer, the whole thing hit. She fell into her chair and felt how hot her face was. That had been just awful, with Philo Righi and that woman. How stupid she'd been to think he'd like her.

Home with her warm folded laundry, she wasn't in the mood for the sheet game. "Sorry, Tess." She smoothed the puppy silk. Loose, it was. "Sorry, Tess." She really did feel sorry for Tess. "Later," she promised, heaving herself on the mattress. Tess seemed to feel her sadness. She stepped on the mattress and licked her cheek and pressed her long body against Hillary's. How smooth the loose puppy silk, from the ears down to the tail. And how sweet, to have a tear dried with a kiss.

"KRMX . . ."

Leslie was busy tomorrow. "But what about tonight? I'm so bored! I need a movie."

"Oh. Sorry," said Hillary. "Can't tonight."

"Well, maybe some other time then. Maybe next weekend? Is Friday or Saturday better for you?"

"Oh! It doesn't really matter. I don't have anything planned yet, I could just work around whatever you want to do."

"Well, let's say Friday."

"Oh, but Leslie, in case something more exciting comes up, you should feel free to cancel. Any time. Don't even think about me. I'll always find something to do."

"Nothing more exciting will come up for me," Leslie said. "I think it's really exciting to get together with you finally, Hillary. I've always wanted to do something with you. I don't know why I get a little shy sometimes. But, Hillary, if something more exciting comes up for *you* . . . you'll have to tell him no."

FIVE, FRIDAY AFTERNOON. Tobin had stayed late today. Hillary stood at the top of the steps, holding Tess back and watching through the trees.

There he was. Married. A secure job, with the city. He was completely absorbed in drawing stripes with his rake. Funny, the difference between those people who knew what their life would be and the people who had no idea.

He looked up. She let Tess free, and Tess ran across the promenade, messing up his stripes.

"Wonder what will happen?" he said.

"To me?" she asked.

"No. I sent some poems off, to a couple of papers. Two, three papers. Ten papers, to tell you the truth. A couple of months ago. Three months. Probably wasted a lot on stamps. Wonder what will happen. Nothing, could be."

He started going over the stripes Tess had messed up. She was off in the woods now, but he knew she'd be back in no more than a minute. Why did he bother?

Tobin looked up and said, "What the hell? I like to leave this place looking good."

The Bolinas Hearsay News

TOBIN'S BLACK BOOTS jumped off the bus in the dark. His steps swung fast up Hyde Street. He was always early, but not this early. Not much point in coming this early. But the woman who owned the flower shop usually came about five. That Ike guy, the piano player, sometimes had trouble sleeping, after a gig. Got up and walked the afghans. Tobin would knock off early today. But he couldn't wait to get started.

He patted the pocket of his jacket. Heard the paper crackle. He'd read it ten or twelve times on the bus. Published poem. "By Tobin de Brettville." Tobin de Brettville. Published. In the *Bolinas Hearsay News*. Not a bad paper.

Pretty good jacket, this. Found it in the bushes. Made in the People's Republic of China. Antique in great condition. Quilted. Fake fur collar. Warm. Paid ten dollars to get the buttons moved over. His wife didn't like that type of work. Ten dollars, that was nothing for a warm waterproof jacket.

And there was a poem in the pocket. Published.

Before he even took out his keys he got the flashlight out of his pocket and took a quick cruise around the park. Both lawns. The red dirt, the lower terrace. The flower store lady always left early. Came early, left early. She'd probably be interested to see this poem.

Nobody there.

Kind of a disappointment. A little deflating, to tell you the truth.

Tobin got out his keys and went to the shed. Turned the light on.

You never knew. Maybe there was an okay bum here tonight. Like that guy a couple of weeks ago who wanted to talk about Kierkegaard. That guy was kind of a surprise. Not just Kierkegaard. These fellows mostly didn't want to talk. Kind of a relief to find one who wanted to talk. Of course, that guy probably wouldn't be a bum long. Too personable. These bums didn't like people, for the most part. Seemed like it. That was their problem.

Well, of course, chicken and egg.

HE TOOK THE flashlight and checked the hutches. Nobody home. Maybe this was his lucky day. Although it might have been kind of nice to see that Kierkegaard guy. In a way. Better, though, not to. That fellow wasn't cut out to be a bum.

On the path up by the tennis courts Tobin heard a rustling. He flashed his light into a bush. Hit two eyes, glittery. Dog. German shepherd, looked like. Plaintive eyes.

"Here, boy. Here, boy," said Tobin, his throaty voice even softer than usual. The dog shook himself and stood up. Hopped. Three legs. The dog had only one back leg. He toppled. Struggled. Three hops then toppled again. One front leg wasn't too good.

Crippled dog. "Here, boy." The dog came forward. Good coat. Tobin felt around the neck for the collar and tags. He ran ten fingers through the pelt at the neck. Rich fur. Downy. Reminded Tobin of a poem he liked. Ben Jonson:

> Have you felt the wool o' the beaver,
> Or swan's down ever?

No ID. Nothing. A kind of anger rushed through Tobin. Ditched dog. What kind of people would do that to a dog? Their dog. "Here, boy." He led the dog along the path to the shed. The dog did pretty good. Maybe dogs didn't need four legs.

Nothing was open. The corner market wouldn't open till nine, for dog food. La Petite Treat wouldn't open till seven. Then Tobin could get him some milk, a bran muffin, even a cup of coffee. Tobin would like to buy this dog a cup of coffee. You never knew. This dog might like coffee. Chantal did. The TV camerawoman's dog liked beer.

He thought about Chantal. The way she loved her poodle? Her roses in England? She'd be pretty mad at whoever ditched this dog. The Englishman too. To tell the truth he was not a bad guy. Seemed to like his wife quite a bit. Showed it more than most guys.

Kind of a lucky guy. At least he knew it.

"Here, boy." The dog, in the shed, hopped closer. Collapsed. Got right up. Hop hop. But Tobin had no dog biscuit. Nothing in here for a dog. "Here, boy." Tobin took out his poem. The dog sniffed. Lost interest.

"Oh well." He closed the door, left the light on. At least the nudie was in there. In case the dog was interested.

THINGS STARTED TO pick up. Here came that psychiatrist guy and the dog with no legs, just ankles in white socks. No woman today. Guess the guy didn't score every night. Psychiatrist seemed to enjoy Tobin's poem, even if it was about a psychiatrist. Not too flattering. And the psychiatrist didn't know what kind of person would take a dog to the park and leave him. The SPCA would be open at nine, and Tobin could use the phone in the shed. La Petite Treat would open up soon, and Tobin could feed him.

Here came the doc with his spade and his rottweiler. He seemed pretty pleased to see Tobin's name in print. "Well done!" he said. He clapped an arm around Tobin's shoulder, to read. Long arm. Read the poem twice. Had a chuckle. "Well done!"

About the dog: "I would advise you to post signs on all the telephone poles. Say 'WANTED. DEAD OR ALIVE. Fifty dollar reward for information leading to the apprehension of the person who abandoned the disabled German shepherd in the park.' I'll put up the money. Make it a hundred. It would be worth it to me to give such a person a brief lecture."

He wanted to see the dog. Tobin took him up to the shed.

"Ironside?" said Tobin, opening the door. No squeak. He'd taken care of that.

"What was that, Tobin?"

"Ironside. The dog reminds me of that old TV guy. Lawyer in a wheelchair. Remember? Ironside?"

"Yes," said the doctor, petting the animal. "Intelligent eyes. A physical disability has not robbed him of his brains or his dignity." He felt about the dog's body. "Ah, but Tobin. I'm afraid you're mistaken about the gender. I'm afraid you'll have to call this dog Mrs. Ironside."

"Oh."

"Here comes the Englishman," he said, looking out the door and through the trees to Hyde Street. The doctor and the gardener stepped out to the lawn, the doctor freeing his rottweiler from the post. There was some tension between the Englishman's male and the doctor's male, so both men gripped their dogs' leashes close to the collar.

"Good morning," said the Englishman, chipper.

The doctor raised his spade. "Already this morning, Tobin has published a poem and rescued a dog. And I have twenty-four patients to see today. If you'll excuse me, gentlemen, I'll leave with the hope of seeing you tomorrow." Wagging his spade, he disappeared.

Fifteen minutes after the Englishman had congratulated Tobin on the poem and taken his poodle home, the poodle was back. "Tobin, Tobin!" Chantal called, jogging toward him. Pretty well-trained poodle. Didn't run any faster than Chantal. "I want to meet Mrs. Ironside."

"La Petite Treat must be opening," Tobin said.

"May I see the dog?" she asked, in her shy way.

He took out his keys and led her up to the shed. She said ooh and *mon dieu* and *ma chérie*. Frenchwomen liked dogs. "Let's buy it some breakfast." She reached in her pocket and unfolded a five dollar bill. "We can chip in."

Sheep een. Nice accent. He'd have to carry the dog, though.

Took a long time to get to the coffee place. Inside, a few people from yesterday were still here today. They looked up from their newspapers. Tobin felt his face get hot. Two days in a row. They maybe thought the gardener and the Frenchwoman were some kind of item. He gave a big smile to the people at one table and extended his right arm in the salute. He didn't say "Raised right arm of Hitler." These people didn't know the poem. Might think he was a little off.

Some of these people stayed here all morning. All afternoon too, seemed like. One group always took the same table. Read the papers and talked. Sometimes about a movie review. Someone from another table would join in. Got pretty loud, sometimes. If it was about movies, they always got back to the old ones. Whether Ingrid Bergman was a sap in *Casablanca*, or whether the guy in *Fatal Attraction* was an innocent victim or a bastard. Funny they got more riled up about old movies. Maybe it was universal themes. Those didn't come up that often, in movies. Not every year. Maybe not every ten. He'd have to think about that. Maybe when he was mowing the lawn.

One guy got out of his chair and went to sit at another table. Wanted to talk to the couple there. Some people sat alone. Some days Tobin counted three laptops. A lot of writers here. That Victoria Chang woman thought this was her office. Reported at seven with her yellow legal pad. Never got up all day except for more coffee or to go to the bathroom. Women in suits waited in line for lattes to go and muffins in white paper bags. Tobin wondered if the coffee'd be cold by the time they got to work. Maybe not. Same women kept coming back. A little later the architects down at the corner shop would come in with their blueprints and stay a long time. Ray and Pete from the drugstore would walk across the street one at a time and get coffees to go. They liked American. Pete liked sugar and cream. He was the plump one. The French people from that food place would walk a couple of blocks in their aprons, to drink cappuccinos. The two Gypsies with the antique clothes store came in with their daydreams. Said they weren't Gypsies. Said they hated Gypsies. But they jangled with jewelry, wore three or four skirts on top of each other, and fancy headdresses. Looked like Gypsies.

70

"What will we give her?" Chantal asked Tobin. The menu was written in bright colors of magic marker on a big shiny board. "Eggs?"

"How does she like them?" Tobin asked. "Not sunny side up I hope." If sunny side up messed up his beard, it'd mess up the dog's.

"Not a cheese omelet," Chantal decided.

Same problem, with the cheese. "Scrambled." Tobin could make a decision.

"Bacon or ham?"

Tobin thought about the dog's cholesterol. "Ham." Could be ham had less fat. Seemed like it.

"Hash browns?" asked the guy behind the counter.

Chantal said yes and Tobin said, "Paper plates."

"The customer wants to eat outside," Chantal explained.

TOBIN HELD OFF as long as he could for his second grapefruit juice. He and Chantal were putting together a found-dog poster to xerox. Just in case someone had lost the dog by accident. Didn't seem likely. They'd reported Mrs. Ironside to the SPCA, and the SPCA said nobody'd called looking for a crippled German shepherd.

Chantal posed Mrs. Ironside on the lawn. Sketched. Pretty good at drawing. Funny what you didn't know about people. Tennis players looked over her shoulder. Admired. She concentrated too hard to notice. Tobin took his time to mow the lawn. Mowed around Chantal and Mrs. Ironside. Forgot to think about universal themes.

The skateboard kid stopped and stayed. Josh. After a long time the kid said to Chantal, "Guess you were good at art when you were a kid."

She looked up. Smiling. Said, "My husband probably looked like you when he had the same age you have. He is English. They all have cheeks like raspberry jam." Kid didn't answer. Studied the drawing. Chantal kept talking. "He was probably serious, too, like you. – But was I good in art? I have to think. Was I? I didn't think I was. Teachers in France are very strict. Full of criticism. But maybe I *was* good at art. I just didn't know it. Nobody ever told me."

71

"I think you were," the boy said.

"If I was, I wish I had known it. I would have taken more art courses."

"It was a waste," the kid said, "if you were good and didn't know it."

"NO SCHOOL TODAY?" Tobin asked. Loud, that lawnmower. Had to ask again.

When the kid looked up, no eye contact. Just, "Gotta rocket." Grabbed his skateboard and took the stairs to the basketball court. A cat climbs a tree like that. Then, sound of skateboard growling on cement. Louder than the lawnmower.

"When I was a kid," Tobin said, "we had to go to school."

"He seems like a nice boy." Dreamy, Chantal sounded.

Tobin sped up the mowing.

Doc was right. Dog had intelligent eyes. Kind of a lovable dog, to tell the truth. Seemed to enjoy breakfast. Enjoyed an ear rub. Gave you a grateful look. Down at La Petite Treat he'd write a description for the post. Maybe a poem.

Might not sound serious enough.

He'd like to get going. Quite a few people would be interested. Probably.

Not much he could do to help Chantal. Got his pen and pad and headed downhill. Passed the top of Filbert. Steepest street in the world, they said.

"Ho *ho!*" Ike yelled, shooting an arm out. "Raised right arm of Hitler!" Raised arm held three leashes with dogs. Voice sounded like Humphrey Bogart. Had a cigarette in his mouth. Just climbed the steepest street in the world smoking a cigarette. Strong guy.

Corner of Union, the TV camerawoman's dog pulled her across the street. Animal was getting big. Could get as tall as the camerawoman. Six-footer dog. Tobin raised his right arm. Kept it raised. She wasn't looking.

Walking into the drugstore, he took the poem out of his pocket. "Something to xerox," he rehearsed. To himself. Ray was listening to a

72

tiny old woman in a big coat and hat. Always wore that same coat and hat, that woman. Probably stylish once. Probably fit once. People shrink. Trouble with her stomach, she told Ray. Took quite a while to describe the symptoms. Ray had a guess about what was wrong. Couldn't say for sure though. Her doctor'd probably prescribe – he named some medicine – sounded like Latin. She said she'd rather not bother her doctor, couldn't Ray just sell it to her?

Most people would rather consult Ray and Pete than their doctors. Couldn't blame them. Nice guys. Helped Tobin with his bad shoulder. Helped Mrs. Leone with Posy's reaction to firecrackers at Chinese New Year's. Helped everybody. So it took a long time to buy a pack of gum.

Tobin was patient. Gardening taught you patience.

"So long, Mrs. Kawalski. Tell your doctor to phone in the prescription and we'll get it right out to you. Say hello to Mr. Kawalski."

To Tobin: "What can I do for you?"

"Got something to xerox."

"She's all yours." Ray gestured toward the xerox machine. "How's it going?"

"Well, you might be kind of interested in this. Could be." He held out the *Bolinas Hearsay News*, opened it to page four.

"Hey!" Ray said. "Hey, Pete. C'mere." Pete was up there on the second floor, kind of like a platform balcony, above the cash register area. Counting out pills. When he saw Tobin, Pete raised his right arm.

Kind of a good day all 'round. Seemed like it. Pete came down the stairs and Ray read the poem to him, loud. Door kept opening. People coming in. Ray stopped at the funny parts so they could laugh. In came the dapper old fellow with the feather in his homburg, and the guy with the beret and the toy poodles, and before the end, Mrs. Leone and Posy. When Ray finished the poem, everyone clapped. The dogs barked. Tobin felt his face get red. "Thought you'd kind of like that." On his way out he saluted. Mrs. Leone saluted back.

On the wall of La Petite Treat was a billboard-type picture of Humphrey Bogart. Looked like Ike, the piano player with the afghans.

Sound-alike, too. They used to have guys like that in America. The fellow behind the counter had an emerald in his nose and about nine earrings in one ear. All little loops. Gold wire. Shaved head. Black fingernail polish. Steam hissing out of the cappuccino machine, he pulled muffins out of the microwave. What was that he was wearing? Pedalpushers. He saw Tobin. Opened the refrigerator for the grapefruit juice saying "The usual?"

"Thanks. Uh, by the way, I've got something here you might be interested in." Young guy had to lean out over the counter to hear. Tobin handed him a xeroxed page from the paper.

"Thanks." He didn't look at the page, just flipped it on the shelf with the mugs.

"HEY, GANG!" IKE shouted to his afghans. "Artist at work." They loped across the lawn for a look. "Nice work. Nice work!" Chantal held her picture in front of her, compared it to Mrs. Ironside. "Hey," Ike said. "What happened to your dog? He used to be a poodle."

Tobin worked on his topiary. Listened. He knew that Ike guy would be mad when he heard about the ditched dog. He liked the way Ike raised his fist. Kind of satisfying. He waited for the right moment to show his poem. Turned out Chantal had to go home to send a few e-mails.

"Got something you might be interested in."

"Oh, yeah?" Sounded just like Humphrey Bogart.

"Yuh. Yuh." Tobin fished a pre-folded copy of his poem from his jeans. "Published a poem. Thought you might like to read it."

"Naw, no thanks," Ike said. "Don't read poetry."

Tobin stood in his boots, the xerox still in his hand.

"No, no." Ike's gravel voice was like a song. "Nope. Don't read poetry. Don't read poetry. Can't stand poetry."

Tobin was surprised. He watched the swing of the legs, the swing of the leashes.

Well, some guys didn't like poetry.

Clothes

"BRING ME YOUR lee-eash!" she said, to give Tess a chance to show off how smart she was. Tess ran to the doorknob and yanked the leash off, whipping and whirling it across the floor. "Good girl! Brilliant!" On the way out she got a look in the mirror and wished she had another sweatshirt. But she still didn't have any credit on her credit cards. This month she'd finally paid off all the over-the-limits, though. She congratulated herself. Life should be fabulous without those fines.

As Tess pulled her up Hyde Street she saw the old woman in the hat and coat too big for her, a hat and coat that had gone out of style before Hillary was born. This is me in a few years, she said to herself. The woman smiled in a friendly way and said, "Who's walking whom?" Hillary put on her smile.

Work tonight should actually be interesting. They were going to Moose's, and the anchorperson was going to interview a bunch of writers who would be eating there. She'd be able to meet all the local names, plus Tom Wolfe, who was visiting from New York. Of course she wouldn't get to talk to them much. It would be pretty much a vicarious pleasure. The thing about her job was, she might as well be invisible. On location, she just carried the camera on her shoulder, crouched down or standing up high, depending on which angle the producer wanted. The reporter asked questions, the newsmaker answered, looking into the camera without even seeing the face behind

75

it. But tonight would be a treat anyway. She was a reader, and she'd never met a writer. Well, not counting Tobin.

Invisible or not, she wished once again that she had another sweat-shirt. Actually, this was once she'd rather have something nicer than a sweatshirt. Well, in fact, she did have a dress. Two, actually. One for interviews, which she luckily didn't have to go on any more, and one for parties, which she never got invited to. The dresses were getting a line of dust on the shoulders where the hangers hit.

Hillary let Tess off the leash at the foot of the brick street. It was a street that didn't go anywhere – just into the park, where it stopped. The only reason anyone ever drove there was to find a parking space, so they drove slowly.

It was always interesting to anticipate who would be here. She hoped Frankie wouldn't be. In a way, she hoped Philo Righi would be, because she was in a fairly up mood. But it wasn't even two-thirty yet, and he would be working. Unless it had changed, Friday was his day off, just like her. Tobin might have left. He came around six, left around three, with a total of an hour off for breaks, but sometimes it was more like five-thirty a.m. to two-thirty p.m. He wasn't supposed to do that, of course. His hours were supposed to be eight to five, but he managed his time like a self-employed person.

From the end of the lawn, down near where the forest began, a very pretty woman in slim pants and a jacket of very soft leather stepped out of the woods with a poodle. Tess dropped to the ground, tail sweeping the lawn, getting ready to charge. "No jumping! No jumping!" Tess's paws vaulted not to the poodle but to the woman's shoulder, so she could kiss the pretty woman's face.

"No!" The woman's voice had an authority to it that gave Hillary a shock. Tess too. She jolted backwards to a sitting position with her ears pressed back. (Were Tess's feelings hurt?) The woman took a lacy handkerchief from her pocket to wipe the dog's saliva off her cheek and to rub the grassy pawprints off her glove-leather jacket. Tess turned her attention to the poodle, who didn't respond. As Hillary got closer, the woman smiled up at her. She wasn't angry! She had delicate features, with shiny hair that kept falling forward, covering one eye. She was tall, but not too tall. Hillary thought again of that Swedish operation, where she could cut two inches off her height. No. She'd need to cut six. Eight.

Her name was Chantal and her dog was Roger. Hillary had seen Roger before. Tess ran circles around him, first darting this way, then pivoting to race around his other side. Roger stood stoic.

"What kind of dog is your Tess?" the woman asked in a French accent, as the puppy's teasing chase sped up like a cartoon – this way? – well, that way? – okay, this way? – that way? – and the poodle's disdain grew cartoonishly haughty.

"A golden retriever," Hillary answered, prepared for the usual response.

"She doesn't look like a golden retriever."

"She is, though." For the gazillionth time in this park, Hillary went into the explanation about silver-whites, et cetera.

Amazingly, Roger crouched and sprang to Tess! The two sped in circles this way, that way, all around the lawn. She never thought that old dog would run.

At the end of the explanation about silver-whites, Chantal said, "She doesn't look like a golden retriever." (Really!) "So skinny and long legs. Such short sleek fur." At this point she was looking past Hillary's shoulder to a spot beyond. Hillary turned and saw Frankie. She carried an upside-down beer can and tried to hold Buster back from joining the chase with Tess and Roger. Frankie didn't say hello. She said, "That's no golden retriever."

"She has papers." Hillary felt a little timid but was firm on this fact. "She's registered with the American Kennel Club."

"Hah!"

"Well, there's another blond one in the neighborhood" (Hillary tried to keep her voice polite) "exactly the same color as Tess. You know Nugget?"

"No, I don't know Nugget." (Frankie didn't try to keep her voice polite.)

"Well, Nugget's owner works in the video store, and he says Nugget looked exactly like Tess until he was a year and a half. And then Nugget got his feathers. That's what they call the curls, the long wavy fur. Sometimes the feathers don't come out until later."

"But so skinny," said the Frenchwoman. "Such a long, pointy face."

"Well, there's a psychiatrist I know named Philo Righi," Hillary said to both Chantal and Frankie. "He has that little Welsh corgi?"

"Yes, I know the corgi," Frankie said wearily. "And I know Philo Righi."

"Well, Philo Righi told me he has a book of dogs, illustrated, from a hundred years ago. It was published in England. And he says golden retrievers used to look like this, back in history. They were all long and more pointed."

"Hah!" Frankie said again. "If you think you've got a golden retriever, you're kidding yourself. If you think you've got a purebred anything, you're just as phony as the people who sold you that dog."

"THAT'S MY LANDLADY," Hillary said to Chantal, watching Buster pull Frankie down toward the promenade.

"Oh well."

"Oh well," Hillary agreed. They both laughed.

It was nice to have someone to talk to. Chantal seemed to feel the same way. Hillary told her about the evening ahead, at work. She hadn't ever been to Moose's, although in Portland she'd seen politicians and football players interviewed there on TV. Tonight, working the camera, she'd be part of the action in this sort of famous place. They said it was where all the writers and journalists went, to find each other and stir up an argument. Her boss said they'd be able to take their dinner break there as guests of the restaurant.

"What are you going to wear?"

"This." Hillary looked down at her flat front.

"Really?" Chantal seemed amazed.

"This is what I always wear."

"You always wear the same thing?"

"I don't have any clothes, really. We dress casually at my end of the camera. The anchors and reporters dress up, and the people doing the office work. But not us."

"Why don't you have any clothes?"

Frenchwomen always cared about clothes. "Well, in the first place, this is just what I wear. I had a bunch of other things, but I hardly ever wore them, so I had a garage sale before I moved here and sold them. I sold all my furniture, my car, my computer, everything, because I needed the money and also because it was cheaper just to buy a mattress here than to move things down from Portland."

"You sleep on a mattress? You don't have any furniture?"

Hillary was starting to feel self-conscious. "I do have a few sweat-shirts and sweaters, but Tess got to them, and they really are a disgrace. I also have two dresses. Really, really pretty ones. You'd be surprised."

"Oh, no. I wouldn't be surprised."

"I guess I could wear one of my dresses tonight if I wanted to."

"Why don't you?" Chantal sounded excited.

"To work?"

"But this is a special night."

"I'm just kind of embarrassed. I mean, I don't like to feel conspicuous."

"Ho-*ho*!" a raspy male voice shouted out. "Looks like Dog City." Chantal and Hillary, who had sat down on the lawn near the dogs, looked up to see the man in the baseball cap, planted on two legs. He had the three afghans, on three colors of leashes. Suddenly the green leash snapped taut and the gray afghan shot at Roger, snarling and growling and barking at once, so he choked, along with the other horrible sounds he made. "Shut up, Moe! God-damned sociophobe." Pulling the dog away, he said in a New York rasp, "Nice meeting you." Moe kept up the noise, until he'd been dragged backwards to the top of the brick street. "What's the matter with you, Moe? Going after a God-damn poodle. Don't you know that's not a dog?"

Yikes. Hillary's watch said three-fifteen. If only she had a ten dollar bill she could take a cab to the station. She'd be lucky if she had enough time to take Tess home and change into her dress.

Dr. Hawthorne

RAYFORD HAWTHORNE OWNED seven pairs of eyeglasses and had eight rooms. He knew which pair of glasses he wanted today, to harmonize with his attire, and Romeo followed him into each cranny of the apartment and observed him rummaging through drawer after drawer and cabinet after cabinet, no doubt wondering what the doctor was up to. Dr. Hawthorne's mind was an exceptionally well-tuned machine, unaccustomed to this poor use of time.

He was giving a talk tonight, in French, at the Alliance Française. When speaking in public, he well knew, appearance was paramount. As he would of necessity progress directly from his final appointment of the day to the school, this morning his ensemble had to be not only assembled but, literally, buttoned up. The highlight was an excellent bow tie with dime-sized red dots on a field of yellow, given him by his mother when he graduated from medical school shortly after the midpoint of the last century. Bow ties had not then been worn by young men, but his mother had a fondness for bow ties and said she knew their day would come again. And it had – when Rayford was no longer a young man. In fact, it had come and gone: indeed a proof of the bow tie's timelessness. Following the fashion of the times had never been a preoccupation of the doctor's. He preferred his sartorial statements to bear the mark of individuality. Hence the ascot that had become his trademark, often worn with the shirt of a lumberjack, on the day-to-day dog walk.

Some might find the colors and dots of his bow tie to be a bit clownish. So be it. No one ever complained of having one more reason to smile.

As he passed a rococo mirror, on his search for the right pair of glasses, his naked eye was good enough to observe that today he looked mirthful. It was unfortunate that under his tweed jacket no one would see the complementary suspenders he had purchased at Macy's, a store he disapproved of, as a matter of fact, because of the prices and the excess of merchandise. It was simply that he had had a root canal at the 450 Sutter Medical Building and had found himself in the position of having nineteen extra minutes to pay for in the Union Square garage, minutes that he would pay for whether he used them to advantage or not. Therefore he'd dashed through Macy's and, at no additional charge for parking, was now the possessor of a handsome pair of yellow-and-red-striped braces. But here he was today, wasting great chunks of time, looking for his spectacles. Fortunately he wasn't being charged for it.

Romeo had apparently lost interest in the pursuit of eyeglasses. His feet no longer trod the hall with his master's, who combed the rooms. Ridiculous, a big place like this for a lone widower. But where else would he keep his treasures, the paintings and tapestries and Louis XIV armoires and highboys he and his wife had collected at auctions, over the years and years, winning each trophy for only a fraction of its worth.

The students in the Advanced class at the Alliance had been given free choice on the subjects of their speeches. He could have chosen something from his area of expertise: People were always eager to hear about viruses and such. Or, he might have expounded on his con-siderable travels: People always had a wanderlust, and Dr. Hawthorne had wandered almost everywhere. But instead he had chosen, as his subject, something of passionate personal interest to him: Garbage.

He had not thrown away an ounce of garbage in thirty years. He had buried his garbage in his garden, rather a large garden, especially for a city garden, located in the back of the small apartment building he owned. And thrive his garden had. By now rhododendrons that had started puny and hopeless had grown into magnificent specimens, some exceeding himself in height. He had a bed of impatiens, a variety that usually grew no taller than the top of your sock, but his had bushed and blossomed to a height far exceeding the knee. These defied all the rules in the *Sunset Western Gardening Book*. He had two rose bushes of a kind that was not supposed to grow at all in San Francisco, and they yielded blooms of competition quality.

He had long been convinced that it was the garbage that had expedited the growth of his plants, that from the garbage the plants received a far more complete diet than they would get from the fertilizers available in nurseries. For the most part he had just theories, verified in the field; but he had done some botanical reading worth mentioning.

Most of his acquaintances (albeit city folk with virtually no gardening experience of their own) were amazed to hear how regular, household-variety garbage contributed to the health and burgeoning of everything that grew. Eggshells, to take one example, contained calcium in a form that was invaluable to insuring both a good pH and an aerated texture to the soil. Orange rinds decomposed naturally, spreading God's good vitamins through the dirt and into trunks and stems and leaves and flowers. Even used teabags made their contribution to organic goodness.

It had been a job, translating all these thoughts into French sentences. The French word for eggshell, for instance, was *coquille d'oeuf*. He should have deduced that one. Primrose was *primevère*. *Bêcher* was the verb that signified "to dig with a spade." *Puanteur* was the noun for stink. It had been amusing to find the different degrees of delicacy with which the French described aromas, scents, and downright odors.

Dr. Hawthorne had often thanked God for his mind, which others had likened, not unduly, to a steel trap: Once inside it, very few things escaped. The same must be true of his apartment, and those damnable specs. And, as if to prove the point, the rimless eyeglasses gleamed up at him from a shelf in the pantry. The glasses sat atop a tube of anchovy paste.

*

THE LOWER TERRACE was free of man or beast. The morning was over-cast, bleak in the social sense as well as the barometrical. Disappointing and deflating as this type of weather could be, it was par for the course in the environs. The only spot of color along Larkin Street was Mrs. Leone's red bathrobe. With one hand resting serene on the balustrade of her high balcony and the other raising a pair of opera glasses, she reminded him of an older Rapunzel with a more restrained coiffeur and a more technological means of surveying the situation. From under a pine tree Dr. Hawthorne waved his spade in her direction. She waved back with her opera glasses. "Fine woman," he said to Romeo. When he heard his voice, alone with Romeo in the wooded air, it sounded English. Almost Shakespearean!

THERE BEING NO other male dogs about, things looked promising today for Romeo; but before freeing him of his leash Dr. Hawthorne had yet to check the upper terrace. It was not easy to say why these male dogs tended to behave uncivilly toward each other, but the fact was there, apparently unalterable. Perhaps he should give this matter some thought and use it as the topic of his next talk at the Alliance Française. Psychology appealed to most listeners, especially if it involved sex.

There being no dogs, male or female, on the lower or upper terrace, Romeo was allowed to run off on his own, unencumbered. He trotted his heavy black body over to the hedge and lifted his leg to give a squirt. Very light on his feet, this rottweiler was, for such a beefy animal. He danced down the length of the hedge, stopping at intervals to sniff and to spray.

Dr. Hawthorne strolled over to the landing that opened onto the promenade and looked up the stairs, then down, where he saw the back of Tobin, descending. Tobin held his arms tight and straight against his chunky body, and his hands, at the level of a ballerina's tutu, fluttered up and down like the wings of a butterfly. Dr. Hawthorne tried to imagine what the fellow might be thinking. Twitter-twitter, twitter-twitter, went the gardener's hands, flouncily. There had to be a daydream going on there somewhere. Of course all of us daydream. Even animals

84

daydream. Romeo was full of fantasies. Often, just walking through the apartment, his head would dance, obviously responding to some imagined doings.

Two paws hopping on the legs of his trousers interrupted Dr. Hawthorne's reverie about what Tobin might have been daydreaming. "Well," the doctor drawled. "If it isn't little Posy." He bent from the waist, controlled as a teacher of dancing, and gave the bichonne frisée's fluffy little head a pat. He straightened to greet Mrs. Leone. She was no longer wearing her bathrobe, of course. She looked very smart indeed in starched white blouse, kilt skirt to mid-calf, short black jacket, and very high heels. He switched the spade to his left hand and took her hand in his right, bowing slightly. "*Enchanté!*"

"*Comment ça va aujourd'hui?*" Mrs. Leone's black eyes twinkled.

"*Vous parlez français?*" asked the doctor.

"*Un petit peu.*" She let her smile break completely full.

Marvelous how a smile from the heart could transform a woman's face. On a young woman the change was not quite so dramatic, but on a woman allegedly past her prime, the sudden radiance was – it actually conveyed something of a thrill. "*Magnifique!*" was the word that sprang to his lips. "As a matter of fact, my dear Madame Leone, I am giving a talk, this very evening, in French!" He felt himself becoming animated, explaining the circumstances surrounding the event, his involvement with this splendid institution over some years, his conviction that shared language was vital to world unity and world peace, and so forth. He couldn't learn all the languages, but he had dabbled in a number of them by now and had made it a point to know one well, in addition to his native English. It might have been Russian or Turkish or Japanese that he selected, and in fact he had dabbled in Turkish for a spell, as he had in German. How he'd happened to choose French as the language to master was probably a simple matter of chance, the fact that it had been offered in his high school in the first half of the last century and that the fine and pleasant opportunity offered by the Alliance Française existed right in this city – in fact within a walk from this hill.

85

Mrs. Leone knew the Alliance well. She had never studied there, but she'd once been "roped into" serving on a committee to raise money for it.

This pleased him. He had always had an inkling that she was involved in projects to make this city an ever more rewarding place for its inhabitants.

Mrs. Leone seemed to conquer a bit of shyness. At least, her voice had a timidity to it when she asked, "I wonder if I might attend your lecture?"

"Oh how you flatter me!" laughed the doctor. In fact he was tremendously flattered. They discussed the time and the room.

"Of course my topic may not interest you."

"What is it?" She was all ears.

A sudden twinge of grave doubt moved through his form. It occurred to him that he might have made an error of judgement. He might embarrass himself horribly.

"Garbage," he replied.

"Garbage?"

He looked down at his spade. Thumped it on his trouser leg. "Yes," he said. He continued to thump his spade on his thigh. "Yes," he said, looking upwards. "Yes. Garbage."

After a deep breath he continued. "You see, I have not thrown away an ounce of garbage in thirty years. Not one cantaloupe seed." He proceeded to tell Mrs. Leone about the endless benefits to his garden. Her enjoyment of his discourse restored his confidence in the fact that this was indeed a most edifying subject. When at last she said, "This is wonderful. I hate garbage and I love gardens," he felt certain that he'd hit on a juicy topic. "Exactly!" His exuberance could no doubt be heard throughout the park.

Consulting his watch, he gave a slight jump. Twenty-four patients to see today. Hitching Romeo's leash, he reminded her, "Seven o'clock. Room C."

He was at the landing when she called out, "I also wanted to say, that's a very good-looking bow tie."

As he gave his spade a wave and called, "*A bientôt,*" his smile didn't have anything to do with being gentlemanly. It spread beyond his control.

The Lawn Itself

TESS USED THE sidewalk as a treadmill, her toenails scraping the pavement. "Slow down!" Hillary yelled from her end of the leash. "Tess. Slow down!" It was amazing Tess didn't choke to death, and that Hillary's leash arm wasn't a foot longer than her other arm. Maybe it was. When a man in polyester said who's walking who, Hillary thought sometimes she'd count how many said who vs. whom.

Oh, well. The fog was giving way to a postcard perfect sky, and she was still a little high from last night. Last night, dressed up, with all those journalists and writers, Hillary was a hit. She couldn't help but notice. People seemed to like her. It wasn't really the dress, probably. It was the way she felt in the dress. Now she was back in her gray sweatshirt, with the wrists flopping around her forearms. Tess was still Tess, totally untrained. But Hillary was a hit last night.

Tobin read the paper, he might know some of the names. He didn't read novels, so he might not be impressed with Tom Wolfe or Herb Gold. Herb Gold had flirted! He was old enough to be her grandfather, and he wasn't tall, but wow. Something about him. And guess who was there, playing the piano! The guy she'd met that same afternoon, when she was talking with Chantal. The guy who sounded like a cabdriver in the movies – the one with the three afghans. Suddenly, for the first time since she'd moved here, Hillary had felt the thrill of having connections. The anchor looked at her with a more respectful smile after the pianist dedicated a song to her. It was a funny, boogy-woogy version of "Walkin' the Dog."

At the foot of the brick street she stopped Tess altogether, holding the leash close to the collar. "Tess. Sit!" Tess sat. This was just amazing. "Wow! Good girl! Whatta good girl!" Tess grinned up with that dog smile that shows a thrill of accomplishment. At the top of the bricks Hillary unlatched the leash, and that was the last she saw of Tess, except for the whipping tail and the hind paws disappearing down the steps.

On the slope below the promenade she found Tobin manipulating a little old-fashioned lawnmower, to cut grasses that grew between rocks on the hill. It looked awkward, but he persevered slowly.

"Why do you have to mow this grass?" She forgot to say hello, just looked at the cherishably green young shoots and thought nothing in particular except, maybe, the more the better. She liked the shoots tall, not clipped.

Seeing her, he stopped mowing and rested his left hand on the handle.

Something was different about Tobin today.

"Why do you have to mow it?" she said, getting back to the grass.

"Oh. People around here. Want it wild, but not too wild." He resumed rolling the lawnmower. She watched the thin green shoots vault in the air, then fall. Most of them landed on the mower blades. Its moving parts were nearly a solid green. "Oh Tobin, I wanted to tell you about what I did last night. I met all these journalists, and famous writers, like Tom Wolfe . . ."

"So you passed the test, I guess."

Sometimes she didn't know how to follow Tobin's line of thought. But she was learning. Maybe. The Electric Koolaid Acid Test?

"You know, a lot of people think I got burnt out on drugs in the sixties."

She hadn't thought of that. Maybe that was it.

"I never went near drugs. Sometimes I think the things people do to be nonconformist are the most conformist things you can do." He pointed a finger straight from the shoulder. "'Thou shalt grow long hair.

Thou shalt eat brown rice.' I never did any drugs. I don't even like coffee."

"Oh."

"I have to admit, I've had a few beers. Back in the old days. Nothing too wrong with that, I guess. Not too many, maybe half a dozen. That's not too bad. In a lifetime." He mowed.

"So what do you think about when you're mowing the lawn?"

"Sometimes philosophy. Ethical questions. I almost had a PhD."

"You did?"

"Yuh. Got the Master's. Got two years into the PhD. Taught. I was good. My classes had waiting lists."

"Really!" Hillary was amazed. "Why didn't you finish?"

"Well, what a philosopher does is ask questions. I asked myself what's the point?"

"So you quit?"

"Yuh. Yuh. Luckily. Except, I could have had a nicer name. Could come in handy in an argument with a C.E.O."

She laughed. But she was fascinated. "So now, when you mow the lawn, you think about ethical questions?"

"Yuh. Sometimes. Most often I think about the lawn itself."

Hillary now felt embarrassed to talk about the trivialities she'd planned to tell him. If he got really involved, mentally, with the blades of the mower slicing off the blades of the grass, it must be like some mantra, some discipline that monks in Tibet worked their lives trying to achieve.

Still, she was Hillary, and she did want to tell him. "You know that guy with the afghans? He's a piano player! And last night at Moose's he played a song just for me. And Herb Gold was there and he was amazingly attentive. I mean, to me. (Me?!!?) We, all the news people, ate dinner there, not even at a back table but right in the middle, and when the writers had finished eating they brought drinks and coffee over and sat for a while. Herb Gold wanted to know everything about my life as a nighttime TV camerawoman, like what I have for breakfast when I wake up at lunch. I had the feeling he was taking notes. Mentally. I think maybe he might put me in a novel someday."

Tobin mowed, but slowly, around the rocks. The lawnmower wasn't loud. She wondered if he'd been listening.

"Someone who worked at the restaurant came up to Tom Wolfe with a book to sign. It was *Look Homeward, Angel.* Tom Wolfe seemed kind of irritated."

Tobin stopped mowing long enough to say, "Could be a little irritating."

"It was a joke!" said Hillary.

"Oh," Tobin said. "Could be he's heard it before."

Who's walking whom?

"I'm a published poet," Tobin said. "Guess you probably heard."

"No! I mean, I didn't know if you were or weren't. Published."

"Yuh," Tobin said, digging a folded copy from the pocket of his jeans. "Came out recently. You might enjoy it."

She smiled as she read. Midway she stopped and looked at Tobin mowing. Every now and then his head gave a nod and a jog. At this moment he probably wasn't thinking of "the lawn itself."

La Pique-Nique

GOING DOWN THE six stairs from her front door to the sidewalk was always a problem, because the height of her heels tipped her forward and there was a good chance she'd fall. She held fast to the handrail and planted each foot soundly, at the same time as she managed Posy's leash and the large basket on her arm. On the other side of the street, she and Posy could climb the twenty-two steps to the lower terrace gingerly. Going up, the height of the heels seemed to help. Maybe they gave her a head start on steepness. The only reason she knew the exact number of steps to the terrace was that she had often counted them, going down.

Today her shoes were a slightly vampish version of spectator pumps, navy blue and white stilettos. Her dress matched: Navy with chalk-white buttons down the front. Too many buttons. She'd counted them, the way she'd counted the stairs, and had reported the number to Morella, as if she needed an excuse for taking so long to get dressed. Nineteen buttons. But it was worth it. The dark color was slimming, and the white buttons up the front had the narrowing effect of a vertical stripe. This was one of those wonderful days when she had some hours off in the middle, nothing to do now until her three o'clock at the museum.

This was a new phase of the project she'd started five years ago, a special project for presenting art to people with disabilities. Today was the unveiling of the most inventive program so far – for the blind. They'd "see" the pictures and sculptures vividly – all without touching. She'd enlisted all sorts of experts, and really, they'd had fabulous ideas –

including music, voices, textures to feel, and even smells. All she'd have to do today was turn the meeting over to them. She and her committee had worked pretty hard on this for almost a year, so today she could do her quick introductions and sit back to enjoy the surprised looks on the trustees' faces.

Meanwhile. In her basket she carried her pocketbook, a blanket to sit on, and her Cassell's French–English dictionary with the scuffed red cover. She'd also packed a simple lunch – and a spanking new copy of *Femme.* "*Le mag de la vie.*" She'd bought it at Smoke Signals (Smoke, for short), that newsstand on Polk Street, where they had magazines in alphabets Anna couldn't identify – Greek and Arabic and every kind of Asian. It filled her with wonder, to think what people here on Russian Hill were reading these days. Down the block at the Boulange de Polk she'd paid seventy-five cents for a madeleine to put in her basket – a lot for a plain little cookie.

Rayford Hawthorne's speech had inspired her. The language. Not the topic. Although, it was true – she'd never in her life thought about how much good could be done by garbage. Someday he might give a garden party. She'd love to see in person how his roses thrived on garbage. He had implored everyone in the class to do as he did and never again throw away a mushy radish or even a used coffee ground. These were God's gifts.

Except for the wisteria and the planted borders in front of her building, which some gardening service took care of, Anna didn't have a garden. It occurred to her that she could save her garbage and give it to Rayford. As she said to Morella, if all the other students in Rayford's class got the same idea, Room C might fill with quite a *puanteur*.

She'd really enjoyed his digression on the various words for smells, odors, and stinks. She was amazed that she'd actually understood one word. But he'd spoken slowly and with clarity – and since he wasn't allowed to explain anything with an English word, and not everyone's French was as advanced as his or the teacher's, he'd pantomimed in a way that had got the class rolling in the aisles. Anna had understood almost half of the speech. Well, almost a third. Or, at least, about a sixth. But that was good! Good for her! It had been years, maybe dozens of years, since she'd spent a minute thinking about French.

When Anna repeated some of Rayford's speech to Morella, in English of course, they'd giggled like little girls. After her evening at the Alliance Française, so lost and confused in a blur of foreign syllables, Anna had decided to spend twice as much time as before talking to Morella. How terrible it must be to live in a country with so much of the conversation a blur. Rayford and his garbage made a great language lesson, because there were plenty of props in the trashcan – for reinforcing new words like lemon *rind* and avocado *pit*.

Before even sitting down on the bench in the park, Anna fished *Femme* from her basket and thumbed through. A picture of a steaming little orange soufflé puffing out of a real orange made her almost salivate. And there was a recipe. Too bad she never cooked. *Tant pis*. As they say. Such a pity. There were movie reviews, spa reviews, instructions for getting "*jambes sublimes.*" With the help of the picture, Anna remembered the word *jambe* was leg. Ah, again, *tant pis*. Legs like that were another never-again. But still. With the magazines at Smoke, and her dictionary, she'd be able to get her vocabulary back, and maybe even get in the swing of the conjugations.

Two little bark sounds from Posy changed the subject. Posy's barks were dog language for "Hi! How are you?" Posy ran to greet Buster. The two dogs swayed tipsily on their hind legs like ballroom dancers, clumsy but enthusiastic. Anna couldn't see Frankie, so she shifted the basket to weigh down the magazine and walked up to the promenade. "Hello!" she called. Frankie leaned on one of those cement garbage cans, smoking. She glanced over at Anna and went back to what she'd been watching. Through spaces between pine boughs, they saw a big ship coming under the bridge. "Probably loaded with Toyotas," Frankie said, "and all those computers made in Japan. Probably Japanese tractors, too. I saw it coming twenty years ago. America going down the drain. And now look where we are."

"Oh, but it's a great day, isn't it? The sky's so blue."

"That's another problem." Frankie stuck her cigarette in her mouth to use both hands to pull the tab off her can. "Global warming."

Anna admitted there were more problems than anyone could count. "Oh! Did you see Tobin's poem? Published?"

Frankie looked her in the face for a moment.

"Yes! Tobin had a poem published. It was really good. Very funny." Seeing a little derision in the smile that was forming on Frankie's lips, she added, "It was meant to be funny."

"What was it published in?"

"Oh, a little paper in Bolinas. The paper has a funny name too. Something like, um, the *Bolinas Hearsay Gazette*."

This hit Frankie just as she was taking a swallow, so her laugh rerouted the beer. She choked and turned pink. "So he finally made the big time." She wiped her eyes with the sleeve of her jacket. "I bet there must be ten people in Bolinas who aren't too stoned to read."

"Oh," Anna said. "We get it in the city, too. I see it in that sophisticated little news place down on Polk Street. With all the European and Asian and Islamic newspapers?" (She was coming on a little heavily.) "Well, of course the Bolinas paper isn't *The Times* of London. But a few people here read it. I was in the drugstore when Ray read the poem out loud. Or was it Pete? Anyway, a whole gathering was in there, and they laughed in all the funny places, and at the end they clapped. They just couldn't help themselves."

"I'll take your word for it."

Just as Anna was thinking of a nice way to say goodbye, Frankie said, "I'm not feeling too good."

Anna felt paralyzed for a second. "What's the matter?"

"Oh, I have gout."

Gout? Anna had heard of people dying of this. She'd seen pictures of people elevating a foot, with pain on their faces. "Does your foot hurt?"

"I wish it was just my foot. It affects the body."

Probably the best way to get Frankie talking might be to say nothing.

Another ship slipped under the Golden Gate now, a huge, whipped-plastic-looking thing, as orange as Tang. They watched. It looked like a giant beer cooler.

"I've had it before," said Frankie.

Anna had heard that you shouldn't drink if you had gout, but she knew she'd better not say that. Instead she asked, "What does your doctor say?"

"I don't have a doctor."

"Oh! Why don't you ask Dr. Hawthorne?"

Seeing the horror on Frankie's face, she hurried on, "He could probably recommend just the right person."

"I don't believe in doctors. When I had this before, it got so bad it turned me against doctors."

Anna kicked herself before saying it, but she said it anyway. Gently. "I remember hearing that if you had gout, it helped if you cut down on alcohol."

"I don't drink! I really don't! Just beer. I'm not even supposed to do that. I'm not supposed to do anything. No red meat, no candy bars, but I don't follow the rules. It's too hard."

"How does it feel?"

"Oh, I'll tell you. What happens is, the cells don't metabolize the nutrition that comes through the blood. They partly burn it and leave the rest. Garbage, I guess. It feels like garbage in liquid and gas form, polluting your whole system. It's muck that festers, carbonating poison. The bubbles can't get out, so this nauseating pressure builds up in every section of your body. You can feel your insides stink. What you feel is all-around horrible."

Both her expression and the grayish color in her skin showed that she meant what she said. Anna tried to imagine feeling this all-around horrible but didn't want to. It was too all-around horrible. She wasn't completely disappointed that Frankie halted the conversation right there, grabbing for Buster and leashing his collar. Anna watched her walk to the farthest trashcan, taking one last swig.

*

ANNA DIDN'T ALWAYS like herself. She wondered what was the matter with her.

"For every virtue, there is a corresponding vice." Henry James.

She hardly remembered anything from college. Nothing from any of the books. The only things she did remember were from conversations with friends – especially with Joe – about the things in the books. Luckily, Joe read most of the books she was assigned, or she might not have gotten anything out of them. One book, *The Art of the Novel* by Henry James, said, "For every virtue, there is a corresponding vice." Meaning, the virtues and the vices were branches growing out of the same trunk. She and Joe talked, over the years, about these corresponding virtues and vices in the various people they knew. Today she thought her virtue was, maybe, that she had a big heart. Her vice was that sometimes it was too big to take in the suffering of other people. At least, she really wanted to turn her back on people who were so badly off she couldn't imagine how to help. She even justified it! If she let herself go, she'd feel so much ache she wouldn't be able to go on with her own life. Her vice was, at a certain point she shut off her feelings.

She hoped Frankie would get better. And that was that. *C'est ça. Tant pis.*

Through a gap in the hedge, the corner of her eye caught something brick-red moving. So slowly, it moved. It was the scab-colored jacket. When he got to the clearing, she put on her glasses to get a good look at the hair, like a hood over his shoulders. It had the texture of a mat you put under a rug, or a filthy old blanket from the bottom of an animal's cage. Maybe his jeans were one reason his steps were so slow. They had so much dirt embedded in the weave they must be as stiff as cardboard. He lifted his head to take a drink from a bottle. When he put the bottle back in his pocket, she noticed it was Evian! He stood facing the Bay, but except when he sipped, he kept his head bowed, so he couldn't be noticing how the color had deepened to a fabulous turquoise. Sadness radiated from his body.

*

97

CAREFUL NOT TO make a sound, she quickly stepped up to the promenade. A high school girl was sitting on a bench, reading. Even though she'd rather be up here, where it was sunnier, Anna knew she could be tempted to get into a conversation, and she wanted to concentrate on her French. So she just stood and watched the lower terrace, waiting for the man with the hair to move down the stairs to Larkin. It took him for ever, but finally she was free to move her things down. One bench had a stripe of sunshine. She unfurled her blanket, and Posy charged at it like a frilly little bull. "No, Posy. No." Getting comfortable, she put on her reading glasses, unwrapped her sandwich, and opened *Femme* to the table of contents. "*Psycho-Test.*" Page *vingt-et-un*. This should be fun. If you met someone intriguing in a bar or on the Metro, one multiple-choice response was that you might give him your "*numéro portable.*" That must be your cell phone. (So apparently you were married? And your husband might answer the regular phone?) In another question, you found your man "*en tête-à-tête avec une ravissante jeune femme.*" (Ahah! *ravissante* = ravishing.) You would do what? None of the answers seemed right to Mrs. Leone. She would have to take the pen and notebook from her pocketbook and find her own words. Good practice. About the *tête-à-tête* with the *ravissante* woman, she wanted to say "join right in," but she didn't know how. Looking here, then there, in her Cassell's, she figured it out. But more and more, this *Psycho-Test* didn't apply to her. Almost every question had to do with "*une escapade extraconjugale*" – something Anna had no interest in. This was obviously for younger women with sublime thighs.

She flipped to "Adjust Your Diet to Your Age." A diet for every decade – up to forty. She thumbed to "The Old Masters Are the New Vogue." To "Cellulite and You." She decided on "The Au Pair and the Husband." Heavens, the author of this article was in a bad situation. She pulled back the tab of her V-8 and almost sucked.

Her peripheral vision told her that Posy had found a friend. The girl she'd seen earlier, on the sunny bench she'd have chosen for herself, had come down to the lower terrace and was holding Posy's chin in her hand. Posy's stub of tail vibrated.

Now Anna needed the dictionary. What was a *poêle*? Ah. A frying pan. She'd never remember that. She flipped a page in her notebook and started a Vocabulary section. Later, she'd give herself a quiz. She went back to the story and with every paragraph felt grateful that when she and Joe were young, au pairs hadn't been in vogue. She worried for her daughter Angela, who had a husband and an au pair. Too bad Nurse Fryckholme wasn't still around. Stern old Nurse Fryckholme had seemed like a pain at the time, but she'd saved Anna from the threat of a gorgeous, seductive au pair.

The girl who'd been reading was scratching both of Posy's ears, and Posy had the expression of a dog who thought she was in heaven. Anna admired the slender young body in slim jeans and a T-shirt that fit like a leotard. Posy ran back and grabbed a thrown pine-cone almost as big as her head. Bouncing back, her shape almost strobed, like a cute dog in a speeded-up movie. Eventually Anna would have to thank this nice young girl. Meanwhile, the au pair. She was glad that forty-seven years ago, when she'd bought this Cassell's, she'd paid the extra eighty cents to get the edition with thumb indentations marking the letters of the alphabet.

Finishing with the au pair, she moved on to "Simone de Beauvoir and Jean-Paul Sartre: the Tristan and Isolde of the Twentieth Century." There was nothing she liked as much as a good love story. This one gripped her so much she skipped over the words she didn't know. Simone and Jean-Paul believed that complete honesty was absolutely necessary for genuine love. They seemed to use "honest" to test each other, meaning torture each other. They brought young women into their bed and shared the young women. (Women! One was sixteen. Anna imagined little Angela, in such a situation.) Feeling a little angry, Anna studied a cluster of pine-cones attached to a bough above her – two big ones and one small. Would what had gone on with Jean-Paul and Simone be what she'd call love? Simone and Jean-Paul seemed to ask,

How much will it take to kill this passion? It was no wonder that early on they stopped making love, and that by the time he died they'd stopped speaking. *Quels monstres!* The funny thing was, both those people were geniuses. Why wouldn't they have been smart enough to know they'd wreck everything by hurting each other's feelings?

SHE LOOKED OVER to check on Posy.

Posy was gone.

Anna stopped breathing.

"Posy!" From back in the woods Posy came bouncing. Her little pink valentine tongue stuck out and her round black button-eyes sparkled. Her stub-tail wagged, if you could call it wagging. This stub-tail was like a subtle comedian, as opposed to slapstick. Anna's arms reached out. And, after grabbing a great gasp of oxygen, she resumed normal breathing. She reached and buried her painted fingernails in Posy's fluff. "Oh, I was frightened." She spoke to the dog to comfort herself. The girl was standing above Posy and her, and Anna said, "I forgot to think about Posy and – oh well."

"Sorry. I don't speak English."

Anna was surprised. "What do you speak?"

The girl apologized with her eyes, shrugging and turning out a palm. "Sorry . . ."

Anna recognized the accent and burst in, "*Vous parlez français?*"

"*Oui.*" The girl smiled first with her eyes and then with her whole face.

This poor girl must need someone to talk to. Anna didn't need to be in the least embarrassed about her French. She reached out her hand and said, "*Je m'appelle Anna Leone.*"

Men

THE BASKETBALL COURT was a map of wet cement and shallow lakes. He didn't care how wet he got. He pushed with his left foot and picked up speed, his board cutting through water, shooting up spray. This was hell of fun. Up in all the buildings around the court, the lights were going out. The one he really liked must be the skinniest skyscraper in the world. This neighborhood had the world's crookedest street and the world's steepest street, so it probably had the world's skinniest skyscraper. It stuck up like a chopstick in a row of matchboxes. Its decoration was lacy, with old-fashioned fire escapes zigzagging down the front. The guy that built it must have had a sense of humor. Josh liked that building. If he didn't take his eyes off it, he could spin up to four twirls without getting dizzy. He was building up to five. Splat. Up again. Hell of cool. The rain had stopped, and now the wind was blowing puffs of white, like chalk dust only wet. Sudden clouds swooped down and almost blinded you. A month ago, he never could have pushed this kind of speed out of his board. He circled the court ten, twenty, thirty times. He wished they had speedometers for skateboards. That could be a good business to get into. He stopped at the corner, over where you could see the Golden Gate Bridge with the lights just coming on, to catch a breather. Down under the trees an umbrella floated along a path. Old lady Leone. Her dog had a raincoat on. Might as well head on down. With a dig of the heel he pivoted his board a one-eight-oh and saw if he could shoot all the way down the court to the gate on only one kick. He got three-quarters there. One more move, a short ride, and he pressed with his heel to shoot the board into his hands.

He was improving, no doubt about it.

She was starting down the steps, so he broke into a run. "Hey, Mrs. Leone! It's me."

She turned. "Well, hello."

He crouched to talk to the dog. "How's business, Posy?"

"How's school, Josh?"

This was a tough one. "I'm working real hard, Mrs. Leone." He didn't feel comfortable talking about it. Oh well, she asked. "I got an F in algebra this last time." She seemed like she couldn't believe it. Neither could he, when he saw it in ink. "I never got an F before. So I'm really working. I think I understand it. I think maybe I'll be able to get a D next time. I'm almost sure I'll rise to a D. I kind of don't think it's fair that the teacher gave me an F. I actually got most of the problems right on the midterm. More than fifty per cent. She said that was still an F."

He couldn't figure it out himself. "The problem is, she's nice. She's way cool. I don't agree with her grading, but I like her. I'm going to do all I can to get a D."

Mrs. Leone didn't look too cheered up. "I always get the end result right. That's no problem. It's just the formula. I get the formula wrong. And the way it is in this class, you have to get them both. I just have a different way of thinking. But I've got to get the formulas straight, for the grade."

She didn't say anything, just kind of scowled down at Posy. He could see she was trying to think of what to say. He didn't want to make her work so hard, so luckily he thought of something else. "Oh! I got an A on my essay in English. I usually do. I remember one time in sixth grade I wrote an essay that was so good my teacher thought I got someone else to write it. She gave me a zero. I had to beg my dad to go in and talk to her." Remembering this, he had to smile. "The wind-up was, the ole man came through. Took off work, went in to school, and she raised my grade to an A. She said, 'I just can't believe a kid could do that.'"

102

This seemed to cheer the old lady up. "Course, that was before I was identified as gifted."

"You've been identified as gifted?"

"Course! Course! Oh, hell yes. You didn't know that? Nice seeing you, Mrs. Leone. Gotta rocket."

A LITTLE RAIN came back to pat the ground. He was hell of hungry – hoped his sister would thaw a good meal. Whatever it was it would be better than what his dad's girlfriend fixed when they were in town.

He was running now, up the steps, past the tennis courts, when a round of barks fired out. He turned to see the piano guy with the afghans, talking to the beret guy with the miniature poodles. "Where's your martini?" Josh called out, still moving.

"I like 'em dry," the beret guy shouted.

"We were just lookin' at that rowboat all alone out there," the piano guy yelled. Josh stopped to look. "See him? Way out past Treasure Island, twilight time, rain pouring down?" Yeah. Cool. Josh sprinted down to join the conversation. "That's where I'd like to be," the piano guy said. "Rowing. With my lady on the prow. Nice exercise. Nice exercise, rowing. – You're not going to a gym, are you?"

Gym? Josh gave his board a pat and grinned: "Don't need it."

"Good. Good thinking. All these guys around here, stinking up a room, checking themselves out in the mirror, see if they're getting 'definition.'"

The beret guy looked down at his chest. Shook his head. "I used to have pretty great definition. I'd be in a gym eight hours a day if I thought it'd do any good now."

Both he and the piano guy had tough-guy voices. Josh could use a little scrape in his pipes. Maybe a hit of New Yock.

"Hey," the beret guy said to the other guy. "I saw you down at the Chinese store, talking to the owner. What language was that?"

"What language does a Chinaman speak?"

"You know Chinese?" Josh almost forgot to make his voice sound tough.

"Oh yeah. Oh yeah," the piano guy said. "Mandarin. Part of my past. My shadowy past. Shad-dowy past." Then he tripped. The big afghan jerked him off his feet – to lunge at a rottweiler.

"Sit!" There was the old doc. "Silence, Romeo."

The piano guy gave the doctor a hello wave, palm circling from elbow. "We were just talking about exercise, Doc. What do you recommend?"

"Pick your pleasure. That's my prescription." His voice carried over the dogs. "Everyone knows by now that the brain has its own pharmacy. But many people are unaware that exercise accompanied by *pleasurable* emotion creates more effective endorphins than exercise accompanied by a grunt and a groan."

The piano guy said, "I hear the brain makes endorphins when you play music."

"Ah!" The doctor was pleased. "But did you know that when the brain is *strenuously* involved, a more elevating form of endorphin is produced. Thus the classical musician gets more of a high than the popular player."

"Aw, bullshit," said the piano guy.

Josh felt embarrassed to say what *he'd* heard about endorphins, so he put some toughness in his voice: "My sister read that cuddling gives you endorphins."

"Ho-*ho*!" The piano guy scratched his stubble. "So *that's* why that's my favorite sport. How 'bout you, Doc?"

"Ah," said the doctor. "I remember it well." He gave an uncomfortable laugh and raised his spade in the sign of goodbye.

The piano guy wouldn't let it go at that. "On the square, Doc. Ever consider the health benefits of a little nooky?"

The doctor made his eyebrows jump. "Perhaps. At my age, however, the risks outweigh the benefits." His back turned. His spade gave a shake.

A Snail

A SNAIL, IN the middle of the path, moved its head out into the air, then its whole neck. It took a morning stretch, reaching east, west, south, up. Felt good. The pine-needles on the ground were wet. Drops still hung on the branches. The air got a bath last night.

The old Chinese gentleman wore a nylon windbreaker over his silk quilt. Poised on one foot, his body, balanced and controlled, helped his hand push an invisible weight away. Very slowly, more slowly than the snail would have done it, he wrestled the air.

Pages of the *Chronicle*, wet, clung to the back of a bench. A heavy, middle-aged woman carried a weight in each fist and jogged in slow motion past the snail, past the Chinese gentleman, past the *Chronicle*. One at a time each foot rose two inches above the ground and stayed, suspended, for more time than seemed right. Gray sweats bulged over her hips, and her red parka only partly covered her sweatshirt. Her red face was in saintly pain.

In stocking cap and rain gear, forest-green, Tobin looked like an elf. The rain gear was new, or new to him – another find from the dumpster. It was a tarp with a hole in the center of his head. The rectangle draped over his shoulders and fell to four points that slapped against the yellow stripes at the knees of his boots. A brass-like ring dangled from each point.

TARP MIGHT WORK better than the yellow slickers the city issued. It worked at the busstops, where rain pelted. Now, drizzle. Cold wet pine air. Nice smell. He snipped a branch of undergrowth. Tossed it on the burlap sheet. Snipped another. Tossed it. Pile got waist high, six feet across. Bundle. Heave ho. Over the shoulder, headed for the shed.

Here came the Englishman. No suit. Old jeans. Not ironed. Old shoes. Mud on his parka. Behind him Mrs. Ironside, hopping down the lawn. "Hello, Tobin."

"Guess you're kind of mad at me," Tobin said.

"Whatever for?" The Englishman looked surprised.

"I could've just given the dog to the SPCA. They would've come up. I should've just asked them." Wet lawn. Wet tennis ball. Hands full. Couldn't pick it up. "I knew nobody'd claim the dog."

"And thank God not! You know how Chantal has fallen for this Ironside lady. You see how the good vet has set her remaining back leg in working condition again? A medical miracle. And Chantal must have told you about Roger. Now that he's gotten used to her, he likes having a big sister, or an elderly aunt, around the house."

"Oh. Oh. I see." Heavy, this bundle. Shifted it to the other shoulder. Trudged to the shed. Came back with another burlap sheet, folded like a flag. Bent to scratch Mrs. Ironside's ear. Nice eyes. Expressive. Obviously liked fondling. Like everybody. "So!" He looked up at the Englishman. "So the Doctor of Despair has lost all his patients." He chuckled. Chuckled alone. Wet tennis ball bothered him. Picked it up. "Guess you were surprised to find out you were friends with a published poet."

"Well I was, Tobin, the first time I learned of it. That must have been about a month ago now."

Oh. Kind of embarrassing. "So many people up here, I forget who I tell."

"Not at all, Tobin. I'm afraid I sounded rather rude. But as a matter of fact you read it to me once, Dr. Hawthorne read it to me, and Chantal has read me that poem half a dozen times or more. She found it in her desk just last night and read it to me again. I'm surprised she hasn't committed it to memory yet. You have a loyal fan club."

"Kind of a thrill, to tell you the truth."

"And another thing, on behalf of the Russian Hill rosarians, meaning Chantal and myself: I've been wanting to thank you for your help with the irrigation."

"Oh. Glad to help."

"The pipes are in. The roses are on their way. There's only enough space for fifty plants, and we have about fifty catalogs and about three hundred favorites. Don't forget, we had acres of roses, back in England. We're not used to limits. We nearly had to call in a marriage counselor to help us decide, for instance, between Elizabeth Taylor and Abraham Lincoln."

"Interesting problem."

"They're both tall and crimson," the Englishman said. "She likes him, I like her."

That explained it.

"I've got to get into my working duds, Tobin, but Chantal will be out soon enough. She'll have some news you might be interested in." He raised his right arm in farewell.

Kind of dated, that salute. Old poem. Unpublished. "The Doctor of Despair has lost all his patients," he said, circling each eyeball with thumb and finger. Glasses. Doctor. Get it?

WALKING PAST THE monument to where he'd left the clippers, he saw Mrs. Leone open the french doors to her balcony. She stuck out a hand to feel the air, then drew the red sleeve of her bathrobe back into the apartment, latching the glass doors. A heavy young woman sat on a bench, jiggling her shoulders and breasts and head. Jiggle-jiggle, jiggle-jiggle, jiggle-jiggle. Wonder what she thinks she's doing-doing, doing-doing, doing-doing. This could be the start of another poem. Poem-poem, poem-poem. A young black woman, thin as wire rope, faced the Bay and did jumping jacks while her red doberman sniffed through bushes. A mother robin led a troop of fuzzy birds across the wet red dirt. She took off, flying low, and the little ones fluttered. After a few bounces they made it into the woods.

Halfway up to the tennis courts, Tobin found his clippers and rested a second to admire his garden. Couldn't remember when the crabapple dropped its blossoms. When did the acacia change its color from canary to green? The big plum tree had dropped its flowers to make a carpet of fluff on the ground. Soggy. The sky was a mix of clouds and blue. The Golden Gate Bridge poked a few points through a sheet of fleece. And here came Mrs. Leone. Hood up. Umbrella closed. Little plaid slicker on the dog. Blue and red. Looked nice with the royal blue leash.

"The Doctor of Despair!" he called out, making those round spectacles with his fingers.

"Hello, Tobin!" She was looking everywhere. "Have you seen my young French friend?"

"Chantal? You know Chantal?"

"Chantal? My friend is Martine."

"Oh. Don't know that one. Unless you mean the one who doesn't speak English."

"Yes!"

"No. Not here."

"Madame Leone!" The one who didn't speak English. Running. Waving. "*Je veux dire* Anna. *Bonjour*, Anna." Fast runner, this kid. Introductions. In French and English. Mrs. Leone introduced him to the girl in French. Switched to English when she introduced the girl to him. Girl stuck out a hand for a handshake. Had a lot of assurance. He wasn't used to shaking hands. Did it, though, since she was French. Mrs. Leone talked French to the girl. He heard "*poète*" next to his name. Kind of nice. Kid said something French. "She says the gardening must be an aspiration for your poetry." "Yuh. Yuh." Mrs. Leone translated "Yuh-yuh" for the girl: Said, "*Oui*." Mrs. Leone seemed to enjoy being the one who knew both languages.

"Can you say, 'Extra, extra, read all about it / Raised right arm of Hitler / Found in a garbage can / In Yugoslavia'?"

"Oh dear."

Probably shouldn't have asked.

108

Fluff dog bopping up steps. Light bouncing off shiny red raincoat. Tall black poodle. Chantal. Trenchcoat. Hair full of drops.

Sniffs. Big handsome poodle and little fru-fru.

"Tobin, Tobin! I've just read your poem again, Tobin, and I love it."

"Oh. Oh. Thanks a lot." Nice yellow tips, his boots had. "Oh. Maybe you'd like to meet Mrs. Leone. And, uh, Martine. Speaks your language."

"*Vous êtes française?*" Squeal. That's what Chantal did. Cheep-cheep-cheep! These two Frenchwomen took off like birds. Peep-peep-peep!

Mrs. Leone? Lost, looked like. Face looked lost. French wasn't that hard though, to tell you the truth. He got a few words. Words like *café* and La Petite Treat. Words like *oui, oui, oui,* and *au revoir,* Tobin.

HE COULD HAVE used a glass of grapefruit juice. He stood with his clippers. Oh, well. He'd wait a few minutes, maybe twenty. Might make them feel bad if he walked in right behind them and sat down at a table by himself.

Crest of the brick street. Long-legged puppy. "No jumping! No jumping!" Braced himself. Didn't like to get knocked over. "Dog's getting strong." Licks. Wet ones, on the cheeks and the nose and the forehead. Dog scampering back to Birdwood, across the bricks. Maserati shooting up. Grazing the dog, almost. Birdwood screaming.

"Right! *Right!*" The big yell of Ike the piano man, running fast uphill. Only one dog today – the little afghan that looked like a mop. Good runner, that puppy. "*Right!*" Ike yells again. Raising fist at Maserati. Maserati spinning into parking slot. "Right!" Ike and puppy running faster. "Just *kill* anybody who gets in your way." Ike sticking his face through the driver's window, into the driver's face. Shouting like from a mile away. "That's right. Time – is – *money!* Life – is – *cheap!*" Following the guy to the door of the condo, door slamming on his finger.

Finger in mouth, shouting, "God-damned C.E.O.! White trash!"

Took a couple of breaths to cool down. "God-damned white trash."

*

COULDN'T STAND HERE all day holding the clippers. Started in on the topiary.

"By the way, kid," the piano guy said to Birdwood. "Got a boyfriend?"

Tobin paid attention. He wondered.

Took a long time to answer. TV camerawoman looked embarrassed. Finally threw her wrists up. "No."

No boyfriend.

"Grrrreat! I've got a guy. I've been wanting to introduce him to someone all year. I keep looking. He's something. I'd just love to introduce him to a woman like you."

Wonder if he's tall.

"He's smart," Ike said, "he's sensitive, he's full of thought, he's straight, he's single, he's a musician, he's employed, he's good-looking, and – he's a man."

Ike made that sound pretty good. A man. Looked like Birdwood thought so too. She was red.

"You're not interested?" Ike looked upset. "You've got some – some something?"

She said nothing. Time passed.

"Oh, I'd be interested." What a grin!

"Well then. I like to do these things right. No pressure. Meg and I have talked about it. You'll like Meg. She'll like you. She wants to have a party. Meg is a great cook. *Great* cook. We haven't set the date yet, but we'll figure it out soon. We know a few people. We'll make sure it won't be a pressure situation for either one of you two. Just cool. We like to do things classy."

Kind of nice. Guy must be tall.

Time to go check out the shrubbery by the monument. Make a work plan, to start on after a grapefruit juice break. On the way down, he passed the snail, which had made some progress.

110

Lumbago

FROM THE BOTTOM of the stairs, ever so slowly, came a lowered gray head. A spade dangled from one hand. The other hand held the railing. His feet gave each step total attention. She wouldn't have been sure it was Rayford if it hadn't been for the spade, the dog, and the ascot. The folded leash poked out of his pocket, and, seeing Posy, the rottweiler sprang from the bushes like a heavyweight in dancing shoes. His owner looked up and saw Anna. The smile he forced to his lips was a weak one. He managed to give his spade a limp wag.

"Rayford! How are you, Rayford?" She tried not to sound too concerned. That made people feel worse. He lifted the heavy spade and seemed to use all his might to give it another wiggle, as if to say just a minute, and used the railing to pull himself up.

At the top he took her hand in his usual gallant manner, looked her in the eyes, and after some seconds expired a sigh. "Oh, my dear lady," he said, shaking his head, "I'm afraid I'm a bit of a crock today."

"A what?"

"Oh, a crock. I have a disorder of the sort we doctors view, if a patient has it, as a kind of neurosis."

"What is it?"

"Oh, it's a damn pain in the lower back. I have no idea where it came from, it just arrived. And, as I say, it's the type of complaint that generally makes us doctors think a patient is neurotic."

111

"But it's real!" She knew this from Joe, who'd had the same pain, sometimes.

"Oh, indeed it is real. And oh, indeed, I wish it weren't."

It almost hurt her to see how much work he had to do to keep his face cheerful.

"In the olden days this was a fashionable ailment. They gave it a fashionable name. Lumbago. 'Oh my lumbago,' they would say. All the fine Victorian ladies had lumbago, and the gentlemen got lumbago. People hobbled stylishly about on gold-handled canes, murmuring about their lumbago." The usual strength was gone from his voice. "I've already had to take codeine twice for this. And I don't like it. In the first place it gives you" – he lowered his eyes to the ground – "constipation." His eyes looked straight into Anna's when he said it, "And I feel like I'm not all there, mentally. I don't like being not all there mentally."

IT WAS TOO bad about formality. The formality of not knowing each other well enough. With Joe, she'd known just where to rub, how light and how heavy her touch should be. Skin on skin did something codeine couldn't. It was a shame that Rayford didn't have an actual person to help him with this pain, instead of just a chemical. "I'm sorry to hear you're under the weather," was all she could say.

Actually, she was more sorry than she could say, because she had had a wonderful idea, and she'd been hoping she'd see him casually, like this, on the chance he might be interested, spur of the moment. Now she probably shouldn't even bring it up. "I've met some new people," she said instead. "French!"

"Ahah." His eyes gave a glint of alertness.

"Yes! I met them right here in the park." She could feel herself getting excited. "The first one I met was just a girl, sitting on that bench, and when I spoke to her all she could say was 'sorry I don't speak English,' which was perfect for me, because after your speech I got interested in brushing up my French, and here she was, this poor French girl alone all day with books and no one to talk to and here I was, trying to learn

112

French with no one to speak French with! So now I see this girl every day (she's only a girl, not even in college yet), and we go to this terrible little place down on Hyde Street called La Petite Treat, where you have to stand in line for your coffee and you have to pay them a tip even though they don't wait on you, and Martine likes to sit right out on the sidewalk, like in Paris, except it's not Paris and there's nothing to see here but Hyde Street and the cable car, and I don't even mind a bit, because she and I talk talk talk. In French! Because the only words she knows in English are sorry I don't speak English. But I'm getting so I can understand her. I know all about her village in France, and the castle there, and the University of Lille, which she's going to start next year, and she always wants to talk about politics, and we disagree, so I have to think. I'm forced to. And she has a boyfriend named Manuel, who I'm going to meet tonight."

"I thought you'd already met him." The doctor looked confused.

"Oh, no . . . I've heard all about him, of course. He's a *dessinateur*. Related to the word design, in English, I guess. He makes cartoons, on the computer."

"But you said you'd met 'some' French people."

"Oh yes! But the other one isn't him. The other one lives right across from the park, on Hyde Street. Her name is Chantal."

"Oh, Chantal! The wife of the Englishman. Nigel. I know him."

"Well, Chantal is lovely. They're all having dinner at my house tonight. It's a shame you can't come."

"It's a shame you haven't invited me!"

"Oh, well, I don't want to invite you now. You belong in bed."

"Madame, you forget to whom you are speaking. As the fellow in Kundera's masterpiece, *The Unbearable Lightness of Being*, so famously said, 'I am a doctor.'"

He laughed along with her. He actually laughed merrily. But she looked him over and saw that his hair most definitely didn't have its usual spring and waviness, or its usual silver shine. It was matted down, combed slick-flat but dullish, gray as an old destroyer. The lack of

113

flounce to his hair made his nose look big. And the crinkles around his eyes looked the way paper grocery bags look when they're overused and ready to split. Still, his eyes had light when he said, "I'd be honored to come, if I were invited."

"Really, Rayford. I'll invite them back another time, when your lumbago is gone."

"*Chère madame,*" he said, making an effort to bow. It looked painful. "You shall be my Lourdes. *A quelle heure?*"

"*Sept heures?*"

"*Sept heures et demi.* I'll be working until six-thirty at least. I'll want to stop home to feed Romeo. May I join you a tad later than the others?"

So it was settled. He shook his spade with some pep. "I have twenty-four patients to see today." Not holding the rail, he descended the steps, but slowly. The rottweiler, a sensitive dog, walked slowly also.

A Lovely Day in the Neighborhood

"WHAT'S GOING ON?" Frankie asked Tobin. Across Hyde Street a couple of workers pulled plants out of the ground, wrapped the roots in burlap, and tossed blue-flowered bundles into the back of a pickup. "Building another condo?"

"Roses," Tobin said. "Englishman and Frenchwoman putting in roses. Pretty good irrigation plan. Designed in Israel. Saves water."

"Roses?"

"Yuh. Yuh."

"IT'S . . . A . . . *LOVE-LY* day in the *neigh*-borhood . . ." Anna had stopped switching on the television in the morning when she heard Mr. Rogers was retiring. She was mad at him. Somehow, it had given her a lovely pleasure to have him in the kitchen as she put things into the dishwasher and ran her bath water. She'd loved the little dramas with the princess and the puppets. In their gentle way, they were actually witty. And even if his voice had been a little exaggerated in its goodness, the things he'd had to say had been such basic human kindness that she'd often been surprised to find herself saying "Yes, that's right!" He was always bringing up simple human truths she'd temporarily forgotten. Sometimes they'd hit like childhood discoveries. Then he said he was going away. Abandoning the children! But then, the happy ending. Like

115

resurrection, he was back. This day, she felt especially happy for the miracle of re-runs. She hummed along with his cheerful little song as she rolled out the dough for her strawberry shortcake. It might have been the first time since Joe died that she'd actually baked something.

She'd already walked Posy in the park, using a shiny red shopping bag from Elizabeth Arden to collect kindling for her Weber on the balcony. She loved gathering twigs from the woods. It reminded her of summers at the lake, of being young. Yesterday she and Morella had put the extra leaf in the table for last night's dinner with the grandchildren, so that part of the work for tonight was done. There'd been a rip in the arm of one chair, and Morella had taken out a needle and thread and made the chair like new. She'd polished the silver, and this morning Anna admired it again as she set the table. She thought she might get a little workout for herself now, so she put on some low-heeled shoes. She and Posy would walk down to Fisherman's Wharf to the wholesale fish place. If the salmon got too heavy on the way back, and the hill too steep, they could step on the cable car. Dogs weren't allowed without a muzzle, but the conductors turned a blind eye on Posy. And they always waved Anna away when she tried to pay. She pressed her money on them, and they never would take it.

A BLOCK DOWN the hill, Rayford Hawthorne stuck a codeine tablet on his tongue and regarded the picture in the bathroom mirror: white dot on red slab. He removed the pill and dropped it in the toilet. He stuck the bottle in his breast pocket, in case he should change his mind. Despite his strong feelings on water conservation, he flushed the toilet, lest Romeo take a drink from the bowl and get knocked out by the narcotic. One might think that closing the lid would be a more efficient solution, but he liked Romeo to have several water sources during the day. If the dog should finish the supply in his water bowl, and if for an unforeseen reason his own return home should be delayed, Romeo would be provided for. His fellow physicians might frown on letting a dog drink from a toilet, but thanks to Mrs. Gomez the housekeeping in Rayford's

116

apartment was near enough to perfection. A few innocent germs? Good for building the dog's immune system.

Rechecking the bow tie, suspenders, and fresh shirt he'd laid out for the party, he was glad he'd had his secretary reduce the patient load to the bare minimum today.

AT RAY AND Pete's drugstore, down on Hyde Street, Ray took out an eighth of a pound of keys and fit one into the padlock linking the two sides of grillework. He wore a sweater he hadn't worn before, the one his wife had given him three birthdays back and that he'd finally kept in the drawer long enough that it didn't seem new. He didn't like wearing new clothes. As the grillework contracted like an accordion, he noticed in the glass door the poster that said, "Remember Valentine's Day." The red in the poster had faded to pink. He remembered Valentine's Day.

WHEN JOSH STEPPED onto the bus, he looked down and saw he had on one brown sock and one green. He could go home and change it, he was going to be hell of late anyway, but he didn't have the energy.

He didn't have to go at all, if he didn't want to. His dad was in Taiwan for two weeks. His business. The good news was his girlfriend had gone with him. Josh hated his dad's girlfriend, but she hated him more. It didn't bother him though. They were gone more than they were home.

He felt hell of bad today. That was why he was going to school. His hangover was so harsh he wouldn't be able to skate. So he stayed on the bus.

CHANTAL HAD THE television on, and her leotard. At the aerobics teacher's command, she stretched out on her back, raised her knees, and pointed her toes. From his height Roger looked down at her. As Chantal set her legs in motion on an imaginary upside-down bicycle, Mrs. Ironside hopped over and rolled onto her back with her three legs in the air. Chantal laughed. "You are so darling, darling." She always spoke to Mrs. Ironside in English. Roger was bilingual, but Mrs.

Ironside wasn't yet. Chantal kicked, and Mrs. Ironside watched with her legs up.

When she turned on the shower, every inch of Chantal's body was already dripping. A network of red chicken wires criss-crossed her white skin. After the shower she'd try on clothes. She happened to know, because Nigel had found out, that Dr. Hawthorne would be at Mrs. Leone's tonight. The only time she'd met him, he'd complimented her on her "handsome jeans." They were actually part lycra. She knew what he really meant was her beautiful figure. It would have been *un tout petit peu gauche* to compliment her on that.

With flounces of silk piling higher and higher on the chintz slipper chairs and on the bed, and with blouse on blouse hanging on doorknobs, she tried one more combination. In cream silk shirt, a sheath skirt of textured cream, and the long pearls, she turned sideways to the mirror. It was like looking at a sheet of paper from the side. Dr. Hawthorne might agree that this was a handsome skirt.

ONE GOOD THING about having hardly any clothes was that you had hardly any trouble deciding what to wear. Hardly any. Tomorrow night was to be the fateful party, where Hillary would meet the Man. The only trouble was, Hillary didn't know whether to go low-key, wear the dress she'd bought for interviews, or go all out and wear the dress she had for parties. The interview dress wasn't Betty Business or anything. She just hated that look. It was a very dark green, almost black ("French green," the sales woman called it), with a skirt that gathered so it almost looked like she had hips. Optical illusion. The fancier dress was like peach clouds. Spun silk. It made her look like she'd gained ten pounds, and yet it was light as air. "No, Tess!" It was so beautiful Tess wanted to eat it. "No! No, Tess. No!"

Hillary hated to do this, but she needed to see herself in the bathroom mirror, and the only way would be to shut Tess in the closet for a sec. "C'mere, Tess." Slam. Scratch! Yowl! Scratches and scratches. A fury of scratches.

118

Such a soft cheerful dress. It made her look so carefree. (Another optical illusion.)

"Okay okay." She slid the dress back onto its hanger. As Tess shot out the door Hillary shoved the dress in and hung it. Slam. Now for the green one, which didn't have the same appeal for Tess. This was the one she should wear. The peach cloud was too show-off. It might make the other guests look bad. It might come off as an announcement that she didn't get much chance to dress up. Looking in the mirror, Hillary thought, You know what this green dress would be perfect for? A funeral.

LEAVING MRS. IRONSIDE lounging sumptuously on her new dog bed, Chantal and Roger stepped out their front door to see Tess pulling Hillary down the stairs from the tennis courts to Hyde Street. From across the street Chantal could see the points of Hillary's knuckles – white from gripping the handrail, because otherwise Tess would yank her to the ground. And down all the steps! This dog was dangerous.

Now might not be the best moment to bring up obedience school, but Chantal resolved to find the right time. She might send off to various dog schools for brochures. There was something about a perfectly disciplined dog, like Roger and Mrs. Ironside, that appealed to her aesthetic. "Do you have to leave the park now?" she called across the street to Hillary. "Or could you . . ."

"It's my day off!" Hillary called back. Tess still pulled, gagging on her collar. Hillary still clutched the rail for dear life. "I have lots of time."

Sitting on the lawn, Hillary told about the decision she had to make. About a dress. Chantal loved this kind of decision. "Why don't we go back to your apartment and you can model them for me?" When Hillary gasped No! she sounded horrified, as if Chantal had asked her to skin her dog. Chantal assumed the housekeeping was not good and said, "Never mind, just describe both dresses for me." She leaned in, all ears, as Hillary began.

"Ho-ho-*ho*!" They turned to see Ike standing above them, with just the puppy Molly. "Ready for the big night? Meg's been cooking since

119

Tuesday. Five courses. A different wine to go with each one. Appetizer? Escargots with artichokes in puff pastry!" He went through each course, punctuating his descriptions with a roll of the eyes or a whistle or an ooh-la-la. "If you play your cards right," he said to Chantal, "you too may someday win an invitation to dine Chez Meg." With Hillary he got serious. "I'm so pleased to introduce you to this guy. He's AOK. He's AOK. And you're a real knock-out." On his way to the other end of the park, he wiped an arc in the air with his palm. "You're a knock-out. A real knock-out!"

"Now I know I was right," Chantal said. "I was going to tell you to wear the dress you like best." She wanted to ask if Hillary could see at all without her glasses, just for one evening. No one could look really glamorous in glasses that thick. She decided to say nothing.

BECAUSE OF THE party tonight, Madame Leone wouldn't be able to meet her during the day, but Martine got on the bus and took her work to Russian Hill anyway. Her work fit neatly into her pocket: Another paperback. After *La Peste*, *L'Etranger*, and *La Chute*, she was glad to leave Albert Camus in the apartment and move backwards to the eleventh century. She sat sipping coffee at a table outside La Petite Treat, smoking and reading *Chanson de Roland* until she feared another *café noir* might destroy her. She took her mug and ashtray over to the sink and threw away her paper napkin.

Waiting for the cable car to pass before she could jay-walk, she noticed the man with three afghans under the awning of the Chinese grocery store. He had just one afghan today, the black puppy, and the puppy wasn't chasing a butterfly. The grocer had on a black watchcap and a jacket like the kind Marlon Brando wore in *On the Waterfront*. The man with the afghan wore the same satin Giants jacket he always wore, and the same baseball cap. His arms moved through the air with those big gestures of his, until the grocer handed him a mug of something, leaving him only one hand to talk with. Since she'd need a new pack of cigarettes in an hour anyway, Martine might as well go say *bonjour*. Close up, she could hear they weren't speaking English. The syllables sang like bamboo chimes.

"Hey!" the man with the afghan shouted. "It's the mademoiselle de Pai-ree. How's it going?"

She smiled. "Sorry, I don't speak English."

"How 'bout Mandarin? Cantonese?"

She shrugged with a grin. She was used to not understanding.

"Meet Ky." With a great, eloquent arm he presented her to the grocery store man like a master of ceremonies. "This is our guest from France."

"Your guest?"

"Yeah. My guest, your guest – our guest."

The grocery man nodded. His cheeks were red. He leaned into the store and took a thermos from the counter. "Tea?"

"Yes!" She could say a word.

Signaling just-a-minute, the grocery man left the store and stepped around the corner.

"Kitchen's in the apartment behind the store," the gravel-voiced man said. "Quickest way to get there is out the store door and through the front door of the apartment building."

Martine just smiled. She didn't have to say sorry I don't speak English again.

"You like San Francisco?" He wasn't going to give up. "San Francisco. You like?"

"San Francisco?"

"Yeah. You like it?"

Guessing, she said, "*C'est beau.*"

"Sorry, I don't speak French." He laughed. So did she. She got the joke!

The grocery man was back with a third mug, this one old, with a blue pattern. The tea he poured from the thermos was almost thin as water.

"Thank you." (Two more words!) She reached in her jeans and took out some bills. "Cigarettes? Camel?"

121

"No," the grocery man said. "No smoking. Smoking is bad. You shouldn't smoke."

Martine looked at the afghan man for a translation.

"He doesn't think you should smoke. No smo-king. Nice young girl like you . . ." He forced a cough and pounded his chest. "It'll ruin your health. – Give her a pack, Ky."

The two of them talked in Chinese for a couple of minutes. It must have been Chinese. It wasn't English. With a big sigh, Ky stepped into the store for a pack. "Bad," he said, shaking his head and taking the money.

MARTINE PUT HER face between bars of iron grillework to see through the window of the little antique clothing store. She moved her face from space to space between diamond-shaped bars to see all the wonderful things there were to see: the life-sized parrot made of tiny colored beads, a lightbulb glowing from inside; the grand Victorian piano shawl with thick embroidery and long silk fringe; the Egyptian wedding veil appliquéd with real silver – a contradiction of gossamer and weightiness; a beaded flapper dress, a poodle skirt, some ancient kimonos; and costume jewelry from the twenties, maybe, and the thirties and forties and fifties.

"Good afternoon," said a woman at her back, jingling a large ring of keys and moving the padlock that kept the grille closed. Beside her was a curly-eared spaniel on a bejeweled leash. The woman looked like a Gypsy, with a pile of black curls on top of her head, dangles of earrings brushing her shoulders, bracelets clacketing up both arms, and rows of necklaces draping her throat and bosom. She wore three skirts, in layers, and three pair of socks – multi-textured layers of hot colors and metallic knits – under her gold lamé heels. Shocking pink, parrot-green, apple-red, brilliant orange, canary-yellow, electric blue: She would waken the dead. And she had made up her eyes and skin with colors almost as dramatic as her costume. "Come in, won't you?"

Inside, every inch of wall was draped with something: Appalachian

122

quilts, Japanese wrapping cloths, a French tapestry, an old American flag with a lot fewer stars than Martine was used to; some Navajo rugs and Chinese textiles, parasols from China and from *fin-de-siècle* France. Lacy dresses and petticoats were pinned up on the walls, and lots of hats. Behind the ornate gold cash register hung a gilt-framed oil painting of a spaniel, looking like a portrait of the curly-eared spaniel that had just been led into the shop, now reclining in a fancily upholstered dog basket. Layered in this tiny space were antique dolls and thin-furred teddy bears and doll furniture. There were exotic shoes and beaded handbags. Martine went to the hat-rack.

"You'd look wonderful in this one," the woman said, plucking off a straw hat with a floppy brim and adjusting it on Martine's head. "Here's the mirror." Martine posed this way and that, then tried on a cloche. She tucked her voluminous gold hair under, which took some time.

"You need hoop earrings with that one." The woman clipped huge gold rings onto the girl's ears, studying. "I think some makeup would help." She dipped into her handbag. "Sit!"

Martine started to feel ashamed, dishonest, to take this woman's time when she had no intention of buying anything. To communicate the truth, she took out her wallet and opened the bill part to show only one dollar.

"Oh, don't worry. I have nothing else to do. This is fun. Sit!" She indicated the needlepoint chair. Martine obeyed. Who needed English?

Finishing with her pencils and brushes, the proprietress led Martine back to the mirror. *Mon dieu.* Who was that? She looked ready to star in an opera. She made faces like glamor shots.

"Try this on." The Gypsy-looking woman took a beaded flapper dress from the window. It fit perfectly. "Shoes!" Black silk with thick high heels and flat bows over the instep. "Maude Frison, Paris, 1926. They're only a little too big." She cut and folded some tissue paper to make padding inside the toes and heels and stood back to admire. "Twenty-three skiddoo."

Martine again took out her wallet to show the one bill.

123

"It's okay. It's fun to see you model. Try this one. This is a French opera coat, created for the opening of the Paris opera in 1932. The debut of art deco. It's woven with gold threads, you see? These flowers were painted on by hand. If you could buy it now, new, it would cost as much money as a Mercedes. Honestly."

Martine caught the words Paris and opera and money and Mercedes and jumped back some.

"Don't worry. Try it."

The gold threads with her gold hair.

Both women sighed. Martine pulled her wads of hair up on to her crown. She was elegant. It seemed sad to try anything else, but the shopowner took out a sheath of embroidered Chinese silk, mandarin collar, frog buttons. She held it up to Martine's reflection. "Nineteen forty-eight, just before the Revolution. That Chinese red looks wonderful with your complexion. Please!" She pointed to the brocade curtain of the dressing-room. "By the way, my name is Sybil." She held out her hand.

"Cybelle?" Martine said, taking the hand. "Martine."

"Hello, Martine."

The bell on the door tinkled, and Martine turned to see a tall man with fiery eyes and beautiful hair, leading a Welsh corgi. "Oh Philo!" Sybil seemed pleased, and Martine slipped behind the curtain with the Chinese dress, the sound of English in the air. When she stepped out, Sybil interrupted her conversation with the man to glance and shake her head no. She came over to take a four-inch fold of fabric between her fingers, to snug the dress to the hips. "Too big," she said.

"Too beeg." Martine could see. Too beeg. She took a very cold, very long dress of black lace from the rack.

"Oh yes. Try it."

From the dressing-room she heard the man in the outer room, quiet but excited. She opened the curtains to peep. He held a necklace up to the light. She closed the curtains quickly and started to work fastening the dress. The cash register rang, and the dainty bell at the door sounded.

124

Right away it tinkled again. When she'd finally done up all the little jet buttons, she stepped out and saw Chantal.

As foreign words cheeped through the shop, Sybil looked confused, then happy. Chantal took a moment out to introduce the two in English and French, to find out they'd already met, and then the two Frenchwomen flew back into French.

For weeks Chantal had been thinking about an evening bag in the window, mother-of-pearl, that snapped shut like a big shell. She switched back and forth between languages to include both women in her thought of how it might be nice to have something from another era tonight, to go with her completely contemporary outfit. What was Martine going to wear?

Martine had a nice top to wear with her jeans.

Oh no, not jeans to a party at Madame Leone's.

Sorry. That was all Martine had. Her *petit ami* Manuel had a suit, because of his job, but Martine always wore jeans. She was comfortable in jeans.

Keeping Sybil apprised of the conversation, Chantal began looking through the racks for the right thing. This was play. Martine held up the flapper dress, the shoes and the cloche.

"Oh yes! Try them!" As Martine disappeared, Chantal spoke English with Sybil. She had an idea. "Okay," Sybil said. "Fifteen dollars."

When Martine stepped from behind the curtain, Chantal and Sybil clapped. Chantal told Martine it was all arranged – she'd rent the outfit. Her treat. "You just have to bring it back tomorrow by noon."

Martine could not accept.

"It will be an honor to Madame Leone." They argued, in French, with Sybil breaking in with "you must" until Martine was worn down. The only stipulation was that she would go home and get a traveler's check. No no no, Chantal would pay. Her husband was doing quite well, he was a C.E.O.! When she tried to explain what that was, Martine got mad, "It's even in all the new French dictionaries!" Chantal apologized but stuck to the point: When Martine was older and doing well she could

125

indulge in treats for someone else. This was for Chantal herself, and Madame Leone.

They finished by splitting the cost, with Sybil chipping in five. "But not the hat," Chantal said. "Maybe we could put your hair in a knot, back here." Martine stood obediently at the mirror as Chantal played. "You will have to come up to our apartment for a few minutes, so I can fix it right. We can take a few strands here to make little spit curls."

"This!" Sybil opened a glass cabinet and took out a black ribbon with a small medallion of rhinestones in the center and tied it around Martine's forehead.

"Perfection," said Chantal.

Manuel would be astonished.

WHEN HILLARY HAD a day off, Tess had a holiday. Today Hillary felt terrible, because she had cheated Tess. Chantal had got so enthused about tomorrow's dinner party at Ike's ("I wish *we* had a man who would be right for you") that she'd talked Hillary into coming up *"chez nous"* with her dresses. "Sorry we can't invite Tess. Our apartment is not, how do you say it, puppy-proof?" Hillary felt awful. "I'll be *right back*," she told Tess. "In *just a little while*." Judging from the hurt expression, Tess wasn't learning these key phrases. And Hillary meant them honestly, when she said them, except that when she got to Chantal's, Chantal was working on a hairdo for the girl who didn't speak English. It seemed hours until she said *au revoir*, and then Chantal handed Hillary her mirror and tested a bunch of looks, and almost forced her to take a shower and use her special French shampoo. Luckily Chantal's taste in hairdos was plain, like Hillary's, but Chantal had huge rollers and a hairdryer that fit like a quilted shower cap. Hillary hadn't set her hair since middle school, but Chantal swore it would look smoother and fuller and more like a party.

It actually was amazing. When the hair was brushed out, she didn't look transformed, she recognized herself, but she looked better. Chantal tried just a touch of her makeup on Hillary and said she looked "*séduisante*." ("What?") "Seductive." (What?)

So not only had Hillary left Tess alone all afternoon, she'd made a date with Leslie to go to another movie. Luckily when they got to the park there was a pine-cone right at the entrance to the promenade, and that toss-and-fetch game could tire Tess out fast. She threw the pine-cone, and out of the bushes rushed the corgi, beating Tess to the pine-cone. Oh no.

Hillary flew to the bench just before Philo appeared on the path. She hadn't seen him since that day at the laundromat. "Hello." She tried to sound cheery and nonchalant.

"Well don't you look nice."

She looked down at her sweatshirt, pushed up the wrists, then remembered her hair. And the makeup. "No jumping!" she yelled. "Tess, no jumping!" Tess had grown so tall she could lick Philo Righi's nose. (Pretty soon she'd be able to lick Hillary's.)

"Oh, it's all right," he said, stroking the dog, who stood with her paws on his shoulders, whipping her tail, kissing his eyebrows. "Hi, baby," he drawled into Tess's face, both hands caressing the soft puppy fur. "To tell you the truth," he said to Hillary, "I love this dog." His fingers were long, going over and over the silky coat.

This man *always* made Hillary dizzy.

He sat down on the bench next to her, and the two sat in silence watching the short dog chase the tall dog. Hillary pretended to be as peaceful as she would be if she had all the time in the world. "It's your night off, isn't it?" he asked. "Mine too. No alarm clock, no necktie, no anorexics."

She tensed. Everyone thought she was one. Then she looked over at his face, so relaxed, and felt sure he didn't think she was.

The dogs chased each other for a few minutes, then ran over together for attention. His corgi put her head on Hillary's foot, Tess jumped up on the bench next to him and kissed his face, banging her tail on the bench back.

"So what did you do this morning, girls?" he asked the dogs, his long

127

arms easily reaching both heads, to pet them with equal affection. "I was out from lunch on. Did you have Tess over for tea and cucumber sandwiches? Did you girls go shopping?"

He was wearing jeans and old scuffed moccasins, and his feet were planted far apart, one knee pointing in the direction of Marin, the other down toward Market Street. It was so masculine to sit so open-legged. The legs were long, and the kneecaps, under the jeans, so thick and strong. She hoped he didn't notice the little pinpoint knees about to pierce through her jeans.

"Did you girls go downtown and try on the new Valentinos at Saks?"

Hillary laughed like a little girl on her daddy's knee.

"My little gal," Philo told Hillary, "had to go to the Pretty-But-Plump Department. Tess has a model's figure. She could wear anything."

Hillary ached to stay here and laugh with Philo Righi. She sneaked a look at her watch and gasped.

"You have a date?" He looked disappointed.

It made Hillary ache even more, to make him sad. But she was so late she couldn't even consider a cordial goodbye. "Sorry." She got up.

"Oh," he said. "I have another damn black-tie party." Still sitting open-legged, he ducked his curly head and rubbed his big hands over the back of it before he turned his eyes back up to her, watching her grab her dog's collar. "Leash?" he said. He picked it off the bench and clipped it on for her. "Sometimes I get sick of parties," he said. "Especially black tie."

"Oh, me too." (Listen to her lie!) "Me too." She took Tess's leash from his hand and shot off without looking back. Otherwise he'd walk her home and find out her date was Leslie, waiting in the car.

Soirée

IF EVER THERE was a day to obliterate all consciousness of lower back pain, this was it. In addition to his scheduled appointments, there had been three unanticipated events. Two had involved patients he'd taken care of for more than a third of a century, whose office visits had come to be like having someone in to tea. Today both of their visits were crises, and the usual pleasure was ruined by anxiety. One, though threatening for the moment, was easily diagnosed: Immediate surgery was imperative, but there was a high probability the outcome would be excellent. The other story was not so happy. Plus, there had been a death, not unexpected, but unexpected today. The woman was not quite thirty, with two small children and an economically unsound husband. In spite of the husband, who was, to put it candidly, a pain in the arse, Rayford had grown to feel for the family. He had a struggle getting ample voice, when the time came to inform the husband – and then two attendants had to be summoned to lead the hysterical man from the room.

When he saw his last patient out at seven-fifteen, pain stabbed his lower back with the force of a pitchfork manned by the Almighty. It took his breath away. With a weak hand, he picked up the receiver to call Anna. He deeply regretted his decision to let her down for the evening, but he was by now in a state unfit for society. He knew that she would forgive him and trusted, even, that she would invite him again one day, under better circumstances.

"Hello? – Oh, Rayford." She spoke in an agitated whisper. She was clearly not herself. "I'm glad you're not here. All the guests came early – actually rode up all at once in the elevator. And you should see how dressed up they are. It's tense. They seemed happy enough at the door, but then a let-down set in as soon as they sat down in the living-room. The conversation is nothing but lulls. I wish I could just ask them all to go home. I'm sure that's what they're wishing, too."

He hadn't expected this.

"Rayford? I hope you won't feel insulted if I suggest that you take a raincheck. I've already told them you aren't feeling well – that you have a bug, I said – and, honestly, you'll be better off home by the fire with Romeo. I'll be more comfortable myself, if you stay home with Romeo."

"Nonsense!" He heard his voice boom. "I only called to say I'll be more than a little tardy, because of unanticipated duties in the service of medicine. And there are yet some details of dress, the dog, and so forth. So I suggest that you serve dinner and keep a plate for me in the warming oven. Regrettably, I'll need a liberal hour and a half."

As she had guests to attend, the objections and counter-objections were blessedly brief. "*A bientôt*," he heard his voice say, sounding as if the back pain were gone. Which it was not.

After pulling his nicked but trusty Subaru into the garage, he limped, both hands on the small of his back, to the unfinished plywood door at the back. He undid the padlock and, to get some light, pulled the chain that hung from the ceiling. The bare bulb might not have been handsome, but it did the job. This was the wine cellar. The organization had none of the efficiency of the Dewey decimal system: The cases were piled in at random, like giant blocks tossed into an oversized toy trunk. He suspected the whereabouts of what he wanted and was nonetheless put out to confirm that yes indeed, each of the two vintages he had decided upon resided at the bottom of their stacks. This presented a problem to the lower spine, but since it was essential to have two reds aged twenty-five years or more – a claret from Bordeaux and a California Cabernet for comparison, he started at the top of each tower and with caution moved boxes to form other towers until he reached the desired cases and extricated a bottle from each. If he had had adequate notice of the doings, he would have taken the wines out seventy-two hours ago to let them rest corks up and drop their sediment to the floors of their bottles, so that with careful pouring there would be no need for decanting. That plan would have been flawed in any case, though, he realized, because in transporting the bottles up the hill to Anna's some jostling would be inevitable.

Climbing the zigzagged complex of back stairs from the garage, he turned the light on at each landing and heeded the reminder by each switch: CONSERVE ENERGY! TURN OFF LIGHTS WHEN NOT IN USE! Twenty-two years ago he'd used a thick black magic marker to advise his tenants thusly and the block letters had lost none of their boldness. At the top stair he heard the tap of Romeo's feet crossing the kitchen, and after a two-minute greeting, Rayford let the dog out to run down to the garden. After scooping kibble into the dog dish, the doctor went to the shelf for a glass and measured two jiggers of bourbon into a small orange juice glass, adding a squeeze of water from the Alhambra dispenser. No ice. The lower back pain had gained some intensity, if that could be possible, but he far preferred whiskey to codeine. He took his bourbon down the long hall into the bathroom, and after a moment's undressing, he stepped with his glass into the shower. Should he shampoo? He was so late as it was, he might as well be hanged for a sheep as a lamb. The Englishman would be there, and, more to the point, his pretty wife Chantal. A shine to the hair could be a social asset. He'd be in need of social assets this evening. He put his head under the nozzle and felt such comfort to his back from the warm water freely pouring that he wondered how he would bring himself to conclude this shower.

Of course, life was full of sensual tricks, various carrots to put before the horse: There was so often another pleasure to look forward to. His inducement to get out of the shower at last was his favorite towel, the gift of a patient (long dead now, unfortunately) – a towel full and fluffy but rough, almost as rough as a loofah. Massaged and dried, still warm and

131

safe within the stall (a precaution he always recommended to patients, for avoiding chill), he carried his towel and what was left of his bourbon into the airy and mirrored main part of the bathroom, where he commenced drying between the toes. Thank God for the steam on the mirror, occluding his reflection. He well knew there was a small bowl, rather flabby, around his navel. It was less than what was referred to as a potbelly, but the word bowlbelly hadn't been coined. Subtle as it was, he didn't like it. And he had what could be called a gardener's tan, extending only to the collar line and the wrist lines. All other skin had the blue-white hue of skimmed milk. The hairs on his chest had grown scant. A clear mirror would have minced no words in announcing once again that he was not the hunk the young girls sought.

Dressed, in fresh shirt and bow tie and suspenders, the mirror had a sweeter tale to tell. Nature had given him height and a broad, well-designed skeleton. With certain parts covered, he appeared to be a distinguished specimen. Putting on his jacket, he felt the pocket to confirm the presence of his complete Swiss Army knife. (Don't leave home without it!) He got his keys and his two bottles of wine and started down the back stairs to the garden. Halfway down it occurred to him that he hadn't asked if Anna had a funnel and a cheesecloth, for decanting. Much as his lower back disliked ascending the flights of stairs yet again, he went up to find these items in his kitchen. And then it was back down to the yard, a jab in the back each time he set weight on a foot. It grated on his conscience to keep the garden floodlit, expending thousands of extra kilowatts each month, but the lights were a necessary security precaution for his tenants and himself. The type of floodlight set off by movement simply did not have the same deterrent effect to the trespasser as lighting that remained constant and visible. The light helped him select five of the most stupendous rhododendrons in bloom, and he used the scissors on the Swiss Army knife to cut them for Anna before departing his property by way of the garage door.

THE BLOCK FROM his building to hers was a steep one, and normally it gave him pleasure, as he felt his motor kick up and start to purr. Perhaps he felt out of step tonight, with a wine bottle plus funnel in one hand and a wine bottle plus flowers in the other. The rhythm of walking was easier with just the spade. After this day, with the back pain and an excess of stress, the hill was a battle against defeat. The bourbon had helped the spinal pain, but no drug was without side effects. Bourbon, when one was fatigued already, didn't do much for the cardio-respiratory system.

For once he was almost glad to see, just up the hill on his side of the street, the dreadful fellow in the blood-colored jacket; because in order to avoid the displeasure of meeting him on the sidewalk, he'd have to cross the street – creating a flat jay-walking path to the other side and another flat jay-walk back, once the wretched creature had passed. Interrupting the vertical with a relief of horizontal helped him get his breath back. Nonetheless, as he rang Anna's bell he gave a little prayer of thanks that elegant urban buildings like this always had elevators.

At the far end of the lobby an Italianate fountain, surrounded by plantings of ferns and violets, tossed sparklets into the light. The marble floor gleamed, a great grand Persian rug in the center. A Flemish tapestry adorned one wall, reflected on its opposite by a large antique mirror. Rayford checked his bow tie, stuck one bottle in a pocket, and freed a hand to open his jacket and see that his suspenders were straight. Ready, he walked with as little limp as possible to the elevator. The carpet inside was red, and on one wall was another antique mirror, flattering to the complexion. From the column of six small, polished brass plates, each with a family name engraved in script, he chose the top one, Leone.

When the back panel of the elevator slid open, without a sound, Anna's private entry hall was revealed, with a needlepoint rug on the shined wood floor and identical Queen Anne chairs on either side of a marble table whose pedestal was a cupid. A silver samovar filled with garden roses sat on the table, and the wall behind it was a patchwork of botanical drawings in gold frames. Anna appeared with a red checkered apron over a silk kimono, a blue and yellow oven mitt on one hand. "*Bonsoir!*" Her face had that radiance it got sometimes. He was suddenly glad he had come. She studied the labels of the wines he presented, her merry black eyes popping. Perhaps she too was a connoisseur of wines. But no, perhaps not. No doubt anyone would be impressed with labels bearing such dates. He hoped his gift was not ostentatious. In French, he explained that he had been collecting wines since the late 1950s, and that this was an occasion that deserved an honor.

Two of the guests he had met, though not so gloriously attired. The understatement of Chantal's pearls on pearl-colored silk showed Rayford that she was, in a manner of speaking, an artist. He noted the vintage mother-of-pearl handbag, shaped like a shell, that rested on the arm of her chair, and mentally gave a thumbs-up. God is in the details. He was introduced to Martine, a little dream of a flapper, and Manuel, a handsome youth in a loose Italian suit and ribbon of necktie. He admired the unbridled imagination of young people today. Or was that young people of yesterday? It did seem that many of the young people he saw this year looked like cookie cutter kids, varying mainly in the number and placement of tattoos and piercings. The young people present at this soirée had originality, and he looked forward to conversing with them; but his immediate interest was in the kitchen.

At Anna's beckoning he poured himself a light drink this time and replenished the guests' glasses. And then, "Corkscrew?"

"*Mais parles français!*" she reminded him.

He would have liked to obey, but for the life of him he couldn't remember the French word for corkscrew. He was saved by remembering the Swiss Army knife in his pocket, whose corkscrew had served him in many another crunch. Luckily, he did remember the French word for decanter; and though Anna didn't know it so could not answer his enquiry, he looked through the shelves and found two.

The duties of sommelier and bartender fulfilled, he folded his jacket and laid it across the stool, observing Anna tediously mincing garlic. "My dear lady," he said in French, rolling up his sleeves. "Allow me to show you a trick I learned in Paris, where I followed a special two-week cookery course for tourists and dilettantes." (Dilettante was a blessedly easy word to translate into French.) "What they did was – would you be so kind as to hand me that knife? – or, if you have a larger one? The biggest cleaver in your kitchen." She fished through the drawer to unearth a tool with the delicacy of a sledgehammer, or an axe, which she told him she'd bought the week she'd thought she might try *cuisine chinoise*. "Well, this might be too big, but it might work very well indeed. First. To peel the garlic." He laid the flat of the cleaver on the clove and smashed the blade with the butt of his fist. "See? One thump and the skin is loose as a chemise." Securing the peeled clove under the blade again, he raised the heel of his fist for a mighty blow. When the clove slipped out and soared across the room, he heroically caught it – demonstrating an athleticism that amazed himself as much as it amazed Anna. With repeated whams, the little clove fell into a rough state of smithereens. "Now. Some salt. Thank you. You see? You pile the garlic with salt and press down with the flat of the blade. Like this. Squished garlic!" He said "squish" in English. Who knows? The word is so onomatopoeic that perhaps it's what the French say too. He kept that thought to himself, because he could not translate onomatopoeic, and two shows of ignorance in two sentences would be more shame than he was willing to display. "You see how it doesn't hold together? It will diffuse" (he guessed at *diffusir* – she'd never know the difference) "—it will almost liquify." Bang! Bang! The garlic was still in rather large hunklets. "Perhaps another tap or two." Whop! Whop! He couldn't seem to get it as diffused and almost liquefied as it should have been, but after all, a great clump of garlic in the mouth was really not as repugnant as they said it was. "Butter? Bread knife? – I find it preferable to slice the loaf lengthwise, like this, and then to slice partway through the crust horizontally, at two-inch intervals, so that each person can tear off a piece shaped like a little boat, hull of crust, interior of softer, buttery-garlicky crumbs. Mmm. Now. Before we melt the butter and crisp the top in the oven, do you have some herbs to sprinkle? And perhaps some Parmesan and paprika? The paprika adds a festive touch. I've experimented: I've offered half with paprika, half without, all in the same basket, and do you know that every guest always chooses the bread with the paprika until all the red-topped pieces are gone?"

Rattling through the spice bottles Anna came up with nothing except cayenne. "*Quel désastre!*" They laughed. He went through the bottles himself. How could there be a home without paprika? "Oh well. We'll try it next time."

No cheese, either. From the looks of things, cooking wasn't Anna's long suit. "You must keep Parmesan in the fridge at all times. Low on butterfat, a gold-mine of calcium – does wonders for a salad, a soup – its usefulness goes far beyond spaghetti."

The ice in the living-room must have thawed. The sounds were lively. Their friends seemed to be having a wonderful time without them.

Anna tore lettuce leaves and seemed a bit panicky. For one thing, the sleeves of her kimono made any task a messy one – even just transferring water from faucet to saucepan. Wasn't the point of such sleeves to indicate that the wearer was of a class above work? Poor choice of costume, for a cook. And if he had been the host here, these details would have been taken care of long before the first guest rang the bell.

"Is this real butter?" he asked, blending it with the garlic.

"It is," she admitted guiltily to the doctor.

"Excellent! These people are French, they'll taste the difference. I myself happen to be of the persuasion that butter is more healthful than margarine for physiological as well as psychological reasons. And given the changes of 'knowledge' the medical field achieves from one year to the next, each year's discoveries canceling out the last, it seems to me the only constant is that butter tastes better. Now what, may I ask, have you planned for the main course?"

"Salmon. I put it on the grill a minute before you arrived."

"Oh, *mon dieu*. Oh, *mon dieu*." He tried to calm himself. "Salmon is done almost the instant you pass it over the flame. I'd better rescue it. Spatula?" Hang speaking French. This was an emergency.

Out on the balcony he was relieved to see the salmon was not steaks

136

or fillets but a whole fish. The coals were quite low. It was possible this hadn't cooked through to sawdust. A slit with the Swiss Army knife – they were in luck! He would need two spatulas to turn it. What she really should have is one of those wire contraptions to clamp around the fish. When was her birthday? A search through her kitchen revealed no second spatula. He would make do with the cleaver. He had to admit he enjoyed the inventiveness such necessity inspired in him. "Are the plates warm?" He shouldn't have asked. He should simply have gone to the shelf and placed a stack in the oven. "Platter?" He found one to slide in on top of the plates.

"I have some fresh lemon thyme sprigs," Anna said with meekness. "I also put lemon slices and a bunch of the thyme in the cavity."

He took in unspoken sentences as she focused her eyes on his, using her oven mitt to wipe her brow. What her face said was that she knew she was deficient as an organizer but hoped to be given at least one point for the lemon thyme.

He hadn't realized what a trial this meal must have been for her. He wanted to put both hands on her shoulders, but of course he put the brakes on that. "*Superbe! Thym citron!*" Her cheeks, already pink from effort, blushed pinker, apparently with pride. Again his impulse toward her, as it was so often with people, was warm and bodily. For the physical encouragement he instinctively wanted to indulge, he substituted his voice: "Our guests are in for a pleasure sublime."

AT THE TABLE people did not talk about the wines aged twenty-six years, they talked about what they'd been doing at this time twenty-six years ago. For Americans over thirty (e.g., Anna and himself), memory was aided by the fact that 1976 had been the bicentennial of our nation's independence. Martine and Manuel couldn't remember a thing about it, of course, because they hadn't been born; but their parents had been doing things. They talked about that. Anna's Joey had been just a little younger than Josh (did they know Josh?) and during the super-duper fireworks that Fourth he'd raced his skateboard down the crookedest

137

street in the world and climbed Telegraph Hill to shoot down the Filbert Steps, breaking his collarbone. Chantal and Nigel vaguely remembered the American bicentennial; they talked about their respective childhoods, in England and France. When it came to Rayford's turn, he was careful to say just enough to entertain and nothing that would betray a sense of loss.

Nonetheless, the topic had obliged him to refer in conversation to "my dear late wife, Jenny." Perhaps if he had spoken of her more frequently, in company, the sound of her name spoken aloud, in his own voice, would not flood him with emotion. As it was, he had voiced it and entered the world of the past. When Chantal went into a little story about something in Paris, Rayford's mind departed from the group for a moment, to indulge a reverie of moments as precious as they were irretrievable.

How he had ached with disappointment for Jenny, as it became apparent that he was not able to give her what she wanted most in life. Of course he couldn't blame himself. His sperm tested out healthy and full of life. If it had been now, they would have tried *in vitro*. As it was, they were given slim chances, and she seized on the narrow range of possibility with all the hope in God's universe. She didn't want to adopt, she wanted *his* child, her child. She continued to believe it would happen. His role was to soothe and shield – and to distract her with pleasures. It wasn't until he'd lost her that he realized: Working so actively for her happiness had protected him from his own grief. Missing out on the pleasures of having a little girl like her, or a boy like himself, was like living only part of a life.

Her death couldn't have come as more of a shock, three weeks after her fortieth birthday. When the obituary printed her age, gasps went out among acquaintances: "Forty? I always assumed she was younger than me!" It was the first case of lamiodemia to be recorded in the United States in more than twenty years – and to date one of the last. What nearly crippled Rayford, losing Jenny, was the loss of someone to take care of. How odd it was, he thought, that it was sadness that had contributed passion to his happiness.

In fact, he'd almost forgotten how much he'd enjoyed the married state. He'd had many years to forget. And in those years, he'd grown to relish the single state.

Underneath his amiable demeanor, he was a bit of a crotchet, enamored of his day-to-day ways. His sister, and even some of his fellow physicians, had occasionally broken the rules of etiquette (in his opinion) and, as they said, "shared with him" their hopes that he would find a new wife – a younger woman. He wasn't interested in finding a younger woman, but he had a hard time getting interested in anyone his age. "Women my age," he confided to a colleague, "always seem to sit in a particular position, with their arms around their purses." His family and associates held firm that he should pursue, if not a young wife, a youngish wife. It would be good for him, they said. A younger woman would keep him on his toes.

The trouble was, he was on his toes too much as it was. In his professional life and his personal life he was forced to strive constantly. Most days he was under stress to be at his best twelve hours a day. Sometimes fourteen. If he checked his watch now (which he certainly would not be so rude as to do), he'd probably be able to chart fifteen hours of either working or keeping up appearances in the course of a single day. Although he didn't feel tired at the moment, he should! The salvation from his long hours of planned activity was that in his solitude, what few hours there were of it, he was allowed to slump. To tread about flatfooted. No one was looking.

At any rate, he had never longed for the arduous climb of setting up a new intimacy. As he mused, swirling his glass and taking the taste of 1976 into his mouth and body, he lifted his gaze and saw Anna across the table, in deep study of his face.

His reaction was to feel violated. He looked away instantly.

THE GUESTS, AND the hostess, stuck to the French-only rule when it was easy for them, which was up to forty per cent of the time. The chief offender was Nigel. "This is a dinner party, not a French class. Chantal, would you go so good as to translate for Martine while I try briefly to hold up my end of the conversation." Chantal did so, in a whisper. Rayford noticed that when a long stretch of English was spoken, fatigue registered on Manuel's face. It was a comfort to see that even someone so young enjoyed the challenge of a new language at first, but grew tired.

ANNA SUGGESTED THAT they have their coffee in the living-room, in front of the fire. She put on an Edith Piaf record. When he took the poker in hand and stooped to stir the logs, pain shot from his back through his entire nervous system so forcefully that it took great strength to resist a collapse.

"Rayford," Anna called softly, tiptoeing in from the kitchen. "Rayford, I think there's something wrong with my espresso pot."

"Ah!" With an agony, he straightened into a position that felt much better – and handed the poker to Nigel. "I have a knack with these kitchen gadgets." Next to the stove, he inspected the Italian volcano pot, which Anna had disassembled. It looked fine.

"It's been so long since I've used this I just can't remember how to fit all the parts back together."

He eyed her with suspicion. The look of helplessness on her face was surely an exaggeration. He couldn't decide how to react to what was obviously a deception: The pot was black with everyday use. He squinted at her, feeling a composite of anger – at having been made the fool – and of a grudging understanding of her understanding. He disliked hypocrisy and manipulation and coddling and patronization. Through his scowl at her sheepish face, he recognized her motive: Empathy. He gave in to a smile. "Ah, my lumbago."

They laughed. He made a flourish of measuring the coffee, ground almost to a powder, and of twisting the top half of the contraption to closure. He and Anna waited for the explosive sound they both knew heralded coffee! and re-entered the living-room, she carrying the tray of demitasse cups and he the pot so black.

With her little finger pointed up, Chantal sipped and laughed with

Manuel about a French cartoonist they both liked. Martine, the flapper, was talking to Nigel and enjoying yet another cigarette. Moving toward the balcony with Anna, Rayford congratulated himself for suppressing the anti-smoking lectures he'd felt coming on repeatedly, through the course of the evening. He would find a more appropriate moment for a message from the American Lung Association.

He was admiring how Martine took care to pronounce each syllable slowly as she spoke to Nigel – when some words stopped him: She said, "*Quand je meurs.*" When I die.

Rather serious. But he saw wild twinkling in her eyes. He had to hear the rest of her sentence. "When I die, I want to go like my grandmother, peacefully in her sleep. Not screaming, like the passenger in her car."

Rayford exploded, laughing.

Nigel sat there kneading his forehead. Was it the word passenger, or the word screaming? Anna too was baffled. He translated it for her and Anna laughed until her mascara melted.

On the balcony she said (mostly in French), "The moon looks like a crooked smile." Rayford knew the word for bent and used it: "*Une sourire courbée.*" He'd have said lopsided, if he'd known the French for it.

The air had a chill that went beyond refreshingly cool into painfully cold. Still smiling inside from the surprise of Martine's joke, he thought about using a hand to pull his hostess's shoulder close to him. It had been some time since he'd felt another person's ninety-eight-point-six against his side. Instead he said, in English, "The moon looks like a Cheshire cat."

Josh

THE MOON LOOKED like the smile his sister had carved in their jack-o-lantern last October. It was a tilted slit, a crazy smirk. He sat in the usual spot, at the top of the cyclone fence that cut up the cliff to the tennis courts. The tree he sat on was way chill, with a low branch growing along the ground, like a bench. He waited, all eyes and ears. The buddies were late.

Looked like ole Mrs. Leone was boogying. The lights were on all over her floor. Once in a while someone walked by the window holding a glass, or a couple would step out on the balcony. Josh raised his brown bag and gave them a toast, before unscrewing the cap inside and taking a swig. This was rye whiskey. He hadn't tried it before. It tasted pretty bad. But he'd already killed a bottle and a half of vodka these last two weeks since his dad had left for Taiwan, and the old man might notice if another was gone. Or, he might not notice. Even odds. Josh took chances, but he had his limits. He'd heard the saying "tempt fate," and it was a good one.

It was something to celebrate, Friday. Friday was the only chill night of the week, except Saturday. Most kids' folks wouldn't let them do squat on the other nights. It was a drag. Especially when his dad and his girlfriend were in Europe or Mexico or Taiwan or the Caribbean, and he was free. Ten days ago they'd touched ground after St. Thomas and had flown right off to the business in Asia. His dad said he'd loafed too much in St. Thomas and had to pay the price by shooting right off to Taiwan

142

for hard labor. He called up a couple of times a week, probably just to find out if Josh and his sister were still living there. Sometimes he called before five in the morning. It seemed kind of stupid that he couldn't remember what time it was for other people. So far Josh hadn't said anything. Some parents didn't take to suggestions from the younger generation. But it was a shock when the phone rang in the middle of the night. He should be used to it, but his first thought was always that someone was dead. Sometimes his sister answered. He got up anyway. She was only twelve. He was going on fifteen. Under eleven months to go. Sometimes when his dad called, Josh was still a little out of it from earlier in the evening. Not usually. He only got wasted a couple of nights a week. And when he was blotto, he could fake it.

Sometimes he thought about going to live with his mom in Arizona. But he hated her boyfriend. Her boyfriend hated him even more. Worse than his dad's girlfriend hated him.

Anyhow, it was time to boogy. Him and Spike. Spike had some good weed, from inside sources. He wanted to come over to Josh's house, but no way. For one thing his sister was home. More to the point, his dad and his girlfriend were coming back Sunday and his dad had a nose that could smell stuff that was gone a week ago. But in the park they were cool.

He didn't want anyone to get wind of this, but the truth was Josh hadn't had a lot of weed experience. Booze was easy. His dad had such a load in his bar he never noticed a bottle gone. But he was one of those fogies who lived in another century and didn't approve of dope. It kind of turned your stomach when he got drunk and slurred his words and got going on how grateful he was he'd never gotten into drugs. That was the signal for Josh to have to go to the bathroom.

This was like being an Indian, up here. Native American. Hiding out, waiting for a pow-wow. Little sticks cracked way down past the hedge by the monument. Feet.

"Hey South!" Spike yelled in a stage-whisper. Coming into view, he kept running.

143

"Hey Pokey!" Josh waved the brown bag with the bottle in it. They didn't use their tags in public, but this wasn't public. Anyhow, Josh was safe. He couldn't get caught now. He wasn't a writer any more.

Spike got close and kick-socked Josh – just kidding. Josh gave a karate chop (Hi-yah!) and took a second out to nest the bag in a pile of leaves before flying forward with his best foot. They had a hell of good fight – not really touching, but showing good form. To talk, though, Josh had to change to boxing. Left hook and fast footwork. "So which do you want to do first? Drink or smoke?"

"How 'bout both at once? And then for dessert – brownies. Guaranteed." Spike unzipped his jacket to show the secret pockets on each side. Out of one pocket he flashed a cube wrapped in aluminium foil. From the other he flashed a silver cigarette box. "Hallucinogenic Izmir." He swore it. "The real thing. None of that Pataluma Green shit." He was trying to get the silver box open. "This is worse than the child-proof cap."

"Careful, man!" Josh grabbed the cigarette box because he trusted himself more. "There." The magic click.

"Now we gotta process it," Spike said. "Gimme that bag." He went to work, making a neat pile of seeds and a stack of flakes. When Josh saw how it was done he pitched in.

"Now the papers." Spike reached into his inside pocket for his packet of ZigZags. It looked like he felt great because he was the one who knew how to do this. "Got matches?"

"Me?" Josh said. "No."

"Well you knew we were going to get stoned, I thought you'd . . ."

Josh shrugged, apologized.

"I always end up having to carry the ball." Spike was irritated. "God, I'd think you'd take some responsibility, feel some sense of par-ticipation." Spike sounded like Josh's dad.

Josh got an idea: "Searchlight's open till ten! I'll make a match run." He took off for the store. Running down Hyde Street it hit him that it might be illegal to sell matches to kids under eighteen. Was it? Then outside the tapas place, he noticed a smoker. She was puffing away and waving her cigarette, talking to that girl he'd seen in the park – the one who reminded him of the skinniest skyscraper in the world. He picked out a few words. Like Oscar. Must've been a movie. "Oh, Leslie!" (So the smoker's name was Leslie.) "Nobel Prize," yada-yada, "schizophrenia . . ." They must've been talking about *A Beautiful Mind*. He saw that last weekend. He waited politely for a break in the conversation. "Schizophrenia" again. It had to be *A Beautiful Mind*. Scary subject, schizophrenia. Finally the skyscraper girl looked over and saw him. "I was wondering," he asked the smoker. "Got an extra matchbook?" She dug in her purse and found one. Cool.

SATURDAY MORNING. HE was frying. He'd gone home around three or four, but you know how it is with drugs. The world was spinning. He tried to get enough breath, but he couldn't. He took in air so fast he gagged, but he couldn't get enough. He sat on the bed and started laughing. It wasn't fun to laugh like this. He couldn't stop. It felt like drowning. His sister came in, in her white flannel nightgown with kittens on it, and it seemed like she was moving in slow motion. Not smooth, but like in the movies when the projector breaks. Her face was out of a horror flick. He laughed till he got a choking fit.

"Please." She was bawling. "Josh. Please."

He started bawling.

THE BUTTONS ON his shirt were too big for the buttonholes. He couldn't get them out. His sister tried to help and he pushed her away.

Out. He had to get out. It wasn't safe in this place.

Top of Filbert. Street like a wall. He blew down so fast the soles of his shoes slapped his butt. Don't panic. Don't panic. What you have to do is not panic.

The streetlights heaved. Straight down. Dangerous. Every thud of his shoes he saw his body topple like a cart off its wheels. Parts split off in all directions. He hit flat land. Red light. Ran through. Up. Coit Tower. A weirdo plunged. Chased. Armed.

Air to his lungs not so easy.

Get me out of here! Reeboks flew.

Up. Home stretch. Hyde. One light on. In the window, a fairy princess walked back and forth, holding a mirror. God, his sideache! He stopped, lungs heaving. It was the skyscraper girl! In a princess dress. What did you call that? Gossamer? It was the color of cloud wisps in a sunset. She was walking back and forth in the middle of the night and looking in a mirror. Like Snow White's stepmother. He was hallucinating!

Get me home. Get me home. I'm coming down with schizophrenia.

Inside, his sister, running to the door, tears on her face. "Joshy. Please, please go to sleep."

"Okay okay." He dived under the covers. Stayed forever, shivering. Tried to sleep. Tried so hard it hurt inside. No point. He had schizophrenia.

Through the cracks in the blinds, a little dark gray in the sky. He let out a laugh. "Time to get up!" His laugh was like in an echo chamber. Turn down the volume!

Another sound. Dad?

The furnace.

Footsteps. Footsteps?

Hyde Street. Nothing open. Except way down at Ling's – the awning cranked open. He ran down, put a quarter in the gum machine. Wouldn't fit. Tears shot out from his eyes.

The old Chinese guy with the leather jacket and the knit cap looked scared of him. Seeing the fear, he tried to make his sobs shut up. Come inside, the Chinese guy said, unscrewing the top of a thermos and handing him a steamy cup. Josh hated tea. He gulped it down, crying.

Outside, the piano guy came up with the shag dogs. Ike. He lifted a *Chronicle*, dug money out of his pocket. Saw the tears. Looked a long time. Said, "Hey." Put his *Chronicle* on the counter and put both hands on Josh's shoulders. "Hey."

Josh honked and took in air, loud like a baby. He choked out the truth: "I'm having a nervous breakdown."

Ike looked scared. His hands gripped harder. Said nothing. Then he said, "This isn't a nervous breakdown. This isn't a nervous breakdown."

How did he know? Through tear wobble, Josh looked him hard in the face, to find out.

"You're gonna be okay." He seemed to know what he was talking about. "You're going to be okay. You're going to be okay. Just, something is wrong today. Where do you live? Greenwich, isn't it?"

Josh felt confused, all of a sudden. He nodded yes.

"They let dogs into your apartment?"

Strange question. "I guess so."

"Mom and dad out?"

He couldn't talk now, but he could nod.

"Where'd they go?"

He couldn't talk now.

"Let's go home." Ike put his arm around Josh's shoulder and put the three leashes in the other hand. At the intersection by the ice-cream store, he said, "Anybody there?"

He couldn't talk. Finally said, "My sister." "Older sister?" Josh answered no with his head. "You get along?" He nodded yeah. "So. Bad trip?" Josh tried to stop the honking from getting so loud again. "What was it? Maui Wowie?"

"Hallucinogenic Izmir. Just a couple of doobies." Ike whistled. "And brownies." "Brownies!" Ike looked worried. "How many?" "Just two." "Two! Ho-ly shit. Two?" He stopped walking. "You've got to be careful with those brownies."

So maybe this was routine, with brownies? The noise from him blared up again. He wasn't causing it. "I'm having a nervous breakdown!"

"Nervous breakdown? Naw. Kid with your character?"

147

The crying stopped. He didn't stop it. It just stopped. He checked this guy out.

Character, matter of fact, was one thing he'd always had.

"I've seen you on your skateboard," said Ike. "Remember? Remember when you could barely get it up on the curb, and you'd fall on your ass and get right up and go for more? Remember that thing you built, that launching pad, that you took up on the basketball court and shot up and flew through the air on, and down like a butterfly? Kind of a loud, klutzy butterfly. I got black and blue just watching. But you're making it. You're practically pro class on that board now."

Josh had to admit, he was improving.

The guy's arm around his shoulder felt okay. If anyone was watching out the window, they probably knew football players and coaches walked around like this all the time.

"This is where I live." Josh stopped.

"Used to sleeping in the day?"

He wasn't. He shook his head. He slept at night.

"It's kind of a trip," Ike said. "Sleeping in the day. I do it all the time. You wake up and it's almost night, you're ready for a little dinner and some nighttime activity, and then pretty soon you're ready for a great day's sleep again, and then you're back on keel. You oughta try it. Oughta try it." Ike gave Josh's butt a pat and was gone, off toward the park with his shag dogs. Maybe he figured out he didn't have to go in after all. Probably figured he'd pull through.

That joke about character was a good one.

Imperfections

WHENEVER IT RAINED you saw how imperfect everything manmade was. The tennis and basketball courts were not smooth, as they seemed in fog or sunlight, but puckered, to make not one slick cover of wetness but a dapple of puddles. The promenade, which was supposed to be flat, sloped to the west, so a long reservoir of liquid sienna filled up on that side. On the brick street water collected over some bricks but not others, pointing out that human hands had laid them, crookedly. Water, when it rested, was absolute in its insistence on forming a horizontal surface. No exceptions.

Tobin noticed this, and how the steps weren't flat. They were slanted. Slanted terraces half full of water. Swimming pools for birds. Birds were having a high time, splashing through all those mistakes. They fluttered their wings to turn a bathtub into a shower, then shot to the sky. Looked like fun.

Tobin picked up a chartreuse tennis ball. Soggy. Squeezed it. Drops sprayed out. Small ones sprayed, big ones plopped. Split seam. Still, good toy for a dog. He gave it another squeeze and shake and put it in his pocket.

The seam of his knit cap came to two points, like mouse ears, over his long gray hair and beard. The green tarpaulin draped from his shoulders. The corners, with the metal rings, dangled by his knees. He flapped, boots making waves in the puddles.

Up in the shed he had something to show people, anyone who was interested. He got it over the weekend. Saturday's mailbox had mail! Both kinds. Fan letters. Hate mail. The *Bolinas Hearsay News* forwarded it in a big envelope. It had been over a month now, since the poem was published. They must've saved these letters up, sent 'em out just in time to improve his weekend. Probably didn't have a large staff, the *Bolinas Hearsay News*. Four letters from people he'd never heard of. Funny what people read into a poem. Pornographic, one said. That tickled him. He hadn't been sure the eroticism would come through to the average reader. Another said it was an assault on Sigmund Freud. He hadn't been thinking about Sigmund Freud.

He worked fast, energized by the morning mess. He wondered who would be the first he could tell. It would be nice if someone came up and asked him, "Any fan mail? Any hate mail?" No one had yet. Not too likely anyone would.

Only trouble with the tarp over his shoulders was, it dragged in the mud. To pick up the weekend trash floating in the promenade he tied all the loose tarp material around his waist so he could go into his squat-walk. Like wading. Pretty ugly, today. The papers were sopped and the beer cans full of mud. The north side of the monument said South in big black letters, running in the rain. Kids' magic marker. The south side said Pokey. Every other bench said one of those names. The rain had turned down to a drizzle, but it would be pouring full blast again before Tobin could get this stuff off. At least magic markers were easier than paint. But the trash containers were cubes of pebbled cement. Pebbles took a long time to rub clean.

These guys were anti-artists. They drained time and energy from an artist. Tobin. It was one of those ethical questions you didn't have to ponder much.

TOBIN WAS WORKING on a Norwegian series. Stories. He'd written to the guy who was head of that Norwegian Seamen's Church down on Hyde, near the water. Big white mansion. Bright. Bright flags in front. Tobin asked if he could use their library. The guy said yes. So he'd spend his lunch hours down there for a few weeks, looking things up. Maybe it'd take a few months. He had a grapefruit, to peel and eat on the way. Kind of a trade-off. He wouldn't get to have La Petite Treat grapefruit juice at lunch. But then he wouldn't be tempted to have the Black Forest cake. And he'd get to be in that library. Beautiful windows. Might lose a pound.

Something different, going to the Norwegian place. Pretty nice, Norwegians.

"I say." It was the Englishman at Tobin's back. "Erasing art, are you?"

"Ever been to Norway?"

The Englishman didn't have an answer.

"I'm going down there today," Tobin explained.

Could be the Englishman would like to see his fan mail. "Want to see something good?" He looked up to see the Englishman was busy. Cleaning up after Mrs. Ironside. Poodle was in the bushes making more work for him.

Next one to come up was the apartment manager woman. Hood up. Her mutt shot into the bushes. Could be there was a cat in there. Or a rat. Lots of rats these days. He used to hate them, but then he got used to them. Rats weren't that different from birds.

He didn't want to show his mail to Frankie right now. Maybe tomorrow. This might be a good time for the Monday morning grapefruit juice break.

When he got to La Petite Treat, it turned out they were just opening. Seven o'clock. Kind of a long morning.

"TOBEEN, TOBEEN!"

Chantal. He was having a hard time with the last trashcan. Porous material soaked up magic marker pretty good.

"Tobeen, we have a new rosebud."

"Nice." He kept rubbing.

"Captain Harry Stebbings."

He kept rubbing. He thought she was talking about roses.

151

"So pretty and pink, like lipstick."

"Who?" He thought she was talking about some Navy guy.

"Ooooh!" she screamed, jumping back. The dog Tess had just galloped up and jumped. Chantal fought to keep her balance, looked down at the muddy pawprints on her nice clean raincoat.

"Chantal!" Hillary panted. Now the dog was washing Tobin's beard with its tongue.

"Oh, Hillary. I'm imagining you in that beautiful frothy dress the color of a peach. I hope you took my advice and wore that to the party."

Hillary grinned: "It took a lot of courage."

Courage. Tobin tried to imagine a dress that would take courage to wear. If you were a woman. All he could imagine was the nudie. It would take courage to wear no dress.

"I woke up in the middle of the night, the night before the party, and couldn't go back to sleep till I'd looked in the mirror for about an hour. I decided it would be okay and then I slept like a puppy."

Proud, she sounded. Courageous.

"Chantal, do you play tennis?"

Hard to follow this conversation. No logic. He stuck his hand out. The rain was pelting now. Tennis?

"Tennis!" said Chantal. "Oh, yes! But I am not an expert." She still had her handkerchief out, still rubbed and rubbed at the pawprints on the raincoat that used to be clean. Used to be a nice white handkerchief. "Are you?" Chantal asked Hillary. "An expert?"

"No!" TV camerawoman sounded proud. "I'm terrible."

Didn't take much to make her proud.

"I just like chasing the ball."

Tobin concentrated on the letter S. Rain had soaked through his cap and gotten to his scalp. Pretty good protection, the tarp.

"Only trouble is I don't have a racquet," Hillary said.

"Oh! We have three!"

A fast rhythm of clattering thunks and a lot of splashing made Tobin look across to the stairs. That skateboard kid was bouncing down, body upstanding. A lot of elastic in the knees. Unsafe! Tobin rushed over to look all the way down the steps to see the boy land, in a kneebend, on the sidewalk. Kid straightened and whipped to the right and down Larkin toward Mrs. Leone's building. Tobin walked back over to Chantal and the TV camerawoman. "When I was a kid we had to go to school." They didn't answer. Kept talking about tennis. How much they liked tennis. How terrible they were at tennis. Both happy about that.

HE HADN'T MENTIONED this to anyone, except his wife, but he had fourteen books ready to print. He'd been working in the dark by himself for years. Quarter of a century. More. While being a philosophy student and a bicycle racer and a ditch digger and a gardener. This thing with the *Hearsay News* meant a lot to him. Four letters. Hate mail! He'd never shown most of his poems to anyone, except his wife, and sometimes his mom when he thought she wouldn't disapprove. And then that one day he sent one out. Look what happened. He thought of those ladies, in the Bible, who held their lights under a bushel. Those guys who buried their talents.

No more. He sent ten poems out last Friday. Five bucks in stamps to Europe. It was Monday. The places could be getting them now. Or at least they'd get 'em next week. On his way home he'd get off the bus at the post office and pop for a whole sheet of stamps and send out ten more. Both poems and stories. He'd be way ahead of the weekly quota he'd decided on last Friday, but what the hay. It was stupid, if you had this kind of talent, to be modest.

If he failed, it'd be because he was human. Or because the editors he sent them to were human. Or because either he or they weren't human enough. That was something to think about on the bus. The rain was pounding, rushing down the brick street. There were oblong pockets where some pools stayed, getting trounced, others that the water slipped over. These bricklayers had put their foibles down for all time. Or until the next earthquake. Tobin had made fourteen books' worth, in his life, and it was time to start laying them out. Crookedly.

Summer

BONJOUR. BUON GIORNO. G'DYE. *Goddag. Guten tag. Arrigato.* There wasn't much reason to travel around the world any more, with the world coming here. Summer, anytime after nine a.m., the only people at the tennis courts speaking American were Hillary and Chantal, Chantal with her accent. "Fuck!" she shouted, missing an easy one.

"Chantal!" Hillary squealed in shock. The players on either side turned to look. Apparently they knew that much English.

Chantal laughed. "I can say it in your language," she said, loud, across the net to Hillary. She took another ball from her pocket and hit it. "I cannot say it in French."

Hillary missed this one. "*Merde!*" she shouted. Both laughed. "I don't know the French word for the one you said," Hillary called out.

"I'm afraid I can't tell you." Chantal sent over another ball. Arms and legs like a disjointed pinwheel, Hillary got this one, shot it to Chantal's left rear corner. With all her energy Chantal ran for it, took the racquet handle in both hands, like a club, and swang. The ball flew far over Hillary's head, over the cyclone fence. "Hole in one?" They watched it go and Hillary ran to scoop up the four balls in her court. They'd started with six. They'd been playing two or three times a week for almost a couple of months now, and what they usually did was play until all the balls were lost. Two balls lost meant their game was a third through. Both were looking forward to the end. Tobin had unlocked the gate to the pen next to the courts to let the dogs in. Roger and Mrs. Ironside

154

could be counted on not to run (or hop) into the street, but Tess couldn't, and she liked company. From behind the cyclone fence Roger and Mrs. Ironside spectated, moving only their heads, like anyone at a tennis match. Tess liked to participate. She chased the ball through the air, shouting her barks. It didn't seem to bother her that the ball was on the other side of the fence. She liked the exercise. (Like Chantal and Hillary.) After the game, Hillary would put Tess to work, going through the woods for balls. She had amazingly keen eyes and nose. Sometimes she found twice as many as they'd lost. Hillary collected them in a big paper bag and later switched six into her two tennis ball cans. She told Tobin not to tell Chantal. She wasn't sure Chantal would like playing with used balls. Anyway, it was nice that Hillary could at least provide the balls, since she used Nigel's racquet.

Tess was growing fast. People said, "Pretty soon she'll be as tall as you." They said it almost as often as they asked who's walking who/ whom. She didn't look like a golden retriever yet, because she was still only a puppy. Apparently silver-whites were slow to get their feathers. Everyone had ideas for what Tess must be. Most thought either an Irish wolfhound or a greyhound. But she was a golden retriever. She had papers.

Hillary was doing a little better in several departments: the money department, the boyfriend department, the friends department, and the clothes department. In order of importance, how would she rank these departments? Clothes should be last and boyfriend first. But she was getting a lot of pleasure from the clothes. Chantal had taken her over to a factory outlet, where she'd got three T-shirts (one pink) practically for free. At the antique clothes store she'd "bought" (i.e., stolen) a soft flowery cotton dress from the nineteen-forties; it was cut so long and skinny not even the mannequin could wear it, and Sybil said it had been on her rack so many years she didn't want to see it any more. She even threw in a pair of fifties espadrilles no one else could wear, because they were size twelve quintuple-A, and no amount of tissue paper in the toes could make those shoes even *look* like they fit anyone. They fit Hillary perfectly.

155

She knew Chantal was a little irked with her for not taking her advice about obedience schools. Chantal had gone to so much trouble, ordering brochures from all over northern California from people who could supposedly teach Tess manners. Chantal could understand why she didn't want to spend thousands of dollars on that dog boarding-school in the Napa Valley, although the course was supposed to perform miracles. But there was one service, where the trainer actually came to your house, a series of twice-a-week lessons, guaranteed, that cost only five hundred. (Can you imagine?) No way. Maybe, just maybe, after a few more paychecks Hillary'd go back over to that outlet, because the compliments she got whenever she wore something other than the gray sweatshirt made her feel like a million bucks. But five hundred dollars for a dog trainer?

She had a hundred dollars of credit available on the one card she was actually paying down. It would've been more if she hadn't bought the clothes, and paid for the vet, the gynecologist, and the birth control pills. Down at the drugstore, when she'd gasped at the cost of the birth control pills, Ray had smiled: "Cheaper than the alternative."

It was embarrassing, having Ray and Pete know about her sex life. On the other hand, it was kind of nice to have them think she had one. She didn't. She'd bought the pills for some future date. She was holding back. It was normal, excusable, with all the sexually transmitted diseases in the air. But it was getting to be time. The guy she'd been seeing, Mike, the one she'd met at Meg and Ike's party, was going to lose interest – give up – if she didn't let this next step happen pretty soon. At least she had the pills in hand. This encouraged both of them.

MIKE HAD A lot going for him. ("Mike," he said to new people. "Not Michael.") Mike was two inches taller than Hillary. It was a relief to look up to someone. Everyone admired his car. It was a BMW, but not a cliché, dot-commer/investment banker car, even though he was an investment banker: It was a very old convertible, orange as an orange, with character. Everyone at the station picnic liked him. He could talk about anything – especially baseball and politics – the things that made Hillary feel like someone from Mars. Leslie was thrilled for Hillary, finding Mike, and was now after her to find one of Mike's friend for her. The night Mike took Hillary, with Chantal and Nigel, to hear Ike play at Moose's, Nigel leaned in to whisper, "I like that chap of yours, Hillary." She felt a swell of pride. This was so different from what she was used to. Another good thing about that night was hearing Ike play. He sounded like he was on fire. The whole room heated up. But the best thing was, she wore that forties dress from Sybil, and the espadrilles, and Chantal said she looked sexy. Nigel said, "I think you're sexy whatever you wear. But who am I to say? I'm only a man."

She was amazed that anyone could think she was sexy. Especially a man. The words that blurted out of her that night were, "Oh, Nigel, I'm in love with you!" The words that blurted out of him were, "Sorry, I'm taken." A little embarrassing. But on the other hand there was something nice about the way Nigel felt proud to make it clear that he and Chantal were each other's one and only. And also, if you wanted to analyze it to death, apparently he'd been serious enough about thinking Hillary sexy that he had to reassure everyone that it was a non-threatening attraction.

And, funny thing, even if she'd been so amazed Nigel would use the word "sexy" about her, it wasn't the first time it had happened. At the party Ike and Meg gave to introduce her to Mike, something almost like that happened.

It was a night full of life, an amazing dinner. How could anyone as chic as Meg be (a) married to Ike, (b) so down to earth, or (c) such a chef? Five courses, ending with something incredible, in flames. A different wine with every course, and cognac after. Ike said he wasn't "into wine," he stuck with gin and tonic and groaned every time some-one commented on the "crispness" of this or the "roundness" of that. Everyone else but Meg and Ike was single: A retired math professor who got totally drunk, a professional dog groomer who'd grown to hate dogs, a lawyer with a ponytail, and an oldish woman who was writing a depressing book about child pornography. She got pretty tipsy. After dinner, there was a Mike 'n'

Ike act, with Ike on piano, Mike on banjo; Ike replenished the gin in his glass pretty steadily. At the door, reaching up to give her a hug, he kissed her ear and whispered into it, "Oh, you sexpot you!"

This was turning out to be her year. And it was nice to have someone to go out with for a movie and a pizza on her nights off. It didn't matter that they didn't like the same kind of pizza. She could peel off the pepperoni. But it did kind of bother her that they didn't like the same kind of movies. He liked those fantastic adventure ones, the ones they made for twelve-year-olds. The way he decided if a movie would be good was to ask around: "How many people get blown up?" Those movies were long. And though it never seemed to bother Mike, those theater chairs weren't built for six-footers.

She was almost sure one of these days he'd see through her faking her interest in the movies, and in rehashing the plots. He was always unavailable when the Giants were playing, because he subscribed to the games on TV. First he watched them, then he talked about them. Inning by inning. She was pretty sure he'd eventually detect her dim feelings for that game. She knew that lots of intellectuals, like John Updike and Roger Angell, liked it. She didn't disrespect Mike and Ike for liking it. I.e., loving it. It was just that even though she tried hard, the game moved pretty slowly. Also, she couldn't quite see the point. Win? Lose? What difference did it make?

The one thing she absolutely loved, though, was the time they actually went to a game. The new stadium was so beautiful and clean and warm (the weather down in that part of the city was so lovely), and the people were warm, too. So many brought kids and babies. She'd never seen so many babies. People hugged their babies to be sure they were warm, hoisted them on their shoulders, explained the game to ears that didn't understand a word. It reminded her of the things she tried to point out to Tess: A pink and blue sunset, a boat on the Bay. It would be nice to have a baby who'd one day understand English. One thing that depressed her about Tess was that she'd never be able to talk. The other thing that made her sad was that Tess would die.

Anyway. Babies. Wouldn't it be nice to have one of those, one of these days. But she didn't think she'd like to have her baby with Mike.

Mike was proud of the fact that he hadn't read a book since college. He teased her for being a bookworm. Bookworm. She only read a couple of books a month. She used to read twice as much. She wished she could get back into reading. He did like to talk about politics (meaning politicians), and at least she could contribute something, thanks to her job on the news. But for her, these politicians were boring enough at work. It might be different if she didn't see so many of them so often. The one she did like was always getting in trouble because he said what he thought instead of what people wanted to hear. He'd never get anywhere.

And there was another thing. She'd made a pretty bad mistake early in the relationship. He was only twenty-five. Since he might run away from her if he knew her true age, she'd lopped off a year. Twenty-six sounded so old to him it was lucky she hadn't said twenty-seven. That's what she told herself. She didn't blame him. For some reason twenty-six sounded like ten years more than twenty-five, and twenty-seven about double. She was glad she'd lied. But then she had to live with it. She lived in fear that he'd see her driver's license. The first night she'd considered inviting him up to her apartment, she had to put the brakes on, because during one of those machine-gun battles in the theater, she suddenly gasped to remember the sight of the invitation on her kitchen counter – the invitation to her tenth high school reunion. The graduation year was printed right on the front. She could say, "I skipped a grade." Graduated at sixteen. Would he believe that? She decided not to ask him up. So for the fifth time they sat in his car, necking like teenagers.

She didn't want to have her baby with him, but God how she loved to kiss him. It was like being drunk and dizzy and hungrier than hungry and she couldn't ever get enough.

BY THE TIME the sixth tennis ball had flown over the fence and into the bushes, Chantal's and Hillary's arms and legs were as blotchy red as their

159

faces. Noon to one was not the best time to play tennis, on a hot day. They really should try to get there before the fog burned off, but that was hard for Hillary after her night job. And anyway, in their physical fatigue they were psychically energized. Chantal wanted to show Hillary the new buds in the rose garden. Mrs. Ironside hopped gracefully, with perfect pedestrian etiquette. The tall old poodle heeled like a show dog. Tess was just the opposite. Hillary dug her tennis shoe into the brick road, leaning back with her body to counter Tess's lunges at the head of the leash. Each step as deliberate as a very old person's, Hillary followed Chantal to the corner.

They had to wait a few minutes to get close to the roses, because a group of men in dark suits were gathered around, speaking Japanese. They changed lenses on their cameras, spun dials and measured light to take pictures of individual flowers and to frame the garden as a whole. Then they almost *jumped* into a line, with each person standing straight, smiling. White teeth. One person would take a picture and hop back into the line so another could step out to snap. After each man had recorded this San Francisco moment, the group stepped, like a body with eighteen or twenty legs, down Hyde toward the crookedest street in the world. With the Japanese moving on, one person remained, the blond boy with the skateboard. Using one foot to hold his board still, he seemed to be memorizing each flower and its name tag.

"Which is your favorite?" Chantal asked.

"What?" He started as if he'd been asleep.

"Do you have some that you like better than others?"

"That's a tough one." He scratched his cheek and looked at each of the fifty bushes. "See, I'm into this for my buddy. Or, my buddy's wife. She wants to plant some roses. They've got this big old back yard full of dirt. You know? I mean, like, dirt. That ugly dried-up kind. Even the weeds die. My buddy's wife, she comes up here all the time to check out these roses. My buddy, he's not too much into flowers. But she says lotta times she comes up with an idea he doesn't like and she does it anyway. Pretty soon he thinks it was his idea. She thinks that's how it'll be with roses. I told her I'd give her a hand with the shovel, and she asked if I'd help her out with the creative process, too."

Hillary could see Chantal glow, hearing this skateboarder talk about roses. From the description of the dirt and the personalities, she knew who this couple must be. She wasn't surprised to learn Ike was buddies with a fourteen-year-old.

"So what are you going to advise her?" Chantal was all ears.

"Oh." The boy moved his hand over his mouth and chin and along his jawline, exactly the way Ike scratched his stubble. "That's a tough one. Yesterday there was a white one, named after some kind of wine. Today I can't find it."

"Chablis!" Chantal walked to a bush and a label. "I picked it."

"You gave it to *me*," Hillary said.

"Yeah, that one was pretty chill," Josh said. "It may be kind of weird to like white. It had some other colors, almost-colors, like a pearl."

"Oh, you *told* me you were good at art. You must be. Most people don't see that rainbow in the white. You can hardly see it, you know."

"Yeah." Color flooded his cheeks. He looked down and put both feet on the skateboard, pressed a heel and pushed off. At the corner he tried a triple pivot and nearly lost it midair, but he caught himself and stayed on the board. When he waved, he used the flat of his palm to make a big arc.

161

Gout

"HAVEN'T SEEN YOU for a while." He let his clippers rest. "Been on vacation?"

"Hah!"

"You look good. Healthy."

She grunted.

"Hair looks nice. Is that a new shirt or something?"

"Oh yeah." She looked down and checked the shirt. "I went shopping."

"Looks nice. You look healthy."

"That's because I've been sick."

"A cold or something?"

"No. The gout."

"Oh. Too bad, I guess."

"Well, maybe not. It's got so bad I had to quit drinking."

"Oh. Must be tough."

"No, not really. I just got so sick I couldn't drink. Not drinking's easier than going to a doctor. Now I don't miss it at all."

"Oh no?"

This was interesting to Frankie, too. She could hardly believe it, in fact. "I can't explain it. I like not drinking. For one thing, I feel better."

"Oh? That's good. You look better. Seems like it. Yes. I'm pretty sure that's true. You look a lot better, to tell the truth."

"Well thank you." She hoped he could tell she didn't appreciate the compliment.

"I didn't mean you looked bad before," he said. "I just notice you look kind of – fresher. Refreshed. Know what I mean?"

"No."

GETTING DOWN TO the terrace, she had to pull Buster's choke chain and bring him close, because those two little French dogs were running around free. The male always tried to make it with Buster. Of course Buster didn't enter in. Bigger dogs looked down on smaller dogs. It was funny that those tiny dogs looked exactly like poodles. Someone must have mated a poodle with a mouse. Eery. Still, Frankie was glad to see the freaks. It meant Pierre must be here, somewhere. Outside of the fact that he was queer, she liked him. Pierre, a big beefy guy from Jersey. He was one of the only people she knew who still smoked. He was the only person she knew out here who was also from Jersey. So what if he wore a beret and changed his name to Pierre. It was his right. There was nothing she hated like a phony, but his name was the only phony thing about him. The beret wasn't phony, it was his logo. And he'd tell anyone that he named himself. It was pretty funny how he'd explained it to Frankie. Calvin was his name, up until 1963, when he got out of Pratt and started his own line of dresses. "Whoever heard of a designer named Calvin?" he said. That was a good one.

"Hey, Frankie." There he came, around the hedge. "Where's your beer?"

"Where's your martini?"

"Too early. I'll get it later. But what about you?"

"Quit drinking."

"Really?"

"Had to. The gout got too bad. But I don't mind. I feel good now."

"Oh yeah?" He looked her over a little too carefully for her taste. "You look good." His belligerent male kept yapping, so he used the leash to pull him close and pretended to mash its head under his shoe. He spent a minute doing this and said, "Don't know what would happen to me if I quit drinking. My liver would go into shock."

He stepped to the nearest bench and sat down. Patting the spot next to him, he said, "Looks like not drinking hasn't hurt you."

She didn't respond.

He said, "Take off your coat and stay a while."

"You mean, put *on* my coat and stay a while." Instead of putting her seat on the bench, she put one of her feet on the bench. "It's cold up here." Leaning on her knee, she took a Pall Mall out of her jeans. "If I'd known I'd be seeing you, I might have brought a coat." As soon as she said that, she wished she hadn't. By the way he looked down and smiled at his knee, she could see he was flattered. Ego-building wasn't her style.

"Here," he said, taking off his leather jacket. "Wear this."

She thought a minute and decided what the hell. Slipping on the roomy jacket and feeling warm all of a sudden, she even thought of saying thank you.

"I don't miss drinking a bit," she said instead. She sat down. "It's been so long I don't remember." She watched Buster and Pierre's female carousing. "I was drinking so much it didn't have any good effect anyhow. Really. I'd be getting at least a six-pack every night. Maybe more. And when you drink that much you don't get a high. To get drunk, I'd have had to drink at least two six-packs in the course of four hours. That might have got me drunk. Or else turn to hard liquor. Or at least wine. But I don't like hard liquor. And I hate wine. Never drink it. Can't stand the stuff."

"I love wine," Pierre said. "I love liquor. I even like beer. I love it all."

"Really? Even wine? You can have it. My boss, Bill, he took me out to dinner one night to that French restaurant out in Pacific Heights, Saint Tropez or something. Real nice. I put on a dress. Wore jewelry, if you can imagine."

He was looking a little too close. It was almost an affront. "Your hair looks nice today," he said.

What hair? Her hair was so short she might as well be bald. She didn't want to get mad and ruin the conversation so she skipped over this whole invasion of her privacy. "Anyhow, my boss, Bill, he said, you've gotta have wine. I said, I want a beer. He saw naw, you gotta have wine. I said no but he ordered it for me anyhow. A jug of it – what do they call it? A giraffe. Well, I meant what I said and didn't drink any of it. So he finished off the whole giraffe, and I tell you I was scared to death driving home with him. We almost didn't make it." She had a sense of humor, now that she was safely out of his car, but it didn't erase the fear from her memory. "I don't like restaurants," she said. "Do you?"

"Well – depends on the restaurant. But I'd say, yeah. I like a good meal out. Candles, good wine, people doing the work for you. I'm not much of a cook."

"Do you eat in restaurants very often?" She hoped he didn't.

"Practically every night. Usually I walk down to the Polk Street Grill, which is like home to me. Or i Fratelli, if I can beat the crowds. But I vary it, go someplace special maybe three nights a week. Have you been to the new sushi place?"

God. She wasn't even going to think about sushi. "I don't like restaurants." She felt her nostrils tense up. "I've worked in them, and I know how slovenly they are, the mistakes they make. Even the best places. The cooks, they wipe their hands on their aprons. They go to the bathroom and don't wash their hands. They drop things on the floor and step on them and put them back in the stew. I can't eat in restaurants."

Pierre seemed to be laughing at her, although he wasn't saying it.

"I used to like restaurants sometimes," she said. "Used to. Before I knew the facts of life. There was a place in Jersey called Haverfords, Haverhills, something like that. You know Jersey. Do you remember?"

He didn't.

"Oh, it was great. They served these slices of liver this thick" (an inch plus) "and it was all tan and juicy inside. Melt in your mouth. I could never eat liver now. No red meat – of course I do sneak a little red meat now and then. But not liver. That's kind of the ultimate. My mother used to fix beef heart. Oh, that was great."

She reached into her jeans pocket for another Pall Mall. It came out broken. She couldn't light that. She shouldn't have sat down. She stood up and fished the pack out of her jeans. The whole pack was bent in half.

"Try my jacket pocket," he said.

She pulled out a packet of heavenly blue. "Gauloise," he said. "I switched to that brand when I changed my name."

Frankie laughed. "Was that when you got your beret?"

Yes it was.

Pierre was no phony.

"I smoke all the time now," she said. "Can't do anything else."

"I'll have one of those," he said, as Frankie started slipping the pack back into the jacket.

"Sorry," she said, handing him a cigarette and lighting it for him, with her own black plastic lighter. When she put the pack back into the pocket, her hand felt his lighter. She took it out and held it in the light. Silver, tarnished, from the twenties or early thirties. One side had the front of some kind of Egyptian type sculpted onto it, the other side showed her from the rear. From both points of view her arms went into that dance routine.

"Deco," Pierre said.

"Deco," Frankie said, like ditto. "As if I didn't know deco." She drew on the Gauloise. Not bad. Couple of these and you'd be looped.

"Ray and Pete down at the drugstore, since I stopped drinking, they can't get rid of their beer. Now that I've quit drinking they've still got the same six-packs on the shelf they had before I quit. Dusty." She studied the filterless cigarette in her hand. It was fatter than American cigarettes. "I'll tell you something," she said to the cigarette, then looked at Pierre. "I'm a little surprised that I don't miss drinking. I thought I needed it, but I guess I didn't. The thing that gets me is I can't eat red meat or chocolate any more. Not at all. But I have a mind to walk up to Cala Foods and buy me the biggest porterhouse steak they sell and cook it and eat the whole thing without putting my knife and fork down. Maybe I will. Probably

166

not today, but maybe tomorrow. Of course a chocolate binge would be easier."

She looked up to see Tobin. How long had he been standing there?

"I just thought you people might be interested, well, I got a poem published. Few weeks ago. Quite a few, I guess. But you might like to have a look." He handed each of them a fresh, unfolded xerox. "I mean, you might want to read it later, maybe at night when you have nothing to do, or something."

"I already saw this poem," Pierre said.

"Saw it?" The gardener tried to hide how happy he was, but it was obvious. "You *saw* it?"

Pierre smiled down. "Yeah. Good poem. Good enough to read again." He held out his hand for the xerox. Frankie took hers and smiled. She was in the mood to be nice.

"You know that Birdwood woman?" Tobin asked. "TV camera-woman?"

It smelled like he'd just cracked a rotten egg under her nose. She could feel her nostrils contract.

"Well, she's getting in with the guys at the *Chronicle. New York Times* even maybe. Could be she can help me market my writing."

"Hah!" Frankie got up and handed Pierre's jacket back to him. "I've got work to do." But she didn't want to seem rude. She tossed her lit butt into the promenade and said, "Nice seeing you."

Words into Cash

DOWN AT THE lower terrace Tobin didn't have to mow grass. The wild blades that used to shoot up around the rocks were dry. Stubs of straw. No more crabapple blossoms, but plenty of crabapples. Not too decorative. You had to look pretty close. Tobin swept the fallen ones into a pile. Scooped 'em into a plastic bag. Enough to make some jelly. His wife didn't spend much time in the kitchen, but his mom made pretty good crabapple jelly.

He'd held off long enough. Time for another grapefruit juice break. When he wanted to see his stomach, he had to duck his head more than he used to. Under the navy sweater, the bulge was flatter. Not flat. He'd brought in his belt a couple of notches. Could be his buns were thinner. He wore his pants around his butt. He'd never had a big butt to begin with, but something was smaller. It didn't matter. He couldn't see his rear. But he could see his belly. And it was smaller. The lunch hours at the Norwegian library paid off double. He was more than halfway through the series. And he didn't miss the bacon and eggs and Black Forest cake that much. Partly because he still had them. Once in a while. Just not often.

Health was all you had. That's what they said.

Could be there were other things. Seemed like it. One of his poems was about a woman who had no chairs. No table. No bed. Just empty rooms except for the paintings. Expensive paintings. "Art before furniture," the poem said. "That's devotion." Could be like putting something else before health. Like Black Forest cake. Maybe that was devotion.

He looked over and saw the apartment manager woman leaning back on her bench, watching a humming bird. She pulled on her cigarette. That looked like devotion.

ON HIS WAY to La Petite Treat he had a check to cash. Magazine in Georgia. Literary journal. Pretty high-class. It was from one of the mailings he'd sent to someplace in America. His gamble for a chance at this Georgia magazine was just over a third of a dollar. Pretty cheap, compared to Europe. The check was for over a hundred times the investment. Good thing it was an American check, because Ray and Pete wouldn't cash checks in francs or yen or Deutschmarks. The time he got a check from Germany it was a pain, until he found out how much it was in dollars. Before, when he got that check in francs, Ray and Pete couldn't cash it, so he spent a lot in bus fares. His bank sent him to another bank that was closed by the time he got there. Had to pay more bus fares on his lunch hour the next day. The francs didn't turn into big bucks, but he had a couple of twenties left, after the bus. About the Deutschmarks, he didn't even ask Ray and Pete, except as a joke. Went straight to the bank. When they started dishing out bills, he thought he should've taken a cab. Eight hundreds, two twenties, a ten, a five, two ones, a dime, a nickel, and two pennies. Pretty generous, those Germans. Of course, this was a story. Could be they'd pay less for a poem. This check from Georgia, for an eight-line poem, was for fifty dollars. No bus fares. No overheads except for the stamp and the xerox.

Meant three tickets to the movies this weekend, plus flowers for his wife. A little payment against guilt. He was spending most of his evenings and weekends on the Norwegian series. Too bad he couldn't just send his wife and his mom to the movies and stay home with the Norwegians.

In a way, this check from Georgia was the best one he'd had so far. No hassle. Plus, he hadn't decided what to do with the eight hundred and fifty-five yet. He'd rolled the bills up and stuck them in a Bandaid box and hid it in the shed, behind some manuscripts.

In a way he should give the money to his mom. He owed it to her. She'd paid his education. Most of it. But in a way he might need the money someday. It was another one of those ethical questions. In a way he'd rather not deal with it.

Fifty smackeroos in his pocket, his boots had energy. They swang forward to La Petite Treat. The Norwegian series could wait. This could be a good day for a hot pastrami sandwich, along with the grapefruit juice. Maybe a piece of Black Forest cake. He'd had that after the Deutschmarks. Maybe today he'd pick up a bag of cherries instead. Down at the organic food store they were five bucks a pound – more than a piece of Black Forest cake – but worth it. It wasn't summer that often.

SHOULD HAVE BOUGHT peaches. It was Georgia money. Trouble was, fuzz in the mouth. Mid-sidewalk, he turned back. He could take the peaches home and wash 'em. Then, as long as he was back in the store, he'd get some milk. Clover. This was the only place around where you could get that brand, made by Sonoma cows. Good milk. Tasted like a trip to the country, drinking in the green hills of Sonoma. Good ads. Billboards up all through those hills, with the goofy-looking cow named Clo. Milk and yogurt and cottage cheese on her clothesline: "Clo's Line." One said "Clo's Encounters." Best one was in a tulip field: "Tip Clo Through Your Two Lips." Half a gallon under the arm holding the plastic bag, he reached for a peach. Hand almost hit another hand. Maroon sleeve. The weird guy. Guy had a basket. Liked Clo's Line, looked like. Both cottage cheese and yogurt. Guy seemed to like cherries and peaches, too. Well, everyone eats food. Tobin had never thought about this. He got away before the guy could shout something ugly.

With a pound of cherries, plus peaches to take home and peel, Tobin almost passed La Petite Treat, but he didn't. He stopped. Went in for Black Forest cake. Why not? He could have it all.

A Series

THE SUN, WHICH had dropped behind the Presidio hills, lit the Bay yellow as a lightbulb. Through the glow a perfect line of seven sailboats moved toward the marina, isosceles triangles of fluorescent white. They looked like floating teepees. Now one slipped a pace eastward, jarring the perfection of the line. It bobbed back into position just as another lagged, to make a gap in the spacing. Anna felt something like suspense as she watched from between trees, hoping to see perfection reinstated for one more instant.

It was unusual to come here with Posy on a Friday evening and find solitude. Pretty soon Martine would arrive, and the two would have dinner, unfortunately at La Petite Treat, because it was the only place where Martine could afford to pay her half. Anna wished she would let her pay. She couldn't imagine what sort of horrible thing they'd have to eat at La Petite Treat. Oh well. They probably couldn't do much to a hamburger.

Anna hoped to talk to Martine about romance. She couldn't figure out if she and Rayford were about to have one. They were, in the old-fashioned phrase, keeping company. She didn't know what sort of advice or insights she hoped to get from an eighteen-year-old, but maybe someone that age was just who she needed to talk to. What she was feeling for Rayford was like a teenage crush. She wasn't sure her sixty-six-year-old constitution could take it.

By now, she could probably recognize some of Rayford's patients on

171

the street. His powers of description were vivid. She felt as if she had always known his college roommate, and his little sister, now sixty-one and living in Virginia. He'd met Angela, and her oldest friends, the Rossis. At the Rossis' house, his heartfelt pronouncements on garbage set up the evening for laughing. Angela didn't seem as enthused about him as Judge Rossi and Maria were. Angela probably measured poor Rayford up against Joe. Or maybe she squirmed, imagining sex between old people.

Right she was. It was ridiculous.

IN A WAY, Anna's life had been a series of lives. They intersected and layered, but in some ways they seemed barely related to each other. Her Italian-speaking childhood, her mad passionate teenage love, college in love with the same boy even though he couldn't go to college, marriage to him, children with him, the widow of him, and what? What was almost like a career at the museum. Some of her programs had been so fabulous she felt like an artist herself. In a way it was more than she could have dreamed of. But more important, she still had her marriage. She talked to Joe every day, every night. He talked to her too. Words worth repeating.

Now Rayford. Getting in the way. Getting in the way of her plans and expectations. But what if? Could there be anything wrong with giving each man a room of his own in the course of her lifetime?

Last Saturday night they'd sat at a back corner table at Capp's, one of the few restaurants in North Beach that hadn't changed since Anna was a high school girl, or since she and Joe had taken little Joey and Angela there for Sunday dinners. They still served family style, the wine tasted as rough as ever, and she still loved the spumoni. Above the bar they had framed photos of boxers and mayors, and wall-to-wall around the booths were snapshots of happy bleached blondes and babies that looked exactly like all other babies.

She was sure he must have come here with Jenny. At least she hoped so, though she didn't want to hear the details. Certain parts of the past might as well stay where they were.

Sex was the problem.

It hadn't come up.

As well it shouldn't.

Still, certain yearnings had started to stir. In her saner moments it felt upsetting. In her insane moments, it felt exciting.

The whole thing was upsetting.

He'd been delighted with the Rossis' house, an earthquake cottage. It was wedged between a block of apartment buildings, so from the outside it looked, as he said, like "The Little House" in the children's book. Inside, it looked like a super-modern loft. They'd knocked out all the walls to turn four little rooms into one big one, with big abstract paintings on the walls. She usually drove to the Rossis', allowing forty-five minutes to look for a parking place; but Rayford preferred traveling by foot to anywhere the foot could go. It took only twenty minutes to get there, and would have taken ten if it hadn't been for the steepness of the hill on the way down, and the height of her heels. On the walk home, to her relief, he navigated a path that avoided the steepest street in the world. The vertical distance they climbed must have been the same, but somehow his route was more gradual, making it not quite *easy*, but at least possible.

As usual, Rayford accompanied her up in the elevator before heading down the hill for home. This time she asked if he'd like a de-caf espresso, and he said he'd like a brandy. She had herb tea. They stepped out on to the balcony, to have a look at the moon. It wasn't there. Fog. The cold in the air shot through her. He must have been cold too, but he didn't put an arm around her. They sipped their liquids and shivered separately. It was the only time she'd spent with Rayford without his filling the air with words.

In bed that night, she hurled herself about. "The toes are sleeping," she chanted. "The ankles are sleeping. The knees are sleeping." She sprang from bed and paced, then forced herself back under the covers. "Resting is as good as sleep. Resting is as good as sleep." She concentrated on the low, nasal bellow of the foghorn. How did it make that sound? She imagined an enormous Coke bottle, big as her building, and

173

a giant blowing into it. Day dawned before the drone of the foghorn rocked her into dizzy drowsiness.

IT WAS HORRIBLE, this over-excitedness she suddenly suffered these nights. She'd been through the same thing before, but that was natural for a seventeen-year-old.

She'd like to talk about sex, with someone. Not Martine after all.

It was good that people were writing, now, about sex among the aged. Since Joe had died in middle age, Anna had had no experience of sex in December. Or November or October, whatever it was. From what she'd read, sexual desire and activity were absolutely normal up to the last gasp.

But how odd.

And Rayford? Did he feel it too? Maybe he wasn't attracted to her. That would be understandable. But it seemed that the electricity she felt with him was coming *from* him.

Maybe he had insecurities. Maybe he had high moral standards.

She had those too. Both.

"*Bonjour!*"

The great stride of Martine's denim airily conquered the distance between them. Posy bounced up the path, stuck her head on Martine's shoe, and poked her butt up for a scratch. Martine obliged, holding in her other hand "*une saxophone!*" She bubbled with news, her French too fast for Anna to follow, but she could make out that Martine had always wanted to play the saxophone and that she'd rented this at a music store on Haight Street. She blew into the mouthpiece, making a sound a little like the foghorn. She handed the saxophone to Anna, who could make no sound at all. Too inhibited, Martine said.

They heard Ike's biggest afghan barking and snarling in the woods, and Ike yelling shut up. Frankie sat on a bench, and Buster lurched into the pounce position, preparing to greet Pierre's poodle. Pierre strolled over with his martini. Anna felt embarrassed to talk in English too long, leaving Martine out, or to speak French to Martine too long, leaving

Pierre out. Even though he didn't cook, Pierre was tired of having no kitchen, his contractor was taking three times as long as he should to remodel. The neighbors were starting to complain that the dumpster had been parked there too long. As Anna dutifully translated to Martine that the La Cournue range hadn't arrived from France yet, and the marble for the counters didn't look quite as good in the kitchen as it had in the showroom, she felt a chill coming over her young socialist friend. Martine didn't need words to communicate that she disapproved of bourgeois chitchat about interior decoration and that she knew of many deserving people who could put the excess money to better use. Pierre looked relieved to spot the corgi and the young psychiatrist coming up the steps, with a woman too gorgeous to be a real person.

Obviously Philo Righi's romance with the tall fragile girl hadn't amounted to anything. But neither had his other romances. With her opera glasses Anna must have seen him with half a dozen women in the last few months. She wondered what was the matter with him.

And then she wondered what was the matter with her. Did every relationship between a man and a woman have to have a goal? Did every living creature need another living creature to devote itself to? It was just this kind of thinking that had gotten her so confused. Maybe Philo Righi had struck upon some other form of happiness than happiness shared with a particular person. If anyone should be able to understand that, Anna should. She'd long ago proved that she didn't need a husband to be happy.

Depression Meat

"IF YOU DON'T eat in restaurants I guess you cook," he was saying, offering her a Gauloise.

"No thanks," she said. "I've got my own." One thing she was not was a leech. "I will take a light though." She pulled a bent Pall Mall out of her pack.

"So what do you cook?" he said.

She looked at him. "You want to know?"

He looked at her. He wanted to know.

"Well, nothing like you eat, in those ptomaine places you go to. I eat healthy. Too healthy. I cook maybe once or twice a week, and now that I can't eat red meat it gets boring. I mean chicken's okay but I get sick of chicken. And I never thought I'd eat turkey except twice a year. But now I get a couple of turkey thighs and cook them up like a potroast, and I have that four nights in a row. Then it's back to chicken. Chicken and turkey, chicken and turkey."

"Can't you have fish?"

"No, I can't have fish." She snapped it. Some people had no idea. "Fish is too expensive. You don't realize I'm on a budget. I get free rent and a few hundred dollars a month. It doesn't go far. I'd say most of my tenants spend that much every week, on their lifestyles. You should see the garbage. They take two slices of these French cheeses with names you can't say and throw the rest of the wheel away. They toss out almost whole servings of Chilean sea bass at eighteen dollars a pound and lobster and crab at five bucks a bite. Chicken and turkey gets boring, but I don't have the kind of money it takes to eat fish."

Obviously this kind of financial information was news to Pierre.

"It's okay," she said. She didn't want to make him suffer too much. "I don't like fish that much anyhow. I used to fix this great hamburger, you know, crackers-eggs-hamburger. Depression meat. Oh, God it's good. You take a slug of hamburger and a roll of crackers, and smash the crackers." She held the imaginary cracker pack in her hands and ground the crackers together through the air, never mind the Pall Mall. "Then I'd chop an onion, mix in a couple of eggs, and make six patties. I like to sear 'em on the stove. You know, cook them real fast so they get black on the outside, or almost black. You put 'em in this pan that I have, that just has room to lay out six, all next to each other. Then I julienne a potato and stick the pieces between the cracks, you know, in the spaces dividing the patties. Then, I open a can of peas and pour the juice over the whole thing. And then, sprinkle just about three tablespoons of milk over it. You put it in the oven, and it doesn't really matter how long you cook it. It never gets tough, because you've got all that liquid in there. At the end I empty all the peas from the can across the top and stick it back in the oven until the peas get hot. Mmm. I could eat for three days on that. Best thing you ever tasted. I'm hungry just thinking about it."

"Hmmm," Pierre said. He gazed at the burning end of his Gauloise before he threw it in the dirt. "You know I eat in some high-class dives. We talked about that. Last night I ate in a place called Masa's. World-famous. They used a different kind of china for each course. They made a sauce from black champagne grapes – little grapes a tenth the size of a huckleberry – floating a dainty brioche. The light sauce, the light brioche – it tasted like a spring cloud." Frankie started fanning her face with her palm, but he went on. "On top of that, they set a hunk of foie gras, like butter with a texture, but so tender you didn't need teeth." She was obviously getting bored, but he wanted to make his point. "It was all I could do not to lick the plate. We had a lobster and avocado salad, and the dressing was made with a reduction of the lobster juices. Dessert was

177

something they call sourdough chocolate cake. It wasn't really like a cake. They served it hot, all soft and moist in the center. The chocolate was so intense – you couldn't have swallowed without savoring."

Frankie held her nose to show what she thought of the whole rhapsody.

"I'm just telling you," he said, "I eat fancy. But I don't think I've ever enjoyed my food as much as it sounds like you like your Depression meat."

"Huh. La-di-da. You should taste my Depression meat."

She wanted to make her point. "Much better than meatloaf. I don't miss my meatloaf. But Depression meat's one of my favorite foods that I miss, now that I can't eat red meat any more. The other food I miss is pork chops. I used to like to cook 'em with a can of crushed pineapple. Can't have that any more either."

He shook his head, reached a hand up to scratch under his beret. "I'm just trying to imagine giving up chicken Escoffier, or eggs Benedict, or sapphire gin."

"Poor baby. My mother was a great cook. Oh, I miss good, unhealthy food. It's terrible, giving things up. I don't even get to drink beer any more."

"But you look terrific. Your complexion, and you've lost some weight, haven't you?"

"Oh, yeah. I don't weigh, you know. But I can feel it. I was getting kind of a belly. And now my figure's got some shape. A waist, almost. It may be the red meat, but I think it's the beer, too. The other night I bought two cans of beer. I watched television and drank 'em. It's nice to have a good cold beer once in a while. I went to the refrigerator after the second one. I was kind of high, you know, drinking as little as I do now. And I wanted another one and I was surprised to see there wasn't another one. I had a little battle with myself. I thought, I'll just walk down to Searchlight and get one. But then I thought. And I didn't."

Heirloom

HILLARY HAD DREAMS of furniture, but no serious thoughts. Every once in a while there would be an ad written on a scrap of paper and tacked on the bulletin board at the Searchlight Market: "Sofa. $1200 value for $250." To write a check for that she'd have to be crazy. Her debts to Visa and MasterCard would go on for the rest of her life. Also, when there was a description, it would be something like turquoise and orange plaid, only slightly worn. Sometimes there was a snapshot which told the ugly truth even more graphically. If she ever got furniture, it would be made possible only by marrying Prince Charming. Meanwhile, you could say the scene in her place was desolate. Or, you could say it was surreal. The bare wood floors stretched on through the two rooms and the hall, polished to reflect the windows, doors, and bare walls. The walls were bare only because Frankie had specified that Hillary could hang no pictures except on those wires you hook into the moldings. No tacks, no tape, no nails. Hillary would have liked to put posters up, but she couldn't afford frames. And she couldn't afford Frankie's anger.

She had one treasure, a quilt made by her great-grandmother, all snowflakes in pink and white. This she kept in a cardboard box on the top shelf of her closet. Since this was a special day, she reached her hand up and plucked the box from the shelf. She was pretty sure it was safe. Tess had grown more selective in what she would chew. She preferred Hillary's sheepskin slippers, and she would only occasionally resort to tennis shoes. She couldn't resist dirty socks, but clean ones didn't appeal

179

to her. She had never liked anything except fur and leather and natural fibers, but now she was bored with sweatshirts and towels, and the only endangered clothes were wool sweaters. If ever she got one of those, Hillary didn't reprimand her: It was her own fault for leaving it out.

This quilt was cotton, maybe fifth on Tess's list. But it was padded, which might make it toothsome. As long as Hillary remembered to put it back in its high box before leaving the apartment, she was pretty sure she could keep Tess from wrecking it. She shut her in the bathroom, scratching, and flung the quilt across the mattress, smoothing the edges and corners. There was something really wonderful about the pink and white snowflakes so close to the wood floor, instead of pedestalled on a bed. Beds were so bourgeois and ordinary. She surveyed the whole apartment through the open bedroom door: The stretch of polished floor, the antique lamp with its hand-painted shade the only piece of furniture in the living-room; the rows of books neatly stacked on their sides against the wall; the little china lamp on the floor next to her bed. At this moment the scene looked to her not like poverty but like minimalist chic. She tried the quilt with the lace-trimmed pillowcases on top, then the pillows covered by the quilt, then the other way, until Tess's scratching at the bathroom door made her hurry her decision: She liked it better with the lacy pillows showing.

Carefully she opened the bathroom door. Tess did not run straight to the quilt but straight to Hillary, jumping in spite of the no-jumping command. The only way Hillary could distract her was to say Sit, an accomplishment Tess was proud to show off. Then Hillary continued with Lie down, something that made Tess's tail bat with happiness as she obeyed, anticipating the next command, which she assumed would be Roll over. The problem was, Tess didn't usually wait for that command but started rolling over as soon as she lay down.

Tess was mid-roll when the sound of the door buzzer shot through Hillary's nervous system. Tess bolted up and barked at the door. Between the buzzer and the barking, Hillary's knees went weak.

The buzzer had an unfamiliar sound. In fact, Mike would be her first guest ever, in San Francisco. She had craftily managed to keep everyone else out, since it was none of their business that she had no furniture. It had taken great bravery to decide Mike could pick her up here, could come in for a minute before they went to the movie. She'd put it off for two and a half months, but she'd known it would have to happen sometime. Over Tess's mad barking, she buzzed him in.

IN A COMMAND that made Hillary jump, he snarled, "*Down*, Tess!"

"No jumping, no jumping," Hillary joined in.

"*Down*, I said!" This time he whacked her across the muzzle. Tess shrank to a fraction of her height, wiggling to compress her body, and walked backwards, stomach close to the floor, tail beating, a look of whimpering confusion on her face.

"And *stay* down!"

No one, not even Tess, would disobey a voice like that. Her ears pressed back against her head in fear.

"Wow!" he said, walking in. "Your windows are clean."

She'd just spent three hours cleaning them. But it was funny he hadn't noticed anything else. He walked to the kitchen, opened the refrigerator door, took out an Anchor Steam and closed the door.

She congratulated herself for buying that six-pack. She'd also bought some corn chips and salsa. Twisting the top off the bottle and taking a swig, he seemed to notice her. "Want a beer?"

"Yes, please," she said.

He opened the door again and handed her one.

She thanked him and reached to the shelf for corn chips and a saucer.

"Tess is the one who really loves beer," she said, taking out the beer opener and pouring a few droplets into the saucer.

"Don't give that dog beer!"

Hillary set the saucer on the floor and Tess hunkered over, ears still pressed back, tail still working, eyes cowering up at Mike. But she was interested in the beer.

"Don't worry," Hillary said, almost cooing, as she watched Tess's

181

fearful approach. "C'mon Tess. – It's just a drop, Mike. It won't get her drunk."

Mike snatched the saucer off the floor and set it on the counter. "I don't care if the dog gets drunk," he said. "It's a waste of beer."

"It's not a waste," she said. "Tess likes it."

Hillary was shocked to see him shake the drops of beer into the sink and say, "It's a bad habit. You spoil her."

She didn't want a fight. She'd do anything to avoid a fight, especially with Mike, whose deep voice could have the same effect on her as it had on Tess. But she looked Tess in the eyes for moments enough to communicate, Don't worry, Tess. After I get home from the movie, I'll open a new bottle just for you. I don't care if we waste all eleven other ounces, you'll get your little bit. Don't worry.

Mike frowned and leaned his shoulder against the top of the refrigerator, taking another swallow of Anchor Steam. "Why didn't she eat her dinner?"

The bowl, a sterling silver serving dish Hillary's grandmother had given her, sat on Tess's placemat on the floor, half full of kibble.

"No eating, only drinking, a sure sign of alcoholism," Mike said, putting his beer down to reach his hand out to Hillary and pull her over next to him.

She laughed. Tess being an alcoholic was a funny thought, and she let him stroke her hair for a second. But he had called her attention to a problem, and she freed herself to open the broom closet and bend into the giant bag of Nature's Recipe Lamb and Rice Kibble. There was a scooper inside, and she scraped it through the rumble of pebbles. Emptying the scoop into Tess's bowl, she explained, "Her dish was half empty. I try to keep it filled, whenever I think of it."

"You just let her eat all day long?"

"Yes!" And Hillary launched sweetly into her feeding theory. "It sounds funny, but it's a good way to keep a dog from getting fat."

"Ho!" Mike thought that was a good one.

"Well, you see how skinny she is." (That was hard to argue with.) "It was my mother's theory, originally, about free-feeding. She thought it was depriving them that made them into pigs if they got the chance. We had a dog, and until she got really really old, she never got even slightly fat. Well, now they've done a lot of studies, and . . ." She could see he wasn't interested. She decided to wind it up quickly. "I know this guy, a psychiatrist, and he told me about all these studies, and how if you free-feed a dog it tends to stay thinner."

He rolled his eyes. She didn't know why she had to convince him, but she had to. "Really! My vet told me, too. My vet told me that if you want a show dog, you shouldn't free-feed it as a puppy because it will never achieve what is considered the ideal weight for the breed, and the ideal proportions."

"Is that what your mother did to you?"

Pain just swept through her. And shame.

"You're so skinny you don't have to take the bus to work. You can just fax yourself."

He went into a convulsion of laughter. She tried to smile, like a good sport.

"Hey where do you sit around here?" He moved his long Levi'd legs from the kitchen to the living-room.

She took some deep breaths to get over her reaction to his mean, cruel joke. If she'd been fat, he'd never ask her why she took the bus instead of just *rolling* herself to work. No one said ugly, heartless things to fat people.

"I don't want to show Tess, though," she said, getting back to a safer subject.

"As a what?" he said. "A golden retriever?"

That was another good one. He laughed and grabbed her hand, pulling her in.

She didn't feel much like kissing him at that moment. But she was beginning to get a little sense of humor about the contrast between what Tess looked like and what her papers said she was.

He wrapped a long arm all the way around both of her shoulders and stroked her cheek with his thumb. "Would you show her as a silver-white?"

He wound his other arm around both shoulders and used that hand to pluck her glasses from her face. Dropping them into his shirt pocket he tipped his head down to find her lips with his lips.

It took a few seconds for her to feel her stiffness melting under the warmth of his arms, to feel the gentle suction of his kiss coax the straight line of her lips to swollen softness, until all she could feel was this hunger for all she could get of his mouth.

By the time he started walking her backwards, through the bedroom door, her head and body were swimming.

His stretched-out arms measured the span of her, from nape of the neck to back of the knees. With the care he'd use to lay out a full-length mink, he tipped her back on her great-grandmother's pink and white snowflakes. There, she gave in to this dizziness, this desire that could never be quenched. She pressed her shoulders and torso and ribs closer, closer into his body, drinking his mouth. It was hard to get breath but she didn't care.

When he slipped his hand under her pretty pink T-shirt, shivering the skin that covered her ribs, gliding under the bra to the shamefully unvoluptuous little-girl bump of a breast, she instinctively buckled to protect herself, but the hand was there, teasing the nipple, teasing out tenderness. She gasped a sigh and let him play. She let herself swoon. Her mind would fight, fight to fight, fight to stop fighting, fight for peace, fight for frenzy, fight to summon reserve, fight to be free of reservation. She wasn't in love, wasn't at all in love – she remembered her saner moments and how not in love she was – but every cell begged for this pleasure.

She jerked her shoulder and head up from the bed. "The pills!" He pushed her back onto the pillow and smothered her mouth to silence with his tremendous mouth. "I haven't started—" She spoke without tongue or lips, so the sound came out like a burble from a jellyfish.

"My pockets are full of condoms! But, you know, we don't have to do anything." He released her lips for just that long, using the hand that wasn't caressing her breast to unbuckle her belt. His strong hand pushed its way under her waistband, under her panties. "Mmmm!"

"No!" Hillary said, popping to a sitting position. He propped himself on an elbow and she saw that his face was red as a crab. "No!" she repeated. Then she felt tears coming into her eyes and she ran her fingers through his hair. "I'm sorry, I'm sorry."

"Christ!" he said.

"I'm sorry . . ."

"You're always sorry!"

"I'm sorry."

"For God's sake stop being sorry." He was mad. "You know, we don't have to get you pregnant. In the first place I don't see why you haven't started taking those pills."

"But you have to wait until the first day after you . . ."

"I know, I know. And I know you don't think condoms are safe enough. I know I know I know! But that's not the only thing we can do. Contraception isn't the only thing stopping you, is it?"

Hillary made her eyes wide.

"Is it!" he accused.

Hillary looked down at her great-grandmother's quilt.

"No," she said.

"Well what is it then?"

"I don't know," she lied, tracing one of the snowflakes with her long, unpainted fingertip.

A Fine Romance

"'A FINE RO-MANCE, my friend, *this* is . . .'" Anna sang along with Louis and Ella. "'A fine *ro*-mance, with no *kiss*-es . . .'" The groceries had just been delivered, she was putting them away, and Posy was helping – treading alongside her from fridge to pantry, not missing a sniff. Anna felt lighter than air, heavier than lead. "'I might as well play *bridge* with my old maid *aunts . . . I* haven't got a *chance . . .'*"

The trouble with hope was, it opened the possibility of despair.

To expose things she'd kept covered all these years was almost unthinkable. Such as her breasts, with their droop. The roll at her waist, the stretch marks. Of course Joe hadn't minded the stretch marks. He'd had something to do with them. And he'd died before the breasts had – sort of – flopped.

Oh phfff. They hadn't *flopped!* They still had a little buoyancy. They didn't *hang*. She was lucky. Swimming at the club apparently paid off. But nothing could bring back the bloom of youth.

Rayford was a doctor. He'd seen stretch marks. He probably saw rolls every day, and baggy thigh-tops and bones that poked out along the shins. But could he love them? Before this silly wish had come along to jostle her, she'd been perfectly happy with her body. She was a normal sixty-six-year-old woman. But now, it seemed sad. Young flesh she couldn't offer. No regime of gym and diet could bring it back. Not even plastic surgery.

Of course he didn't have young flesh either, but men didn't trade on that. And he'd done an amazing job of keeping up his physique. She'd never seen him without a shirt, but it was obvious he was trim. And tall and broad-shouldered.

She felt the nudge of Posy's cold nose through her stockings and saw that her water bowl was empty. "Oh, sweet Posy! How long have you been dying of thirst?" She didn't know how to check a dog for dehydration, but felt fearful, as she filled the bowl and listened to the loud lapping – and put the last packet of peas in the freezer.

"Be careful what you wish for." She was a college girl when she first heard that. Joe sent her those words on a postcard. Her spirits shot to the sky, leaving an empty head down on the ground. He knew what she wished for. The next day another postcard came: ". . . For it might come true." He was telling her she could have it. He was warning her. It was the happiest she'd ever been.

Joe wasn't in college. He had a family to support. When his dad died, his mother went to work at Stella's bakery, starting at five but getting home before the kids. In high school he worked every Saturday for the plumber across the street. When Anna and everyone else went to Cal or Stanford, he went to work for the plumber fulltime. Honor roll, football star, student body president, he could have gotten into any college. But he didn't apply.

Since he couldn't make school his job, he made it his hobby. It was like going to night school, he said, with professors like Bertrand Russell and Shakespeare and the *Atlantic Monthly*.

Anna was impressed with his paycheck, but the money had to go in a lot of directions. It ended up putting his sisters and brothers through college. In those days, he had to be thrifty. Since phone calls across the Bay were expensive then – maybe a quarter for a conversation – he and Anna sent penny postcards back and forth to each other. It was like e-mailing is now – except now everybody's e-mailing. Then nobody sent quick little messages back and forth every day.

Sometimes he'd just tell her an amazing fact he'd learned that night: "'Love is blind.' Guess who said that." She'd write back one word:

"Who?" He'd write, "Shakespeare! (*As You Like It*)" Later she got a postcard with the pen digging into the paper: "Guess what! *Chaucer* said 'Love is blynd.' (*Canterbury Tales*)"

He liked to copy out things other people said, things he'd been thinking about, but they could say it better than he could. So Anna got postcards from famous people.

Courage is the greatest of the virtues, because it makes all the others possible.

Winston Churchill

She went to the closet where she kept her old tax returns and big envelopes full of articles she'd torn out and hoped to read someday – and shoeboxes full of memorabilia. Reaching to the box marked "Cal," she shuffled through all sorts of postcards. She laughed to find a picture of Joe that was all nose, and smiled at one of her in her bathing suit. A postcard tumbled to the floor. She picked it up and read:

The lyfe so shorte, the crafte so long to lerne,
The assay so hard, so sharpe the conquerynge.
Geoffrey Chaucer

Putting the top back on the shoebox, her eyes welled up. She and Joe hadn't had any idea how shorte the lyfe would be.

SHE HAD CHASED him. Everyone could see it. The friends from home in North Beach thought she was brazen and the friends from Cal thought she was crazy. (A plumber!) She didn't care what anyone thought. Except Joe. He didn't seem to mind.

Believe it or not, in those days, the word cellulite hadn't been invented. Anyway, she didn't have any. She had nothing at all to be ashamed of, except not being as smart as Joe, or as hard-working or as earnest. He knew too that he was smarter and more hard-working and more earnest. He liked her anyway.

In the case of Rayford, the problem was more than what was on the outside. It was what might be on the inside. As she went to the recycling bin on the back steps of the building, she stood by the garbage chute disassembling the box the groceries had come in and thought about Winnie Schindler's stroke. Winnie was three years younger than Anna. And the office administrator at the museum, Mavis Chang, two years younger than Anna, had osteoporosis so bad she broke a rib just by coughing. In a few years, Anna could imagine Rayford having to take care of her.

Well, he was a doctor.

How could she distort reality. One thing Rayford didn't need was another patient. When she got back into the apartment Louis and Ella were singing "Can't We Be Friends." A sign.

But then that song ended and the singers crooned, "'It isn't your sweet conversation . . . that brings this sensation . . .'"

But it *was*.

"'Oh, no. It's just the nearness of you.'"

Well, that too.

DOORBELL. BARKING THAT funny little rough-tough-cream-puff bark, Posy jumped off the sofa and sent a couple of cushions flying. Over the intercom, a just-cracking young male voice said, "Delivery. Ray and Pete's." She buzzed him into the building and got to her entry hall just as the elevator opened. "Josh!"

His face was one big proud grin. "Hey, Mrs. Leone." The four paper bags in his hand were stapled shut with the pink sales slips attached on the outside. He found the bag marked Leone. "You're not sick are you, Mrs. Leone?"

"Oh, no no no. These are just everyday pills. About fifty years from now, you'll have to take everyday pills too."

"Hope I live that long, Mrs. Leone."

Yes. "But Josh. What are you doing, with these bags of pills?"

"Guess I'm working now, Mrs. Leone. I've got this buddy, Ike, who

189

got wind of a job at the drugstore. You know Ike? The piano player? I went in and had an interview with Ray and Pete, of course they've known me since I was born, it was hell of funny, and the wind-up is, here I am. Not exactly nine to five, but four to six is a start. Works out pretty good, since I'm in summer school four days a week. Every day but Friday. So. Got a tip?"

"Oh!" She was so surprised she'd forgotten. Where was her handbag?

"No, no, Mrs. Leone. Just kidding. I don't want no tip from you."

"*Any* tip," she corrected, before she could stop herself.

"Yeah-yeah," said Josh. "You don't need to worry, Mrs. Leone. I speak English pretty good when I have to. Got a whole stack of A compositions to prove it. Say. This is a pretty cool pad. Hell of chill."

She was still looking for her handbag.

"Forget it, Mrs. Leone. You really feeling okay? Because I was thinking, you might like to go out on my rounds with me. I only have three more stops. One on Lombard, two on Chestnut. Ten minutes at the most. You'll see some mighty fine lobbies, Mrs. Leone."

One thing Anna hadn't been thinking she'd like to do this afternoon was go out and make deliveries for the drugstore. But then, she hated to disappoint a young person.

She noticed the fascination on his face when she took the needle off the record. Maybe he'd never seen a phonograph before. "Do I need my coat?"

"Hell no. Hell no."

She appreciated the way he didn't talk down to her. Or up. "Just let me get my keys."

In the elevator he said, "Hey I got a new tape, Mrs. Leone. Paid for it with the paycheck. It's dirt rap."

"Dirt rap?" Did they still have that? They had something like that when Joey was just a little older than Josh.

"Yeah, dirt rap. Hell of funny. Every cuss word you can think of. You're not allowed to buy it unless you're eighteen. But I passed, at Tower Records. They didn't even ask for my ID."

Anna felt sure they had sold it to him because no one over eighteen would want to buy it. "Do you get to write compositions in summer school, Josh? Or are you taking algebra?"

"Oh! Got a C-plus on my last test. Had a celebration last night." They were on the street now, passing the park and turning the corner up Lombard. A line of cars idled their engines all the way down to Van Ness, filling the air with foul smells as they waited to drive down the winding street. "I treated the family to Chinese food. Delivered from Wah Sing. Plus a DVD. I went in and rented an old flick called *This Boy's Life*. Did you see that?"

"Oh, I miss so many movies – but I *loved* the book!"

"Oh. I miss so many books. – Just kidding. – But you gotta see the movie! It was my fifth time." They were in front of the brick house with the columns. Josh sprinted to the front door, and Anna waited at the gate. This elegant Virginia-style house looked so odd and picturesque, squeezed between two big apartment buildings. Anna admired the rose trees lining the path through the lawn and half expected to see Thomas Jefferson answer the door.

"Only two stops to go," Josh said, moving to the top of the hill. "Wait'll you see the lobby of this next place." They turned left at Hyde, where the cable car was stopped to let the passengers get out to play with their cameras. "Did I tell you I've been writing poetry, Mrs. Leone?"

"Heavens. What inspired this?"

"Well." Josh stopped, so he could look straight at her. "I've got a girlfriend." He started walking again, so she did too. "I think the poems are really good. I might get 'em published next semester in the school paper."

"And the girlfriend?"

"Oh, she's real nice. First place, she likes poetry. And she wants to learn to skate. And let's see. She loves *This Boy's Life*. She's only seen it twice. And she's pretty. She gets better grades than I do but I think I'll be improving some. Looks like it. And, what else? Her mom and dad still live together, which is a trip. And they're nice. You know I'm going on

191

fifteen now, Mrs. Leone. So this is the one," he said, stopping. "Get a load of that marble. Be right back."

It was strange how many times Anna had passed this building without looking inside. The floor, so vast, was marble; the walls, which went up two stories' worth in the lobby, were marble. The elevator doors were tremendous sheets of polished brass, matching the banister railings that undulated up the marble staircase. Anna wrinkled her nose.

Josh seemed to be on pretty good terms with the doorman, who handed him something.

"One buck," Josh said. "Sometimes when I get in to see the customer they give me two. One old guy gave me a twenty, and then he died the next day. Last stop." He jogged up to another tall door, making an exchange with another doorman.

"I'll walk you home," he said now. "Oops. Cross here."

"Why?"

"Didn't you see that weird guy?"

She turned and saw the poor man with the horrible hair. "Oh." She stepped faster across the street.

"Don't worry. He won't hurt you with me here. It's just nicer to be on a different sidewalk. You know what, Mrs. Leone? When I told my friend Spike about my girlfriend, he cried."

"He cried?"

"Yeah! He bawled like a baby."

"Why? Was he afraid he'd be losing your friendship, or . . ."

"Hell no, Mrs. Leone. He cried because he was happy for me. I read him my poem and he cried." Josh's long footsteps came to a halt in front of her building. "Well, guess I better get back to the old sweatshop. Thanks for the talk, Mrs. Leone."

"Wait. Josh. You don't want a tip. But I have something you would like. Come on up and I'll give it to you. It's a book. Way back when it first came out, I bought another copy for Joey, but it turned out he'd already read it." Upstairs, she went to the library and found what she was looking for.

"Shit! Are you kidding me, Mrs. Leone? *This Boy's Life?*"

What she felt, as she watched the elevator door shut behind him, was thanks. What luck. The serendipity of being able to give him that book made her happy.

She turned over the record. This time it was Louis, without Ella: "In My Solitude."

Engraved Invitation

WITH BIG SWEEPS from the shoulder he unreeled the hose, tossing it forward up the lawn. His feet hurried to keep up as he threw out yards more. He was descended from a high-class family. Nobility. Of course somewhere along the line some de Brettville in America had messed up economically. Before that they were rich. But to tell you the truth, he could feel the noble blood running through his veins. He'd always felt it. He was born with it. He bent from the hip to give the hose a shake. Now it lay straight. He walked to the faucet and let her rip. From all the little holes, shots of water rose and formed arcs. He liked the way they sparkled. With his hand on the faucet he could make the arches taller and wider, their formation perfect. He could turn the faucet the other way and make them miniature and wobbly, unsure of themselves. He could turn the whole thing into magnificent architecture, or glittering little dribbles, or he could make the sparkles disappear. Tobin the Magnificent.

"Hey, Tobin!" Ike and the dogs. "How's it goin', pal?"

"Ever read Miss Manners?" Tobin answered in his hoarse voice.

"*Miss Manners?* Naw." Ike turned up the path through the woods.

"My wife thinks I should." Tobin watched Ike's back go out of view.

IT MIGHT NOT be what you'd call an engraved invitation. It was a card. Bigger than a business card. Just the right size for the little envelope. Name and address. Engraved. You could feel it on the front and the back. Said "Mr. and Mrs. Nigel Webster Uldrich Chillingsworth." The Mr. and Mrs. part was crossed out with a fountain pen and "Chantal" was written in. Handwriting at the top: "At home, Friday, 8 August, 6 to 10 p.m." Bottom left, Chantal wrote RSVP and the phone number.

His wife thought he should take another lunch hour off from the Norwegian series and walk down to the North Beach library. Check out the etiquette books. Find out the proper form of reply.

Sometimes he wished she'd go to the library. But she had all these complaints. Her back. His mother. Her work. (She was a weaver.) Tobin thought it would be good for her to get out of the house. But she didn't.

He didn't know if they'd let you take Miss Manners out of the library. Could be a reference book. And if you had to use it there, he didn't know what to look under. He could waste a whole lunch hour. Maybe the index would have something like "Invitation, engraved." Or "Home, at."

Maybe he'd go to the North Beach library. Or maybe not. It wasn't even seven yet. He had over four hours to make up his mind.

Could be he'd write a poem about this. Could be just right for the *Bolinas Hearsay News.*

Hillary came up the stairs, asked him how he was.

"I'm kind of looking forward to it," he said. "To tell you the truth."

Looked like she wasn't following him. "I guess you got your invitation?" he asked.

"From Chantal and Nigel! Will we get to meet your wife?"

"She's deciding what to wear." He was on his way to get the clippers. He was starting to get behind in his work. You could get overwhelmed if you didn't keep up. "A gardener has to govern himself," he told Hillary. "This is a big park. Doesn't look so big from a distance, but it's pretty good-sized. And you don't have some boss following you around and making lists for you. It's kind of like being self-employed. Some gardeners don't see it that way, but I've always been pretty good at managing myself. You have to be." Turning up to the shed he said, "She looks pretty good when she gets dressed up. I think you'll be surprised."

195

"I can hardly wait," she called after him, but he was halfway up the stairs and didn't see any need for answering.

NIGEL HAD GONE to work, and with Mrs. Ironside sharing her pillow, Chantal kept her eyes closed and worked on her menu. The dishes would marry the tastes of California with the tastes of France. Mussels steamed in vermouth, to be sure, and *pâté de campagne* – along with the green, yellow, orange, and Burgundy tomatoes she'd been so amazed to see here, some of them with stripes! The local crab was not in season. *Tant pis.* But they might have toasted goat cheese from Pt. Reyes on oak leaf lettuce from Sonoma. Napa Valley wines would be a necessity, along with champagne from Champagne. Chantal put her arms around Mrs. Ironside's neck – her "ruff." It was the opposite of rough. "Today, darling, Nigel is taking the afternoon off to drive us to the new doctor in Palo Alto. Palo *Al*-to. He's a *ca*-nine oph-thal-*mol*-o-gist." She repeated canine ophthalmologist a couple of times, to fascinate Mrs. Ironside. "We hope he can make you better, so you won't bump into the furniture any more. So much energy you have to spend to move across the room, only to bang your beautiful head." Roger put his chin on the covers. "*Je t'aime aussi, chéri,*" she said, and he touched her cheek with his nose. *Ice cube!*

"Now, children," came a woman's voice from under the window. "This is our rose garden. You must be very careful not to touch."

Chantal sprang up. Pulling on her robe, she peered down on a long-haired woman poking up from a crowd of heads. The children looked like toys, holding hands. Three or four heads had Asian black hair, one had cornrows, a couple were blond, and one had lots of little pigtails with bright pink bows, like a birthday present.

"The stems have thorns, which are sharp and can make you bleed," said the teacher. "And the flowers are very, very fragile. If you touch them they may get bruises or even fall apart. You must enjoy them only with your eyes, and your noses. Can everybody smell the roses?" Hands conspicuously clasped behind her back, she bent forward to sniff a

196

Prima Donna. The children were just the right height for smelling the roses, but they tipped forward too – all still holding hands. "All of these roses have names. Just like you, Joey, and you, Heather, and you, Cimba. You see this white one? Its name is Love! And the one next to it is named Honor. Do you see this peach-colored one?" She leaned way across to point. "This one is called 'Just Joey'!"

"Just Joey!" yelled the girl with bows. One boy ducked his head when the others laughed. Joey?

"This little pink one – do you see how tiny it is? It has a funny name. Puppy Love." Again Chantal was tickled by the tinkle of laughter. "And do you see how curly all the petals are on this red one? Its name is Permanent Wave!" More giggles. "Here's a nice name. This one is called Captain Harry Stebbings. And this one is called John F. Kennedy. Does anyone know who John F. Kennedy was?"

"Oh!" Chantal squealed, pirouetting into the bathroom.

AT LA PETITE Treat she shifted her balance from one size twelve quintuple-A shoe to the other. A whole line of people with cameras had come in before her, and they were making noise in various languages. Five minutes passed while someone from some place like Turkey tried to understand the difference between a full-robustity cappuccino and a skinny latte. Getting a cup of coffee had never been such a project in Portland. But she'd started feeling guilty about slipping in to sneak newspapers off the tables and decided it was good policy to buy something once in a while. She could afford a cup of coffee. Five more minutes passed. She calculated that at this rate, in only ten minutes more she'd be at the head of the line. Her eyes moved to the stack of *Bay Guardians* near the counter. These were free for everyone. She took one and left.

Crouching by the No Parking sign to untie Tess's leash, she felt a tap on her shoulder. A huge masculine face with freckles and straight red bangs smiled down from a great height. When she stood up, the face continued to smile down from on high. The man was huge.

197

"Help?" he said.

She felt frightened. "What?"

"Help?"

She took him in. Camera, short sleeves, enormous long arms with curly red hairs. He pointed to her, then to his chest. "Help?"

"You want me to help you?"

He nodded his head up and down, really grinning. He held a fist just below his ear, alongside his cheek. He made pokes in the air with his index finger.

"Phone? You want to phone?"

He shrugged his shoulders and kept up his pantomime.

"You need a telephone." This must be it. "There's one in there," she said, pointing to the laundromat. "Just go in there." She pointed again and started up the hill with Tess.

His hand on her shoulder. "Help?" He took a piece of yellow paper out of his pocket, unfolded it, and showed her a phone number.

"You don't know how to use the telephone?"

He nodded with vigor.

She and Tess led him into the laundromat. "You need money."

He looked puzzled. She pointed to the slots in the pay phone. He took a handful of metal discs out of his pocket, a jumble of sizes, some with holes in the middle. She counted out some American coins and handed them to him, pointing to the slots. He pointed to her and again poked at the air with his index finger. She punched the keys to get the number and when she heard the ring signal handed him the receiver. "*Manitak, manitak*," he said, blushing with happiness. He began to say lilting syllables into the phone and reached a long arm out to grab her hand and pump it.

This would never happen in Portland.

IF YOU'D TOLD Hillary three months ago that she'd someday be happy to have a Friday night to herself, she wouldn't have believed it. But it was true. She had two good books going. One she was reading for work, about how to produce features for TV news. The other was the novel she'd started yesterday in the park and hated to put down. It was about Catholic girls – their aunts and their mother – about women and how much spirit they had and the mystery of why they cared about men. It related to Hillary, because she'd just begun to reflect on the mystery of why she cared about men, considering how disappointing they always turned out to be.

Up Hyde Street, the troupe of three afghans rounded the corner. Tess bounded forward. Luckily, it wasn't Ike holding the leashes. Any other time, Hillary would be glad to see Ike, but not today. It was the skateboard kid, for once without his skateboard. Molly was scraping her claws on the sidewalk to get to Tess, who of course scraped hers too. Lagging way behind the group was Meg.

"Hey!" The skateboard kid made that big arc wave from the elbow. Cute. But Hillary wasn't in the mood for talking. Especially to Meg. After Meg had gone to so much trouble introducing her to Mike. Five minutes after he'd slammed the door that night, he'd opened it again. To say his famous last words "See ya 'round campus."

"Hello, Teresa," Meg called out, getting close. Hillary loved the way she always called Tess Teresa, in that hoarse and loving voice. But today Hillary pretended to be in a rush. "Sorry, can't talk. I'm late for . . ."

Molly and Tess had tangled their leashes. Frenetically Hillary untangled as the puppies retangled. "Wish I hadn't made this appointment . . ."

"Step aside," said the kid, making a Harry Potter flourish. He did the trick.

"Thanks." Hillary went on with her feigned hurrying and disappeared through the door of her building. "Don't worry, Tess." The poor little puppy face looked totally confused and crestfallen. "As soon as the coast is clear." Two minutes later Hillary peeked out and saw the group turn the corner and disappear down Filbert. She opened the door and Tess bolted out fast enough to take her arm off. A man waiting for the cable car asked who's walking who and for once Hillary openly sneered. Then she felt awful. She almost pulled Tess back so she could apologize to the man. But what would she say? That was really a funny joke?

What a relief to get to the park and free Tess and open the *Bay Guardian* to the personals at the back. "W/M, 5′ 6″ but with great build." Maybe she should meet him. If she wrote an ad, she'd probably announced herself as 6′ 2″ but nice.

5′ 6″ W/M was "35, extremely successful entrepreneur, hoping to find woman to jog with, and things." If it hadn't been for the "and things" she might have answered the ad. Well, she didn't like jogging either. "Man who appreciates a disciplined woman," she read, "seeks younger partner (30s to 40s) who takes direction well."

"*Ho!*" It was the skateboard kid. This boy was almost *becoming* Ike. She shut the paper fast, hoping he hadn't seen what she was reading. He asked, "How'd your appointment go?"

"Oh, it was over in no time."

Heading off, he gave the Ike wave.

Leslie had met someone on the Internet who'd turned out pretty frightening. Another guy at work had paid three thousand dollars to join a dating club. (So he'd meet someone who could also afford three thousand dollars.) It didn't work out, but maybe the *Bay Guardian* would work for her. One thing she had to admit: Her opinion of herself was changing. It might have been Nigel and Ike telling her she was sexy. It might even have been Mike. In spite of her defects, he had desired her. Or it could have been something as superficial as Chantal nudging her to have the nerve to wear some pretty clothes.

Somewhere in this paper there must be someone okay. The ideal thing would be to meet someone before Chantal and Nigel's party. She had two weeks.

Luckily most of the men in here gave some information about their height. Quite a few seemed to be "tall."

Fairies

NORMALLY, HE COULDN'T afford to let his male off the leash. Napoleon didn't know he was a *toy* poodle. He'd take on a great dane. But a stroll through the woods showed no sign of dogs anywhere, so Napoleon and Josephine could run. But they didn't. They exercised their nostrils. Neither of them ever ran any more, unless there was an instigator around, like that speed-freak Tess. A quail, head thrusting forwards-backwards forwards-backwards in a rhythm like in an Apache war dance, bopped right up to Josephine. Josephine just looked at it. Napoleon ambled over for a look and lost interest. The bird got bored and chugged away, neck still jerking to the silent tom-tom.

Now that he'd turned over half his day-to-day operations to his new production manager, he could knock off early. For the dogs' sake, he liked to get to the park when Tess was tearing through the woods. For his own sake, he liked to time it so he'd see that young guy with the Australian shepherd. Rob. Rob used to keep a pretty regular schedule, but he hadn't been around lately. Pierre wondered if the dog was still alive. Very old animal. Dizzy spells. He sat on the bench that faced the hedge and lit up a Gauloise, remembering his active days. Even if he hadn't done it in twelve years, going on thirteen, he hoped the day would never come when he didn't get a hit from talking to a great-looking man.

Tobin did a nice job with this hedge, but Pierre always wondered if he couldn't do something about those gaps that came at irregular intervals. Through the scrappy holes you saw pale blue, and it was hard to make out if it was sky or water. Pretty peek-a-views, but he'd like a neater hedge.

Shrill barks erupted from the little poodles. "Cut the noise." He lunged to grab Napoleon. Down the steps came two of Ike's afghans. Not the male. So Pierre could let go of Napoleon. A gorgeous brunette held the two leashes, the green one relaxed and the red one taut as a line with a fish on it. The comical puppy at the end had a soprano bark. "God, I wish I could let her go," she said. Her voice was rich and low. "But if I did, I'd never see her again."

Pierre stood up and held out a hand. "You must be Ike's beautiful wife."

She had a throaty laugh. "Does Ike have a beautiful wife?"

"That's what he tells us, but until this minute, no one believed him."

Tying the puppy's leash to the back of the bench she plonked herself down on the seat, spread her legs like open scissors and flexed her heels. "I want to tell you, I'm a big fan of your work."

"Me? Mine? How do you know . . . We haven't met, have we?"

"There aren't too many people in berets around here, puffing on Gauloises." She had a chesty laugh. "I get a rundown on every dog person at least twice a week. Of course, I've been mad about your style since way before we moved to San Francisco."

He'd been ogling her own style. It wasn't like his. The slim tunic she wore over her skinny black pants looked like Ohashi, but it could have been Yamahito. He'd been thinking about a mustard like that for next spring. Well, not mustard. More like the yolk of a brown egg. The texture seemed like a silk-and-linen weave. Her earrings were asymmetrical – multicolored geometrics dangling like miniature mobiles under slices of gloss black hair. She was young, fifteen or twenty years Ike's junior. Not the type he'd imagined, for Ike. She wasn't the type he'd think would like his stuff, either. "Did Jason Spence do those earrings?"

When she shook her head the plastic rattled. "Shelly Seth."

"I was close," said Pierre. "Those new Brits are classy."

"I think your stuff is the definition of class," she said. She looked him straight in the eyes. "I mean, it's the grace. I've always wanted to meet you. We're in related fields."

"Rags?"

"Yeah. I'm textiles."

He checked out her nails. Nice to see red again. "You got a studio, or what?"

"Oh, I work at home. We have a huge old flat. Completely broken down when we moved in, but the rent was right. We had to practically rebuild it."

He thought about how he never even wondered about what kind of places the dog people lived in.

"Of course," she said, "when the landlady saw what we'd done she tried to get us out so she could double the rent."

"Come on!" He was a landlord himself. "People like that give a bad name to people like me." Better change the subject. "You pretty busy?"

"Busy! There's no end. I hardly ever see Ike any more. I'm still working when he goes out to play at night. I konk just before he gets home. When I wake up he's gone – out playing golf at sunrise, walking the dogs. I work while he catches a nap in the afternoon – after he rows, or drops in on his cronies, speaks a little Chinese . . ."

"What's this speaking Chinese stuff?"

"Didn't you know? That used to be part of his job. International banking. First he majored in Asian Studies at Yale . . ."

"Yale?"

"Oh, yeah. Then Wharton. Master's in Finance. Then New York. Hong Kong. He married a socialite. Big house in Scarsdale. Then all of a sudden he flipped the other way. He doesn't like to talk about it. It's his 'shadowy past.'"

"I'll be God-damned."

Under her makeup, which was a little heavy for his taste, Pierre could see crescents like bruises. "Who do you sell to?"

She shot him a look from the corners of her eyes. "Brace yourself."

He used both hands to hold his beret down.

"Would you believe Kathleen Garth?"

"You?" He was amazed. "I mean, it's pretty, but—"

"You're right. It's not me."

"All those faint little – posies?"

"That's me. I mean, it's not me. But I need the money. I'm so sick of violets I could go out and stamp on some."

"Is that all you do?" He wished he hadn't put it quite that way.

"No. No. Thank God. No, I'm starting my own line. That's one reason for the hours. I've been back and forth to New York all year."

"Hey!" He spotted Mrs. Leone. "Join the party." The poodles would get a workout after all, with that popular Posy. Dust flew. Pierre started introductions, but Meg interrupted, happy to show off that she knew Mrs. Leone already, from word of mouth. She even knew Posy's complete medical history.

"Anybody know a good housekeeper?" she asked out of the blue.

"Oh!" Words poured out of Mrs. Leone. "Morella mends upholstery, fixes the garbage disposal, and tells me when my shoes need repairs. She takes them to the shop. I think she loves taking care of me the way she loves taking care of her children. She's smart and well educated – you'd want her as a friend! She works one day a week for a monster who is – well, I have to say, *cruel.*"

"Why doesn't she quit?" Pierre asked.

"Her husband had an accident at work. He's paralyzed. She can't quit. Unless . . ."

Meg's eyes were getting round. "How much does she charge?"

"I'm not sure." Mrs. Leone looked bewildered. "You see, I wouldn't think of paying her as little as she told me she wanted. After all, I don't need a psychiatrist . . ."

"Psychiatrist?"

"Well, whatever Morella told me she charges for a whole day is about what a psychiatrist gets for just an hour. It's less than a lawyer gets for *half* an hour. And that is unfair."

"I could pay more than the monster! Right now, with my Kathleen Garth gig, money isn't my problem. Time is."

"Exactly!"

And on and on, buzz buzz tweet. Pierre remembered that he hadn't had a drink yet. He touched his beret, a gesture to the ladies, who barely noticed. But at the bottom of the steps, the poodles spun on their leashes and shot up, jerking his arms back from his shoulders. Oh my God. The Australian shepherd was there.

"PIERRE!" MRS. LEONE said. Luckily Meg and the afghans had gone, and Mrs. Leone acted like she hadn't seen him in ages. The old girl was on to him. A diplomat, too. He could feel a flood of heat in his cheeks as he asked Rob, "How's your kid?"

The Australian shepherd, a female, teetered over to bat Napoleon with a paw and stumbled off into the ivy. Squatting was a problem, and her knees shook. When she made her way back to the bench, she listed to the right and her eyes were paler than they had been – like cloud cover over blue sky.

"The vet was afraid it was a brain tumor. I was prepared for the worst, but it turns out to be some inner ear thing. I have to force six pills a day down her throat, but I think there's hope." The dog moved toward a pine-cone. Each step took a while.

"Old age," Rob said.

"You wouldn't know about that," said Pierre.

"Not yet."

"You will."

"Hope so." Rob's tone was serious.

This was getting heavy. There was something to be said for not having done it for a dozen years and more. "Well look who's coming!" Pierre rose to his feet to show respect, and so did Rob.

"No, no," Frankie said, taking out a smoke. "I've been sitting all afternoon. Working on my drawings."

"She says she draws," Pierre told Rob. "I've never seen any proof."

"Well, it's awkward, bringing my drawings up to the park. The wind would blow them around, the dogs would kick dirt on them. They're pretty good I think, but no better than what you see in the magazines and the art galleries."

Pierre sneaked a grin at Rob.

"I just do it for myself," Frankie explained. "I like to see what I can do, how much I've improved over the years. I've kept all my drawings. When I compare what I do now to what I did even one year ago, I see a big difference. From 1977 – there's no comparison. You learn. That's one thing I can say for aging."

"Yes," Anna said.

"I've never seen any of your drawings either," Frankie said sarcastically.

"Oh, I don't draw!" Mrs. Leone looked embarrassed. "I just mean, I can see improvements, over the years, in my museum work and the things I do. Nothing important, like art. I must say I envy you, that you have something concrete, like drawings, instead of just kind of vague memories of mistakes you hope you don't make any more."

"Pierre draws too," Frankie said. "Or so he tells me."

Pierre didn't want to talk about his drawing. "Rob and I both collect comics. Do you remember Jane Arden?"

Anna and Frankie remembered. Rob knew them from the dealers.

"I liked Jane Arden," Pierre continued, "because she was a brunette like my mother. I was a mama's boy. Remember how the Jane Ardens used to have paperdolls? I'd cut them out, and I could have spent all twenty-four hours a day with my paperdolls. Drove my stepdad crazy. He'd catch me and whip me till I couldn't sit down. He was a trucker, and he thought the job of a man was to be tough. Get out there and do hard labor, education meant nothing to him. I guess I can't blame him. That's all he knew."

"Guess he wasn't too crazy about your choice of careers?" Rob asked.

"Ho!" Pierre roared. "He nearly croaked when I got my first job. My very first job, before I went to art school, was out here in Frisco – a trainee

206

with Elizabeth Levine. He thought I had a desk job, which was bad enough. I don't know how he found out the whole story, but when he did it was hell for my mom. He told her it was all her fault I'd turned into a fairy. Oh, he really gave it to her."

Rob and Pierre laughed a big one, but Mrs. Leone sat there biting her lip. You couldn't blame her. Stuff like this was probably new to her.

"I think it was worse when my stepdad found out I was a dress designer than when I actually broke the news that I was a faggot."

"How'd you do it?" Rob asked.

"Oh, I couldn't avoid telling them after a while. My lover and I went back and visited. Christmas, summer. One time we got in a fight that was so violent – jealousy, you know – they couldn't help hearing what we were yelling, and it wasn't hard to figure it out."

"After that could you be open about it?" Mrs. Leone asked.

"Are you kidding? After that we couldn't go back. I couldn't even call my mom. At first I would call, and I'd hang up when he answered the phone, but he figured that one out pretty fast. It got to where the only way I could talk to my mom – because he went over the phone bills – was if she'd go to a pay phone and call me."

Rob seemed to be enjoying this tale. He probably had some of his own to tell, but they'd had enough tragedy for one walk in the park.

"So how's the apartment business, Frankie?" Pierre asked.

"I thought you'd never ask. It's hell."

Tall, Dark, and Allegedly Handsome

THE AD HAD a thick black border and said, "Tall, Dark, and Allegedly Handsome." The rest was interesting.

> MD, PhD, 43, with extraordinary financial success, seeks permanent union with slim, good-looking, intelligent woman, 28 to 42, personally and financially able to travel and seek adventure. I am taking an early retirement and desire a companion with whom to enjoy life and possibly marriage.

She'd used up half her notepad, and she couldn't get her letter right. This was once she wished she hadn't sold her laptop – but the computer might not be right anyway, for a letter this intimate. The most recent approach said:

Dear Tall, Dark, and Allegedly Handsome:

I have never responded to a Personal Classified, in fact until today I had never read one with myself in mind. Today, though, I decided to answer one ad in the *Bay Guardian*, and yours was the one I picked.

I chose it because I wonder what you are going to do with the rest of your life. There are so many kinds of adventures – I wonder which one you'll choose – you're in an exciting spot.

As for me, I suppose I could arrange to be "personally and financially able to travel," if I gave up my apartment and took my dog and somebody else paid. Even England might be okay now, for an extra-long stay, since I understand they've revised their strict laws to prevent rabies, so that instead of the six-month quarantine they used to require (a deprivation that would kill most dogs) they now allow dogs into the country if they have some kind of computer chip embedded in their flesh certifying that they are rabies-free. I'd have to check into how this is done, but I assume it would be possible, and therefore my dog and I would be able to accompany you. I hope so, because I'm sure I would love England. I am always reading books about it, from the Brontë sisters through James Herriot.

Since in your list of qualifications you put "slim" first, I can say I certainly fit that bill, although I may actually be slimmer than you might like. Also, I think I should warn you that the fashion magazines say, "Slim is no longer in." I mention this because I fear that a person who puts slim foremost may be fashion-oriented, and the fact is that fashion changes. My best friend, a Frenchwoman named Chantal (whom I'm sure you would like very much – she is married) is also slim, although not as slim as I am, and she is mad at this new trend. "Now they're dictating that we be something even more unachievable than what they demanded before!" she complains. (She's afraid that they'd want you to be fat in places where she wouldn't be fat, if she were fat. Myself, I can't imagine what parts of me would be fat, if I were fat, and whatever places did get fat on me, I would welcome them.) In any case, I agree with her that all this emphasis on slimness or "voluptuousness" is a bit beside the point, as far as "seeking permanent union" with another human being is concerned. Also, it seems odd, the order of the adjectives you specified: first slim, second good-looking, third intelligent. Don't you agree that was odd? I mean, putting good-looking after slim seems a funny priority. But I was especially puzzled by the way you put intelligence last.

In this case it doesn't matter that you put slimness ahead of intelligence. As luck would have it, I'm much more slim than I am intelligent.

Also, I am very tall. This does not affect my personality and should not affect our relationship, should we have one, but I think I should warn you, in case you might feel intimidated (6′ 1″).

Also, how did you decide on the upper and lower age limits in your ad? I see that your upper limit is one year younger than your own age. This struck me as peculiar. And in answering your ad at all, I am assuring myself that you would be somewhat flexible in your numbers. (I am one year shy of your lower limit – or a fraction of a year. My twenty-eighth birthday will be on Valentine's Day next year.)

For some unknown reason I have always liked doctors. (What's your PhD in? I think I'd like PhDs too, although I don't know any very well.)

I am a TV camerawoman. I work for the evening news in San Francisco. Our station has the top rating! I am not wedded to my job, although I like it more and more, as I get to know the people. Also, I'm branching out. I'm thinking up ideas for features to suggest to the producers, and these features could be very much fun.

One reason I'm writing you is that it occurs to me that you have this new freedom and want to do something new with it, but travel may not be what you need at all. I live on Russian Hill in San Francisco. (I see in your ad no address, just a *Guardian* box number, but for some reason I assume you live in Berkeley. Do you?) On Russian Hill I have a life which you probably would not believe. My friends here are from all over the map, in terms of class and age. There are quite a few foreign people. You can pick almost any major country and find someone from it, right here. As for my friends, each one of them is someone you could travel thousands of miles and never meet the likes of.

I can imagine that you're tired of Berkeley, or whatever town or neighborhood you live in. But you might find that in San Francisco, especially on Russian Hill, there is much of interest. This might really be the adventure you seek. I would love to share it with you.

Sincerely,

Hillary Birdwood

SHE DECIDED TO scratch out the last sentence. How did she know she would love to share it with him?

And she decided to add a P.S.:

P.S.: I really respect the fact that you didn't ask for a picture. I am sending one anyway, maybe just because you didn't ask. This was taken in the park where I live, practically, by my friend Nigel (husband of Chantal, mentioned before). (He is English!) I'm the tall one in the gray sweatshirt. The other woman is a society woman named Mrs. Leone (she represents the high class, of the many classes I told you live on Russian Hill). I actually don't know her as well as some other people, but I'd love to. She has a heart of gold. The man with the long gray hair and beard is Tobin, our gardener. (I mean, we think of this park as our garden, and he works for the park department.) You might think he represents the low end of the class range, but that would be a mistake.

Even though the sweatshirt I'm wearing here is huge, I think you can still see I am "slim."

READING THIS OVER, Hillary added something more:

P.P.S.: By writing this letter, I'm not seeking a permanent union, I'm just thinking it might be nice to meet you.

And then, there was something else to say:

P.P.P.S.: I wonder why, since you have achieved "extraordinary financial success," you specify that the woman you seek must be "personally and financially" free to travel. Do you mean that, even if you fell in love with her, and had oodles of money, as you seem to, you would still demand that she pay her own way? Even considering that she may not actually want to go anywhere, but would go just to be with you?

On reading this, Hillary had one more thing to add:

P.P.P.P.S.: As a doctor, isn't it a betrayal of your Hippocratic Oath to abandon your patients in the prime of your life and go off traveling and seeking adventure? Maybe you could at least be a ship's doctor, or join some organization like Doctors Without Borders.

IT WAS LATE. The day was almost gone. Hillary had wasted so much time on this letter, to this incredibly selfish, rigid, lookist creep, that she had completely forgotten Tess's absolute need to be taken to the park. It was nearly nighttime. How could she have wasted her time this way, on a letter it was pointless to mail?

"Tess! Bring me your lee-eash!" As Tess clattered the clasp across the hardwood, Hillary put the cap on her pen. Then she took it off. She walked to her closet, reached up to the top shelf for the box that held envelopes, and plucked one out. "Just a minute, Tess." She addressed the envelope with the box number and printed her own address and phone number underneath the signature on her letter. In her wallet she kept several stamps, and she tore one out to stick on. The letter was four pages, messily written with a few sentences crossed out, but he didn't deserve another rewrite. She used her thumb and index finger to press four folds into the sheaf. Adding the snapshot, she had a pretty fat envelope to fit in the mailbox. She tore off a second stamp, just in case. She licked the flap of the envelope and just after she'd closed it she remembered something else. Luckily the glue was still wet so she could gently pull the envelope open without tearing it, just warping it a little. She found the place where she'd shaved an inch off her height, crossed out 6′ 1″ and wrote in 6′ 2″.

AT THE BLUE mailbox, she jammed in the letter and slammed the lid shut to make such a furious clank that two people waiting for the cable car jumped! She scowled at them and stomped up Hyde Street, jerking Tess from her greedy sniffs at the fire hydrant. At the brick street she unlatched the leash, kicked a pine-cone, and kept stomping.

"Well I declare," drawled a male voice. At the gate to the tennis court stood Philo Righi, whose corgi scuttled over the lawn to jump up to Tess's hindquarters. "Hey." Tossing a chartreuse tennis ball for the dogs, Philo strode over to Hillary saying, "My, my. The lady looks angry."

Her reflexes pulled her down at the knees and shoulders and made her voice chirp, "Oh, hi." The cheerfulness she was trying for didn't come out sounding very genuine at all.

He ambled closer, until he was near enough to smile lightly down into her face. "What's his name?"

This did make her laugh a second, before slipping back into her frown. She sifted through the answers that criss-crossed her brain. This man I've been seeing wants me to drop my career and travel around the world with him. This man I've been seeing is ridiculously jealous of all my other boyfriends.

"What *is* his name?" Philo Righi asked, sounding serious.

She was sick of contracting like an inchworm. With a large inhale of grass-scented air, she straightened her knees and spine. She shook her head so she could feel her hair brush against one cheek and the other, and her nose. She lifted her hands and shrugged. "I don't know his name," she admitted.

His chin stretched up some now, to examine her face. He was ignoring his corgi, who jumped on the knees of his jeans to present the tennis ball she'd fetched.

Hillary bent down to take the ball and toss it. "You're a psychiatrist," she said, from her full height. "What do you think of a doctor who ditches his patients at the age of forty-three and runs off to seek adventure? Who demands that his wife come along and pay her own plane fare? Who picks his wife first for her weight, second for other things, including her money! Even though he is 'extraordinarily' rich?"

Philo's face showed real sympathy. "So your boyfriend is married?"

Hillary smiled a real smile. "No. At least it's not that. No. No, this man is not my boyfriend and he isn't married. Yet. This is all predicated on his finding somebody thin enough and rich enough."

Philo Righi shoved those big expressive hands of his into his pockets and looked up at her with bemused puzzlement. "This is interesting. Why don't you tell me from the beginning?"

She'd forgotten how large his eyes were. How even the whites sparkled. The whites set off the irises so dark she couldn't name the color. Not chocolate, not onyx, not jet, not anything but this amazing complexity of colors and lights that would be called, on a driver's license, brown. Maybe the color was black fire.

She didn't think about where to begin her story, because she knew she wasn't going to tell him.

"Tess!" she yelled. She was sorry to go, but, "Tess! Tess." She ran to the tennis courts, knowing Tess would stop rolling on the lawn with the corgi and follow. When Tess was inside the courts Hillary stepped out and closed the gate, to trap her. Tess sped over to the gate, frantic to get out. Hillary opened it a crack and attached the leash to the collar. "C'mon, Tess." They walked to the brick street.

"Wait!" Philo Righi called out, leashing his corgi. "I'll walk you down."

On the way, every word she could think of to say was too

insignificant. He didn't say anything either, even at her front door. When she looked down into his eyes, the black flickering there was so bright she had to turn away. "'Bye."

French-Fried Roses

ANNA LEONE WAS not on a diet. It was just that she didn't have any interest in eating. Last night at Chantal's party, there was all this lovely food, catered by the new bistro on Hyde that was getting all the write-ups. Chantal had a black bowl, big as a coffee table, that worked like a round frame for concentric circles of mussels and prawns and grilled peppers and saffron rice. Even the outlandishly oversized serving spoons (sterling) were works of modern art. The most surprising salad was blood oranges and lemons, with olive oil and a sprinkling of edible flowers. Another platter was garnished with French-fried roses. Rayford ate three. ("Delicious.")

"Where's Meg?" Anna asked Ike. She and Rayford had been the first to arrive. Ike was next, looking crisp in a seersucker suit. Meg was in New York on business. "Work, work, work, that's all she does any more. It's a God-damned bore. A God-damned bore." And that was almost all the talk he had time for. He'd just stopped by on his way to his piano gig down the hill.

Tobin spent the first half of the evening with a dancer who'd been in a Dr. Pepper commercial. He seemed to be trying to get her life's story. Tobin's wife, magnificent in a black mantilla they'd bought in Spain, back in his bike-racing days, pretended to listen in, her eyes roving the room. When Anna went over to rescue her, Tobin's wife all but winked and whispered, "He's researching a poem." When Nigel interrupted and took the dancer away to meet his old school chum, visiting from

London, Tobin found Martine. They didn't speak the same language, but they had a high time pantomiming dog barks and jumps, the saxophone, and a bicycle race. Since Martine regarded poets as the highest humans, she was thrilled to "talk" to Tobin. Soon a publisher from Switzerland entered as translator and Anna moved on to introduce Tobin's wife to a potter from Ukiah. Out of the corner of her eye Anna saw the Swiss publisher reach in his pocket and hand Tobin a business card.

Pierre looked very much at home, holding a martini glass. He found a tan, muscular man to talk to. Anna wondered if this man's eyelashes were real. She'd wondered the same thing about Elizabeth Taylor. Implanted? Pierre was up on these things. She'd ask him tomorrow in the park. Would they come out when she swam?

Josh, almost bursting out of a suit that pulled at the shoulders and crotch and showed a lot of sock, brought his girlfriend! She was a chubby thing who blushed like a Renoir. Anna worked at drawing her out and was just beginning to think it would have to be some other time when Josh said, "Mrs. Leone's the one who gave me *This Boy's Life*." The girl said "Oooh!" and told how Josh said it was the best book he'd ever read and how she didn't want to read it because it didn't have any girls in it, but he said she had to anyway so she did and she *loved* it, even if there weren't any girls – well, there was the mom . . . Then, to Anna's amazement, the girl took Josh's sleeve and walked right up to Ray and Pete from the drugstore. Of course, Josh took it from there. He certainly knew how to carry a conversation. Ray's wife was just what you'd expect: a marshmallow with glasses and a silk print. She was warm, and Anna saw a pleased look on Josh's face when he noticed his girlfriend seemed comfortable with her. The amazing thing was Pete's wife. She was a bombshell. Her skirt was almost as short as a bathing suit, and her top was tight and sequined, showing lots of cleavage. For a while – a little too long in fact – Rayford couldn't take his eyes off her. Anna finally found a moment to lead him away to Philo Righi, who wasn't joining in. Philo seemed edgy. Amazingly enough he'd come on his own. He wasn't

217

wildly gesturing with his hands the way he usually did. Maybe he was self-conscious to be seen in public without the usual babe. Rayford talked to him sort of doctor-to-doctor, but Anna noticed Philo kept losing track, and Rayford had to repeat some of his questions. Philo jumped every time the doorbell rang. Maybe he was hoping to see the tall girl, Hillary? She was the one person Anna was puzzled not to see. Frankie wasn't there, but of course so few people liked her. (Of course, it worked both ways.) But Hillary. Anna was sure she didn't work Friday nights. Did she have flu?

With all that beautiful food, Anna had nothing but a few slices of blood orange, a taste of striped green tomato, and a couple of mussels. She kept the same glass of Chardonnay with her throughout the evening. This loss of appetite had been recent, but already her clothes had begun to hang.

MORELLA HAD TUNED the radio to an old rock station, and she stroked her silver-polishing cloth in rhythm with Marvin Gaye: "Let's Get It On." Anna's hips swayed with the song as she fixed a pot of coffee for both of them. She told Morella she was not on a diet, but she was losing weight. Morella told Anna she *was* on a diet, but she was *not* losing weight. She'd started going to Weight Watchers, and all the women weighed in, and some of them lost five pounds, three pounds, at least a pound or two, each week. Morella had never lost more than a quarter of a pound in a week. It had been four weeks, and she still hadn't lost a whole pound. "They tell me," she said, "it's slow for some people."

Anna knew this was true. Slow and steady was good. "I'm thinking about my French. It was almost impossible to talk with Martine at first. But little by little . . . It's like you and your English. Last year we could never have had a conversation like this. We couldn't tell the difference from one week to the next, but it added up, and here we are. We understand each other perfectly. It'll probably go like that with the diet."

"But I have to lose *fifty* pounds!" ("*Feef-dy.*") She burst into that ticklesome laugh, and Anna laughed too. She handed Morella a steaming cup on a saucer and poured a cup for herself, sliding into a chair and setting both elbows on the table.

"I have to lose the weight," Morella said, "because of my kids." ("Keeds.") "My little one" ("leedle") "he say to me one day, 'Mommy, all the kids have skinny mommies. Why do I have a fat mommy?'"

"Oh, dear!" Poor mommy.

"Yes!" agreed Morella. "So I *trying*. But it hard."

Anna told Morella about how she was not trying, and it was easy. She wasn't bragging, she was trying to figure the whole thing out. Instead of swimming for twenty minutes two or three times a week, she found herself swimming a mile every day. Well, almost every day. She could see a difference in her stomach. Also, she needed the extra lung capacity, since Rayford wasn't one for driving or taking cabs. They walked to the Marina, and once all the way to the Palace of Fine Arts. Sometimes they walked to Chinatown – so pretty, with lantern light on some streets, but so much of the neighborhood still a little sleazy, the way San Francisco used to be before all the well-to-do young people started prettying it up. Rayford led her up all sorts of routes home, some steeper than others, but all of them up. She would have thought that would make her tired and hungry, but it was just the opposite. Her body seemed to be manufacturing energy on its own, not wanting calories except the kind in carrots and celery and things she used to eat only as a duty. "I have no will power, but I don't need any. When my stomach growls, it doesn't seem to say Feed me. It seems to say Congratulations."

"I wish that would happen to me," Morella sighed.

"Maybe it will."

A song came on the radio. "Let's Get Physical." It made Anna smile – partly because of what was happening to her, and partly because it brought back a memory of the last trip she and Joe had made to Bologna to see his Aunt Rosa and the kids. Rosa's little granddaughter had just changed from wanting to be that pretty ice-skater with the haircut, whatever her name was – you know, in the eighties – to wanting to be Olivia Newton-John. Anna didn't know how to react when the little

219

innocent waggled her hips and threw her whole body into a shockingly good imitation of Olivia singing this song. "Oh, honey!" Anna had said. But now she wanted to say "Oh, honey!" to herself. If Rosa's little granddaughter had been too young for "Let's Get Physical," Anna was too old.

About the weight loss, maybe there was another explanation. Maybe her body was adapting to the other change she'd just gone through: She'd lost a few inches in height. The heels she'd loved so well had had to be replaced with flats, for all that walking. A sacrifice. She did wear the high ones for special occasions. She wore her Blahniks to Chantal's.

MORELLA WAS TELLING her about the super-rich lady she worked for on Tuesdays, in Pacific Heights. "I have problems," Morella said. "I have terrible problems, and sometimes at night I cannot sleep, and sometimes I cry, and I cry. But I don't have problems like most of the rich people I working for. This lady in Pacific Heights, she always in Europe, and her son, fifteen year old, he home all day. He never go to school. He take drugs. And do you know, he wet the bed. Every time I come, the sheets are wet, not changed since the last time I come."

"Oh!"

"Fifteen year old," Morella said. "But that not the worst. He wear his mama underwear. I find the panties, wet, in the bed."

"Oh my goodness."

"He know I know. He asked me not to tell. So I don't tell." She started to giggle. "I see so many people, in my work. So many problems. At night I tell my husband, and he say, 'Morella, you know so much about people. One day you going to have to sit yourself down and write a book.'"

Through the window Anna caught a glimpse of Ike herding the afghans across the promenade. "I have to go out!" She dashed for Posy's leash.

Breathless from the stairs, she called out, "Ike! Ike. Ike, I meant to ask

220

you, did Meg ever decide whether she needs the housekeeper we talked about?"

"Naw." Ike growled it. He screwed his face. "No way. A housekeeper? How bourgeois." He started to the other end of the terrace, led by his three shaggy dogs. "How bourgeois," he called over his shoulder. "No thank you. No servants in our house. No servants in our house."

Well. Anna was disappointed. The whole thing seemed like a nice exchange. Meg needed help, Morella needed money. She needed an alternative to the monster who didn't pay because all Latins were stupid and lazy.

She was overqualified for this kind of work, but she was working on her English. Anna was helping her, and Meg might help her too, just in the natural course of a day. What Morella needed most was practice. Even Ike would probably help her with English, just being there. She'd have to mention this benefit, next time she saw him.

And Morella was dieting! Pretty soon she'd be able to compete for a really good job. She was a master organizer. She could be an executive. She was bilingual! More or less. More and more.

When the time came, Anna would give her some expensive clothes to help make a knock-out impression. But Meg could help even more in the clothes department. Anna could just see Morella, twenty-five pounds thinner, in one of the outfits Meg designed. The most important thing, for this period when Morella had to earn her living this way, was that she work for nice people.

Anna sat on the bench and vowed that the next time she saw Ike she'd fly down and catch him. He was a reasonable man, he'd see the light.

Light. The wind was kissing the Bay, making sparkles like sequins of gold. Sitting in this exact spot reminded her of summers at the lake with Joe and the kids, except that here, you didn't hear motor boats.

MOMENTS OF EROTIC bliss may be like illness or pain: The mind retains the fact that they happened, but the memory can't recreate the

221

sensations with all the feeling that was there. Even last night had lost its vividness by morning. The thought of it, though, gave her a shiver. She savored the shiver, but it wasn't the same shiver.

After Chantal and Nigel's party, Rayford wanted to extend their walk home. She didn't groan about her heels, she just wouldn't pay attention to her feet. She did steady herself by taking his arm on the way down the cable-car route past Ghirardelli Square. The other time she'd taken his arm he'd tensed up. This time she explained and said, "This is survival." He chuckled. On level ground, and on the way up, she let go. And she actually did forget her feet.

They walked through the empty bleachers that overlooked the Bay, the bleachers where last Sunday they had heard the steel drums play in the sun. At midnight, they were the only ones there, except for the moon, veiled by a sheer canopy of clouds. The surf had a slow beat, and three or four big boats rocked in the harbor. The S.S. *Balclutha* was lit up, with stacks of yellow portholes and streamers of tiny bulbs.

She felt herself jump when he wrapped his long arm around her back and clasped her waist with his hand. It took her a second to relax and let her body drink in the pleasure of how her shoulder fit perfectly into the hollow of his.

Today it occurred to her that maybe it was lucky he'd waited so long to put an arm around her. A month or two ago she hadn't had a waist.

Last night in the bleachers a thrill buzzed inside her and grew till she thought she might burst, or cry. Dim, from a distance, music was coming toward them. They turned in the direction of Fisherman's Wharf to see a figure with a jaunty step walking along the edge of the water in baggy Bermudas and a baseball cap on backwards. He carried a gigantic radio like the kind Joey used to lug everywhere. Soon they could hear Louis Armstrong's voice, making its way across the beach to them. "I see friends shakin' hands, Sayin' *how*-do-you-do, They're really sayin' – I love you. And I say to myself . . ." Rayford put a rasp in his voice and sang out the next words along with Louis Armstrong: "'What a wonderful world.'"

222

This seemed to be their song.

They walked on, past Fisherman's Wharf, its bustle dwindled out, and farther down the Embarcadero with its finger piers poking into the Bay and water lapping against them. This sound took her back to Joe, to the two of them in the moonlight with the lake slapping the dock. Here, though, the water stretched out black as oil, reflecting lights like yellow paint spilled and smeared.

When a talker like Rayford stood wordless, a new electricity filled the air. They climbed back up Russian Hill by way of Chestnut Street, past the Art Institute, to Anna's.

Sitting at one end of the sofa, with her on the other, he reached across to take hold of her ankle, to lift it from the floor and lay it on his knee. He took her shoe off and placed it on the coffee table. All this with no words. Starting with the heel, he massaged every tiny bone and muscle, moving to the arch, and eventually to the ball of the foot – finally giving complete attention to each of the toes. He moved that foot closer in on his lap and picked up the other foot, undressing it. Having pleasured both feet, he set them on the floor, stood up, and extended his hands to help Anna up. He walked her, in her stockingfeet, to her front door. There, he walked out, leaving her spinning.

Dear Hillary Birdwood

WOULDN'T YOU KNOW it would arrive a week after Chantal's party? More. It took him three weeks to respond to her letter. He'd probably put it in his B stack. Not that she was the least bit interested. But if he'd answered right away, and if he actually had been as tall, dark, and allegedly handsome as he said he was, she could have gone to the party. Introducing Dr. So-and-so.

That had been the most horrible night, hiding in her apartment with all the lights off, afraid to open the refrigerator door for fear someone passing (Philo Righi) might see the kitchen light up. She'd just sat on the lid of the toilet with the bathroom door shut, holding her pen and notepad, trying to concentrate on the hypothetical assignments she'd given herself for practice in writing featurettes. All she could do was stare at that ugly army-green shower curtain. She turned off the bathroom light to tiptoe into the dark apartment to find her book about the Catholic girls. After reading a paragraph twenty times, she'd give up and go on to the next. The worst thing was putting on a pathetic voice and lying to Chantal – even calling Saturday morning, pretending to be still "a little weak."

Dear Hillary Birdwood,

Who are you? What are your parents like? Of all your travels, what has been your favorite place? What was the last book you read, and what did you think of it? If you were to have your life story filmed, who would be the star you'd choose to portray you? What did you dream last night? Did you grow up in a religion, and if so do you still believe? What sign are you, and what are your feelings about astrology? May I see your stock portfolio? (Just kidding.) Will you have coffee with me, and tell me about yourself?

Please call me, at 650-668-8750. I want to hear your voice.

Sincerely,

Tall, Dark, and Allegedly Handsome.

So he didn't live in Berkeley. That was 510. He lived on the Peninsula – like Palo Alto or something in tech-land but not so deep into it there was nothing else. (That area code was 408.)

He didn't even sign his name. How embarrassing, to call and ask for Tall, Dark, and Allegedly Handsome. He'd obviously printed out sixty of these. Sent thirty to the A list, and when they bombed, sent the remaining thirty. Or maybe he'd printed ninety and was finally getting down to the Cs.

There wasn't one word about her letter. The only possible reference would have been the question (joke? – hah!) about the stock portfolio. That might have been a subtle answer to her irritation that money had to be part of his dream woman's package. More likely a lot of the women answering had objected to that, and he was killing a bunch of birds with one stone. At least he was staying in character, the egoist. The solipsist. He wanted to hear their voices. To judge them. She took the letter right to the phone and sat next to it on the floor, punching the numbers. She wished she could afford a cordless phone, so she could walk around while she talked. This guy made her nervous.

Of course. The answering machine. "You have reached 650-668-8750. Please leave a message." Beeep.

That was quick. What was she supposed to say? "This is Hillary Birdwood." She listened to the echo in the empty room, wondering if the machine would pick up that she had no furniture. "I'm calling in response to your letter. Since you left your number, I thought I'd find out if you'd

225

thought about any of the questions I asked you. I'm the one on Russian Hill. I'll leave my number, but I'm not here after four p.m., and I don't have a machine. It's not that I have anything against them, it's just that . . ." a laugh bubbled up: "I'm saving up for all the trips we're going to take. So. Now you've heard my voice, and I've heard yours. It sounds like you're from New England. Are you? My number is 415-118-5678. So long."

Luckily she didn't have time to think about this creep any more. Today she was going to work overtime. Now that Mike wasn't wasting her precious hours with baseball and stupid movies, she had time to work out those little features she'd assigned herself, and the station was finally going to do one! A three-minute segment on "The Poet-Gardener." If it worked, they'd do a series called "Citifolk" – just quick little portraits of regular people in the various neighborhoods. Her favorite producer, Jade Wu-Henderson, loved the idea and came up with her own list of characters. Since Jade *lived* at work, her neighborhood was the Financial District. Though all of Hillary's were people who made a contribution to the community, like Mrs. Leone with her bichonne frisée and her museum programs for the disabled, Jade wanted to do one on the blind man who for twenty years had laid out a plaid blanket in front of the Bank of America Building with his guide dog, Lopez. He worked a ten-hour day making friends and collecting quarters. Jade said his contribution was that he made people feel good. (It was true. He once told Hillary he knew what she looked like and described her. It turned out he'd asked a man, and the man had gone into every detail, including a guess at her height and weight – wrong, too kind, really – and this guy had told the blind man that Hillary was "beautiful." Talk about making someone feel good.) Pretty soon everybody on the crew had ideas of people from their own neighborhoods. A bus driver who passed out sheet music for carols at Christmas and drove the loudest, happiest bus in town. A woman in Hunter's Point who'd started a jazz workshop for kids, with guest teachers like Herbie Hancock and – believe it or not – Ike! There were so many. "Citifolk" would be an intimate overview of the city, Jade said, and featuring regular people

226

would make all the regular-people viewers think about who was special in their neighborhood and – the really important thing – what was special about themselves.

SINCE ALL THESE stories had to be taped during the subjects' working hours, and Hillary'd be the producer/camera for the pilot, she'd be working extra hours. If the series went, she'd be working half-days, as well as longer nights – maybe until she was promoted to daytime producer/camera, or even to Producer. For sure she'd be working long hours today, taping Tobin and attending the edit after her regular work was done. Someday, maybe, she'd be *doing* the edit.

It was amazing what a good month Hillary had had, since Jade had lent her that first how-to book on producing. She'd given herself pretend assignments and planned the footage and imagined it edited and televised. Although none of her victims knew what she was doing, she had secretly interviewed a bunch of people, including Nigel, Pierre, and Dr. Hawthorne, before deciding on the three she eventually handed in. Just the act of doing this had made her suddenly popular. She was talking with people about their favorite subject: themselves.

For Tobin, like the others, she'd made up a list of questions for the on-air guy to ask.

Jade was fabulous. She thought Hillary would be a good producer and said she (Jade) needed help. It was true, she really had too much to do. And actually, she probably should have been a teacher. She *loved* to see Hillary learn.

The plan was to shoot Tobin on his rounds, to interview him about the European magazines that had been taking his poems, and about the first prize he'd just won in the Oakland Museum's Painting and Poetry contest. She knew he'd want to tell about the travel and the bicycle-racing and maybe the near-PhD in philosophy, but gardening and poetry seemed enough for three minutes. She went through pounds of his poems and chose three of the shortest, funniest ones.

*

"YOU LOOK NICE," Tobin said. "Nice to see you in a dress."

"Thanks," she beamed. "Doesn't Tess look nice too?" She'd splurged three dollars and eighty-five cents on a bandana at Ray and Pete's. It looked as pretty as the thirty-five dollar scarf Chantal had bought at Nordstrom for Mrs. Ironside. "Tess just loves it when I tie on her scarf. She sits there, with her nose up, waiting. She knows I'll say 'Prit-ty girl.'" The crew laughed when Tess heard those words and bolted across the lawn, tail waving, so the prit-ty girl could get cooed at.

"Let's get him down there in the glen, clipping the hedge with the tiled benches in the background," Jade said, waving her clipboard toward the promenade.

"Well, the light's better up here," said Hillary, "and the topiary's really special, and we can get the cable car passing. It's nice to see Coit Tower, and the brick street."

Jade seemed to respect that. Maybe she didn't realize Hillary virtually lived in this park and knew everything.

Hillary admired the way Jade gently coaxed Tobin to get more volume out of his voice. After just a couple of minutes with her, he lost his shyness completely.

She saw the rushes that night and went in at noon to watch Jade edit, reconstructing the order almost the way Hillary had planned it. She had to work during the six o'clock news, so she couldn't see her darling broadcast live, but Jade gave her three cassettes of the air check: one for her parents, one for Tobin, and one for herself, should she ever get a TV. When she hopped off the bus at one in the morning, she skipped up the block and past her building to Chantal and Nigel's, to see if their lights were on. They weren't. Chantal and Nigel had said they were going to tape it too, and they were going to save theirs for everyone to see. Probably they'd want to keep it and play it again and again for the rest of their lives.

IT WAS THE sixth grade talent show. She was the bride (five feet ten already) and little Midgie McDonald (a sixth grader the size of a second grader) was the groom. Midgie wore tails and a stovepipe hat and very polished black shoes. The parents and kids in the auditorium roared with laughter as the groom reached up to unveil the bride's face and couldn't reach high enough to get the netting over the top of her head. As Hillary helped Midgie pull the veil back and looked down at him, Midgie changed into Philo Righi and was standing on his toes and reaching his lips up. He started a kiss so consuming she had to fight for breath. The phone rang. She pulled the pillow tight over both ears and tried to get back into the kiss, but the telephone kept ringing. Tess's tail banged the mattress and her nose probed the covers, and the phone didn't stop. The little clock next to her, on the floor, said nine-thirty.

Owww. She rolled off the mattress, staggered to the tall closet shelf where she kept her slippers out of Tess's reach, and shuffled to the damn phone. Tess's nose stalked the sheepskin slippers, teeth nipping. "Stop it, Tess. Hello?"

Too late.

What a weird dream. She hadn't thought about that skit since sixth grade. It was amazing the teachers had let them do it. The laughs were rewarding at the time, but the experience had scarred Hillary for life. Hadn't the teachers known that would happen? It was bad enough being a freak, without flaunting it in front of a whole auditorium. Laughing at her! And what about poor Midgie McDonald? Hillary put her slippers back on the high shelf and got back under the covers, trying for a better dream. The phone rang.

"Hello, I'd like to speak to Hillary Birdwood."

"Yes, this is Hillary . . ."

"This is Hampton Blake."

"Hampton . . .? Oh, my gosh!" She was starting to wake up. Or was this the next dream? "You mean, Tall, Dark and Allegedly Handsome?"

"I don't know what you're talking about," he said, "I was calling about . . ."

"Oh my God."

"I was calling about your stock portfolio." He had a rich chuckle.

229

"So you remember me?" Hillary said.

Again he chuckled. "I don't believe we've ever met."

Oh my God.

"Oh, I am sorry," he said. "I couldn't resist. It is a funny situation, don't you agree?"

Well, yes. Sort of. "I guess it is. But do you remember me? I wrote you a – the letter was a little embarrassing. I don't know why I sent it."

"Well, I liked it up to the P.S.s. Frankly, I wasn't going to respond, because I sensed some anger there, and I'm not good at dealing with anger."

She could feel herself getting angry.

But he continued. "In the main part of your letter, I found myself wanting to meet you. You seemed to have such a love of your life, I could imagine you being a refreshing change from the dozens of others I've met through the *Bay Guardian* ad."

"So you saved me for last?"

"Oh no. I ran the ad three times – and got seventy-one responses. Most people thought it was a rather good ad."

So he was from New England. The way he said rather. A lot of people thought New Englanders and Oregonians had a lot in common, though she wouldn't know. They did name their towns Medford and Salem and Springfield and Portland and – "Did you know I'm from Oregon?"

"Sorry, I'm not following you."

"Oh. Yeah. I'm not actually awake yet. It's only about five a.m., my time."

"You've been traveling?"

"Oh, no. You see—"

"It doesn't matter," he said quickly. "I'm going to have to cut this short. I'd prefer to talk to you face to face. Could we meet for a coffee?"

"Well that would be fun!" Maybe they could go to La Petite Treat, and he could see the neighborhood first-hand.

"Good," he said, in a tone she knew meant let's hurry this up. "I'm in

Palo Alto. There's a nice little spot I can bicycle to. What would you say about Saturday morning at ten?"

Palo Alto? She'd never been to Palo Alto. She'd heard it was at least an hour by train, and the train station was at least three bus transfers from here, and the trains hardly ran at all on the weekend. What she wanted to ask was How tall are you?

"Are you there?" he asked.

"Oh! Yes."

"The place I had in mind is the Café Verona. You know it?"

"No," she said. Asking directions would give her time to decide whether to say yes or no. Everything in her wanted to say yes, but not because she wanted to spend all day getting to and from Palo Alto for a cup of coffee. It was that she had a weird, lifelong need to accommodate. She always wanted to say yes while the person was there and then have some leisure to change her mind and leave a message on a machine or something. This desire to please never had anything to do with whether the person deserved to be pleased or not. Or whether she intended to go through with accommodating the way she said she would.

She got an idea! "Do you have a car?"

"Well yes of course. But I bike whenever I can. Why?"

"Oh, I was just thinking, maybe you could come up here. You see, I have no car, and it's a long way, I mean in terms of hours, getting to the train, and so forth. Maybe you had some errands you wanted to do in the city? Maybe you'd like to catch the new photography show at the MOMA? It's supposed to be terrific. I know quite a bit about two of the photographers showing, since that's my field . . ."

"I'm afraid my schedule doesn't allow much time for pleasure," he said.

"Oh." Suddenly she didn't have that urge to accommodate. "Neither does mine. Thank you for calling, though. And good luck. Maybe we'll bump into each other in Bangkok or something."

Quite a few pulse beats took place before she said, "Are you there?"

"Mmm. Just a minute." She could hear another voice in the room. He came back to say, "My assistant is just reminding me of the time."

Apparently she was supposed to say something here, because he didn't. All her muscles felt brittle from trying to come up with some appropriate words.

Finally he spoke. "Are you free for dinner, in San Francisco, Saturday night?"

She hated to admit it, but why not.

The Great Dog Spirit

WHO SHOULD SHOOT from under a bush but the corgi, presenting her sweet face to Posy's ruffled rump. Buster ran up to share a sniff. Actually, Buster hopped! His front right paw was tucked up, as if in a sling. "What's the matter with Buster?"

From the bench, Frankie took time out from her conversation with Philo Righi to yell back, "Nothing's wrong with Buster."

His mood seemed frisky. "Did he break his leg?"

"No. There's nothing wrong with him. You should be more worried about me." Frankie held her palm across one eye.

"What's the matter with you?" Anna was all sympathy.

"Oh, that terrible dog Tess hurt me."

"Really?" The puppy was huge and out of control, but Anna couldn't imagine her hurting anyone. That dog had an uncanny sensitivity. She only risked knocking over people who could afford to be knocked over. And she certainly wouldn't bite.

Frankie kept her eye squeezed shut when she lowered her hand. "It was my own fault. I shouldn't have come up to the park. I should just stay home in my basement and let Buster go to the bathroom on the gravel roof outside. The park is a public place, and I have a right to be in it, but I'm not safe here."

"What happened?"

"Oh, I got careless. This happened once before."

"What?"

233

"Tess jumped up on the bench and slapped my eye with her tail. The last time she did it, it hurt so bad I couldn't sleep. I had to keep one eye shut when I drew, so I couldn't get my perspectives right. I had two free days to make some progress and she wrecked them. I couldn't draw and I couldn't go to the park either. I was scared to death that dog from hell would be back. But I guess my memory is getting dim, because I came up here just now and my worst fears came true. The damn dog was on the bench before I saw her, and she whipped me again."

She stood up to leave. "What that dog needs is a kick in the stomach." Seeing the shocked expressions on Philo and Anna she said, "I'm telling the truth. And I'd like to be the one to kick her, but I don't like training someone else's dog."

No one seemed able to say anything, so she went on: "You people have lived in neighborhoods like this most of your lives, so you don't know how good you've got it. Me, I've lived all over, and I can tell you, there's a difference between places. Different neighborhoods have different classes, both people and dogs. We're lucky we only have one Tess. The longer I live here, the more of a snob I become. Breeding shows."

Anna watched the dogs, playing together. Buster's paw was still tucked up. "I have a wonderful vet," she said. "Dr. Rhonda Stallings. Dr. Hawthorne recommended her."

"I don't believe in vets. They're all robbers."

"I know what you mean!" Anna did know. She told about one vet who urged her to give Posy a series of shots to prevent a winter cold. "A thousand dollars! Imagine that." She took out a card and a pen and wrote Dr. Rhonda Stallings's phone number on it. "This is one you can trust."

"Thanks but no thanks." Frankie was reaching to grab Buster's collar. When she pulled him out of the pile, she did it more gently than usual.

SO HERE ANNA was, alone with the man she had marveled at. Could it be that he'd found the secret of making a completely satisfying life by himself? He had women when he needed them, but they seemed to bop

234

in and out of his life like tennis balls over the fence. Always glamorous. No real-person-ness seemed to show, from under all the varnish. One day, she'd have to do some subtle inquiries to figure out his secret.

What was wrong with today?

What was wrong with today was that she hadn't "prepared her interview," as Hillary would say. Hillary had prepared her interview with Tobin by following him around the park and asking questions. She'd prepared an interview with Anna while Anna was right next to her on the bench. She'd admitted to Anna that she knew nothing about the museum program for the disabled except that it existed and that it had been Anna's idea – but what better way was there to find out the whole story than to ask Anna herself, right that minute? She said she'd get the basic information, talk to a few more people, and refine the on-camera questions later, after she had a good idea what the answers would be. ("It's a structure, with steps leading up to it. Let's do the first step.") But Anna couldn't just ask Philo Righi, "Are you truly happy not having someone to share your life with?"

She sat beside him in silence, watching his corgi use her feet like paddles to scrape her stomach along the ground, shooting this way past Posy, then that way, trying to get something started. Posy sat almost prissily, until all of a sudden she sprang at the corgi and chased her into the woods. When they reappeared it was the corgi chasing Posy, round and round the monument.

"I have a confession," Philo Righi said.

"Yes?" She could hardly believe her ears.

"I really like that dog Tess."

Anna smiled. Philo didn't.

"I mean it." He spread his ten long fingers, feeling for words. "Tess," he pronounced, "is The Great Dog Spirit."

Interesting.

"Don't you think?" He really seemed to think he'd put his fingers on the truth. "All the dogs have personalities. Mine has hers, yours has hers. And they're all dogs. But there's something about Tess." With his chin on his hand, he looked like The Thinker. "Maybe it's that she's unobstructed. Maybe I like her because she's untrained. My theory is that she's naturally sweet. Hillary doesn't try to train her and change her, she just lets her be what she is."

"The Great Dog Spirit?"

"Yes." The fire in his eyes shone on a spot in front of him, as if he were seeing Tess right there – as if he were observing her fly without a care into somebody's solar plexus.

"Remember the time," he said, "—we were both here – when that old, old couple teetered in on canes? They were so fragile they had their arms locked together, hanging on for life. Remember how Tess sped at them?"

How could she forget? Everyone got up and held their breath.

"And," Philo said, "Tess did not jump on them. She stopped just short of the couple and sprang up and down in one place."

"I was praying," Anna said. "When she didn't jump on those people it seemed like proof that there is a God."

"Right! The Great Dog Spirit."

"You think she knew they were frail?" Anna asked.

"I have no doubt. And I knew she would never hurt them."

"Remember when I used to wear high heels?"

"Yes. She never jumped on you."

"But now she does," Anna said.

He looked down at her flats and smiled.

"In your work," Anna asked Dr. Righi, "I suppose you see a lot of *people* who are overtrained?"

"Oh. Don't get me started."

"Do you have a girlfriend?" (She said it!)

He laughed a kind of no-no-no laugh. When he shook his head, he really shook it. "No, no time for a girlfriend."

She just looked at him, to get the answer.

He pushed his hair back behind his ears. "I have too many interests. That's my problem. I sail, I ski. I love flyfishing. I go to the Art Institute

236

Tuesday nights for a photography class. I bike, I travel, I play the piano. Which means I get invited to parties, and I go – even if they're stuffy black tie. I love playing for people. And I have my girl . . ." He smiled over at his corgi.

"The dog must get in the way," Anna said.

"You're not kidding. But I couldn't live without her." He got thoughtful. "It took me a long time to get a dog. I knew I didn't have time. The worst thing was, I knew myself. I knew if I got a dog, and it turned out to be too hard – you know, walks when it's raining, even at three a.m. in my tux, dogsitters when I travel, vet bills, surgeries – even if it turned out to be too much, I knew I'd never give the dog up. I'd be making a promise. And I know myself. I'd never turn my back on someone who depended on me for love."

Was this what kept him from a serious romance? She knew better than to ask a pointed question.

"That's why I can't have a girlfriend." He stood up and did a stretch from his waist to his ten fingertips. The whites of his eyes flashed, along with his teeth, when he gave her a shy smile. "Session's over."

Since he was clipping on his corgi's leash, Anna called Posy over. It was time to go home. She walked with him as far as the brick street.

"Want some firewood?" he asked her. "Hold this." No sooner had she taken the corgi's leash than she saw him take one strong leap and disappear, into the dumpster parked by Pierre's house. Hanging by his waist over the top, he handed her a slab of lumber the length of a fire log. She took it and watched him dip, filling her arms with short boards, then flying off the rim with his own arms full. "This is where I get the wood for my fireplace. Those too heavy for you? – Let's go. I'll walk you home."

Inside, he set his armload on the hearth and unloaded the wood from her arms. He gave her Tobin's Doctor of Despair salute (fingers forming two circles where glasses would be) and said, "Pretty good deal, you think?"

It's fun to be young, Anna thought, watching the elevator close behind him. He made her feel young.

On her knees by the fireplace she took newspapers from the basket and then kindling. She liked building fires. Joe had taught her well. Building her pyramid, she found herself talking to him, in her head. Now that Rayford was such a big part of her life, she wasn't seeing as much of Joe as she used to. It was a treat to be with him. It happened when something they'd talked about came up. This time it was Churchill – the postcard with his quote about courage. "I wonder," she said to Joe (silently, of course), "if he was right. Maybe courage *isn't* the greatest of virtues. Maybe loyalty is. Or, fidelity? Being someone it's safe to trust. Maybe that's the greatest of the virtues, because it makes all the others possible." Aloud she said, "What do *you* think, Posy?"

Saturday Night

HER EYELASHES WERE so thin and blonde that putting on mascara took about half an hour. In the first place she had to work without her glasses, which made every brushtroke a long, scary process. While one set of lashes dried, she did the other, then built thickness with coat after coat. It wasn't until after about four coats of mascara that she could begin to see any eyelashes at all. Theoretically, if she spent enough time, they would finally get to a point where they looked the way eyelashes looked in magazines. In her whole life she'd never had the patience to verify this theory. Tonight she was trying.

Buzzz! Damn doorbell. The wand jabbed her eyelid. Oh, no. Now she'd have to start all over on that eye. She wet her finger and rubbed. She wet a washcloth and scraped until her eyelid was red. *Bzzzz!* Shut up. She kept wetting the cloth in new spots, putting her glasses on to check, taking them off to scrub some more. The buzzer blasted a third time as she set to replenishing the losses on the eyelashes, but this time she was braced and the wand didn't jump. She ran on bare feet to the intercom to croon, "Just a *minute* . . ."

Early. Typical of his personality type. Anxious anxious pushing pushing. If only she had some furniture she could buzz him in, but she didn't even know this man. "Tess, where are my shooooes?" Tess didn't know that word. Hillary felt along the top shelf until her hand hit an espadrille. Where was the other? She crisscrossed the laces up one ankle and hopscotched back to the mirror for another layer of mascara, on the theory that if she stopped looking for the shoe she'd find it. And there it was, high up in the closet, in the envelope box. "Be right down," she said into the intercom. "Where are my keeeeys?" Tess knew this word and ran to the leash, pulling it from the doorknob. "No, sweetie," she said, spotting her keys. "We can't go for a walk now. I have to go out. For *just a little while.*" Tess's ears went back in that broken-hearted way. Hillary steeled herself and promised, "I'll *be right back.*"

That probably wasn't a lie, she thought, flying down the stairs.

He was wearing white pleated pants and Birkenstocks. No socks.

"Hi. I'm Hillary."

He put out a hand. His height, she judged, was about five-eleven. His build was definitely mesotomorph. His dark, grey-threaded hair was thick and crazed, like one of those etchings of Beethoven. "I'm glad you finally got down here," he said. "I had to park about four blocks away and I don't like leaving the Mercedes out in the city. How can you stand it here? Parking is impossible."

"I don't have a car. I'm dying to find out about your life. Those questions you asked me – or that you asked all of us in your form letter – were really interesting. They gave me a lot to think about, and I want to ask you the same questions. But I have a bunch more, too." She'd be darned if she'd let this turn into an evening of conversations about parking spaces. She had her conversational agenda pretty well planned. She'd use some of the interview techniques she'd been practicing for the job. She smiled comfortably down into his eyes, which she could see without her glasses were brilliantly blue, with lashes she'd never be able to accomplish with an hour of mascara-ing.

"THE SEASONS CHANGE so fast now I barely have time to catch the nuances," she said to Rayford. It was only the middle of August, but by quarter to eight, they stepped out Anna's front door into graying, left-over daylight.

And who should round the corner a block down but young Hillary Birdwood. She looked wonderfully free, without Tess directing her

240

footsteps. Laughing down into the face of a swashbuckling man, she tossed her hair and her hands, almost as animated as Philo Righi. With their polite dogs, Rayford and Anna paused at the wrought iron gate and waited for the young couple to notice them. The breeze fluffed the skirt of Hillary's flowered dress as her arm wagged high. Still waving she danced forward, beckoning the man at her side to speed up. Seeing her look so pretty, and with a man, gave Anna cheer. The best thing was, she towered over him. Well. She was inches taller.

Rayford's "Well well well" crossed with Hillary's "This is Mrs. Leone, the one whose picture I sent you. Mrs. Leone, this is . . . ummm . . ."

"We're the ones who are supposed to forget each other's names," said Rayford.

"She knows me by a nickname," the man explained. When Rayford and Anna showed an interest in the nickname, he ducked his head and Hillary laughed.

"We're headed this way," Rayford said with the tone he used to announce that he had twenty-four patients to see today. As he and Anna rounded the corner toward his place, he said to her, "In our day a girl that tall would have trouble with the gents. But I suppose nowadays women's rights extend to height. Remember how it used to surprise everyone to see Woody Allen dwarfed by his heroines? Now you see it everywhere. In this girl's case, though, the height is exceptional. I wonder if it's hereditary or pituitary."

"You know what I think?" Anna said. "I think it's that everything in her wants to defy gravity. She used to try to quash herself, but now she's letting go. You see how she soars?"

ANNA LOVED RAYFORD's gallantry. He'd left his duck in the oven to walk up the hill and escort her down. He'd arrive with a gift, as usual, this time a cartoon from the *New Yorker*, with a small dog standing meekly at attention in the courtroom and a big-dog judge banging a gavel. "Not guilty! Because puppies do these things."

Rayford had dressed for the occasion, looking both smart and daffy in his yellow bow tie and, as she saw when he hung up his jacket, the coordinated suspenders. Cracking the oven door to reveal the fat duck, its cavity sewn shut with kitchen string, he said, "My surgical training helped considerably, boning this bird. I confess to having spent most the day on this meal. I walked to Chinatown at the break of dawn and bought the duck at Fah Ling. In another place on Stockton I got the ground pork, and I went to another, on Pacific, for the dried cranberries and the pistachios. Do you know, in Chinatown you can get a pound of pistachios already shelled for what it would cost for four ounces, shells on, in our neck of the woods? I can't remember for how many years I've wanted to try this Ballotine of Duck." She sat on a stool at the kitchen counter and sipped a glass of Sauvignon Blanc as he gave her a minute-by-minute description of his culinary preparations. She sighed at how lucky she was that when he was with her, he felt perfectly free to be boring.

The meal was stunning, but too much. Try as she would, her stomach had shrunk. She did manage to eat half of what he'd served her, including two of the French-fried roses. "Quite a simple garnish to emulate," he said, "if you happen to have a rose bush. I could probably be sued for serving this menu to a patient."

It was funny how often they both seemed to be thinking the same thing at the same time. Duck, stuffed with ground pork and pistachios. Potatoes chewy-soft inside but burnished to a crisp outside – so tasty because – they'd been browned in duck fat! He'd used the rendered duck fat to sauté the chard, too. And he'd drizzled all that extra-virgin olive oil on the heirloom tomatoes. Not only that, but chocolate mousse.

"I advise my patients – most of them, anyway – to learn the rules and apply them, but not to base their lives on them. Some of the young people today have developed a fear of food that borders on the pathological. Present one with a crisp slice of bacon and provoke a heart attack. It's the anxiety! I believe happiness is vital to health."

He presented the dessert with wonderful news: "You know, do you not, that chocolate is nature's richest source of Vitamin E?"

Over espresso he admitted, "As a matter of fact it wouldn't appeal to me to eat this way on a daily basis, but why deny the joy of it on a special occasion? I advocate moderation in all things, including moderation."

WAS THIS A special occasion? Well. With Rayford every day was a special occasion.

His living-room was enshrouded, the foghorns moaning, the yellow dots of city lights dim and furry. Rayford struck a long-stemmed match to the fire he had laid and went to his Bechstein grand for a Bach fugue, textured with a sprinkling of wrong notes that didn't seem to bother him. He moved into "Alexander's Ragtime Band," the volume of his left hand as booming as his voice in the park. The dogs pushed their heads near Anna on the sofa, where she curled up, drinking in the jewel patterns of the Persian rugs, careful to stroke Romeo's ears for as long as she stroked Posy's, and vice versa. The vases, the statues, the slightly nicked Chinese screen overlaid with gold leaf – this place was rich as Ali Baba's. He played for half an hour before pouring each of them an ounce of brandy. As he sat down next to her, his eyes locked with hers. A flash of honesty lasted a fraction of a second or less. It betrayed naked – what?

The emotion bared was hope. It was hope so vulnerable it almost frightened.

The kiss that followed lasted through eleven chimes of the grand-father clock.

Twelve chimes had come and gone before they stirred into consciousness of anything but the tension and warmth of each other's bodies. "It's time for me to walk you home," he said, sitting up and putting his shoes back on. Anna groaned, and noticed that both dogs' ears cocked when they heard her quiet laugh and his belly-deep chuckle. The dogs had been watching the people with the intensity of playgoers on the edges of their seats. When laughter came, it struck the dogs as a new development in the plot.

"IT DIDN'T WORK, darling." He was out of breath, and beads of sweat stood out on his forehead as he carried Mrs. Ironside over the threshhold and deposited her in her basket. "If this goes on much longer I'll be able to give up my membership at the gym." He couldn't count how many times he'd carried her downstairs and across Hyde Street to the park, these last few days, hoping she could finally do a bizz.

"How long has it been?" Chantal asked. She stood in her nightgown, putting her take-the-client-to-dinner dress on its hanger.

"The last time was Thursday morning. That makes three full days."

"Poor, poor darling." On her knees by the basket, Chantal plunged her lacquered nails into Mrs. Ironside's ruff. "Her pelt is so rich, Nigel, the warmth goes all the way into my heart."

"I understand the university hospital is open all night," Nigel said. "This is beginning to feel quite serious."

Oh. The thought of driving all the way up to Davis, at midnight. "Let's call them," she said, handing him the Post-it from the fridge.

Touching in the phone number, he said, "I've heard about massage. Perhaps someone will at least be able to instruct us. Did you say your appointment with the neurologist there is Tuesday? Let's make it first thing Monday morning, if possible. – Hello . . ."

There is no reason to go into detail about the massage, except to say that it would take until three a.m. to succeed. For what remained of the night, Mrs. Ironside would sleep in their bed, with four arms around her.

FRANKIE LOVED THAT statue of David. She hadn't seen the real thing, because she hadn't been to Florence, Italy. But she had art books full of photographs, both color and black-and-white. This was at least the hundredth time she'd tried to draw it. She'd saved one drawing per year since 1974, and it looked like every year she was getting closer. Maybe by the time she died, she'd be able to get her charcoal on paper to capture the feeling Michelangelo got in his statue. It was a combination of power and vulnerability. And the hard part was the hand. The hand said it all. But she couldn't get the hand. It was almost three o'clock in the morning. Buster and the cat were curled up, but she'd be working at this till ten

244

a.m., when she'd have to take Buster out. The thought of breaking at ten for Buster really pissed her off. Maybe she should get it over with now. Buster didn't like being roused from his sleep, but it might be a good investment.

It was dark in the park, except along the brick street. She stayed there and let Buster off so he could go into the bushes and do what he had to do. Three blocks down, passing under a street lamp, a man took long strides. He got closer – wearing a tux. And closer. Philo Righi. He stopped at the corner of Greenwich to have a look at the view. Not a bad view. Coit Tower centered. Its lights were off, most lights were off except street lamps, all lined up on Telegraph Hill – and the lights of the Bay Bridge swooping like jewels. Philo stood just under a lamp, so she could see one hand, hanging relaxed at his side.

It wasn't David's hand. But it had the same power. It was out of proportion with the rest of his body. Too big. But Philo's hand was thin, like a Giacometti version of David's.

Back inside, Frankie didn't tear up the drawing she'd been working on. She took loving care to put it in a folder and took out a fresh sheet. Maybe what she needed to do was not copy David exactly. She was going to do a new David, with a Giacometti hand. And of course a more wiry body. Not too wiry though. It was flesh that told the story.

IN THEIR FLAT down on Filbert Street, two doors up from the North Beach Shoe Repair, Ike's eyes popped open. It was still dark. Without looking or reaching over, he could feel that Meg was stiff and awake on her side of the bed. On top of his feet, through the covers, he could feel that the big cat was stiff and awake. He could feel him standing up on the quilt, four paws walking to the center of the bed, to stand on the space between Meg and himself. There was a lot of space between them, these nights. The cat pulled the center of his back toward the ceiling, straightening his tail like a Halloween cat. When Ike put a hand out to touch the fur, the cat shot down the hall. The kitten yowled and fled after him.

He and Meg were alone now, and he knew she could sense his muscles were rigid, the way he could sense hers were.

She didn't move. "I have something to tell you." Her voice grated. It always grated lately. Now it was even more of a monotone that it had been for the last few months. "I'm moving to New York."

He didn't fly off the bed like the cat. His bones might break from not moving. He said, "Good."

"I've been thinking about this for a long time," she said. No emotion at all.

"I've been thinking the same thing." His voice didn't have any lilt in it either.

"You have?" She sat up slowly, not sounding surprised. Same dead-sounding voice. "You've been thinking I should move to New York?"

"Yeah. You've got *work* to do." He made that word sound as dirty as he meant it. "New York's where it's at, isn't it? You practically live there already." He held on to his self-control. "Don't worry about me."

"I won't."

"So. You leaving this morning?"

"Well, no! Of course not!" Finally she had some life in her voice. She switched on her lamp. "We have to talk."

"Why?"

"There's a lot we haven't said!"

"I don't have anything to say." He studied the crack in the ceiling. Seemed like it had grown since the last time he looked. "Book a flight for this afternoon."

She got out of bed and put her hands on her hips. "All right. I will! Right this minute. But I'm coming back in a week." She didn't even put her slippers on. Just walked barelegged in her nightshirt to the studio. She was mad, but she was calm. Like him. He heard the orchestra fanfare the computer played when she turned it on.

He followed her in there and watched her click this, click that. Change of screens.

"I think I'll enjoy living alone," he said.

"Me too." She made more clicks. Punched in her credit card. "There."

From the doorway he watched her reach to the top of the closet. He watched her legs and her tiptoes as she hauled down her suitcase. Nice legs, he used to think. When she heaved it onto the bed and opened it, he ran to the dresser and yanked open a drawer. He grabbed a handful of bras and panties and threw them across the room at her. "Here!" He hurled until he'd emptied every drawer. "Take everything. Take everything!" Tearing the closet door open he swept out an armful of clothes. "Here!" Three fell swoops and the closet was empty. He banged the door shut and picked up his clothes from the chair. "Don't forget your toothbrush!" he yelled, pulling on his jeans. Zipping his jacket he yelled, "C'mon gang" and grabbed all three leashes. Before he slammed the front door he yelled, "I'm gonna enjoy living alone." After he slammed it he said to the dogs, "I'm gonna enjoy living alone."

Tess

"IS THIS PRIVATE territory?" A pretty woman, making a slight bow, peeped through the hedge at Tobin. Looking down from the ridge above the promenade, Hillary said, "C'mon, Tess" and started down, fascinated by this woman's look. She wore a sharp yellow jacket of leather, yellow leather shoes to match, and carried a yellow leather shoulder bag. Her haircut looked expensive. So did her camera. Tobin kept clipping.

"Is this private territory?"

What an interesting question, Hillary thought.

"I'm trying to find the crookedest street in the world."

"Oh." This seemed to interest Tobin.

"Do you know how to get there?" The woman kept smiling.

"Yuh. Yuh."

Patient, the woman smiled, "How do you get there?"

Tobin pointed a finger to the sky.

The woman looked puzzled.

"Up. Just go up. After the tennis courts, left one block along the tracks." His voice was so soft the woman had to lean forward. "Crookedest street in the world. They say it is. I'm not sure. Could be there's a crookeder one somewhere."

Hillary was mesmerized by the bounce of the yellow shoes along the pine-needled path, when it hit her. "Tess? Tess!" No response.

"Tess!" Fear ripped through her veins. She angled her legs like a pole

248

vaulter over one bush and another, holding her glasses in place with one hand. She tipped like an antenna to miss a branch, sprang back, bent and bobbed. She raced up to Hyde Street. "Tess?" Running away was the only discipline problem Tess didn't have. Tess with her eyes always turning to Hillary every few seconds, terrified of losing her.

At the top of the crooked street a cab gunned up to pass a cable car and screech-stopped just short of hitting the woman in yellow. It shot again and spun the corner of Chestnut.

At the bottom of the park, Hillary stood on the concrete wall eight feet above Larkin and looked down on that old man with a pheasant feather in his hatband. "Have you seen a dog?" "Dog?" Across the street, Mrs. Leone, in a very fancy outfit today – high heels – sorted through a sheaf of mail. Too polite to shout, Hillary flew down to her. "Have you seen Tess?"

"Over there." She used her handful of mail to point across the street. There, on the rim of the wall, eight feet above the sidewalk, stood Tess. The anxious eyes. The tail beating. A red Alpha ripped past.

"Stay!" screamed Hillary, tearing her vocal chords.

Tess ran. This way. That way. Back and forth high on the wall. A black Boxter roared round from Lombard.

"Stay!"

The dog jumped. Plummeted eight feet to Larkin.

Hillary hurled herself into the street, arms outstretched in front of the car. "Stop!" That one syllable threw itself up and higher and on into space until her voice shattered like a lightbulb.

Rip of rubber on cement. Squeal of brakes.

The louder, shriller, more horrific scream of Tess.

TIME PASSED. HILLARY let her hands fall from her ears. She opened her eyes. No Tess.

"She ran over there." Mrs. Leone pointed to the driveway that led to the back of her building. "They do that," she said, her voice a whisper. "They run off to die."

249

Behind the garage, Tess was propped against the wall. Hillary ran to touch her. Tess didn't move. No recognition in her eyes. "Tess," Hillary breathed. "Tess, Tess, Tess." The dog stared ahead. When Hillary stroked her, her body stayed stiff.

"I'll find a cab so you can get to the vet." Mrs. Leone's high heels hurried her body back to the street.

Hillary was absorbed in Tess, lavishing her with love and reassurance, holding her and checking all over her coat for blood. There wasn't any blood. She felt the stiff body for broken bones and didn't know how to tell. She put her nose to Tess's nose and whispered, "Tess, Tess, Tess." Tess stood, with the help of the wall. Her eyes were open. But she seemed not to be awake.

"I got one," Mrs. Leone called, as a cab pulled into the driveway. She set her stack of mail on the ground and took off one shoe to weight it. She hitched Posy's blue leash to a stripe of wrought iron and rushed on one shoe like Diddle-Diddle-Dumpling to help lift Tess.

"I'm fine," Hillary said, folding her confusion of arms and legs down to lift the puppy. Everyone always perceived her as weak.

"I know how to do this," Mrs. Leone said, hanging her purse around her neck and almost falling off the point of her one heel as she crouched to demonstrate. "You put this hand under here, supporting the abdomen from beneath, and this arm under the chest. That way you can move her without jarring anything that's ruptured." With haste she added, "If anything is ruptured." She was trying to sound hopeful. She teetered under the weight of the dog as Hillary opened the back door of the cab, embarrassed to have an old lady labor for her. "Pretty heavy for a puppy," Mrs. Leone puffed. "Hope she doesn't grow any more."

This stabbed Hillary.

"I mean – I mean, I hope she's reached her full growth and . . ." She gave up. "Do you have plenty of cab fare?" She opened her purse, which still hung from around her neck.

"I'm fine," Hillary said. "Thank you so much." They had to hurry.

250

"Fillmore and Jackson," she said to the driver. On her lap, she could feel trembling. By the time they crossed Van Ness, Tess's shiver had become more like a rattle.

Maybe she should have accepted some cab fare. She'd just been embarrassed. To ask so much of someone. Or, not to ask, but to accept. As it was, she was fully guilty of getting into this cab knowing she had no money. She had also made a conscious decision not to ask the driver to take her by her apartment so she could run up four flights to get her ten dollar bill, which was the total amount of cash she had. She knew it would be pointless to stop by an ATM, because the machine knew as well as she did that she had less than twenty dollars left in her checking account.

"My dog just got hit by a car."

"Hit and run?"

"Yes." All of a sudden she felt mad. That driver heard Tess scream. A death scream! He had to feel the impact.

"Did you get the license number?"

"I wasn't thinking about that."

She was not going to say a word about not having the money until he had delivered her at the vet's door.

Tess's body was beginning to vibrate with a force like rigor mortis. Hillary heard her own teeth chatter.

"Here you go," said the driver, pulling into a spot. The meter said eight dollars and sixty cents.

"May I carry her in and come back?" She spoke with all the innocence of the innocent.

"Sure, kid, sure." He darted around the cab to open the door. "Take your time." Piling another debt upon her mountain of guilt, she thanked him as he transferred the dog's weight to his own arms and carried her in.

As the glass door closed behind them, she gasped, "Oh my heavens!" She made a show of digging through her pockets. "I had a ten dollar bill in here! Oh, my God . . ."

251

"That's okay, kid. Let's get the dog seen. You'll need a ride back home, and you can give it to me then."

"But if you wait it'll cost a fortune!" Finally honesty poured out of her. "I won't even have enough money at home, or in the bank, to pay the round trip." To the woman at the desk she said, "Dr. Stallings please. Emergency!"

"Have a seat please." The receptionist had a maddening calm.

"Dog's got the shakes pretty bad," the driver told the receptionist, sinking into the plastic upholstery and getting the huge puppy settled on his lap.

Cold linoleum. Cold, no-color plastic chairs. Convulsing dog. She watched the jerks. Brochure rack. "Helping Your Dog Reduce." "How to Break Your Dog's Bad Habits." She stood up and plucked out that one. The room was so silent she heard the paper crackle in her shaking hands.

"Hi," said the cheerful voice of Dr. Rhonda Stallings. "Got a hurt baby?"

With gratitude, Hillary took in the plump, feminine body under the white polyester jacket, the limp blonde hair, the eyes as blue as the Pacific Ocean.

"A car," Hillary began.

"Let's see." Dr. Stallings sank to her haunches in front of the driver's chair, smoothed the puppy's ears, stroked under her chin, used her thumbs to roll the eyeballs around in their sockets. "Let's set her down. There. Let's see you walk, baby." The puppy moved four stiff legs across the linoleum, her body dipping to the right.

"Got a shock," Dr. Stallings said, down on all her fours, feeling. "See this?" She pointed to a stripe of black on the left haunch. "That's where he hit her." She felt every joint and bone. "No breaks. Though there could be a fracture, or internal injuries. Let me take her back for an X-ray."

As fast as she'd gone, she was back, without Tess. "It takes a few minutes. I don't think she's too bad. If it's a hip fracture, the worst that could happen would be we'd have to put in a plate. I don't like to do that, when she's growing so fast, because it would mean a second surgery later to put in a bigger plate."

"How much?" She tried to show no panic.

Dr. Stallings shook her head, looking grave. "Could be a couple grand. Worst case, three."

It wasn't that Hillary was surprised. It was just that she didn't know where she'd get it.

"The hospital takes Visa and MasterCard."

Too bad it wasn't a year from now, when she might have that much credit.

She might be able to borrow from her parents, but she still owed them a ton, and they'd been so against her getting this puppy.

"Let's not worry about that yet," Dr. Stallings said. "It could be that all we have to do is rest her. At her age the bones and organs are pretty good at mending themselves." She pulled back a wisp of hair that had fallen across her forehead. It was so pale it was almost transparent. "And anyway," she said, "we don't even know if there are any fractures. The X-rays will be out in a minute." Moving her eyes across Hillary's face, and the tension there, she raised two eyebrows, so blonde they were almost invisible, and smiled: "You haven't asked me how *I* am."

Hillary liked this doctor. Another time she'd been here, for shots, she'd heard a patient call her Rhonda. She hoped that someday she would be invited to call her Rhonda. She was only about six or seven years older than Hillary, and even if she was overweight, she was beautiful. Even the overweight was beautiful, very soft. Last time, she'd had snapshots on her wall – kittens and puppies and funny-looking older animals, some dressed up in hats – and along with them, there were pictures of a baby. Her own new baby. With an epiphany of memory, the name came to Hillary. Such a good name. "How's Abigail?"

"Wonderful." Dr. Stallings looked down at her hands, her papery nails with no polish. Using her ocean-blue eyes to look straight into Hillary's, she said, "No one prepared me for what happens, with a baby."

Her voice hushed, all of a sudden. Hillary had to lean in to hear. "No

253

one ever prepared me for this. This falling in love."

Hillary's heart gave a slip. This was how she felt about Tess. She wouldn't tell anyone about it. But she knew she knew what Dr. Stallings meant. If it was more intense with a real baby, she might not be able to stand it.

The swing door slapped open, and another white coat, over jeans, walked in and handed a manila envelope to Dr. Stallings.

"Ah. Thanks." To Hillary, "Follow me." In a back room, Dr. Stallings switched on the lightboard, clipping an X-ray to the top. She bent from the pelvis and studied with a frown. Removing that negative she flipped out the next, and the next and the next, examining each one with her nose about an inch from the picture, following the lines and shadows. Switching off the lightboard, she turned and raised her hands to hold Hillary's shoulders, way up there. "Yay! It's a *small* fracture! She won't need surgery."

Hillary held the doctor's soft body, as her arms hugged back tighter. A new flood of feeling began within Hillary, and she could feel tears piling up. She rushed the heels of her hands up to her eyes and used all her mental might to stop the flood before it got loose and overtook everything.

If Dr. Stallings noticed how fast Hillary kept blinking, she didn't show it. She ran through the details of Tess's special care, over the next two weeks, and said, "Pay at the window." She was gone before Hillary could tell her, "Say hi to Abigail."

NOW. PAYING AT the window. Embarrassing. She threw up her hands and whispered her apology. "No money. No credit cards. No wallet. No checkbook."

The receptionist gave her a blank look.

"My dog was hit by a car, we were on a walk, I didn't have my handbag—"

"Can you bring in a card or a check tomorrow, please." The clerk was weary.

"Yie!" Hillary gaped at the print-out. "An X-ray costs *how much*? – And the shot? – Oh, my *gosh*! I can't believe it."

"We open at nine on Saturdays."

After all this, trying so hard, paying every free dollar to the credit card companies, even paying her dad back *a thousand dollars*, she couldn't even pay a vet bill. She had felt so proud of getting down below her limits on all her cards and keeping up with the minimums. She'd paid the one down so she had almost enough to pay this bill! Almost was not enough.

She'd just have to write a bad check, tomorrow. They couldn't possibly deposit it on Saturday, and maybe they wouldn't on Monday either. Tuesday the computer would deposit her paycheck. Maybe she should just not show up at this desk until Tuesday. Maybe she could call and say the check was in the mail! That would work. She might have to skip a credit card payment this month – but that was far in the future.

The cab driver's body left an imprint in the plastic upholstery. He stretched. "Good news, I guess?"

On to the next insurmountable problem. "But I only have ten dollars at home."

He looked up at her and smiled. "That'll be okay."

My heavens.

Bending her legs like hairpins to fit in the back seat, she helped him settle Tess in her lap, she thought, I really have to pay him more. "I have that ten dollar bill at home, and my checkbook. I can cash a check at the drugstore on the corner." It was too late Friday for the drugstore to get the check to the bank. And if they waited until Tuesday it would be fine. She really shouldn't be thinking of herself as the kind of person who writes bad checks.

He actually carried Tess up all four flights and set her on the mattress. She handed him her ten and said, "Let's just walk down to the drugstore so I can cash a check and give you another twenty."

"Forget it, kid. For you, ten bucks and that's it."

"No, no, I insist." She was looking for her checkbook when she heard the cab shoot away.

SHE AND HER puppy lay on the mattress, two long bodies. "Pooor puppy." She felt Tess's silk from the crown of the head to the round of the haunch, and down the length of the tail. "Poooor puppy." Tess enjoyed the sympathy. "Pooor poor poooor puppy."

She'd have to call Hampton and cancel their date for tomorrow night. She couldn't leave Tess alone. She'd be working extra hours all week, and it was criminal to leave Tess alone more than she had to.

The rules were, no playing with other dogs for two weeks, no walking at all off-leash, no walking down or up steps. At least Hillary hadn't had to buy a crate, which was what Dr. Stallings said she should do, because it would be dangerous if she got on the furniture and jumped off. Hillary didn't bother explaining to Dr. Stallings that, luckily, she had no furniture.

Carrying seventy pounds up and down four flights would be hard. But oh, how lucky Hillary was to be such a resourceful person. Like, problem: What's she going to eat from now until Tuesday, if she isn't going to write any bad checks? Solution: Cash one at Ray and Pete's and hope they won't take it to the bank until Tuesday. Or! They take credit cards at the grocery store. She can buy more food than she can eat. Never worry, Tess. I'll get you up and down the stairs. She cuddled closer and listened to the rhythm of soft snort sounds that meant air was coming into the lungs and soft whistles that meant air was going out. "Pooooor puppy," she cooed. The tail gave a hint of a thump, as the sleep sounds continued, regular as heartbeats.

The Pursuit of Happiness

THE DOGS SAT in front of Rayford's seasoned leather sofa, still as oil paintings. They watched him reposition the throw pillow to lift Anna's head a little. Sitting up, he twisted his fingers through her hair and said, "I'd like to make a modest proposal."

What shot through her was something like fear.

"It doesn't seem to me that we know each other well enough yet to make love." Some of his syllables reached above the whisper, most didn't. "What I would like would be, to spend the night together. Without . . ."

A long breath exuded itself from her lungs. She burrowed in closer and whispered back, "That's just what I would like."

"It occurs to me that it might be more comfortable for you to wear a nightgown, and to have your things at hand in the morning." With his large hand she positioned her face so he could see her eyes. "I take it you haven't brought your toothbrush?"

They laughed like children. Both dogs' faces grew more alert.

To the face he held in both hands he said, "And so my proposal is that we collect ourselves and walk the hill to your place."

"Ouch," she whined, fitting her body exactly to his and wrapping her arms tighter.

However, he did have a point about the nightgown. And she'd hate him to see her in the morning without her makeup. "Oh, all right." With tiptoe tenderness he pressed her head into the hollow between his chin

257

and his collarbone, and there the two of them stayed, silent, for a long time. It was she who summoned the momentum to stand, step into her shoes, and pull him up.

"For the sake of propriety," he said, "I'll pack a valise with pajamas." She stood by the fireplace as he moved to the bedroom. She judged that the embers were almost out, but she didn't like the idea of leaving a house with the fire still going. He returned with a canvas bag printed with the Air Force logo and a saucepan full of water. Sprinkling to hisses of steam, he said, "Safety first." After he'd taken his empty pan to the kitchen and she'd leashed both dogs, she heard the growl of the dishwasher building to a roar.

As it happened, she had just bought an Egyptian cotton duvet cover with a spattering of faint violets on pristine white. It was delicious and expensive – a Kathleen Garth. Under its airiness, her hands went over every bone and muscle of him, every round and point. The skin at the back of his neck was loose. She smiled at the phrase that popped into her mind. Well, who wanted to go to bed with a spring chicken anyway?

His mouth and whiskers and prickly eyebrows tickled her forehead, her wrists, her ankles, and the tops of her toes. She laughed, and they both looked over at the dogs, to see if they were enjoying this. Both were asleep on the floor. "How interesting," he whispered, "that dogs, when they're awake, react the way they do to laughter. I think they're puzzled, because it's a language different from English. They think if they listen hard enough, they can slowly learn this language the way they gradually went from 'good dog' to 'breakfast.'"

A whale of a sigh came out of him. "I don't know how I could have made a promise not to make love. I'll never make such a promise again."

Between the sheets, they exulted in desire. A rhythm of whirls became regular: A dizzy spell of passion, a spin of drowsiness – and a new surge of desire wheeling in. They would not sleep one minute this night. "I feel drunk," he said. She spun.

*

"WHEN I WAS a boy," he whispered, "my mother wouldn't let us have a dog."

"Why not?"

"She said, 'The dog will get run over, or it will develop a disease and have to be put to sleep. And even if it doesn't, it will die of old age long before we are ready to see it go. And we will be sad. It's best not to have a dog.'"

"Oh!" Anna disagreed. "All that love and pleasure. To deny yourself – and the dog – that happiness, because it will end. Even if you know you will lose it, and that the pain will be worse than you imagined, it doesn't mean you should never have the thing you're afraid of losing."

Rayford stiffened. He spoke aloud: "I have a condition."

Anna sat up. "A condition?"

He pulled her down and close, so he could go back to whispering. "I have the usual vulnerabilities of aging. The spine. The likelihood of prostate problems. The hardening arteries. You have comparable vulnerabilities. We all do."

"But the condition?"

"I had a cycling accident twenty years ago. My head hit a rock. At the time it seemed to be a minor concussion, and that's what it was. But there were complications."

"What kind of complications?" Fear made the volume of her whisper go down.

"I am fine, most of the time. Except for some runs of headaches that can be controlled with Darvon. But the scans show an aneurysm in the brain." He sat up and talked out loud. "Actually it's so small only repeated MRIs could detect it. In the early days the MRI was like a James Bond torture contraption, where you were put into a capsule and shut into darkness as intense as in the womb. You were then fed through a tunnel of banging terror. Many patients couldn't go through with it, and I have to tell you, I couldn't the first time. I called the procedure to a halt. But the headaches I had were sometimes close to making me blind. They frightened me. I steeled myself and scheduled another test and

259

completed the job, with the help of some drugs that would cost a pretty penny on the street. As it was, I had to go through it again and again. At last the aneurysm showed up. The bad news is, they can't do anything about the headaches. Except Darvon. The good news is, the aneurysm might just exist for years and do nothing but cause a headache. On the other hand it might burst into a stroke. Or conceivably, if you believe in magic – which I confess to you, Anna, I sometimes do – it could heal over."

"Meanwhile?"

"I have to be careful. The main thing is, I have to avoid stress."

"It reminds me of what you said at dinner, about anxiety over bacon being the most dangerous thing about bacon. And also, what you said about the health benefits of happiness."

"Yes, I plan my happiness. I live, in fact, in the conscientious pursuit of happiness. But I must tell you, I don't avoid stress. I work to control it, but I can't do my job without going through stress. What could I do? Limit my practice to well patients?"

"Hmmm," Anna whispered, moving a pillow so she wouldn't put so much stress on his shoulder as she moved in tighter. "But you love your patients. It seems sometimes you especially like the sick ones."

"I know. That's my problem." He got silent. "I love the ones I can't afford to lose. Then I lose them."

"You shouldn't have let yourself get a dog."

"And I shouldn't let myself get a wife."

Suddenly she couldn't breathe. "Would you like a wife?"

His answer came from his body. She kept all sound from pouring out of her, but she felt tears stream from the corners of her eyes and disappear in the hair at her temples.

Posy and Romeo's snores syncopated, as they curled together on the floor, at the foot of the bed that had been specially made, extra long, for Joe.

Adversity

WHAT SHOULD SHE think of Philo Righi? He went to all these black-tie parties but never even invited her to walk down the street to Za Pizza. Maybe he didn't know that she actually owned a beautiful dress that would fit right in at a black-tie party. But he knew even her gray sweatshirt would fit in at Za.

And then. When he went to the drugstore and found out from Ray and Pete that Tess was hurt, he went to the trouble of calling Frankie to find out her work number. He got her at the station and said she should get an answering machine. He'd made nine calls to her home number. Wasn't she there in the daytime, until about four p.m.? (She wasn't, any more.) He was worried about Tess. Was there anything he could do to help?

No, not really. But it was incredibly great that he asked.

But he'd heard Tess couldn't go up or down stairs on her own. He'd heard she had to be carried.

"Who did you hear this from?"

"Ray and Pete." He said, "It must be hard, that Tess must weigh quite a bit."

"I'm really strong." She was proud of it. "You'd be amazed." But in fact, she staggered, and last night she fell and was barely able to keep Tess from tumbling down all the steps, which would have fractured the fracture. She managed to keep Tess tight in her arms, but the bruise on her own thigh spread seven inches, and it had all the colors of a peacock feather. She whacked her elbow, too, which made it excruciating to carry Tess, now. And the bloody scrape on her ankle hurt so much she had to limp.

"I saw Frankie today," he said, "and she told me she had to go up yesterday, about five, and carry Tess down to the street to go to the bathroom, and then carry her back up. Because you were working all afternoon and all night."

"It's amazing, that she did it for us," Hillary said. "Because Frankie doesn't like Tess. Or me, actually."

"Oh really?" Then he laughed.

"I don't know why she did it. I didn't ask her. After I filled the prescription for dog tranquilizers, Ray and Pete told her. She called me up and said she was going to take care of Tess for *just one day*. She said I'd have to make other arrangements to get Tess taken care of for the next two weeks, but for one day she'd help. It was just completely out of character for her to volunteer like that."

Philo said he thought it might have something to do with how sad Frankie felt about Mrs. Ironside.

"What?"

"Mrs. Ironside."

"What?" Hillary had been working all the time, and of course Tess couldn't go to the park, so she hadn't seen Chantal. "What do you mean, because of Mrs. Ironside?"

He told her.

While they were talking, while she was hearing the story, she opened the phone book and found Chantal's number. Funny, she'd never called Chantal before.

She knew they'd taken Mrs. Ironside to every canine orthopedist, ophthalmologist, and gastro-enterologist from Palo Alto to Davis. But she thought Mrs. Ironside was getting better.

"She was, till a couple of weeks ago."

Had it been that long since she'd seen Chantal? "What happened, exactly?"

262

He told the story, ending with Wednesday. That's when they had the vet come over to their apartment. "They held her in their arms while he gave her the shot, and for half an hour after she'd stopped breathing."

Instant tears. She jammed one hand into her mouth, to block her sounds, and used the other palm to blanket the mouthpiece.

"You there?" he asked. "You there?"

"Mmm."

"You know how Frankie is," he said. It was so nice of him to keep talking. To spare her. "Frankie says she likes dogs better than people. Yesterday morning she said gout was nothing. Any human sickness was nothing. She said Mrs. Ironside was as sweet as a dog can get. She was drinking a beer."

What a good idea! Hillary stretched the phone cord and made it to the refrigerator door. She still had a beer in there. But the cord was too short. She couldn't make it to the drawer that had the beer opener.

"On top of that," Philo said, "Buster."

"What? Buster?" This made the sobs stop squeaking.

He told her all about Buster. She'd had no idea. Poor Buster. Poor Frankie!

"So about Tess," he said. His plan was, Hillary should give him a key, and he'd stop by before and after work every day and carry Tess down to the street for a walk. "I won't wake you up in the morning." Well, Hillary could get her down and up in the morning, but she had no idea what in the world to do about the afternoon. "Forget it," he said. "I'm coming twice a day, for the whole two weeks. She's heavy. If you drop her, I'll never forgive you."

He always made her laugh. "I must warn you," she said, "I don't have any furniture."

"No furniture?"

"No."

"That sounds interesting!"

The arrangements were made. She won, about the morning. He'd only come in the afternoons while she was at work. And he'd see how interesting everything was.

The Sun Rises

"*LE SOLEIL SE LÈVE.*" Ever since Anna had surrounded him with all these French people, these were the words he stated aloud to greet a new morn, the minute he woke up, every day. Rain or shine – or, more likely, fog. In his west-facing apartment he couldn't see the sunrise even with his eyes open, but he felt the brightness through his eyelids. *Le soleil se lève!* Minutes later, he said to his toothbrush, "*Je me brosse les dents.*" In the shower his baritone rang from wall to wall of the steamy concert hall: "*Allons enfants de la patrie-ee-ah!*" He continued to belt out "*La Marseillaise*" as he rubbed down with his special rough towel. Romeo helped him out by licking dribs from his calves. Moving his long-boned legs down the hall, accompanied by the rottweiler's thick four, the doctor announced, "*Je désire un café.*" In baby blue and white striped undershorts, he measured out kibble from the bag and meat from the Cycle Three can. "*Voici ton petit déjeuner. Manges!*" Romeo vibrated his tail in anticipation as the dish moved toward the floor. The joy the dog took in eating humble dog food never ceased to touch Rayford with a sensation of shared pleasure. There must be a French equivalent for the phrase, "The tail wags the dog." The black stub at the base of the spine wiggled with such exuberance it shook the whole rear half of the animal.

"*Et maintenant,*" Rayford announced: "*Pour moi, peut-être un banane sur les* cornflakes." *Est-ce-qu'il y a un mot français pour* cornflakes? He even thought in French, he said to himself in English – and hastily restated it in French, as he reached for his kitchen copy of Cassell's

French–English English–French. It had dozens of words for corn, entirely different words for when one talked about ears of corn, or corncakes or corn-cockles, whatever those were, or Indian corn or the corn exchange, cornflour or cornflowers, corn stacks, corn pipes, corn poppies, corned beef, but no cornflakes. No corny jokes, either. Nor popcorn. Perhaps this dictionary had been published before the invention of cornflakes.

For the moment he would have to settle for *céréales* and later ask Martine or Chantal about cornflakes and – the ring of the telephone blasted from every direction. Drat! Who came up with these cordless phones? Never where you could find them. Chased by rude bleeps sounding from all points, he loped from room to room, perusing bookshelves and tables, opening closets and armoires – you'd think he could find just one of the eight he owned. He opened the lid of the piano and *voilà*.

"*Bonjour!*" he sang out, voice full of cheer.

"*Bonjour. C'est moi.*" Anna. *En français* they affirmed their evening plans, in which he would be *M. le Docteur Chef* at a barbecue in the back yard with Martine, Manuel, Anna and himself. Martine would bring her saxophone. She was learning. He wanted to try a trio, himself at the piano, Manuel on his tablas – *un combo éclectique*. The poor girl hadn't actually mastered any notes at all, but this made no difference. Rayford held fast to his belief that the spirit of bravado and the sense of humor were as basic to musicianship as the treble and the clef. Assuming that Martine would progress as normally as any novice on an instrument, there would never again be a time as appropriate as the present for developing either bravado or the ability to laugh at oneself.

He would have made a magnificent father. He had often observed fine paternal qualities in himself, but as he did so today he was past the age of ache. This day, the statement was simply a proud, flagrantly immodest utterance of probability. One could not fulfill every one of the potentials one had been granted. Today, buttoning his plaid flannel shirt and tying his ascot, he mused, in French, upon how he would never have thought that in the latter half of his seventh decade he would become as proficient in this foreign tongue as he had become in the last months. Speaking aloud, to give good practice to his accent, he told Romeo that these days he rarely thought in English until he got to the park, where it was necessary to exchange greetings in the language of this land. After their jaunt in the fine air, after satisfying himself that the dog was duly exhausted and comfortably snoozing in his blanket-lined basket, after changing into coat and tie and starting his Subaru toward the office, he spoke in French to his windshield. It wasn't until he had donned his white lab coat that he re-entered a world where English was spoken.

In addition to this new mastery of language, there were other proficiencies he had achieved by this point in his life, not the least of which was his professional success: He had often observed, with compassion, how few of his fellow human beings looked forward to a day of work the way he did, how few could feel the sense of accomplishment he did, reflecting simply on an average day. It was not, though, professional success that stirred up the greatest feelings of pride in him of late: It was his incredible fortune, at the age of sixty-six, in the Dept. of Romance. To be so much aroused, and to have his ardor returned, was a happiness he had not dared anticipate at this late date. He had passed through the Christmas-is-for-children and love-is-for-the-young phase of thinking to a revelation that joys of many varieties were open to, quite possibly, anyone who was open to them. He had a friendship that was like no other, made sweeter yet by delights of the flesh.

HE HAD GROWN! At an age where dogs were not supposed to learn new tricks, he had defied the rules. As a young husband, he would never have dreamed of being as considerate of Jenny, as concerned with her wishes, as he was with Anna. Take the simple matter of cooking. On the occasions during his marriage when he had donned his chef's cap, he would never have thought of asking Jenny what she would like to eat. It had been sufficient to him to know what he would like to cook. Of course

Jenny hadn't minded. Or had she? She hadn't said she did. But Anna he asked. And often he was amazed to find that what she would like to eat was far from what he had in mind. It started when he made his famous pesto-scallop-bowtie pasta. Heaven on earth, in his opinion. In noticing that she left most of the scallops on her plate, he thought to ask what else she didn't like. Oddly, he found she didn't like lettuce. Well, going without lettuce was contrary to the laws of nutritional science. He had begun to compose his lecture when it occurred to him he might find an alternative form of Vitamin A-packed roughage. He found that virtually every other type of vegetable, either raw or *al dente*, appealed to her. And so he started going through his recipe books and recipe box (all those clippings of things never tried) and found delicious salads that called for no lettuce. There was celery root and carrots, julienned, in a mustard dressing. There were heirloom tomatoes with basil and mozzarella. There was fennel, mushroom and parmesan, all shaved. Besides that, he found that Anna enjoyed participating in the cooking, as long as she didn't have to labor on the kinds of meat-and-potatoes practicalities that she'd endured for so many years as family nurturer. He had introduced her to the magic of the sweet soufflé, had guided her into inventiveness that had resulted in the most glorious version of the Grand Marnier soufflé that man or the angels had ever tasted, as well as a chocolate soufflé like air-light brownies and a raspberry soufflé whose recipe they were thinking of submitting to *Gourmet* magazine. This newfound thoughtfulness of his, which amazed him in that it hadn't been in his nature before, extended to every area, not the least of which was the mysterious realm of sexuality.

In his marriage, he had prided himself that his education as a physician had given him privileged information on the nature of the female's sexual nervous system, so to speak; and he had had every confidence that he was satisfying Jenny. With Anna, the situation was different. Age had given each of them what could be called, if one were to view it negatively, certain physiological dysfunctions inconceivable in youth. And yet this devil, age, had within it another aspect – highly advantageous.

Call it enlightenment. Call it inspiration from a more highly evolved resource. Call it what you will, it made possible great enjoyment.

With Anna, he had tried something new, rather an erotic little experiment: He had pretended to be more naïve than he was and asked her to give him lessons in pleasuring. She enjoyed the game. To understate hyperbolically, she enjoyed it. As for himself, he had to admit, he had learned a thing or two.

He had also sensed, early on, that she was somewhat ashamed of her body. Of course! She wasn't sixteen. She wasn't even sixty any more. Closer to seventy, by God. Of *course* she was no longer nubile. She had a different sort of loveliness now.

It was true, he had had to work some at getting her to stop losing weight. Didn't she knew that as a female got older, she should get plumper? It puffed out the wrinkles. If she had been truly fat, it might have been another matter. But within limits, a woman was better off being a bit "overweight," by the standards of current fashion or – in his opinion – even the standards set on the health charts. He reminded Anna of the words of the late Jackie O.: "There comes an age where a woman has to choose between face and fanny."

Besides, he told her, he had a selfish motive in encouraging her to stay the way she was. He liked something to hold on to. Whoever heard of cherishing a skinny teddy bear? He searched through his library to find his dear copy of Brillat-Savarin, *The Physiology of Taste*, in which the ancient philosopher-chef includes the essay, "On Thinness." Here it was: "Thinness is no great disadvantage to men; they are no weaker for being thin, and much fitter." Et cetera et cetera . . . "But for women it is a frightful misfortune; for to them beauty is more than life itself, and beauty consists above all in roundness of form and gracefully curving lines." Et cetera . . . "A thin woman, however beautiful she may seem, loses something of her charm."

This gave Anna a healthy laugh.

Ah, what a wonderful world. This was the thought on his mind almost each new day, as he plucked his spade from the table in the front hall and attached Romeo's collar to his leash. Fog always freshened the morning air at this glorious time of summer. His feet, in high-laced gardening boots, always sprang up Filbert Street to the park – just as his Subaru later sprang from the garage and purred sweetly up Broadway toward his office, the Japanese vehicle perhaps stimulated by the pleasure of learning a little French.

This Is Important!

AFTER SAYING À *bientôt* to Rayford, Anna passed the dining-room mirror and said, "*Je porte le pyjama.*" She flexed her heel and gave a little Asian kick. She liked these crisp new peppermint p.j.s. She'd got them to wear for Rayford, because he seemed to appreciate a little dash. For her, bedtime was the best time for dressing up. And after a while those Christian Dior nightgowns got to looking alike.

Of course the nights with Rayford were top secret. Martine was the only one she'd told. She'd even had to break down and buy a cell phone, so her kids could reach her without knowing where she was. Suddenly she had something in common with the wife who was having the *escapade extraconjugale*.

She slept better on the nights when she was with him. It came as a shock when he told her he didn't sleep at all. "We have to work on this!" she said. So they set about analyzing. First, her down pillows were too soft for him. He got a crimp in his neck. She had to buy him a foam one, which nearly killed her, since down was so much nicer. And he felt obliged to lie on his back so she could sleep with her head on his chest. He'd never been able to sleep on his back. What she had to do about that was to forbid him to let her fall asleep while they cuddled. He didn't like that, but she said, "This is important!" And worst of all, he said she snored. She couldn't believe that, but he seemed to know more about it than she did. He said she made quite a disturbance. So, she made him promise to wake her up whenever the snoring started. Again, he didn't

271

like to do that, but she was almost fierce when she said, "This is important!" And so, sleeping together got to be nice for both of them. In fact, he said to her the other morning, "There is no pleasure greater than waking to feel your warm gluteus maximus butted against my own."

The only thing that would be nicer, she thought, would be sleeping together every night. After only a few weeks, she began to feel that the upset of being together one night, apart the next, wasn't good for people their age. Habit, routine, were part of comfort. From there you could go off in all directions, but your basic home life needed stability. He hadn't mentioned that the upset bothered him, but she thought it must.

There was only one serious problem. She liked her place much more than his. Her feelings went deep. She loved her home so much it felt like part of her self. Body and soul.

Phfff. Her apartment wasn't her body and soul. She'd have to do some work on herself. Because Rayford had even more of his spirit invested in those eight rooms of treasures bought at auction. And his garden. He'd spent more than half his lifetime lovingly feeding it garbage.

Now Chantal and Nigel had ignited him with rosarian zeal. He'd bought five connoisseur rose books and had almost eaten them. By now he knew so much he felt he deserved an honorary degree in botany. But he told Anna he'd be damned if he'd duplicate the species Nigel had planted – those fussy hybrid teas. For one thing, Nigel's reached the standard of perfection in the bud stage. At the bud stage, the old-fashioned roses hadn't even begun. With the old-fashioned roses, the beauty of each bloom intensified as it grew more mature. The ruffled layers of petals grew more and more heart-rending as they grew older, until at their peak they fell apart as if the poetry of their lives had been too much for them.

And to boot, he told her, the old-fashioned teas, musks, and rugosas were far less finicky than Nigel's hybrid teas. Rayford bought a Ferdinand Pichard, with candy-striped petals; a Mabel Morrison, whose flesh-pink buds started out globe-shaped, like peonies, and burst open into layers of scallops you'd swear were made of silk; a Mme Alfred Carrière with a smell that hypnotized you; a Souvenir de Malmaison (the classic, from the Empress Josephine's garden); and a Cécille Brünner, which he was training up over his back door, because its buds were just what the top buttonhole of his lab coat had been crying out for. The first day he wore one, he told Anna it was true! Almost every patient had smiled and commented. A pink baby rose lifted everyone's spirits, naturally.

He did make two concessions to Nigel's beloved hybrid teas: Rayford planted a Priscilla Burton, one of the great hybridizer Sam McGredy's "hand-painted" series, and a Captain Harry Stebbings, because it had a name Rayford might have chosen for himself. These modern roses he liked, but philosophically he was an old-fashioned guy. He liked Captain Harry and Priscilla, but he was always pointing out to Anna how quickly their flowers fell into the past tense. He said the old-fashioned roses were "always climbing to a higher concept of prime, reaching sensuous complexities unheard of in the lesser hybrid teas."

They'd spent lots of days in the country, visiting rose ranches, and this weekend they were going to drive to one called Roses of Yesterday and Today. He was going to pack a picnic to eat at a redwood table set, he said, amidst forty-foot Mme Alfred Carrières, and Gloires de Dijon. He wanted to pick out one of the David Austen series for a spot near his Captain Harry. Lots of the David Austens were named after characters in Shakespeare or Chaucer (he liked The Wife of Bath), and he was curious because they were supposed to have some of the good points of both the old-fashioneds and the moderns.

At first she tried to work with him, clearing space for the newcomers. It made her feel terrible that she didn't like that kind of labor. He said nonsense, he didn't need a field hand. He loved to sweat. And he said he took more pleasure in his garden now than he ever had.

EDITH PIAF FILLED Anna's apartment with song. "*Je vous connais, Milord! Vous ne m'avez jamais vu . . .*" The percussion in parts sounded a little like tapdancing, and Anna worked her feet as she put on makeup. A couple of times she put on her glasses to consult the *New York Times* and her battered red Cassell's before returning to the mascara or the blusher brush.

She took out her opera glasses to look through the park. Nothing of interest. But down on the sidewalk, walking back and forth past her little front garden, was the man with the horrible hair. His steps were so slow it took him for ever to go from one end of the wrought iron fence to the other. His heart must be heavy. At the trunk of her wisteria vine, he stopped. He turned to look around. When a car passed he took a few steps toward the corner of Greenwich, then moved back to the wisteria, slow as a snail. Seeing there was no one around now, he pressed himself close to the fence. He faced the wisteria for about forty seconds. She assumed he was urinating. He took an Evian bottle out of his pocket and poured some on the spot.

She went back to the *New York Times*. She was planning part of a conversation she hoped to have with Martine this afternoon at La Petite Treat. Yesterday they'd argued about new developments in "*L'Afrique du Sud*," And Anna hadn't had enough facts or French to state her opinions right. Of course Martine's facts and French had changed a few of Anna's opinions, but she still had some worth saying that she couldn't get across yesterday. Thanks to Martine, the little French radical, Anna had had to do a lot of homework this summer. And some thinking. Anna was so happy Martine couldn't speak English.

WHERE WAS SHE? Anna walked through the lower and upper terraces and the woods. Martine was nowhere. She wasn't up on the lawn by the tennis courts.

There was Hillary, being pulled down the brick street this way and that way by Tess. "Hello!" Anna called. Hillary turned back to wave just as the door of Chantal's building opened and Nigel rushed out shouting, "Hillary! Hillary!" He ran up the street and grabbed the leash. "Hillary." His voice was louder than it had to be. "It's time you taught that dog to heel." He gave the leash a jerk, so the dog would get a jolt in the neck. Her face turned plaintively up to him. "Heel!" Tess looked back to Hillary, and Nigel held the leash close. "Heel!" He forced her to stay in step with him. Hillary followed close behind. Anna followed farther behind, as Nigel ordered, "Heel. Heel!" Tess zigzagged as far and wide as possible, her range becoming more and more limited as Nigel clenched the leash closer and closer until his hand was nearly on her collar. He jerked it enough to give her pain. The dog looked up at him, not pained but interested: "What are you trying to say?" Trying something, Tess walked forward, in step with him. "Good girl!" he said, patting her head. "What a good girl." She seemed to like that. She kept walking in step, checking up at his face now and then. Hillary stayed behind. Something on the sidewalk caught Tess's eye, and she lunged for it. Nigel jerked the leash, and she looked up, puzzled, then got her attention back and fell in step. "What a good girl!" he crooned. At the stoplight he handed the leash to Hillary, who mimicked what he'd done. Anna watched them progress, Nigel coaching, Hillary and Tess working hard to please him.

What would Philo Righi think of this? The dog seemed delighted.

Martine must be in the park by now. But no, she wasn't. The best thing would be to go home and wait, with her opera glasses. Inside, when she finally found the glasses, there was a new scene on the promenade.

"*PAUVRE PETIT!*" MARTINE was cooing at Buster, who wore a little cast. "*Pauvre petit.*" Frankie was there, and a girl – a young woman with a purple crewcut, saying "Awww." If ever there was a sight to tug your heart, it was Buster in a cast.

Seeing Anna, Frankie said, "Buster's enjoying this!" Buster hopped over to say hi to Posy and Frankie said, "Everyone on the cable car points and says, 'Cute!' Cars on Hyde Street stop, so the people can roll down their windows and say 'Aww. Cute!' So many people see him and say 'cute,' I think he thinks his name is Cute." The purple-haired girl called out, "Here, Cute!" And Buster hopped over. "*Mignon,*" Anna translated, for Martine. She laughed.

The girl with the purple crewcut said, "Let's take a photograph of Buster in his cast and sell it to Hallmark as a get-well card."

"Have you met my friend?" Frankie asked. "Her name is – What is your name?" She said it was Felicity. "Felicity," said Frankie. "She's a professional dogsitter. Works in the neighborhood sometimes. You see the dog she's taking care of now? It's your dog's cousin."

It was a bichon frisé. (Male.) But clipped so oddly. The body was sheared close, so it was much smaller than Posy's. But the head was left all huge and frizzy. Its eyes, gleaming out from the wild froth, looked fiercely intelligent. "The dog's name is Einstein."

"Einstein," Anna translated for Martine. She got it instantly.

"By the way. I went to a vet," Frankie told Mrs. Leone. "Had to. Went to yours."

"So I suppose Buster will get better? What was wrong, exactly?"

"Nothing was wrong with him. Just a broken leg."

ROUNDING THE CORNER after her session with Martine at La Petite Treat, her heart gave a jump. The man who'd just urinated in her garden was moving toward her. Whenever he appeared, jay-walking to the other side of the street was routine. But it was hard to do it inconspicuously. She was creative, so she usually found a plant to study across the street, or a piece of litter to pick up, even a doorbell to ring. Luckily, today there was a stack of *Nob Hill Gazette*s on the opposite sidewalk – free newspapers. She was just leading Posy off the curb when she changed her mind. She stayed on the same sidewalk with the man and didn't avert her eyes. It turned out she didn't have to, because his glance avoided hers.

Up close, his skin was bleached the color of a white pumpkin, stiff but seeming to sink, the way a carved-out pumpkin collapses eventually. She saw eye holes and a triangle nose. When she pulled up her courage and smiled into the blank face, the mouth hole formed the shape of a tiny half circle, the top sliced straight. There were no teeth.

Was it a smile?

After he'd passed, what came at her was something almost as frightening as she used to think he was. It was her dangerous old friend, hope. Hope and all the threats of disappointment it brought with it.

She wasn't going to *do* anything. Not at the moment. She wasn't going to talk to anyone about it, except maybe Rayford. And Morella. Morella had so much wisdom. Also, she might call Dr. Lemanski, the best resource on psychological disability she'd come across in her museum project. Maybe they could have lunch in a month or two. She'd turned down his idea on a program for psychologically disabled adults and wasn't going to start out on the one for kids until October. But she might have lunch with Dr. Lemanski sometime in the fall and just try to learn something. She should know more about people like this man. Because it was a smile. It made her want to cry.

Fall

"HEY. WHAT'RE YOU doing? What're you doing?"

Tobin sat on a branch, the first in one of the columns of sycamores along the promenade. He moved his saw and watched the limb crash. "Pruning."

"Why?"

"Because it's fall."

"Whaddya mean it's fall? The leaves are green. It's too soon to prune."

"Some of these leaves are yellow. Some brown. Time to prune."

"But this is still September. Best month of the year. Best month of the year! This is San Francisco, man. Autumn doesn't come till November. Why don't you wait till the leaves get brown, crumble up on the ground, so we can get the pleasure of crunching them with our sneakers? Then you can cut."

"Kind of a waste of labor. If the leaves fall I have to rake every day. I rake today, I rake tomorrow, I rake the next day. Goes on through October, November. Then I have to prune. Best to cut back the branches now, get ready. Winter comes. Every year. A gardener has to think ahead."

Ike walked away with his black puppy Molly and Goldie the blonde. "God-damned Nazi," he said to Goldie. "Efficiency above all. That's what counts. Never mind if summer isn't over. Prevent the waste of raking autumn leaves. Cut off the branches now."

Down at the lower terrace he swooped an arm down to grab a pine-

278

cone and hurl it. Made it out of the park. "Tobin the God-damned gardener is just like Chantal and the fucking Englishman," he said to Goldie. She was the adult. "They killed their dog before nature said it was time to die. Put it to sleep, they call it. The word is kill. So what if the dog can't walk. So what if it can't shit. So what if it can't fuck! It can still breathe, can't it? It can still feel the sun on its ruff. It can enjoy the pleasures of sleep. Of looking out the window."

And now Meg's cut out. Sure, she came back. They talked. She came back again. They talked. They felt the same kinds of emotions. They cried like kids.

She needs to be alone awhile and get to know herself better. She said. They might get back together. She said. She'll be back next weekend and they'll talk again. Bawl again.

She took her clothes and the second TV. Took Moe. Left him the good two. At least she took Moe. Nobody said she wasn't generous. But God. After all these years. After they'd come out to California without two twenties in their jeans.

Oh yeah. They'd grown their separate ways. Trend-setter, she liked to be – and the latest trend was money. Just one more fad he couldn't get into. Trends were something he didn't want to set and didn't want to follow. He stayed the same. Except his eyes never used to have these red rings around them. He hadn't cried like this since he was twelve. And he never used to hang out in churches. God, he'd spent a lot of time in churches. When she came back, and when she left again. When she came back again, and when she left again. He was in church every day but Sunday. You didn't have to kneel, you didn't have to douse holy water. You didn't have to listen to sermons. You just had to be there, with God. With whatever made sense. If anything ever made any sense. Her face looked even more beat-up than his.

THE WEDDING WAS this weekend. The Doc and Mrs. Leone doing their number in Doc's yard. Oh well. You had to hand it to these old birds. After all, they met in a yard. Our yard.

279

Shotgun affair. At their age. Doc says that's why they have to move fast. They're in their last decades. Plural, if they're lucky. They've lived long enough to know how fast a decade goes. They don't want to waste any part of one. So it's like – tomorrow.

His house. Never mind how much she likes hers. She'll get used to it. She's the female. In his anatomy course at Yale he figured it out. The vagina is the most accommodating organ in human physiology. It must apply to the whole female organism. Any age.

Meg was pretty accommodating. God. She took Moe.

Leone's place is more luxurious, but Doc's is huge. Eight rooms, plus garden. Plus Doc's attached to it. Not that Leone doesn't like hers. Maybe she should rent it out to him for a discount, being a friend. Seriously, he needs a change of place. Maybe he should offer to house-sit until the divorce.

Just kidding.

Doc said he'd cleared the way for Leone by putting some of his furniture in the basement. She'd bring her best stuff and store the rest down in his basement. Tough compromises, the rich have to make.

She wasn't going to give up her maid, though. Gotta draw the line somewhere. He was keeping his, too. Why not? It was a big house. Plenty of room for servants. Actually though, Leone was right about one thing. Her maid wasn't cut out for lowly work. She was getting out of the maid business. She got some fancy-schmantzy job as an "administrative assistant" in a Latino mental health clinic. No longer a servant. Except on Saturday. He knew this from the doctor. Doc said the maid had confided in him that she was afraid Leone couldn't make it without her. The doctor and the maid had a laugh. Must be nice to be needed, Ike thought.

He wouldn't be at the wedding. No. No way. Not in the mood for to have and to hold, for better for worse, for richer for poorer, in sickness and in health and all that crap.

He liked it once. Meant a lot to him. The second time. First time he was going through the motions. All her rich relatives, all that

280

money, the bride–groom thing, actor–actress thing, he couldn't remember a minute of the first time. But the second time, in City Hall. With Meg.

For better for worse.

Ha. That was a good one.

Doc and Leone wanted him to play electric keyboards, down in the yard. If he didn't feel so lousy, he'd bring his bass player. But he was gonna cut out before the action started. Last night he and the kid put tapes together, according to the wishes of the bride and groom. Edith Piaf, Gilbert Becaud, even Maurice Chevalier. Plus Duke Ellington, Marlene Dietrich, Bix, the mix. Doc asked to hear two particular numbers twice – once at the beginning and once at the end. One was an old blues singer, Alberta Hunter, belting out an anthem: "I've got that *old*-fashioned *love* in my heart . . ." The other was Louis Armstrong, "What a Wonderful World." Oh yaaa? Whatever. Tomorrow they'd get the sound system going and split. Or, he'd split. Josh would stay. Said he'd never been to a wedding. Wanted his girlfriend to see it. Poor kid.

Chantal and Nigel went to the country today, Sonoma, some rose ranch. They were buying their gift. Three rose bushes, all whites, named Love, Honor, and Cherish.

Ike felt the corners of his mouth jerk down again, remembering his own love, honor, and cherishing. God, he'd fucked up.

Meg said it was all this bitterness. All this anger, toward everyone. It felt like anger toward her. She said it made her insecure about herself. It made her think she wasn't worth anything.

But she was worth the world! And that anger wasn't him. It was an act. To cover up how insecure he was about himself.

He forgot to tell her that. Or, he hadn't forgotten. It hadn't occurred to him. He should tell her. Sure, he didn't like ex-dot-commers who retired at twenty-five with twenty-five million bucks, or C.E.O.s or investment bankers. Especially investment bankers. He should know about those guys.

281

He didn't like Russian Hill. Frankie thought it was great, this so-called high-class neighborhood. He'd rather live in the projects. This place was phony.

See? There I go again. It might be phony and it might not be. It just makes me insecure about myself.

Am I secure enough to tell Meg that? If I tell her, it won't make it less true. I like the common people's world. She likes Russian Hill and money.

HERE CAME MRS. Leone with her frilly little dog. "Nice shoes, Mrs. Leone. Flats. That's smart. Red's a good color. Good color!"

He had to admit he liked her. Even if she was rich and happy.

"Ike!" She reached into her pocketbook. "I'm glad you're here. I have something I want to read to you." She pulled out a fat envelope. "Do you remember Martine, my French friend?"

"Lady Godiva? Sure I do. Sure I do. Nice girl. Nice girl."

"I just got this letter this morning." She slipped a folded page out of the envelope. "We'll read it after the wedding, but since you won't be there . . . She's back at Lille now, you know. France. She's started the university there, and her boyfriend Manuel is back at his job, and she's learning English, and, well . . ." She put on her glasses.

My dear Anna,

You astonish you that I write in English? I am very fortunate to have a teacher, woman, not many more years than I have.

On our voyage home we see the Grand Canyon, the Rocky Mountains, and New York.

At Lille all the world want to know about America, and especially the Americans. I tell them of you, Anna, and the Docteur and Ike and Tobin, and the Gypsies who are not Gypsies and Frankie the concierge.

In France we had a famous writer, Marcel Proust. He has special biscuits – madeleines. He eat a madeleine and he remember of

282

many things. For me, my madeleines are McDonald hamburgers. I eat and I remember of La Petite Treat and you.

A bientôt, Anna!

Martine.

"NICE," IKE SAID. He felt his throat getting thick. "Aw, McDonald's!" he growled. "Nice girl," he admitted. "Very nice girl. What else is in the envelope?"

"Oh." Anna had started to put it back in her purse. "Pictures." She took the envelope back out. "Here. The Grand Canyon, the Grand Canyon, a river in Colorado, a meadow in Colorado . . . And here's Rayford – and me . . . Here's Tobin . . ." While he looked at that one, she thumbed through a bunch and found another. "This is yours, to keep."

He looked at it. It was Meg and him and the three kids, taken here in the park. "Good picture," he said. "Good photograph. I'll send it to Meg." He concentrated on the pocket he was putting the snapshot into. He turned away. "C'mon, gang." When he and Goldie and Molly got to the landing, he gave Mrs. Leone that wave, the big flat palm moved from the elbow. "Break a leg."

"OH!" SHE GASPED. "Oh!" She staggered back to the tiled bench for support.

"No jumping! Tess, no jumping!"

"I'm so glad you're coming to the party," Anna said, now safely seated on the bench, sharing it with Tess. "We got your reply." Tess was kissing her. "You and I certainly did a good job of saving this puppy, didn't we?"

Hillary let her smile out. She sat down next to Mrs. Leone and Tess, inviting Posy to hop up and join the group.

"I have opera glasses, you know. So I watch you."

"You watch me?"

"Yes. And I see you like that Philo Righi."

"What?" Hillary seemed amazed.

283

"Yes, I've noticed."

The girl seemed embarrassed, but Anna had been prepared for this. "I like him too."

"You do?"

"Yes. He's coming to our wedding. We just got his reply card."

"Did he accept for one or for two?"

Anna said, "That's what he asked about you, before he mailed his reply. I told him you'd replied for one. And he replied for one."

FRANKIE HAD REPLIED for one. And she had decided to wear a dress and her jewelry. "When I managed that building in the Tenderloin I used to get invited to my tenants' parties all the time," she told Pierre. "This is the first time I've been invited to one on Russian Hill. I don't like weddings. I've only been to one wedding." Without bothering to say thanks, she picked a Gauloise out of the pack he waved. He lit it for her, with his deco lighter. All three dogs were up in the woods, and Pierre had taken off his beret. She'd always assumed he was bald, but this was the first time she'd seen his dome with her own eyes. It was not shiny, it was soft-looking skin, like a baby's. She felt the sweet pungency of the French smoke coming in, going out. "Life is a big bore," she said.

He looked at her. Took a sip of his martini.

He probably knew what she was talking about. He seemed a little down himself. "I get a kick from my drawing and painting and all," she told him. "Sometimes I'll stay up all night two nights in a row. I was up till five this morning, trying to get a figure right. But I'm not kidding myself. If I died tomorrow I wouldn't be missing anything."

"Oh, no, you're just going through a tough time, Frankie."

She could tell he wasn't convinced. "I mean," she said, "I'm on my own. I haven't got anyone."

"Oh well," he said. "I usually don't think that's so important."

"Usually? How do you feel right now? You're on your own. I've been yacking, why don't I shut up and let you talk for a change?"

284

He smiled at that. "Actually, I'd rather listen. Funny, but that's how I feel."

"Oh, okay. Life's a bore and I'm a bore." She tossed off her French cigarette before smoking half of it. "I don't want to be a drunk, though. So it's lucky I got the gout. I'm just damn lucky I got sick." She looked out at the water. "Otherwise it could have gotten out of hand and I'd be out on the street. And I couldn't handle that."

"I couldn't handle it," Pierre said, "if I had to give up my sapphire gin. I don't know what I'd do if it ever got to that point." He knocked the wooden bench with his knuckles.

"Two things have affected me lately," she told him. "First, Ike and Meg. I see what he is going through. I know what it's like to be lonely. But of course I started out being lonely at a younger age than he is. I started going through it first when my real dad split. The killer was when my mom died. So, I've been in training for loneliness a long time. I'm better equipped to handle it than Ike is. He's just my age, he's fifty-four, and he's never been alone before. He's got a lot to go through."

She looked over at Pierre, who seemed to know what she meant. "I've learned a lot from watching him," she said. "All that sour stuff, all that hate. I mean, I hate yuppies and dot-com millionaires or young handsome C.E.O.s or whatever name you give a certain type, depending on the times. And I know Ike doesn't mean it. He mouths off in an angry way, but he's not really full of hate. It's just a way he's got used to acting. Like me with my beers, ten a.m. to midnight. It's his style. But I see how hard it must be for Meg to live with that, day after day. It's been interesting to me, because I used to be kind of like that myself. But why? People are people."

Both of them just sat there, the fog blowing down its usual path over the Bay, cooling everything off.

"You said two things have been bothering you," he said. "What's the other one?"

"The other thing that's bothered me," she answered, shaking her head back and forth slowly, looking at the striped dirt, "is the death of this dog, Mrs. Ironside. It's not just that it was such a sweet dog. All dogs are sweet – except Tess. But in fact when I get honest, even Tess is sweet. The whole problem is her mistress. I had to look after Tess for one day, so I found out. Her basic nature is good. But this Mrs. Ironside was really sweet."

Pierre took the olive out of his martini. He put it back in.

"Thank God I saw the light in time and got Buster to the vet. Of course it doesn't make any difference in the course of a lifetime. He'll be dead too before you can wink. Just like my cat. The cat'll go first. It's best not to get attached."

Pierre offered his heavenly blue pack to her, and she refused. He lit another.

"Do you think you might be interested in some sort of romance one day?" he asked her. "I mean, you mentioned not having anyone."

"A romance? No! What do I have to offer? I don't have youth, I don't have money, I don't have beauty."

He couldn't say anything to that. After a long time, he ate his olive. "I'm kind of in the same boat, except maybe financially. At least, I've got money enough for myself, but I'm not rich enough to buy love."

He finished the martini. "You," he said. "You can be a pleasure to be with."

"When I'm in the mood," she said.

"There must be any number of people who also need companion-ship," he said.

"As a companion, sure," she said. "I'd give anything for a good companion. I think I'd be good in return. No sex, of course. I have nothing to offer sexually."

"I'm the same way. I haven't had sex for going on thirteen years."

"But you have companions. Isn't it about time for dinner, in one of your *restaurants*?"

She despised restaurants. "C'mon, Buster." She headed for the mound just below where the cyclone fence bisected the cliff from the

286

tennis courts. One last look at the scenery and it would be time for dinner. Last night's turkey.

From up in the woods near the tennis courts, she looked down on the bench and saw Pierre sitting, twirling the stem of his empty glass. He put his beret back on his head. He clipped his female to the leash and led both toy poodles over to the landing, where he stood.

It had turned into a misty night. Frankie's wool jacket was covered with droplets, loading on so that after this hour or so with Pierre she could brush the wool with her hand and send off a spray of water. Looking down to the path, she could see him. Standing. Still.

The bridge. It was an indication of a shape, blurred but strong, against a fuzzy backdrop. In this light the spires had no color. The color not being there added to the power of the architecture. The spires seemed like symbols. The vision had a liquid feel, but all was still.

It was funny, about the Bay. As far as she could see, it didn't change much. It kept the same shape. Her uncle had built a house alongside a river in New Jersey, and the river had changed course and washed the house away. Rivers, bays, all bodies of water did this. Maybe this Bay was changing, it was just too slow to see.

She led Buster over to the stairway and saw that Pierre wasn't moving toward his house at the edge of the park. He'd turned the wrong direction. He was walking her way.

A struggle started in her chest and stomach. He was crowding her.

But then she remembered what she'd been saying just now. People are people. He was a person.

"What do you want?"

He got closer. "I was just thinking I might cancel my evening plans."

"Why?"

"I was just going to eat alone at the Polk Street Grill again. I thought I might have dinner at your place instead."

Was he crazy?

"Come on. I've never seen your art. For all I know you've been bulling me, and you aren't an artist at all."

287

"You know I am!"

"Seeing is believing. The plan is, I buy the ingredients, you make that Depression meat you've been telling me about."

"That's not on my diet."

"Neither is beer, but you told me you drink a couple of beers on Friday nights or something."

"That's different."

"Well, we'll have chicken then. Or turkey. Or hey! We could have fish. I'll pay."

"No. I told you about my place. The walls are black from the smoking I do."

"I smoke too," Pierre said.

"I only have that one chair. The chair I draw in is the same chair as I sit on to eat."

"I've got a nice cushion I carry around behind me," he said. "I can sit on the floor, if I've got it with me now." He craned his neck backwards to check.

"Oh, Christ," Frankie said. "Depression meat. But don't say I didn't warn you."

At the top of the brick street, looking out at the Bay Bridge, there was a lot more lavender to the sky. Down Hyde a kid, six or seven, pushed a skateboard. Josh's board roared down to catch up with him. When the boy fell down, Josh gave him a hand up. Showed him how to get more speed. "Oh no," Frankie said. "Here comes another ten years of hell on wheels."

Pierre didn't talk. They walked. His little high-class dogs heeled. Buster hopped. He'd be using all four legs again pretty soon. But then, pretty soon too, he'd be dead.

Still. This was today, and he was full of life. Her cat was alive at home. Probably. Through the fog, tail-lights slipped straight up the streets of Telegraph Hill – stripes of fuzzy red vibrations. Probably she was wrong, but from here, in the hush, the blurred lights in the windows looked warm and inviting.

288

One More Thing

HILLARY HAD A new dress, for the wedding. Silk, but not shiny. China red. It was high-necked and modest and sophisticated, all at once. She got it from the Gypsy place. This time not cheap. That was okay. She didn't even mind paying extra to have it taken in. She'd never noticed till she tried on this dress that her hair had some coppery glints.

On the way to the park, Tess heeled! (Well, for a minute.) Hillary was thinking about a chair. Or two chairs. Maybe even a table. It was lucky she didn't want a bed too. At least she wasn't that bourgeois. But maybe instead of chairs and a table (say she did want a table), she should just buy a painting. An expensive one, to hang from the moldings, so she wouldn't have to put a nail in Frankie's wall. She could go the way of the woman in Tobin's poem – the art-before-furniture poem: "That's devotion."

But there was something nice about furniture. People like chairs. They're something to sit down in, and talk. It would be nice to have someone over.

She'd have to think about this. Or, rather, she'd have to keep thinking about this. With her Ikea catalog, her Horchow catalog, and her indecision, she reached the top of the brick street and freed Tess to run.

For Hillary, a solution to her worst problem had just – materialized. Like a genie, rising from a bottle. One unsolvable problem solved. And then here she was again, tense with the next problem, created by solving the last one.

289

All week she'd been trying to figure out what to do.

Jade Wu-Henderson had called her into her office, her smile almost filling up her whole face: "Usually you just get either a raise *or* a title," she said. "You're getting both, Producer Birdwood." The new little series was a hit. Well – kind of a hit. People noticed it. People talked about it. The TV editor of the paper wrote about it!

The raise was way too big. And retroactive from June, which really wasn't fair, because the series wasn't even a twinkle in her eye back in June. But Channel 12 and Channel 9 had both tried to hire her over, and Jade Wu-Henderson used the offers to get Hillary what she deserved. Or, what Jade said she deserved. ("We had to beat the competition, Hillary.") Amazing.

With the one-time-only sum for the retroactive, the amount the computer deposited this week was enough to pay off two and a half credit cards. Or, she could pay off just two and buy a very nice chair. (A starter chair.) Or, she could pay off just one and a half cards and buy two good chairs and a table. The annual amount of her new salary had a fabulous ring. Too bad the station couldn't just pay her the whole thing right now.

Anyway, she'd bought a shower curtain. How could she have lived with that ghastly one that looked like army surplus? The white duck with the white tiles just lifted your spirits. It was like getting a whole new room.

As she stood at the top of the stairs leading down to the woods, a quiet voice from below cut into her new decor dilemma. Ears perked, Hillary peered down through leaves. Tobin stood at the monument – making it a podium. Whatever he was saying, he said it a little louder.

Whoosh! There went Tess, scrambling the Friday stripes in the dirt. She vaulted to the monument, pushing her nose into Tobin's beard.

"Good girl," he seemed to say. But so softly.

Hillary trotted down. Tobin looked up. The color in his cheeks shot red. "Rehearsing," he said.

"Rehearsing?"

"Yuh. Yuh. Mrs. Leone's wedding."

"One of your poems?"

"No. No. Not mine. Doc found another one. Good poem. Good poet. He thought since you'd gotten me on TV, and I was used to appearing in public, I might like to present the poem. For the wedding. To read the poem he wants. She wants. By William Carlos Williams. Good poet. Poet calls it 'Love Song.' Kind of appropriate."

"Are you presiding over the ceremony, Tobin?"

"No. No. Judge Rossi. But they want this poem. Asked me to read it. He says I'm Poet Laureate of the Park. Seems fair. I'm the only poet in the park. Wanna hear?"

Hillary leaned back on the tiled bench and closed her eyes, to listen. Tobin had really become pretty good at making his voice heard.

Tess barked. A bird had taken off. To compensate for her thundering paws and her loud cries, Tobin raised his voice: " 'Who shall hear of us – In the time to come?' "

Hillary stopped listening to the poem. Her mind went to Tess, leaping to catch the bird that hovered above the highest tree. The bird floated down closer, teasing. Tess ran in a circle to build enough momentum to thrust herself higher. And higher! If birds could laugh, this bird must be laughing. With boundless hope, Tess seemed to think she could accomplish the lift that this bird got from its wings. Body and soul, she put herself into chasing after what she could never possibly catch. Funny how it made her so happy. Except – this bird was bringing her as close to flying as she'd ever get.

291

Acknowledgements

I want to thank Alison Samuel, at Chatto & Windus, in London. I've never met her or seen her picture. All I know first hand is that she knows what I'm trying to say. Thanks to her, the book you're reading is the book I wanted to write.

The other person I want to thank is my London agent, Teresa Chris. She never doubts that my solitary scribbling will eventually become a book she hates to finish.

*

Grateful acknowledgement is made to the following for permission to quote from copyrighted material:

Lines from "The Nearness of You", from the Paramount Picture *Romance in the Dark*; words by Ned Washington; music by Hoagy Carmichael. Copyright © 1937, 1940 (Renewed 1964, 1967) by Famous Music Corporation. International Copyright Secured. All Rights Reserved.

Lines from "What a Wonderful World"; words and music by George Weiss and Bob Thiele. Copyright © 1967 by Range Road Music Inc., Quartet Music, Inc. and Abilene Music, Inc. Copyright renewed. International Copyright Secured. All Rights Reserved. Used by Permission.

Lines from "A Fine Romance", by Jerome Kern and Dorothy Fields, © 1936, from the film *Swing Time*. Permission from Universal MCA Music Publishing.